GREY MAGIC

BONDS OF MAGIC
BOOK THREE

BY
JEFFE KENNEDY

The epic story of Nic and Gabriel concludes…

His Darkness, Her Brightness… Together They Defy the World

Lord Gabriel Phel at last holds his dream in his grasp—and faces losing everything. He's finally won the love of his wife, familiar, and mother of his child, and she offers him a heartfelt commitment he can truly believe in. Together they're building a true house, one with a growing family of friends and allies that can help them stand against their enemies. And he's learning to master his magic, to use it as the powerful tool and weapon it should be. But old and new enemies array themselves to take it all away.

Lady Veronica, now fully of House Phel, is doing her best to embrace happiness. After all, she has her hands full managing her mercurial and powerful wizard as he navigates taking his place as the head of their house, and with learning her own extraordinary ability. But she fears whatever peace they win won't last long. When their enemies inevitably strike—including, perhaps, her own father—they must be ready to defend all they hold precious. It doesn't help that her idealistic husband insists on making foolishly noble decisions that put them at even greater risk, nor that she loves him all the more for it.

As Nic and Gabriel struggle to put their household in order, giving ill-advised safe harbor to Nic's runaway sister and risking their lives to save Gabriel's sister's sanity, their enemies draw the noose tighter on their well laid plans. When the unthinkable occurs, it's up to both of them to trust in the nascent, unknown magic they've woven together.

DEDICATION

To David,
because it's been a while since I dedicated one to you,
and because you know me better than I know myself

ACKNOWLEDGMENTS

Thanks to Carien Ubink and Marcella Burnard for that last-minute critical read. Thanks to Darynda Jones and Kelly Robson, too, who never doubted that I'd finish on time.

And love to Grace Draven, because, because, because...

A round of coffee to the Writer Coffee peeps—Emily Mah, Jim Sorenson, and J. Barton Mitchell—for weekly doses of peopling. You all are awesome.

Shoutout to the staff, board, and key volunteers of SFWA. It's amazing to work with all of you who make my job so easy. Special thanks to Terra LeMay, for asking about the book and rooting for me to break the curse.

Thank you for reading!

Credits
Proofreading: Pikko's House (www.pikkoshouse.com)
Cover: Ravven (www.ravven.com)

~ I ~

"ARE YOU *SURE* we can't stay in the arcanium forever?" Lying on her back on the tiled floor, Nic gazed up at the curved struts of the dome still flickering with silver moon magic, the circular lens of the topmost window illuminated with a softer glow. Beyond the thick glass, the shifting water of the lake rippled with deep blues.

"*You* were the one who painted dire fate of starvation and desiccated bones if we locked ourselves in here and never emerged," Gabriel observed lazily, stroking a hand down her naked flank and snuggling her more tightly against his side.

Explosive sex following taking her alternate form for the first time—a large silver bird that might be a phoenix, which was a strange development—had left her mind considerably muddled. "Maybe we're just not thinking creatively enough. You're a wizard. Can't you magic us food?"

He chuckled and, to her great dismay, shifted to a sitting position, bringing her upright with him. "All the creative thinking in the world won't save our people if we abandon them to hide away in here," he pointed out.

"There is that," she replied glumly, unwillingly contemplating the host of problems that awaited them outside this idyllic bubble.

"And," he said, patting her back encouragingly, "recall that you wanted to practice taking your alternate form while clothed before we confront the Convocation proctor, which means you need to get dressed."

"Since when are *you* the practical one in this relationship?" she grumbled, pushing to her feet and stretching.

"I've been learning from the best." He muttered a curse, and she turned to see him wrestling with his leather pants, which had tangled around his knee-high boots when she'd yanked them down. Above them, he was naked, silvery hairs bright against his darker skin, his moon-pale hair wildly tousled from her fervid hands. Though she'd thought herself sated a moment ago, the sight of him so thoroughly ravaged had her blood heating. Gabriel caught her looking and cocked a brow, lifting his hips to yank his pants up the rest of the way, then firmly laced them. "No," he told her, "or we will emerge to a barren landscape scoured clean by your Convocation and all our people taken prisoner."

"It's not *my* Convocation," she reminded him, tempted to try his resolve anyway. Not that she was dreading facing exactly the scenario he predicted or anything.

"Even so, we know what they're capable of, and I'm not excited to stage a rescue at this point in time."

"We *are* going to have to retrieve Selly before facing the proctor," she observed. Gabriel's sister was a familiar—at least half mad from having untapped magic build up in her all her life with no release—but her family hadn't had the knowledge to identify what corroded Selly's physical and mental health.

When Nic arrived at House Phel, she'd known immediately what the problem was, and that Selly couldn't go on that way. Unfortunately, Selly had a propensity for running wild in the Meresin marshes, and she'd eluded their attempts to help her. Even worse, the tracker Gabriel sent after her, Rat, had brought Selly back just as the Convocation proctor arrived to challenge whether Gabriel had properly bonded Nic. The proctor had also seen what Selly was: a rogue, unbonded, untapped familiar. Before the proctor could take possession of Selly, intending to convey both Nic and Selly back to Convocation Center, Selly had escaped again.

Seizing the opportunity, Gabriel promised they'd retrieve Selly, but then dragged Nic off to the arcanium instead, hoping to provide conclusive proof of their bonding by demonstrating he could put her in her alternate form.

"We're not risking bringing Selly around that proctor," Gabriel countered. "I want that odious woman off Meresin land. We'll just say Selly gave us the slip, which is the truth."

"Because we didn't actually go look for her."

"Nevertheless true. Besides, Rat will have gone after Selly. He won't like that he lost her again, and if anyone can find her, he can. Now, get dressed so we can finish this."

"All right, all right." She paused to mess with her hair in one of the reflective silver surfaces. Her short, dark hair curled wildly, in such disarray that only a grooming imp could fix it.

"Nic," he said, a warning in his tone, "if I have to haul you out there naked to prove to that proctor that you're properly bonded and can take your alternate form, I will."

"No, you wouldn't," she retorted.

"Don't test me on this, Nic," he ground out. "I value your life over your dignity."

"Fine." She found her lingerie and gown in a heap by the arcanium door, where they'd fallen when he'd practically ripped them off of her. If not for the Ophiel magic that made the bindings loosen, he might have torn them. Good thing they'd survived intact, as she didn't have many decent gowns. "You know," she said as she dressed, "it's overly dramatic to say that my life is at stake. I'm too valuable to be killed. The Convocation would only discipline and retrain me so that—" She ended on an undignified squeak, as Gabriel was on her in a flash of movement, seizing her in a ruthless grip and kissing the words from her lips. His mouth was hard and the fire in her leapt to his demand.

He ended the kiss as suddenly as he'd begun it, but without releasing her. He'd leaned his forehead against hers, his breathing ragged. "Nic," he ground out, "if you love me at all, please don't ever again speak so casually of those monsters punishing you and breaking your mind to make you obedient to me."

Her soft-hearted wizard. Easing back enough to frame his face in her hands, she caught and held that wizard-black gaze with hers. "No one is taking me away from you, Gabriel. And I do love you, with everything in me."

He let out a breath, softening under her hands. "I love you, too—and it makes me crazy."

Laughing, she stepped back, triggering the magic toggles to seal her gown, the fabric tingling as it adjusted to fit her figure perfectly. She hopped a bit, tugging on one boot, then the other. "I refuse to take the blame for that. There's considerable evidence that you were crazy long before you met me. Like the moment you decided to decimate House Phel's coffers to pay the application fee for me."

"I should've known you'd have made your way through all the house ledgers by now," he said wryly.

"To be fair, there wasn't all that much to get through."

He winced. "Sorry about that."

"No need to be. I intend to make your investment in me well worth it. But first things first. Let's test the alternate form change. That proctor will find nothing to justify questioning our bond."

"All right." Gabriel's magic braided around her. "Ready?"

"Yes, wizard," she purred, deliberately using the name that indicated they were drawing lines of power.

His magic tightened on her in response, a silver web that he'd laid into her with deft and devastating thoroughness as he sensually tormented her. It was as if all his cool water and shimmering moon magic had become part of her body, underlying her skin with an intimacy unprecedented in her life. She didn't know how it felt to other wizard–familiar pairs, but this went far deeper than the bonding, as if Gabriel had wrapped his mental fingers around her very soul instead of simply taking her by the hand.

She shivered at this final loss of autonomy. Not that she'd go back and change anything. Gabriel had already muddied the waters with the Convocation by insisting on a reciprocal wizard–familiar bonding that had confused the proctor's oracle head. Demonstrating that Gabriel could push her into alternate form would be the incontrovertible proof they needed. Despite her brave words, Nic had no desire to be returned to Convocation Center for punishment and retraining.

"Something wrong?" Gabriel asked with a frown of concern.

"No. It's just... a disconcerting feeling. I'll become accustomed to it with practice." She hoped. And if she didn't, she certainly wasn't going to tell Gabriel. The last thing he needed was something else in their wizard–familiar relationship to obsessively fret over. "Do it," she told him.

The silver net flexed, strumming her nerves with a sensation very like orgasmic agony. The first time he'd shifted her into alternate form, she'd been out of her mind with frustrated desire, so she'd attributed the sensation—what little of it she'd been cognizant enough to track—to their erotic play. This... this was something else entirely. Sensual in nature, but with visceral intensity. Her body convulsed with it, then dissolved.

Once again, she was in her alternate form. A creature Gabriel had described as a silver phoenix, which wasn't something she'd ever heard of. She'd really like to get a look at herself in a mirror and compare the image to the book he'd mentioned seeing it in. Convocation knew the House Phel library had all sorts of oddities secreted away, as did the house itself, along with its lone wizard.

But that would have to wait. All she knew was her vision was very different—more acute and also disconcertingly... globular. Sounds came through vividly and smells did not. She shifted, feeling the thousands of pinpricks where her feathers protruded from her skin, each exquisitely sensitive. That would take getting used to.

Gabriel, sharply delineated in grayscale with a magical aura that radiated well beyond the confines of the arcanium, gazed on her with a smile so satisfied she'd call it smug on anyone else. For him, however, she knew the bland expression covered a wealth of relief. She'd love to find a way to prevent him from worrying about her so much. It simply wasn't natural for a wizard. The typical Convocation wizard took their familiar for granted for a good reason: so they could focus on more pressing concerns. If Gabriel faltered in the defense of House Phel because he was distracted thinking about her safety... well, it didn't bear considering because she'd make sure that didn't happen.

Somehow.

Gabriel laid a hand on her feathered breast, the silver net of magic tightened on her again, inexorable and impossible to resist. The contraction of pleasure-pain wrenched through her, and she returned to human form. Naked.

Planting her hands on her hips, she glared at Gabriel. "Forget something?"

He gaped at her in dismay—and the beginnings of debilitating guilt. "What happened?"

Though he wasn't asking her, she answered before he could go into a spiral of doubt and defeatism. Wizards shaped magic with their minds, so belief in themselves was critical to successful incantations. There was a reason the most arrogant wizards were the most powerful. "If you want to get me naked, all you have to do is ask, wizard," she murmured, deliberately striking a seductive pose.

His jaw firmed, wizard-black eyes sparking with indignation. A much better emotion for him to work with. "I wasn't trying to—"

"What *were* you trying to do?" she interrupted. "What did you picture when you summoned me back to human form?"

Puzzled, he knitted his brows. Then his face cleared. "I was thinking of how it worked before."

"All right, then. So, put me back in alternate form, and this time when you summon me, be careful with the details."

"Wait a moment." He held up a hand, his frown deepening. "If I have this much control over how you return to your natural form, then I must have similar influence over sending you into your alternate form. What if I do something wrong and harm you?"

She tried to swallow her heavy sigh, she really did. But it escaped anyway. "Do we need to have another conversation about you having confidence in what you're doing? Because, as you've repeatedly pointed out, people are waiting on us. They could be in trouble even now while you dither."

A low growl escaped him. "Being concerned about not killing my wife is hardly *dithering*, Nic."

"It *is* dithering," she snapped. "You did this before. I was fine. You can do it again. Nothing has changed except a few pieces of fabric."

"That's a vast oversimplification."

"To counter your vast overcomplication of what is instinctive for you!" She stomped her foot, considerably less effective barefooted, her naked breasts jiggling enough to draw his lustful eye, despite his resolve. His magic flared with his arousal, which was at least something. "Do it. Now. While you're not overthinking it."

He looked like he might balk still, so she skimmed her hands over her breasts and down her hips, shimmying a little. "Saving my life, remember?" she purred.

That did it. He grabbed her hand. Though the fist of silver magic netted her with considerably less finesse this time, the contraction dissolving and explosion downright painful. She barely had a moment to register her transition to alternate form before his argent grip yanked her back, turning her skin inside out as she returned to human form. Her body throbbed in every pore, her heart pounding and breathing ragged. But she was clothed. Still barefoot, as he'd forgotten about her boots, but she could hide her bare feet under the long skirt and call it a victory.

Except her head swam with dizziness, and she had to bend over, bracing her hands on her knees.

"Nic!" Gabriel swept her up into his arms. "Asa. We need Asa."

"I'm all right," she protested, wriggling. She would have the Refoel wizard healer take a look at her—later, and without Gabriel there to panic. "Just dizzy. That might've been a lot of back and forth in a short time."

"Is there precedent for that?"

"Yes, they mentioned it at Convocation Academy," she replied, which wasn't technically a lie. It had been mentioned in passing, though in the context of a wizard being ham-handed with their magic and using more force than technique. She could work with Gabriel on this. "We only need do this once more today, to satisfy the proctor, and then we can make haste more slowly." He still held her, showing no sign of setting her down, so she laid a hand on his cheek and kissed his pursed and unresponsive lips. "I'm fine, Gabriel. I'd tell you if I wasn't."

"We have yet to establish that you will," he countered, "as you've been evasive with me in the past about the toll our magic work takes on you."

"I've promised to do better," she replied with all the sincerity she could muster, well aware that she wasn't being perfectly honest at the moment. There would be time for honesty later.

He hesitated. "It occurs to me that in your twisty mind there's some distance between doing better in the future and adhering to your promise in the moment, especially if you think you're doing the right thing in managing me."

The man knew her far too well. How had that happened in such a short span of time? She scraped her nails over his cheek, just sharply enough to make him flinch. "How unfortunate that we have no time for self-excoriating philosophy." She sighed as if in deep regret. "You know how I love it so."

"Ha-ha," he muttered, but he set her on her feet—though he kept steadying hands on her.

She brushed them off. "I'm fine. See?" Determined to stay upright, she marched to the magically sealed arcanium door, then held out an expectant hand. "Let's go kick that proctor in the teeth."

Gabriel took her hand, interlacing their fingers while watching her intently, and she knew he was sampling her magic, testing her strength. At least he knew to do that now. Fortunately, whatever he sensed seemed to satisfy him because he nodded minutely. "Ready?"

"Yes." She faced the door, a seemingly solid circle of silver. Gabriel sipped at her magic, just enough to mix with his, the tendrils winding out to make contact with the enchantment embedded there by his Phel wizard ancestors. She paid close attention to the transition of the dense metal back into the moonlight it had been woven from. Or, at least, as Gabriel had guessed that was how they'd done it. It was truly a miraculous enchantment—both in its original creation and that it had endured for so long without a living wizard to maintain it. Once again, she marveled at the ingenuity and power of the ancient House Phel wizards.

And she wondered at their precipitous decline. Gabriel possessed off-the-charts levels of magical potential and, from the evidence, so had his ancestors. How had such a powerful house gone from that to magic too minor to register above a three on the Convocation's MP scorecards, and in just a couple of generations? Houses declined in power, sure, and were removed from the Convocation roster when they no longer had at least one wizard with sufficient scores. But usually they decayed gracefully, a High House drifting into second-tier status, and thence to the lower tiers where they scrabbled along, their production license greatly reduced but still viable to sustain a small household.

But House Phel—they'd gone from High House to nothing. Their people had become farmers largely ignorant of magic and the distant Convocation, not even aware of the minor magic still lingering in most of the population. Yes, rumors had it that madness had played a role in the fall of House Phel, but that didn't explain the enormity of the precipitous fall.

"Nic?" Gabriel prompted, tugging her hand. "Do you need to rest?"

The long tunnel under the lake glowed ahead of her. "Just thinking." She kicked her feet into gear. They had a number of pressing issues to handle, far more immediately important, and yet… "Is there a history of House Phel in the library?" she asked Gabriel as they walked, side by side, their fingers still interlaced.

He didn't answer for a long moment. "That's not what I expected you to be thinking about."

"That's promising." She gave him a cheeky smile. "I'd hate to be predictable this early in our relationship."

"Somehow I suspect you will *never* be predictable," he muttered under his breath.

"What's that, darling? I didn't catch it." She beamed innocently.

"Never mind. There are histories, yes, some quite old. What era are you interested in?"

"The, ah—" She caught herself before calling it the "final" one. Nothing ominous in that. Besides, it hadn't been so final after all. "The most recent, before House Phel's status was revoked."

"That's still a couple of centuries old," he pointed out.

"I didn't ask if it was new," she replied patiently.

"I don't recall reading one," he answered slowly as they

reached the end of the tunnel, unlocking the next door. "It could've been among the tomes ruined by floodwaters."

Hmm. She really wondered. "How about family gossip?" She picked her way carefully over the cellar floor, hoping she wouldn't step on anything disgusting—or venomous—with her bare feet, but still unwilling to call Gabriel's attention to his error in forgetting her boots. "What tales are told of the end days of old House Phel?"

"They aren't," he said abruptly. "We don't talk of the past."

Maybe Gabriel's parents would know. "Do you have any living grandparents?"

He bit out a sigh. "No. Do you want to tell me what you're getting at?"

"Just mulling a few things. In History of the Convocation, my professor emphasized learning from the past to predict the future." Thankfully they reached the rickety stairs up to the kitchen without anything chomping on her toes.

"We're still in the process of reestablishing House Phel," he replied, sounding cranky about it, "and you're already researching our downfall?"

"Well, clearly I'm not," she countered primly. "As there aren't any books to read on the topic."

"What about in the Convocation archives you mentioned?"

The back kitchen was silent, empty of people. Though the old manse was coming to life, housing more wizards and familiars by the day, Nic had decided to keep the old kitchen in the central part of the house as a staging area. The kitchen in the north wing was being outfitted for the primary meal activities, which she hoped to enhance with magical conveniences. Eventually they could add a kitchen annex to the south wing, too. But it would be best for Gabriel's temper—and would be in service of keeping the location of the arcanium secret—for this space to remain a glorified pantry.

"I wouldn't mind taking a look in the Convocation archives," she mused, eyes and ears alert for trouble. Everyone must be still out front, awaiting Nic and Gabriel's return with Selly. "It's your right to access House Phel's records."

"*Our* right," he corrected, squeezing her hand, then releasing it to rest his on the hilt of his sword.

"Sure," she agreed easily. "As long as you don't mind me making a trip to Convocation Center so I can—"

"Out of the question," he growled. "You're not going anywhere near those savages."

That was what she'd thought. She'd have to think of another way. Alise and Nander were enrolled at Convocation Academy and could potentially access the archives, given a seal of permission from Gabriel. *If* they were willing to help out. Her brother wasn't likely to do it. A newly minted wizard, Nander was tragically self-involved, not to mention replete with the fundamental laziness of a fifteen-year-old boy.

But Alise might do it. She'd been a wizard only a little longer than Nander, but Alise was older, more mature, and less taken by the sudden elevation in status, even though it meant their papa was now grooming Alise to be the next head of House Elal. Unfortunately, Nic and Alise didn't have a close relationship. They hadn't talked in ages.

It could be that Alise felt bad that it was her and not Nic who'd manifested as a wizard. They hadn't really spoken about it. Looking back, in fact... the lack of communication was probably Nic's fault. She'd been so crushed at the oracle's declaration that doomed her to be a familiar, so humiliated that all her grand dreams were nothing but dust, that Nic had thrown herself into finishing her studies. She'd cranked through the advanced courses for familiars in record time, taken her final exams, graduated, and promptly locked herself into the Betrothal Trials, determined to get the rest of her life going, however dismal it might be.

Now she considered that, even if the rumors of Nic's unwise escape attempt and subsequent recapture by her vengeful wizard husband hadn't gained much traction in the wider gossip circles, it was likely that Papa had at least contacted Alise about it, if only to interrogate her on what she might know.

Which would be nothing, because Nic hadn't confided in Alise. In fact, Nic couldn't recall the last real conversation she'd had with Alise, the kind that didn't involve polite greetings and discussion of family business. She should write to her sister. Nander, too, regardless of whether he'd care. With a twinge of unaccustomed guilt, she realized she should've done so a long time ago.

There: Gabriel would be pleased. She'd engaged in some self-excoriating philosophizing worthy of her wizard at his most angst-ridden. She had to say, she didn't at all understand his fondness for the depressing preoccupation.

As they came down the hall toward the front of the manse

with its expansive front porch, it seemed little had changed in their absence. Though the great front doors were closed, the flanking wide windows—newly unboarded and glassed in by the Byssan sisters, bless them—gave them a good view.

Everyone remained out front, on the porch or on the soggy lawn beyond. It had stopped raining, and some of the House Phel denizens appeared to be engaged in a game where a ball was volleyed or kicked about. The Convocation proctor had taken a seat, if stiffly, on the wide porch steps, the oracle's tabernacle beside her. Gabriel's parents stood to one side, looking worried.

"Will your parents be prepared to see me take alternate form?" Nic whispered to Gabriel.

He'd already fastened his wizard-black gaze on his folks, his pained expression a mirror of theirs. "They're not prepared for *any* of this, unfortunately."

She squeezed his hand in sympathy. All the people of Meresin had been so uninvolved in the Convocation for so long that they were largely ignorant of so much of what was common knowledge in Elal, where Nic had grown up. Their ignorance may have been bliss for centuries, but things had changed, and the monsters they didn't know about absolutely could and would hurt them.

"What do you plan to tell the proctor about your incantation?" she asked in a low voice, only partly to divert his worry. She also needed him to be prepared with a good lie, something that did not come naturally to her ethically moribund wizard.

"Incantation?" He frowned at her. "For your alternate form, you mean."

"No. The one you told the proctor you needed me for, in order to recover Selly."

"Oh." He waved off that consideration. "I'll say it didn't work."

"I see."

"What?" He stopped just shy of opening the doors.

"Nothing."

"No, that's your oh-so-neutral voice that means you think I'm being foolish but you don't want to openly disagree with me. Spit it out."

"You've been going to considerable effort to establish yourself as prideful, powerful, and scary Lord Phel with your new minions," she pointed out. "Which I know has strained your moral code. By admitting to failure—one that doesn't exist, by the way, as you didn't even try—you risk undermining all of that."

He sighed in annoyance. "Why do you even bother to ask me? Just tell me what I should say and I'll say it."

If she wasn't barefoot, she'd kick his shin for that. As it was, she'd only bruise her toes. "Because you're not my puppet, Lord Phel. I'm giving you advice, as you requested I do, I might add, not shoving my hand up your ass so I can work your mouth with my hand."

His mouth gave up its flat, irritated line, sensual lips quirking into a reluctant smile. "As charmingly filthy as that image might be, I agree it's not ideal for the partnership we're developing. I'd much rather have your hand working other parts of me." He lifted their joined hands and kissed the back of hers. "I apologize."

She actually flushed in pleasure and arousal, his moonsilver essence sparkling through her blood, cool and effervescent. "Accepted."

Still bent over her hand, he raised a brow. "And you suggest that I say…"

"Oh!" Where was her head? He smirked a little, well aware of how easily he'd flustered her. "Say that the incantation is in place but takes time to work. If questioned, make up something arcane and twisty that no one will understand. Make sure it's enough time for us to find her again," she added.

"I'm not handing Selly over to the Convocation," he warned darkly, straightening at last.

"I understand," she replied, not bothering to explain—yet again—that they might not have a choice in the matter.

~ 2 ~

EVERYONE CAME TO attention as Gabriel and Nic opened the front doors and walked out onto the graceful porch of House Phel. Though it gratified some small and mean part of him—the overwhelmed and ignorant farmer boy he'd once been—to have the instant and immediate attention of this cohort of the Convocation's finest, he also didn't much care to be under scrutiny.

Was it too much to ask to be left alone to enjoy his wife and family in peace and quiet? Apparently so.

Reading something of his regrets in him, Nic gave him an assessing sideways look from her canny emerald-green eyes. *You're the one wanting to dash yourself brainless fighting the Convocation,* she seemed to say in his mind, though they did not have that kind of telepathic communication. He didn't need Nic's remonstrations in his head for her to make her opinions clear. The look in her brilliant, knowing eyes was more than enough.

How he loved her.

"Lord Phel," the Convocation Proctor declared, as if identifying an odd species of fungus, rising to her feet. The ornate tabernacle containing the oracle head sat on the wide porch rail, its doors locked again. "Where is the rogue familiar you promised to retrieve?"

He banished the urge to cringe like a disobedient schoolboy caught out by sharp-eyed tutor. Instead he fluttered the fingers of his free hand, imitating what he imagined a lordly noble might do. Nic's fingers remained firmly entwined with his other hand. She'd repeatedly warned him that keeping physical contact with her made it look as if he were prepared to access her magic as his familiar—a sign of weakness or aggression—but he didn't care. He liked holding her hand, and doing as he liked was the soul of wizardly arrogance, wasn't it?

"The incantation has been enacted," he intoned, trying to sound powerful and enigmatic.

The proctor narrowed her eyes at him. "Forgive me, Lord Phel," she said, her tone clearly unapologetic, "but I am well aware you did not attend Convocation Academy and lack, if not the training for a proper incantation, then at least the language to describe what you've done. But indulge me. What sort of spell, precisely, have you enacted to retrieve the rogue familiar you endangered through willful concealment?"

Nic's magic warmed his hand, filtering into his blood with rose-dark, bloodred warning. *Make up something arcane and twisty that no one will understand.* He raised a hand and pointed to the moon, invisible behind the cloud cover, yet vivid in his mind. He always knew where the moon was. "The moon shines her face upon the land and none may hide from her reflection." He swept a hand at the lake and the marshes beyond. "Likewise, water infiltrates all, seeping into every crevice, and no force may keep it out." Beside him, Nic snorted softly in wry agreement. He'd been sure her alternate form would be a feline, like her mother's, what with the way Nic loathed getting wet. "And none may hide from it," he finished on a low note.

The watching wizards—among them Asa, the Refoel healer; the glassmaker, Sage; the furniture maker, Wolfgang; and the enigmatic El-Adrel spy, Jadren—exchanged bemused glances. *At least they seem suitably confused.*

The proctor waited a beat longer. "That's all you have to say?"

Gabriel pulled icy arrogance around himself. "I don't expect a mid-level wizard such as yourself to understand."

She huffed out a breath, setting a hand on the tabernacle containing the oracle head as if considering asking it. "How long am I to wait for a result?"

"As long as necessary," he replied coldly, allowing some of his water magic to chill the humid air around the loathsome woman.

"I am expected at Convocation Center." Though she shivered, the proctor lifted her chin and firmed her lips. "I cannot dally here."

"Then by all means," he returned, "do not dally." He swept a hand at the carriage she'd arrived in just a few hours ago, then cast a jaundiced eye at the overcast, twilit sky. "Feel free to depart immediately. It looks like rain."

"Does it ever *not* look like rain in this miserable swamp?" she snapped back. "I am not leaving, Lord Phel, until I've completed my duties." She slid her disapproving glare onto Nic. "As you've failed to demonstrate that this recalcitrant and demonstrably disobedient familiar is properly bonded, I shall send a Ratsiel courier to Convocation Center. They will dispatch an escort to take Lady Veronica Elal into custody and return her for disciplinary action and retraining, while I wait here for the other one."

Nic made a sound of distress—not for that prospect, but because he'd vised his grip on her hand. Making himself relax, he stared down the proctor. "Lady *Phel* remains with me. I have need of her. And you were allowed on my lands only on the contingency that those Convocation hunters do not step one hairy, clawed foot here."

That got their audience's attention. The familiars, gathered into their own little group—though Asa's familiar, Laryn, stood well apart from them—in particular looked keenly interested. It seemed the hunters were kept somewhat secret. With common folk, he could see how that was possible as they couldn't see the creatures, but magic wielders, whether wizard or familiar, seemed able to detect the presence of hunters easily.

"The Convocation agreed to your terms on the premise that I'd be welcomed here and allowed to observe. So far I have not been offered lodging or refreshment, and I hardly feel welcome." The woman delivered her remonstration slicingly, but beneath, her magic, weak as it was, quaked slightly.

And Gabriel actually felt a hint of remorse. Glancing at Nic, he found her deep-green eyes fixed on him—with some of the same feeling in it. "My apologies," he said, returning his gaze to the proctor. "Our hospitality has indeed been remiss. Mom?"

His mother, Daisy, jerked in surprise at being noticed. She and Gabriel's father had retreated to a far corner of the porch, observing in appalled anxiety. No wonder. Their daughter had been found, named a familiar, and proclaimed insane as a result of it, lost again, and now arguments raged that they could barely understand. His father, too, looked confused and more than a little sad. Gabriel grieved at how he'd turned their lives inside out—and he saw an opportunity to at least spare them the sight of Nic taking her extraordinary alternate form.

"Mom," he repeated, more gently, extracting a tremulous smile from her. "And Dad—would you two see about finding a room for the proctor and a snack to tide her over until she can..." He set his teeth and will against the prospect of the odious woman at his dining table. "... join us for the evening meal?"

They nodded in the unison of a long and harmonious marriage. "Daisy, you know more about the room situation," his father said. "I'll round up *refreshments*." The old farmer made the word sound overly dainty, but it was easy to forgive. The proctor had made many enemies quickly.

"Acceptable?" Gabriel inquired of the proctor as his folks slipped inside.

She sniffed. "You have yet to demonstrate the familiar is properly bonded and obedient to your will."

"She looks obedient to me," Gabriel said, unable to resist teasing Nic with an assessing look. Her expression remained carefully schooled, but her eyes held green fire.

"That remains to be seen. Regardless, it would be irresponsible of me to allow her to remain free if she is not under a wizard's *complete* control." The proctor eyed Nic with false sympathy. "If only for her own safety."

"Ah, yes." Gabriel snapped his fingers as if only then remembering. "I recall you suggested a demonstration of Lady Phel's alternate form, just before we were interrupted." By the untimely arrival of Selly, trussed up in ropes and fighting like a marsh cat. He'd desperately wanted Selly to be found, but that had been the worst possible timing. "Familiar," he said to Nic, using the word to harness her attention. This had to go smoothly. And he couldn't compromise this little demonstration by asking her permission. This was as close as he could come.

"Yes, wizard," she replied calmly, her eyes full of perfect trust, her magic a billowing counterpoint, summer roses, fiery heat, and spiced wine filling him with heady power.

He reached for the silver strands of his magic that connected them, following the rich, wine-red channels of her magic that flowed back to him. Gathering them gently, he held her hand, feeling as if he'd leashed a wild horse by fragile silver ribbons. Wrapping them around his mental fist, he tugged, sharp and swift, willing her to become something *else.*

If she thought he didn't sense how it pained her, she was wrong. He was also aware that she attempted to conceal it from him, but nothing could disguise the convulsion of self that disrupted her, that pulled the internal to the external, a wrenching dislocation of her human skin.

Their audience gasped, murmurs of surprise and speculation rising into louder conversation. Gabriel ignored them, his attention trained on the proctor's reaction—and on the glory that was Nic's alternate form.

A majestic and shining silver bird, she stood with her head level to his. Without the erotic haze clouding his brain, without the cloying worry that he'd perform the magic wrong or somehow harm her, he was able to observe her more closely. Though clearly not equipped for standing on flat ground, her silver talons dug into the soft lawn, gripping with strength to allow for her poised posture. A crest of shimmering shades of crystal crowned her proud head, cascading down her long, arched neck. Wings that looked large enough to carry even her considerable mass in flight were folded sleekly along her body, and a long tail flowed to the ground, trailing in glittering argent shades. Here and there, he caught a shimmer of rose red. He got the impression that, if she chose to spread her tail like a peacock might, that the fan would show more of those rosy shades. Perhaps her wings, too.

Nic cocked her head, turning it so one emerald eye was fixed on the proctor, her lethally curved beak in profile. She trilled a question at the obviously flummoxed wizard, seeming to ask if the proctor was satisfied.

The proctor seemed to be momentarily incapable of speech. "That... This..." she stammered. "This is *not* an appropriate alternate form," she nearly screeched.

Uh-oh. Nic had worried that Gabriel's insistence on recip-rocal bonding would manifest in odd ways. And here he was, too ignorant of the arcane information taught in the academy's advanced wizard studies to know if this form truly was a problem.

"A point of order, if I may, Lord Phel?" Asa asked in a

raised, polite tone. At Gabriel's nod, the Refoel wizard strode forward, coming near Nic, but not touching. He held up his hands, his healing magic palpable to Gabriel as it condensed over Nic. "She is perfectly healthy," Asa announced.

"She is a mythical creature!" the proctor hissed, appalled and affronted. Gabriel was especially glad his parents had left.

"Unusual," Asa replied placidly.

"A monster!" she retorted.

"I realize you are not a high-level wizard, proctor," Asa said, not without sympathy. "So you would not be aware of the information we have access to in the more advanced classes. This alternate form is not monstrous."

"So you *claim*," she muttered.

Asa eyed the proctor, then beckoned to his familiar, Laryn, without looking, but with an unconscious expectation of obedience that set Gabriel's teeth on edge. He wouldn't make an issue of it now, however, especially as Laryn complied immediately, coming to Asa's side to slip her hand into his, lending him her magic. Asa looked to Gabriel. "May I conduct a more in-depth examination?"

He had to bite back the retort to ask Nic herself, and simply nodded, not trusting his voice. The sooner they got through this, the sooner he could restore Nic to her native form and they could move on with their lives without Convocation interference.

To his credit, Asa approached Nic slowly, holding up a hand that contrasted darkly with her shining silver. She curved her neck, dipping her beak, and the healer smiled. Laying a hand against her feathers, he closed his eyes, a reverent expression transforming his face. "Oh, you are a beauty, indeed," he murmured, and Gabriel fought the irrational and wildly jealous urge to wrench the other wizard away.

It's in a wizard's nature to be possessive, he heard Nic observe in his mind, and her emerald gaze, the same color as her human eyes but foreign to him in their avian shape, seemed to sparkle with amusement at his expense.

"The alternate form is sound," Asa informed the proctor.

"But what *is* it?" she hissed, fingers digging clawlike into the tabernacle.

Asa dipped a chin at the tabernacle. "Why not ask?"

"I will!" The proctor busied herself with unlocking the tabernacle doors, and Asa took the opportunity to slide Gabriel a dark-eyed look. One he couldn't interpret, however. A warning?

"I have to say," Jadren El-Adrel drawled in a bored tone, "I've never read of precedent for the Convocation questioning a familiar's alternate form. It's well known that the shape a familiar takes is innate. I can't imagine what you believe Lord Phel may have accomplished here." He grinned at Gabriel. "My mother will be most interested, however."

House El-Adrel would no doubt eat up every scrap of information Jadren fed them.

The proctor paused. "Wizard El-Adrel, I do not question the alternate form itself, but whether this inconclusive bonding is legitimate."

Jadren raised a supercilious brow. "That's not how it sounded. You stated that demonstration of alternate form would be proof of bonding."

"The alternate form is irregular," she protested, but her argument lacked force.

Jadren and Asa exchanged glances, then shook their heads in unison. "That's not in your authority to decide," Jadren informed her, pity in his tone.

"If Lord Phel does not have control of this... this beast," the proctor persisted, "imagine the damage it could do."

"But Lord Phel obviously has control," Asa inserted. "As he can demonstrate by returning the familiar to human form, fully dressed."

He gave Gabriel that look again, so Gabriel took the hint and hastily complied. Drawing the silver net of magic tight as he laid a hand on her sleek feathers, he envisioned Nic in all her fiery beauty, fully clothed.

"Wait, I—" The proctor protested too late. Nic stood where the silver phoenix had been, her gown rustling as it adjusted to her shape, emphasizing her lush figure. "I didn't get to ask the oracle what that bird is," the proctor finished unhappily.

"Some other time, perhaps," Gabriel replied loftily, offering Nic his arm, seeing the weariness in her. "I must check the incantation now. I will see you all at dinner."

Turning to the steps, he brought Nic along, concerned by the way she leaned heavily against him.

"Lord Phel, if I may have a word?" Asa inquired.

Gabriel nearly said no, then caught the look in the healer's eye. He nodded stiffly, then proceeded to the library. The fire crackled cheerfully, the armchairs, freshly upholstered by the House Ophiel Wizard Dahlia, still where he and Nic had vacated them upon the proctor's arrival. It felt like days ago, not hours. He helped Nic settle into one of them, his alarm increasing at her vacant expression. "What's wrong with her?" he demanded.

Asa crouched before Nic, studying her face. "May I have your permission to touch Lady Phel?" he inquired carefully.

Gabriel nearly snapped at him but recalled his reaction at finding the healer's hands on his wife before and grudgingly nodded.

Asa took Nic's unresponsive hands in his. Laryn stood close behind him, ready to serve, no doubt, but Gabriel knew Nic wouldn't like for the other woman to observe her debilitated state. Nic didn't like anyone to see her as weak, no matter how much she proclaimed her comfort with her subservient status as a familiar. Besides, Laryn in particular was no friend of Nic's. If Gabriel had known, he wouldn't have accepted Asa's application to be the House Phel healer. Water under the bridge.

Unfortunately, short of playing arrogant wizard to the hilt, Gabriel couldn't banish Laryn from the room. And if Asa needed to access his familiar's magic to help Nic, then any amount of embarrassment would be worth it. He only hoped Nic would see it the same way.

"Alternate form is tricky," Asa answered, though sounding almost as if musing to himself. "Even with long practice, the process can be draining and difficult. I surmise you two haven't had extensive practice yet?"

If he only knew *how* little, that he and Nic had only figured it out a couple of hours ago. Rather than explain, especially as he wasn't sure how much Nic would want anyone to know, he simply folded his arms and grunted. Asa accepted that response, and Gabriel had to give Nic credit: the taciturn and broody image she'd encouraged him to cultivate came in handy in circumstances like this.

"I can tell you that the pregnancy is fine," Asa said, fortunately intent upon Nic and so missing Gabriel's start of guilt and surprise.

He hadn't thought about the pregnancy, nor had Nic mentioned it as a problem when he forced her into alternate form. Of course the pregnancy could be at risk. So unutterably careless of him. And yet... with Nic's well-being at stake, he'd make the same choice again. With nothing to do but wait on her wizard, Laryn watched him closely, her serious eyes resting on his face, something of a knowing smirk on her otherwise pretty mouth. She rested a hand on her own noticeably rounded belly, beaming with superiority.

No wonder Nic didn't care for the woman.

Just then, Nic inhaled sharply, jerking from her slouch, color flooding her cheeks. Asa smiled broadly. "There we are. How do you feel?"

Gabriel had opened his mouth to ask the same question, and closed it again, irritated to be edged out.

Nic curled her fingers around Asa's. "Better now. Thank you. That was... a very strange experience."

"I'll bet." Asa rubbed Nic's hands between his, then stopped and slowly released them, casting a wary look at Gabriel as a low growl escaped him. Laryn gazed at Gabriel with increased interest, pursing her lips thoughtfully.

"Lord Phel," Nic said softly, holding out a hand to him. "Do you have need of me?"

He did, but not in the way she intended their audience to believe. But he seized the excuse to touch her, taking the proffered hand and enfolding it in his, like he might hold an injured bird that might further harm itself by trying to flap away. Nic met his gaze, a world of reassurance in it. She said she loved him, and he wanted to believe it. Mostly he did believe it, though he would likely never forget how the Fascination drove her to cleave to him whether she chose to or not.

"What happened?" he asked.

Asa answered. "Taking alternate form, as I said, is a powerful experience for a familiar. You both have plenty of magical potential to perform the feat, obviously, but sheer power—while it gets the job done—isn't all that's required. It takes getting used to, and I don't recommend practicing to excess."

Gabriel bit down on the retort that the healer's contradictory advice was hardly helpful.

"Second," Asa continued, "being in what is essentially an animal mind is disorienting even for an experienced familiar. With Lady Phel's... unusual form, it's not unreasonable to expect a greater level of dislocation."

Nic nodded. "I feel like I'm still not thinking straight."

"Food and rest should help," Asa told her. "If you still feel off, or in any way not yourself in the morning, come see me. The final consideration for Lady Phel's present difficulties," he said, turning to Gabriel, "is the matter of your nonstandard bonding."

"There is nothing wrong with our bonding," Gabriel growled.

"With *your* bonding, Lord Phel," Asa emphasized gently. "It's not reciprocal. A wizard binds a familiar. The very fact that you don't speak of it that way gives me pause." He looked between Nic and Gabriel. "Is there anything you two would like to tell me?"

Nic curled her fingers against his palm, a subtle warning he didn't need. He produced a puzzled, hopefully innocently bemused frown. "I can't imagine what?"

Asa sighed. "I'm under contract to your house, Lord Phel. You should be able to trust my loyalty."

Gabriel highly doubted that. Nic had certainly made it clear that trust was a liability in the Convocation, not a strength. He regarded Asa impassively, offering nothing more.

"I'm concerned that…" The Refoel wizard paused, clicked his tongue against his teeth, considering his words. "No insult intended, Lord Phel—and I hope you know I mean that in all sincerity—but it's common knowledge that you did not attend Convocation Academy. While you've clearly developed impressive skills outside of a conventional education, there remain… gaps in your advanced understanding, particularly as applies to working with a familiar, especially one as powerful as Lady Phel."

In short: Gabriel was a shitty wizard who had put his familiar in jeopardy. This wasn't the first time Asa had implied as much, though this time he spoke far more baldly. Nic squeezed Gabriel's hand, still gazing up at him, her expression warm and loving. "Understood," he grated out.

"Good." Asa dusted his hands together. "For example, it seems you pushed Lady Phel into alternate form without using a compulsion spell?"

Shit. It hadn't occurred to Gabriel to use compulsion, though the application was obvious, and he'd witnessed Lord Elal using one on Nic's mother to put her in alternate form. "You're correct," he admitted. "But my compulsion magic isn't strong."

"It would be more appropriate to say it's not as strong as your other magics," Asa replied easily. "Still, I must admit I have no idea how you performed that feat *without* using compulsion."

Gabriel exchanged a long look with Nic. Neither of them knew the answer, as she wasn't trained in advanced wizardry either, and they'd simply... improvised. "And your point is?" he asked Asa.

"I don't want to presume to offer instruction, as you are obviously far my senior in rank and power, Lord Phel. I am only a simple healer. I did, however, complete my advanced wizardry training at the academy with high marks, and I'm an adequate tutor. I feel strongly that you could use advice from a friendly quarter, from someone who will keep your secrets."

Gabriel raised a dubious brow. "You won't be relaying information back to House Refoel?"

Nic winced, making a low sound—no doubt appalled at his lack of subtlety—and Asa glanced at her, grinning. "I'd be surprised if Lady Phel wasn't educating you in how the Convocation runs on gossip and spies."

Nic rolled her eyes at him, but didn't comment, so Asa

returned his gaze to Gabriel. "I am expected to pass information back to my house, yes, but it's also understood that I
belong to House Phel. If it increases your confidence in me,
you can add a nondisclosure codicil to the contract we have yet
to sign."

Nic sat up straight, tugging her hand from his, eyes flashing. "You haven't signed the contract yet?" Her glare was all
for Gabriel.

Amused that house business was what snapped Nic out of
her stupor—and trying not to cringe like a kid caught slacking
on his chores—Gabriel gestured to the desks stacked with
paperwork and missives delivered by the seemingly unending
stream of Ratsiel couriers. "We've been busy," he pointed out,
sounding only a little defensive.

Nic popped out of her chair, apparently fully recovered by
the galvanizing effect of critical business left undone. "This is
not something you can let fall through the cracks, Gabriel," she
scolded, striding over to the paired desks, one hers and one his.
He studied the desks more closely, realizing that furniture
wizard Wolfgang had been at work there, too. The wood
gleamed like new, and the one no longer listed alarmingly on
its splinted leg.

"Aha!" Asa said, raising an amused brow as he walked
alongside Gabriel, hands casually tucked in his pockets.
"There's the spirited woman I recall from the academy. I had
wondered." Laryn trailed behind them, her meekness irritating
Gabriel, but he was also unclear on how to address the issue.

Caught out, contract in hand, Nic actually blushed faintly,
sending Gabriel a rueful look. As if he cared that her pretense

at being *his* meek and subservient familiar had collapsed. "We can't get this nondisclosure agreement signed quickly enough, apparently," she replied with admirable composure. She raised a brow at Gabriel. "Is the contract otherwise agreeable to you?"

Since they seemed to have abandoned—at least with Asa, and inevitably, Laryn—the subterfuge of making Gabriel out to be lord and master of everything, he shrugged. "You know better than I what should be in the contract."

"Then I'll add the codicil." She sat at her desk, giving Gabriel a grateful smile when he lit the oil lamp for her.

"Is this nondisclosure agreement enforceable?" Gabriel asked, mostly of Nic.

She tapped the self-inking quill against her lower lip. "Yes and no. The Convocation *should* regard it as legally binding, but most of its power will reside in you and what you will do to anyone who dares break their agreement with you. The Convocation would back whatever retribution you deemed appropriate in that case. Fear of what you might do is a powerful motivator."

"Good enough," he decided, surreptitiously stroking the velvety nape of her neck before stepping away to let her concentrate.

"You're not using Elal elementals for lighting, I noticed," Asa said as Nic wrote.

Nic's magic, which had been blooming rosily, contracted at Asa's words. "No," Gabriel replied for her. "We have yet to reach... an agreement with House Elal."

"Pity." Asa nodded knowingly. "And no surprise there,

though I'm sorry to hear it."

"Care to review this, Wizard Asa?" Nic inquired, holding out the contract.

He took it, laying the document on the desk in the pool of warm light and bending over it. He straightened, looking between Nic and Gabriel with considerable surprise. "You're asking your wizards to agree to share all income, including royalties from products developed, equally with their familiars?"

Laryn startled visibly in Gabriel's peripheral vision, and Asa turned to look at his familiar as if just then remembering her existence. Gabriel set his teeth. Asa wasn't anywhere near as arrogant and self-involved as most Convocation wizards, but he still had a distressing tendency to treat his familiar like an appendage, rather than as an independent human being.

"Where would she keep the funds?" he asked, studying Laryn. "And how would she use them?"

Mastering his temper, Gabriel looked to Nic for help. She blinked at him with wide eyes, smiling with patently false innocence, making it clear he was on his own. *This was your idea,* she seemed to be saying, *so you make the argument.* Clearing his throat, he recalled what Nic had said when he proposed the idea. "To begin with, we're aware that familiars wouldn't be able to spend their income outside of Meresin. House Phel could, however, keep accounts for familiars who are uncomfortable keeping their coin any other way. We would then make purchases for familiars via our house vendor accounts, so they can acquire what they like from their credit."

For the first time in their brief acquaintance, Laryn looked something less than dour.

"I'm frankly a bit insulted by the implication that I wouldn't provide for my own familiar and wife," Asa said, but not angrily.

"Don't be, Asa," Nic put in. "No one is questioning your ability or willingness to provide for Laryn. Think about other wizards we've known who are not so generous as you."

Asa, still studying Laryn, nodded thoughtfully. "It's a radical idea," he said. "I suggest that your nondisclosure cover the contract terms as well, or you may see trouble from this. In fact, you'd be wise to seal the nondisclosure *before* you show anyone the contract, in case they decline to sign and carry the tale back to the Convocation."

Nic raised her brows at Gabriel, managing to both seek his approval on the tactic and remind him that she'd told him this move would create trouble. "Excellent idea," he replied to Asa, wondering if the wizard would now be one of those who refused to sign, the first to carry the tale to Convocation if allowed—and what lengths Gabriel would be willing to go to in order to silence the man.

Asa seemed to read Gabriel's darker thoughts, because he chuckled, holding up his hands in surrender. "You can pull back your magic, Lord Phel. I'm not going to betray you." Reaching for the quill Nic offered him, Asa flipped to the final page and signed with a flourish. "I assume you want Laryn to sign also." He beckoned to her, handing her the quill when she stood there, unmoving. "Read it, of course," he prompted her gently, running an affectionate hand down her arm.

She tried to hand the quill back to him. "My signature has

no legal significance."

"It does here in Meresin," Nic told her firmly. One thing about Nic—when she gave her loyalty, she gave it absolutely. She might argue Gabriel to death about bashing himself brainless against the walls of the Convocation, but she kept those arguments private. Before others, they were a united front, something he hadn't known to value until she gave it to him.

Laryn eyed Nic with obvious, even virulent, dislike. "It's foolishness," she told Nic. "I am a *properly* bonded familiar, and thus could never go against my wizard's wishes."

"Then why haven't you read the contract, as Asa directed you to do?" Nic replied softly, giving no indication that Laryn's insulting implication had registered.

Flushing, Laryn bent over the contract, reading with such grim intensity her eyes might've burnt holes in the paper, flipping the pages with more force than necessary. Then she signed beneath Asa's signature, dropped the quill on top, and turned to face Gabriel and Asa. "Any further instructions?" she bit out ungraciously.

Behind Laryn's back, Nic wrinkled her nose, smoothing her expression before sliding the contract to Gabriel. "You'll need to sign and seal this."

He spun it around, plucking up the quill Laryn had dropped and offering it to Nic like a gift. "You, too."

She opened her mouth to argue, realized her predicament, and shook her head slightly. Gabriel smiled to himself as she signed. The easiest argument he'd ever won with her. When she handed the contract back to him, he took it to his desk and opened the drawer. Well oiled and now with convenient compartments, the drawer held the House Phel seal in the same spot. Very interesting wizardry on Wolfgang's part. Did the wizard leave everything in place and shape the desk around it?

Shaking off the musings, he withdrew the silver seal with a sense of reverence. When he'd finally grappled with his new, hugely changed life as a wizard, and had determined to restore House Phel, he'd gone to Convocation Center to complete the paperwork. They'd given him the ancient seal, which had been returned to the Convocation, they explained, when the Phel family lost their house status. From Nic, he now understood that the Convocation should've given him full access to the House Phel archives at the time, instead taking advantage of his ignorance by omitting that bit of information.

Still, receiving that heavy silver seal had been a thrilling moment, one whose shine had yet to fade. Despite everything he'd learned since, he still experienced that sense of gravity in using the seal, the excitement of realized ambition, and anticipation of the endless possibilities the future held. Nic had told him that part of his inheritance of the Phel magic was a connection to his ancestors. Even though he had reservations about who those wizards had been as human beings, that sense of connection trilled through him through the silver.

Generations of magic, of wizards and familiars, building to this moment to carry forward. Catching Nic's eye, he saw a glimmer of similar emotion in her gaze, understanding him well, as always. With a dip of his chin to her, acknowledging all she'd done to bring this about, he signed, then sealed the contract.

House Phel had its first official minion. Minions, he corrected himself with a mental head shake. If he wanted familiars to count, then he needed to remember to count them.

~ 3 ~

Nic's head still didn't feel right, but she put herself to drafting the nondisclosure agreements, making sure she had one to pair with each of the contracts she'd drafted. She also made a note to buy a copying gremlin from House Xerograf. The things could be a terrible pest if not well-bonded, making copies of everything in sight, then balking entirely for days on end, but the expense for a good one would be worth the trade for her time.

She included signature lines for the familiars as well, should the wizard be bonded to one, as it had become rather frighteningly clear what a risk the familiars posed to House Phel's secrecy and security. Naturally, the Convocation expected that wizards would control their familiars and prevent them from acting—or passing along information—without the wizard's knowledge, but how much of that was true in reality? Until Nic had noted the way Laryn observed everything that passed with glittering intensity, it hadn't occurred to her that the woman could, and likely happily would, betray Nic, given half the chance. Familiars were so often in the background, so often ignored and forgotten, that they made perfect spies.

Foolish of her not to consider that before. Fortunately, thanks to Asa's quick wits, they'd caught the problem in time. She hoped. And with Gabriel's magical seal on the nondisclosure, Laryn not only wasn't allowed to pass along information, she should be physically unable to do so.

Nic really wanted everyone they'd brought into House Phel to sign one of the NDAs immediately. They all already knew too much about her and Gabriel's unusual bonding. Still, nothing would seal the proctor's mouth—short of the woman's death, and Nic wasn't going to put *that* idea into Gabriel's head, if it wasn't there already.

As she worked at her desk, she half listened as Asa instructed Gabriel on the finer points of evoking alternate form from one's familiar. They'd all decided—even Nic—that Nic was in no condition to transform again that night, so Asa limited himself to repeating the lectures he'd received in the advanced wizardry practicums at Convocation Academy, and to a single demonstration with Laryn.

Laryn's alternate form, it turned out, was a small falcon. Nic rather envied the other familiar for that. She'd wanted wings, yes, but it would be far more convenient to have a winged form that was less... conspicuous. She wasn't sure if her fuzzy thinking came from being in alternate form, full stop, as Asa had indicated, or whether the phoenix's mind wasn't somehow *very* different. Nic rather thought it was the latter, but she obviously had no basis for comparison. So far, Laryn was the only familiar in House Phel who had taken alternate form, and she didn't see them having a cozy chat between familiars.

If only Quinn had taken her alternate form, but she hadn't and likely wouldn't. Being her sister's familiar made their relationship necessarily nonsexual. Besides, for a glassmaking duo like them, alternate form wasn't a priority. Still, Nic wondered if Quinn wasn't wistful about it, as having an alternate form was one of the few perks of being a familiar.

Finished with enough nondisclosures to cover their current group, plus a few extra—it would be good to have Gabriel's parents sign them, too, though she doubted she'd get any of them to agree to that—she began her letter to Alise.

Dear Alise,

I hope you will forgive…

And there she stopped. The empty space glared at her accusingly.

Would it be tacky to include a bullet-pointed list of all the transgressions Nic hoped Alise would forgive? Starting with their childhood and all the innumerable ways Nic had been overbearing to her little sister, so certain of her golden future as the head of House Elal. Looking back, she cringed at her own behavior. How could she even begin to make that up to Alise? As she stared at those brief lines, the conspicuously empty space after that innocuous word, "forgive," the letter began to seem like a gargantuan task. She dropped her aching head into her hands.

"Ready for dinner?" Gabriel asked.

Startled, she looked up to find him standing on the other side of the desk. Asa and Laryn were gone. She groaned, folding her arms and collapsing onto them. "I cannot face formal dinner with all those people."

"Surely that's my line." Gabriel sounded amused, though not unsympathetic. He came around behind her, brushing soothing hands over the back of her neck, bared by her short haircut, digging his thumbs into the tense ligaments at the base of her skull. "You could probably claim feeling unwell and skip it. No one would blame you."

For a brief, giddy moment, she considered that option. She could go take a hot bath and read her new book that she'd barely had time to get into, and go to bed early. Then Maman's voice scolded her sternly about her duties as Lady Phel. "No." She sighed and sat up, her groan turning to a purr as Gabriel slid his arms around her in a loose embrace, his lips nuzzling her temple. "I should be by your side, particularly in these early days, especially with all that happened this afternoon."

"Pity," he murmured, kissing her ear. "I was going to take the excuse to stay with you."

She laughed throatily, not at all surprised. In fact, knowing Gabriel would try to avoid dinner if she wasn't there was a large part of the reason she knew she had to go. "I should check on the progress of dinner. I hadn't realized it had gotten so late." The overcast sky outside the windows had darkened to full night. It had been an incredibly long day, and she was still wearing the gown she'd worn to assist Gabriel with the levee repair. She probably looked terrible. "But I also need to clean up and change for dinner."

"You go change," he told her, "and I'll check on dinner."

She raised a brow at the offer. "Are you sure?"

He raised a mirroring brow. "I can terrorize staff just as well as you can."

Laughing, she acknowledged that truth, accepting his hand to get up from the chair. "I won't be long."

He drew her to him, lips brushing over hers in a light kiss that quickly heated. Firmly setting her away from him, he shook his head. "Just don't take too long, or I'll have to come find you, and we'll no doubt end up in bed."

She put the back of her hand to her forehead and sagged dramatically. "On second thought, I think maybe I *don't* feel well enough to attend dinner. Maybe you need to carry me up to bed." Nic secretly relished it when Gabriel carried her, his easy strength so deliciously compelling.

Gabriel laughed and waggled a finger at her. "None of your tricks, familiar. I'm wise to your seductions."

A susurrous of need thrilled through her at him calling her that. "Seductions don't require a bed, wizard," she purred, swaying toward him and reaching to undo his pants. Perhaps she'd kneel and...

He stepped back, deftly evading her. "Later," he promised.

"It wouldn't take long," she protested.

"Maybe we can share that bath," he said over his shoulder as he strode for the library doors, casting her a wicked grin.

"But you promised me the arcanium tonight."

He paused, looking blank.

"Right before Lady El-Adrel arrived," she prompted, though that brought to mind that whole set of problems, with Lady El-Adrel blackmailing Gabriel over the enchanted knife he'd made and forcing him to take on her wizard son, Jadren.

A wizard with no MP scorecard—impossible—and who Nic had no idea about—almost as impossible. She should ask Alise. After she got through the long, complex, and complicated apology portion of the letter. Maybe her sister could dig up some gossip about the enigmatic, auburn-haired Jadren El-Adrel. Though Maman would frown on asking favors in the same letter as an apology. Nic would have to send two letters, with a respectful time in between. Speaking of which, maybe Alise would be able to check on their mother and determine if Papa had really kept her in alternate form all this time.

And if Alise didn't respond, well… that would be an answer too.

"That was before we ended up in the arcanium this afternoon," Gabriel said, and she had to wrench her thoughts back to the subject at hand.

"Guess what?" she asked, gliding toward him and hooking a finger in the open neckline of his shirt, his skin hot as fire-warmed velvet beneath. "We can go to the arcanium multiple times a day."

"No," he replied firmly, grasping her hand to hold it in place and sliding the other behind her neck. He kissed her, soft and deep. "I love you, Nic," he said, catching and holding her gaze.

Her heart turned over with a dreamy sigh. "I love you, too."

He smiled, boyishly pleased. "New rule: we visit the arcanium once a day only, at most. Less often if I deem it would be too hard on you."

"Look at you being the autocratic wizard," she complained. "What happened to partnership?"

"The care and feeding of familiars," he replied, his smile warm and affectionate. "I reserve the right to protect you from your worst instincts."

Her body thrummed with disappointment even as the rational part of her acknowledged he was probably right. She needed to take a break from all the magic inflow and outflow.

Gabriel drew her closer, placing a lingering kiss on her forehead, then on both eyelids as they fluttered closed. "I'll still make love to you, my heart," he whispered. "It's my turn to tend to you, and I plan to take very long time with you."

Oh my. He released her and strode out of the library. Well, that parting line certainly helped salve her disappointment, though it did the opposite for her state of arousal. Alas for that. At least her head felt clearer. She followed Gabriel's path out of the library and turned in the other direction for the stairs up to the master suite. Reaching the bathing chamber, she caught sight of herself in the age-spotted mirror and gasped in dismay.

Though the Ophiel gown did its best, apparently no amount of magic could withstand the rigors of the day she'd spent in it. Mud spattered the hem, no doubt from the morning's work at the levee, not to mention standing outside in the rain greeting their various visitors, most of them unwelcome. Gabriel's magic may have kept the rain off, but he hadn't wicked the water out of the soaked lawn. Then there had been wild sex magic in the arcanium, and several transitions from human to alternate form and back again. It all had left her pale, with shadows under her eyes you could hide an army of wizards in, eyes that were red and puffy from her crying jag in the library over her father's cruel message, and strained lines around her mouth from... who knew? Repressing the sarcastic remarks she longed to make, no doubt.

And her hair... well the short cut wasn't the miracle she'd hoped for back when she'd struggled to manage it long, dreaming of the day she'd be a bonded familiar and at least be able to cut her hair. The wildly curling mass had a life of its own. Losing the length made it easier to comb out, but that much more difficult to control.

It had been vain to keep the upper locks long, softening her too-high Elal forehead and beaky nose. And the price of that vanity was apparently a bristling halo of dark curls that made her look like the miniature troll dolls she'd played with as a girl. *Not* a good look.

Muttering imprecations at Gabriel for not mentioning her ghastly disrepair—though no wonder he hadn't been tempted by her—she triggered the fastenings on the gown and stripped it off, along with the sweat-soaked lingerie beneath. Unleashing the grooming imp on her hair, she dipped a cloth in a basin of water to sponge bathe, gritting her teeth at its chill and missing her water elementals who'd bathed her so thoroughly, and *warmly*. It was almost enough to make her want to reconcile with Papa. Almost.

Not that it was within her power to do so.

Besides, Gabriel, as impossible as it seemed, was even more stubborn than she was. When Lady El-Adrel had delivered Papa's message—*drink water*—Gabriel had understood its meaning as well as Nic had. More, he understood how ruthlessly Lord Elal had cut ties with his eldest daughter with those simple words. He would not be sending Nic's trousseau, nor the grape vines she'd requested as part of her dowry, or any dowry at all. She'd defied her father and her house by trying to escape Gabriel, then again by cleaving to her water wizard instead of returning obediently to House Elal. *Drink water.* The message was clear. She didn't want it to hurt, but—oh, how deeply that had cut.

Exactly as her father intended. And Gabriel, in all of his protective fury on her behalf, would never forgive him for it. The only way House Phel would be acquiring helpful elementals was buying canned ones retail, an expense she did not relish absorbing and, besides, the canned ones never worked as well.

With her face clean, Nic reapplied her makeup, not trusting the grooming imp with the task, though it had restored her hair to a semblance of order. She found some thoughtful soul had left her velvet robe on a hook in the bathing chamber—her efforts to enlist help in running the house were beginning to pay off—and shrugged it on. Deciding what to wear to dinner wouldn't take long, as she still only had only a few gowns to choose from and only one warm enough for the chilly, rainy evening. Thankfully, another kind and helpful soul, or possibly the same one, had laundered the burgundy velvet.

Nic sniffed it suspiciously, wary of the thing, as the last time she'd worn it, the gown had been soaked in fetid algae marsh water. It smelled fresh and clean, however, and she happily laid it on the bed. She was shrugging out of the robe when a knock sounded on the door.

Reflexively, she glanced at the balcony doors, black with

night and sheeting rain, but they remained firmly closed. Not Selly, then, who had a penchant for climbing the manse and slipping inside. Though Selly wouldn't knock anyway. Nic opened the doors and found Gabriel's mother wringing her hands, expression tense.

"Daisy," Nic said in some surprise. "Won't you come in? I was just changing for dinner."

"Oh, I won't keep you," Daisy replied, hesitating on the threshold.

"You won't be, as long as you don't mind me changing clothes."

"All right, then." Daisy went straight to the fireplace, holding her hands out to the cheerful blaze. "I swear, spring is the coldest season. The chill goes right to the bone. All that damp."

"I wondered about that." Nic doffed her robe and slipped on the fresh set of lingerie, shivering. "It's full winter still in Elal, but somehow I'm colder here." Of course, House Elal was heated by fire elementals embedded in the floors. The fireplaces there were all for pleasure, the temperature of the house not fluctuating much. She'd actually take the fire elementals—for both heat and light—before the water elementals for washing, and that was saying something.

Not that she'd have either anytime soon.

"Do you need help with your fastenings?" Daisy asked as Nic pulled on the gown.

Nic shook her head, smiling. "It's magic." She triggered the fastening, and the gown sealed itself, fitting to her figure.

"How clever," Daisy said, but she sounded unhappy about

it.

"Wine?" Nic asked, joining Daisy by the fire and picking up the carafe on the table between the chairs there. Not Elal wine, but that was another luxury she'd have to learn to live without.

"Oh, no, I really shouldn't keep you." But Daisy didn't move.

"Want to walk with me?" Nic ventured.

"What I want to ask is, ah, private."

"I see." Nic sat and poured them both wine. "Is this about today, with Selly?"

Daisy plopped into the chair, taking the wine and drinking it down, then stared into the glass. Nic helpfully refilled it. "Is it true?" Daisy demanded. "Is my daughter a familiar like…" She didn't finish, blanching as she realized the insult she'd been about to give.

"Like me," Nic finished, cupping her hands around the metal goblet. "Yes, she is. I'm sorry that you had to find out like that. Gabriel and I planned to tell you and GF, but we were waiting for the right opportunity. And Gabriel needed time to accustom himself to the news as well."

"How long have you known?" Daisy asked, not sounding friendly at all. Gone was the affectionate mother-in-law, and Nic sighed for that loss.

"From the moment I met Selly," she admitted.

"And yet you said nothing!" Daisy drank her wine, mouth puckering.

"It was a party, and I'd only just met you," Nic pointed out calmly. "I knew the news would be unwelcome. And I chose to tell Gabriel first."

"I don't know what I did," Daisy said bitterly, staring into the fire. "First Gabriel and now Selly. Both of my children, *contaminated* with magic. I don't understand why this happened, after all this time."

Contaminated. It would seem like contamination to the folk of Meresin, living generations without magic, far from the Convocation. "No one knows why magical potential wanes in a family," Nic said gently, "nor why it suddenly reappears, as it has in yours. But the magic breeds true, which means you and GF carried the potential for it."

She snorted. "Nonsense. Neither of us has a lick of magic in us."

Which wasn't true. Daisy and GF might have low MP scores, but they had some. Why their pairing had produced progeny with such wildly high scores, well... no one knew. Though Nic was certain the Convocation very much wanted to figure it out. "The important thing to remember," she said, "is that we can help Selly. Now that we know." *If we can recapture her.*

"Help her," Daisy echoed in patent disbelief. "What would that entail?"

Argh. Nic wasn't really in shape to explain the physiology and mental and emotional health of familiars, but this was apparently falling to her. "The difference between wizards and familiars is that wizards can express the magic and familiars can't. I have a great deal of magic, and I generate more all the time, but I can't use it. That's why I was paired to Gabriel, so *he* can use my magic."

Daisy looked dismayed, her spine unstiffening for the first time since she'd entered the room. "You're not husband and wife?"

"We are that, too," Nic hastily assured her, although that was a bit of a lie, since her imprudent escape meant they'd never had an actual wedding. In the eyes of the Convocation, however, as soon as the oracle verified that Gabriel had successfully impregnated Nic, they were as good as married. Not that she was going to explain that bit to her mother-in-law. Come to think of it, Nic wasn't at all certain how Gabriel had explained the Betrothal Trials to his parents to begin with. Probably not with the bald truth. "When the Convocation pairs wizards and familiars in heterosexual teams, they want to ensure their compatibility in fertility as well as in magic."

Daisy's gaze fell to Nic's still-flat stomach. "So your child will be..."

"Also a wizard or familiar, almost certainly very powerful," Nic confirmed. Daisy's unhappy frown wasn't encouraging, so Nic plowed on past the point. "What that means for Selly is this: A familiar can't express their own magic, so they need a wizard to do it for them. Selly's magic has been building up inside her for years. Without a channel to express that magic, it becomes, well, like a bog. It's not healthy."

Daisy gazed at her with a wrenching combination of horror and hope. "Then... Selly isn't crazy?"

Oh, Selly is crazy all right. The question was, could she be returned to sanity? Nic discreetly didn't say that, however. "She isn't. She's just an untapped familiar."

Daisy nodded, clearly not fully comprehending. "And what

they said today, about you. What does it mean, you taking an alternate form?"

Nic smiled weakly. "Some of the stories are true. Familiars can become an animal, if their wizard provides the magical push to do it."

"And that would happen to my Selly?"

"It depends, but probably. She would need to be paired with a wizard first."

"That Convocation proctor—that's why she wants to take Selly, why she accused us of neglect or deliberate cruelty."

Wincing, Nic nodded. "She doesn't know. The proctors have certain inherent biases. It's as unusual for a familiar of Selly's power to turn up among nonmagical folk as it is, well, for a wizard of Gabriel's power to manifest. Selly's was just different enough that you didn't observe it in the same way."

Daisy nodded ruefully. "Gabriel becoming a wizard was hard to miss."

Nic laughed softly. "He's told me the story."

Shaking her head, Daisy studied Nic. "And your own people—they knew you for a familiar right away?"

Deciding not to explain that Nic's family had believed her to be a wizard until they were all disabused of that notion, Nic nodded. "Growing up among wizards and familiars, my magical potential was noted early on. I started attending Convocation Academy to learn to control my magic when I was five."

"You were so young, and you've studied so long. How can my Selly ever catch up?"

It was a good question, and one with perhaps a distressingly negative answer. "Gabriel did," she pointed out. "If he did, Selly can, too."

"I don't want her going to that academy," Daisy burst out. "I don't like that vicious proctor woman. I won't have her taking my daughter away."

Clearly Gabriel was an apple that hadn't fallen far from this tree. "Gabriel feels the same," Nic replied with gentle firmness. "You should discuss it with him."

Daisy set her wineglass down and dusted off her skirts. "That boy doesn't listen to me," she said with some irritation. "I'm proud of him, of course. We both are. But when he turned into a wizard, he—" She caught herself and stood.

"He's the same person he always was, Daisy," Nic said, standing also, stung into defending Gabriel. She knew it pained him that he no longer fit in with his nonmagical family.

"You didn't know him before," Daisy retorted, eyes bright with tears. "He was such a sweet boy. Such a good heart, loving, kind, generous, and—" She dashed the tears away with the back of her hand.

"Gabriel is still all of those things." More so than anyone else she'd ever known.

"I don't know." Daisy searched Nic's face. "It's a strange thing, to be frightened of your own son. He used to have the prettiest blue eyes like his father's, and black hair like mine. Now I look into those dark, dark eyes, see that hair that turned white—overnight!—and sometimes I don't even recognize him. All I see is a monster. I lost my son to your magic. And now my daughter, too."

Nic took a chance and reached for Daisy's hand. "They're

the same people they always were," she said with urgency, needing Gabriel's mother to understand this. She squeezed the woman's hand. "Flesh and blood, *your* flesh and blood, just with a bit of magic thrown in."

Daisy pulled her hand away, not ungently, but with deliberate firmness. "I can't—" Her gaze jerked up to a point over Nic's shoulder. "Gabriel!"

Nic closed her eyes in pain. She should've been paying attention to the feel of Gabriel's approach. They must not have shut the doors completely.

"I came to see what was keeping Nic," he said flatly.

"I'll go check on the meal," Daisy said, flustered, practically running out of the room. Gabriel barely acknowledged his mother's departure.

Nic followed her and firmly closed the doors, then turned and leaned against them. "How much of that did you hear?"

"Enough," Gabriel answered, still in that toneless voice, his back to her.

She went to him and put her arms around his waist. He remained rigid, so it felt like hugging a tree. "She's overwrought. Upset about all that happened today. Worried about Selly."

"She didn't say anything that wasn't true." Gabriel's voice rumbled through him. "Or anything I didn't know. I've felt her fear, seen how she looks at me sometimes."

"Gabriel…" She hugged him tighter. "You are not a monster."

He unbent slightly, putting his hands over hers. "In the eye of the beholder, I suppose."

"No," she said firmly, ducking under one big arm to circle in front of him. "Beholders don't always know. Don't people label something monstrous out of fear and ignorance?"

"I don't know about that."

"In all of the stories," she insisted, "the monster is unknown, all the scarier because it's always in the shadows, barely glimpsed. Once it becomes known, it ceases to be frightening. It even ceases to be monstrous."

"Clearly I haven't read as many stories as you have."

"Clearly that's your problem," she replied with impish humor. But he didn't respond in kind. His wizard-black eyes regarded her gravely, a world of sorrow in them.

Nic knew she was more accustomed to the change magic wielding wrought, turning wizards' eyes to that unfathomable, starless blackness, but it grieved her that Daisy only seemed to mourn the loss of blue and wasn't able to see how beautiful Gabriel was. Yes, an accident in moon magic had turned his hair silver-white, but for the one black streak at his temple, but he was strikingly handsome, even more so for the startling contrasts. She framed his beautiful face in her hands, then combed the fingers of her left hand through the black streak that echoed his intense gaze. "Our actions define us, Gabriel. Not our potentials, even the magical ones."

His lips twitched in a sorrowful, crooked half smile. "Is that Convocation wisdom?"

It wasn't, actually. And Nic had surprised herself with it. "That's Nic wisdom."

"Even better." He sighed and gathered her close, leaning his cheek against her hair. "What would I do without you?"

"Fortunately, you'll never have to find out," she answered, hugging him tightly.

"We should go to dinner," he finally said. "Everyone is waiting. I had to authorize a second round of wine."

"They'll all be drunk."

"No doubt." At least he sounded drily amused. "They were well on their way when I came to find you."

"Apologies," she said on a wince. "But Daisy wanted to ask about Selly, and I didn't feel I could walk away."

"I appreciate that you handled that conversation." He let her go but tucked her hand in the crook of his arm, escorting her out of the room.

"I was happy to."

He glanced at her with a sardonic expression. "*Happy* to?"

Well, happy to spare him the pain of it. She gave him a bright smile. "A happy wizard makes for a happy familiar!"

He groaned, shaking his head at her, then sobered. "I'm not, you know. A happy person. Or wizard. I don't want you to be forever bashing your own self brainless trying to change that."

"You're wrong, you know," she replied quietly, because they were approaching the dining hall. Though the loud conversation rolling down the hall would've made it impossible for anyone to overhear her.

Gabriel snorted. "You were the one to call me brooding, self-loathing, sullen, and prone to sudden explosions of anger."

"That was before you discovered true love," she informed him archly.

"Is that so?" He paused outside the open doors to the dining hall, just out of sight of the occupants, and feathered gentle fingers over her cheek.

"Yes." She kissed those fingers, the callused hands of a working man and sword-wielder. "Just as Lyndella softened Sylus, turning him from raging wizard to gentle lover, I am transforming you."

"Sylus needed transforming," Gabriel noted with a grimace. "The guy was a serious ass."

That Gabriel had taken to reading her favorite wizard–familiar romantic epic meant everything to Nic. She patted his cheek. "He was only a bit broody and misunderstood. Our love story shall be equally epic."

"Without the tragic ending," he cautioned her.

"Only happiness for us," she agreed. "After a suitable set of hardships." A raucous laugh rang out of the dining hall, followed by the clatter of something breaking.

Gabriel winced. "Speaking of which…"

"Let us brave the enemy," she declared, pumping her fist into the air.

This time, when he laughed at her, it came from the heart.

~ 4 ~

GABRIEL OBSERVED THE crowd of wizards and familiars lining the long dining table, grimly wondering exactly how his life had come to this. Though Nic had done a considerable amount to lighten his heart, he couldn't get his mother's words out of his mind. *I don't even recognize him. All I see is a monster. I lost my son to your magic.*

It didn't help that the cursed proctor had been invited to join them at dinner. Nic no doubt had some reason for including the woman that had to do with convoluted Convocation social etiquette, but he didn't much care to dine with the enemy. Nic, seated to his left, set her hand on his thigh under the table. "Your magic is getting all spiky," she murmured under her breath. "You might reel it back a bit."

He'd like to send a silver spike through that proctor's forehead, but he took his wife's point, along with a deep breath, and turned his attention away. Unfortunately, that meant it lit on Jadren El-Adrel, seated on his other side. Apparently Nic had given up leaving the seat open for Selly, no doubt since everyone had witnessed Selly's insanity—or had heard about it by now, if they weren't there—and had also decided that Jadren's rank put him at Gabriel's right hand.

He had no idea when Nic had found the opportunity to alter the seating arrangements, but he also had no doubt she was behind it. When his step had faltered at seeing the irascible El-Adrel scion at the chair next to his own, Nic had simply given him a serene smile, her green eyes full of warning.

Fine, then. Fortunately, the man seemed equally uninterested in idle chatter, focusing on eating with single-minded intensity. Unfortunately, that didn't last.

"You don't lay much of a table, Lord Phel," Jadren commented, pushing his empty plate away. It was as clean as if a dog had licked it.

Gabriel set his teeth. "We are in a rebuilding phase. I believe House Phel's missive inviting junior wizards such as yourself to apply for a contract specified as much."

"I wouldn't know." Jadren replied, stroking his neatly trimmed beard, trying to appear nonchalant, though his jaw was tight.

Ah, yes. Lady El-Adrel had decided for her son. "You are, of course, welcome to go," Gabriel commented mildly. Nic observed him closely, knowing that tone for what it was. "You have not yet signed a contract."

Jadren's eyes flashed with anger. Gabriel could see how the wizard-black could be intimidating, though the El-Adrel wizard didn't concern him. Especially as, he realized, that anger wasn't directed at himself. "You agreed to my mother's terms, Lord Phel," Jadren gritted out. "We are both trapped in this arrangement, so we might as well go forward. If it's agreeable to you, I'll sign the contract after dinner."

"It includes a nondisclosure agreement," Gabriel mentioned, taking another roll and smearing it with butter fresh from the dairy. It was simple food, yes, and not exactly bountiful due to Nic's careful budgeting, but it was nutritious, satisfying, and tasty. Farm food, he supposed, was not up to the elegant standards of House El-Adrel. "You'll have to sign that before you can see the contract."

Jadren's eyebrows rose, and he stared stonily across the table at Nic, who had her head lowered over her plate in a pretense of meekness. The El-Adrel wizard had said something to her earlier. Nic had brushed it off, refusing to tell Gabriel the details, but he'd sensed her unhappiness. "An unusual gambit," Jadren noted. "One that smacks of Elal guile."

Nic didn't react, so Gabriel said nothing. Ostensibly, and according to Convocation norms, as the wizard heading House Phel, he was the final—more correctly, only—word on house policy. Jadren shouldn't expect Nic to have a role in those decisions, so Gabriel wouldn't take the bait in that particular trap, no matter what the El-Adrel scion, and spy, suspected.

Asa, seated beside Nic and across from Jadren, had been listening. "I've signed both the NDA and the contract," he told Jadren. "I had no issues with either, if that's any reassurance."

"It isn't," Jadren replied shortly, with an unfriendly glower. "House Refoel is hardly known for its political savvy."

Asa smiled thinly, black eyes glittering in his dark face. "And yet we manage to make ourselves of critical importance to the Convocation, regardless."

Gabriel sensed Nic's amusement in her magic, the scent of roses blooming lightly in the air.

Jadren apparently chose not to address that argument,

turning pointedly back to Gabriel. "Let us stick to conversation not covered by your NDA, Lord Phel. Might I have the key to the workroom in the north wing?"

Gabriel sipped his wine, aware of Nic's sharpened interest, along with the alert expressions of the wizards nearby. Not that the existence of the locked workroom at the end of the north wing was a secret, but he was somewhat surprised that it seemed to be common knowledge. He and Nic had not yet had the opportunity to revisit the large room in daylight, to discover if it held anything more than empty space.

"I'll consider it," he replied judiciously, and loud enough for anyone nearby to hear, "for anyone who has signed the NDA and is duly contracted."

Jadren set his jaw, folding his arms. "How am I to discover if our magics can combine to create these water-related artifacts if I cannot practice in the workroom? Unless you'll allow me to use the House Phel arcanium." His expression was stoic, but something in his manner held a hint of slyness.

You never want to bring another wizard's magic into your arcanium, Nic's voice whispered in his mind, and he caught a glimpse of an emerald-green side-eye. Yes, he realized Jadren was baiting him.

"Careful," he growled, allowing his magic to sharpen. "You risk angering me, junior wizard."

Jadren's black eyes hardened further. "You don't frighten me, Lord Phel."

Gabriel picked up a sharp knife, spinning it between his fingers before using it to slice off a bite of poultry. Nic might scorn his tendency to reach for physical weapons before magical ones, but he estimated he could slit Jadren's throat before the arrogant man knew what had happened. This Convocation nicety of sitting down to dinner with your enemies made no sense to him. You dined with your friends and killed your enemies.

Whatever Jadren gleaned of Gabriel's intentions, it made more of an impression than anything else had thus far, because he cleared his throat. "Perhaps we can discuss the products you have in mind, Lord Phel. I understand you'd like to make flasks that are always filled with clean water?"

Gabriel dipped a chin. "To begin with, yes."

Jadren grunted thoughtfully. "Shouldn't be too difficult, as you'll handle the water magic, I assume. I can enchant a flask."

Gabriel didn't reply that he knew that. He'd used an every-day, unenchanted flask to hold the spell that kept it ever full of clean water, but Nic had explained in excruciating detail that House El-Adrel held the monopoly on all enchanted artifacts. Having Jadren "assist" with that product line—and not incidentally giving El-Adrel a chunk of the profits—was necessary only to abide by the legalities. The trick would be discovering what else Jadren could truly contribute. "We'd like to offer clean wells, too," he added, remembering Nic's suggestion.

Jadren frowned, though thoughtfully this time. "Now there's a greater challenge. I don't know how you'd accomplish that without going to the well." Nic had said the same thing, so Gabriel nodded. "Perhaps a device that could be installed in the well," Jadren mused. "What other ideas do you have?"

Reflexively, Gabriel glanced at Nic, the font of revenue-producing ideas. "Nic?"

"Waterproof footwear and clothing," she reminded him. "Perhaps Wizard Dahlia can collaborate?" She smiled down the table at the Ophiel fabric wizard who, having been listening to the conversation along with everyone else, looked intrigued.

"Familiars should be seen and not heard," Jadren snapped dismissively. The entire table fell silent, only the proctor looking pleased.

Gabriel held onto his temper with a silver sliver of control. "You will respect Lady Phel," he instructed quietly.

Jadren's lip curled. "I realize you are ignorant of Convocation ways, Lord Phel." Jadren made it sound like a fatal personal failing. "But I would advise you to have a care how much leash you give your familiar. Such laxity could turn out very badly for you."

Gabriel sat back, considering the man, acutely aware of the raptly listening audience, and Nic's plentiful advice on playing arrogant Lord Phel who must keep his minions suitably cowed. He also felt Nic's intent gaze on the side of his face, burning with warning. "You are in *my* house, Wizard Jadren," he said softly. "House Phel is mine, as are the rules. I am thoroughly uninterested in your opinion of my rules, but I do require that you follow them. You are, of course, free to decline my contract and depart."

It seemed the entire room held their breath. Jadren narrowed his eyes. "You don't have the latitude you seem to think you do, Lord Phel," he replied, not putting the threat into words, but implicitly reminding Gabriel of the enchanted dagger—evidence of license infringement—that Lady El-Adrel kept in custody to compel House Phel's acceptance of her agent. "Your house is still on probationary status. Would you truly risk that to coddle a familiar?"

Down the table, the proctor leaned forward, expression keen with curiosity. Nic didn't move, but Gabriel felt her alarm prickle along his skin.

"For my wife? Yes." Turning to Nic, he took her hand. "You, and everyone who wishes to be a member of House Phel, will treat Lady Phel with the respect and deference due her station as an equal head of this house." Nic's hand spasmed in his, but he squeezed it, casting his gaze down the table to ensure everyone present knew they were included in this edict. Nic wanted him to be king of this castle? Then he would be, particularly on this. There were some concessions he simply would not make, not even as a pretense.

Jadren's face was a picture of incredulity. "You'd destroy everything, for *her*?"

"No," Nic said at the same time he said, "Yes."

He caught and held her gaze. "I don't care what the Convocation says about familiars," he told her, then deliberately looked down the table at the proctor. "In Meresin, everyone is a person first, and their magical inclination second. If you don't like that, you are welcome to depart. Immediately."

"You might've waited until they all signed the NDA," Nic muttered, but emotion shone in her green eyes, and it wasn't anger.

He smiled at her. He might've started this venture to restore House Phel, but she'd become the means and the meaning. Without her, it could all sink back into the marsh. Besides, the proctor would never have signed the NDA anyway. Nic had accused him of wanting to go to war with the Convocation, and that wasn't wrong. It was also sounding better all the time.

Jadren sat back in his chair, a strange expression on his face. "I can't decide if you're courageous or a fool."

"Lord Phel can be both," Asa noted wryly, without rancor, and Gabriel found himself unexpectedly grinning back at the healer.

"Regardless," the proctor spoke up, her voice ringing with authority, "the Convocation's laws take precedence over house rules, Lord Phel. You are already on tenuous ground, given your nonstandard bonding of your own familiar and your house's willful concealment of an untapped rogue familiar, jeopardizing her health and sanity. Those are grave trespasses, Lord Phel, and the Convocation will not take them lightly when I report back. I will verify that you have no regard for Convocation law. You won't have to be concerned with Lady Phel when your house status is revoked and both Lady Veronica Elal and Seliah Phel are taken into protective custody by the Convocation." She smiled in smug triumph.

Gabriel gave her a cold look, barely containing the urge to kill.

"Don't do it," Nic warned under her breath, clutching his hand tightly. Someone gasped as silver condensed in the air, shimmering down onto the table like a gentle rain.

"Why are you still here?" he asked the proctor conversationally.

She lifted her chin. "As you are well aware, Lord Phel, I'm awaiting the return of your sister, so that I can—"

"That's not what I'm asking," Gabriel said, cutting her off and, letting go of Nic's hand, rising to his feet. More silver condensed in the air, along with a silver spike that hovered menacingly before the proctor's right eye. Outside, the downpour increased, thundering on the roof high overhead. "What confuses me," he added silkily, "is why you value your own life so little."

Her mouth fell open. "You wouldn't dare!"

He solidified a second silver spike to hover before her left eye. "By your own words, you've judged me as a scofflaw. And you're right. I don't care about Convocation law, which means you have no protection."

"Murdering a Convocation proctor would result in…" She trailed off.

"The same consequence you just threatened," Sage Quinn put in softly. "Lord Phel, with all due respect, I feel I must point out that everyone in this room would be judged an accessory to that murder if we don't attempt to stop you."

"How can we stop him?" Jadren asked in a newly respectful and hushed tone. "Look at what he's doing. And he's not even touching his familiar right now. This is all him. That's serious power."

"The Convocation won't see it that way," Wolfgang, the Ratisbon furniture wizard observed, sounding not at all concerned, though he put a comforting arm around his familiar, Costa.

"Lord Phel." Nic had risen to her feet also. "You've made

your point."

Keeping his gaze on the proctor, he slid the silver spikes slightly closer to the woman's tightly closed eyes. As if that could protect her. She was pressed, tense and terrified, against the high back of the chair, with nowhere else to retreat, clawed fingers digging into the arms of the chair. Someone whimpered.

"Gabriel," Nic said, her voice warm, pushing through the sharp silver roar of his magic. "I'm asking you to stop now. Trust me. Stop it here."

A bit of sanity returned with her steadying presence. "I want her out of my house," he gritted out. "Now. Tonight. House Phel doesn't dine with its enemies."

"She'll go straight to the Convocation," Nic warned.

"Let her," he growled.

"Proctor, I apologize for the inconvenience, but would you be willing to depart without staying the night?" Nic asked with elegant manners, sounding for all the world as if she were offering the woman dessert.

The proctor squeaked out an affirmative, barely moving.

"All right, Gabriel?" Nic asked. "Drop the spikes, and she's gone."

With effort—not magical, because his blood sang with furious power, but emotional, denying himself the visceral need to kill—Gabriel drew back the spikes. He didn't drop them, however, as Nic suggested, but sent them spinning through the air, circling the gathering.

"Anyone else?" he demanded. "If you are an enemy of House Phel, declare yourself and die, or leave now."

His gaze settled on Jadren, who held up empty hands in clear surrender. "I am trapped by my mother's machinations as surely as you are, Lord Phel," he replied in a steady tone. "I will sign your documents, no matter what they contain." His lips twisted wryly. "Surely there's no greater loyalty than from someone who has no choice but to throw in with you."

Gabriel glanced at Nic, who nodded slightly. Jadren marked the exchange but said nothing.

"Under the circumstances," Nic said to the room at large, using her gracious, highborn manners to the hilt, "I'm afraid we'll hold dessert. I'm asking a page to circulate our very simple NDA. Lord Phel requires everyone to sign, whether you stay or depart, if you haven't already." She bestowed a dazzling smile on Asa and Laryn. The boy who Nic had apparently conscripted to serve as a page was distributing copies of the NDA. Gabriel had missed when she'd given that instruction. "Once you've signed, as Wizard Asa and Familiar Laryn have, you may collect your dessert and carry it back to your rooms, along with some brandy."

Another servant was setting out individual snifters of brandy on a side table. Gabriel noted that with additional bemusement.

"Familiars, too?" someone muttered in incredulity. "Is that even legal?"

"Lord Phel's house. Lord Phel's rules," Nic replied.

"And if we choose not to sign?" someone else asked.

"Absolutely your prerogative," Nic answered smoothly. "You may depart with the proctor. I'm sure she'd be delighted to share her conveyance. Isn't that so, Proctor?"

The woman nodded stiffly, her eyes wide and glassy, fingers still clawed into the arms of her chair.

Nic laid a hand on his arm, and Gabriel started slightly at the contact, his magic reaching for hers with instant greed. He found himself glaring at her, enraged for no reason at all. "Lord Phel," Nic said with infinite gentleness, meeting his gaze with deep forest-green calm, no fear in her at all. She used to be afraid of him. He'd sensed that fear in her from the beginning, and it had lasted up until just a few days ago. Now, when she should be truly alarmed, she gazed at him with calmness and perfect trust. "Lord Phel," she repeated, as if speaking to a wild animal. "Your instructions are being carried out. You needn't remain if you don't wish to. I know you have a great deal requiring your attention, and I can handle this."

"No," he ground out, taking her by the wrist. She gasped, just a little, a sound only he could hear, her magic heating and bowing in submission. His own magic, that greedy, fearsome beast in him, leapt in ferocious glee at her response. "I have need of you."

"I'll take care of this," Asa offered. "Laryn and I can, as we're under contract. Might as well start delegating to the minions," he added cheerfully, but there was a note of wariness in his voice.

"Thank you, Wizard Asa." Nic kept her gaze on Gabriel, watching him like a beast about to attack. "Shall we, Lord Phel?"

Without a word, he turned and strode out of the room, nearly dragging Nic with him. He didn't care what any of them thought. He wanted out of that cloying room, away from those shocked and staring gazes. *I don't even recognize him. All I see is a monster.* His mother was right to loathe him.

"Gabriel!" Nic hissed, and not for the first time, he realized, as she uncharacteristically resisted his pull.

He wheeled around, glaring at her. "*Now* is when you decide is a good time to cross me?" he demanded in a hoarse, whispered shout. "After all your talk of—"

"No!" She laid her free hand on the bare skin just below the hollow of this throat, where his shirt parted. Her magic swam into him, calming rose, soothing like a draught of fine red wine. "Never," she averred, holding his gaze. "Drop the spikes, or they'll be too afraid to move."

He gazed at her for a long moment, uncomprehending. *The spikes?*

"Circling the air above the dining table," she reminded him, as if it were the most normal thing in the world, "like a pair of hawks eyeing their prey below."

Ah. Right. He hadn't even realized he was still feeding their flight. With a thought, he dropped them, their clatter on some dishes followed by a small scream of dismay, quickly silenced. "Anything else?" he gritted out.

"No." She smiled, curling her nails against his skin. "Take me wherever you need me to be."

The beast in him leapt, salivating, and he swept her into his arms, ignoring her startled squeak. He wanted to devour her right there in the hall, uncaring who saw. *The predator can have no mercy in its heart for the prey*, Nic had once told him, and he'd been appalled. But that had been his better self, and that fellow seemed to have disappeared somewhere in the incandescence of his rage and need. Still, part of him remembered that he shouldn't drain her magic as he craved to do. But he would have everything else of her. Because their bedroom was too far away, he turned the other direction to the library, making it there in several long strides.

Fortunately the door stood open, and he kicked it closed. "Lock it," he ordered Nic, moving to set her down.

But she wound her arms behind his neck, her green gaze as feral as he felt. "Do it yourself, *wizard*."

With a snarl, he flexed his magic, manifesting a set of silver pins from moonlight and nailing the door shut. She laughed, a wild, delighted sound that ended in a gasp as he flung her over his desk. Pushing her down with a hand at the nape of her neck, he was vaguely aware that she'd taunted him with this very thing. *Next time, try bending me over the desk while you hold me down by the back of the neck and toss up my skirts.* He'd been shocked by that, too, horrified by the suggestion—and something of that self stood by in that same aghast horror.

But that self was his mother's son. *He was such a sweet boy. Such a good heart, loving, kind, generous, and...* "And gone forever," he growled, pulling up Nic's skirts and kicking her feet apart as she squirmed under his grip. Finding her lacy, silky panties, he ripped them off, hearing her moan. She lay over the now-glossy wood of the desk, one cheek pressed against it, her face turned away and her arms stretched to grasp the far side. Her perfect ass, round, gleaming pale in the faint light, was splayed before him, vulnerable and enticing. He slapped it, hard, savoring her cry of pain and desire, loving how she writhed, whimpering.

Dragging his fingers through her spread sex, he found her slick with passion, hot, fluttering beneath his touch. She pressed back against his hand, wanton, needy, offering everything. Ripping open his pants, he freed himself and thrust into her, viciously pleased by her wailing cry and the way she convulsed, bucking under his grip. He had to take a moment to master his own shuddering need, deeply shaken by the heated welcome of her body, the tight returning grip of her sheath, her back arched to take him in, to yield him everything—including her magic, which poured into him with intoxicating strength.

Ruthlessly, he held her down, penetrating deeply, digging deeper with every thrust. Her magic billowed and bloomed, warming his icy fury. And she moved with him, flowering, opening with every stroke, harder, faster, deeper.

Until he exploded, ramming himself home as she screamed her climax, silver falling around them in a torrent that echoed the raging storm outside. Semen, moonlight, argent rain, it all poured out of him and into her. In one corner of his soul, he sensed the arcanium pulsing in time with their orgasms, streams of silver light charging through the arched beams.

At the last moment, he interlaced his fingers with hers, so they both held on to the edge with the same desperate grip. With red and black edging his vision, safe in the embrace of Nic's prone body, he collapsed, giving himself over to the solace of senselessness.

~ 5 ~

NIC SHUDDERED WITH the aftermath of Gabriel's primal, nearly violent lovemaking, barely able to drag in a breath, her throat sore from her screams of ecstasy—which she hoped no one had heard over the storm. Gabriel lay over her like a deadweight, his ragged breathing and pounding heart confirming that he lived. That and his magic, streaming bright and hard-edged in the air. Silver gleamed over the surface of the desk, gritty under her cheek and hands.

And the rain outside poured in a deluge, unleashed, as wildly loosed from control as her wizard.

"Gabriel," she murmured, and he grunted, unmoving. She wriggled, not able to do much, his muscled body so dense, so much larger than hers. Besides, with him still buried deep inside her, quite hard despite his recent climax, the movement sent aftershocks of enervating arousal through her. Her breasts were crushed against the desk, erotically aching, her taut nipples compressed, and she wanted nothing more than to stay exactly as she was, pinned and utterly vanquished, even her heart obediently synchronizing to the rhythm of his.

But there were other considerations, and apparently it fell to her to remind him of them. She unlaced her fingers from his, pinching the back of his hand. "Gabriel!" she said more sharply.

He tensed, then nearly leapt off of her, withdrawing from her body so abruptly she cried out for the loss of him. "Nic! I hurt you." His hands settled warm on her, pulling her skirts down again and bodily lifting her, though she'd already begun to stand on her own. Gabriel sat her on the desk, running firm hands over her as if checking for bone breaks, then he cupped her face in his big hands, thumb traveling over her cheek where it had been pressed against the wood, no doubt leaving a mark. He searched her eyes, his own flat black with despair. "You'll never forgive me," he informed her.

"Is that so?" she asked with deliberate archness. "Will you also instruct me on exactly what it is I'm supposed to never forgive?"

His expression darkened, thunderous, echoed by the storm outside. "Don't toy with me, Nic. We both know what just happened here."

"Really excellent sex," she agreed, wriggling a bit, as her sensitive sex still throbbed and tingled from his passionate assault. "But," she said as his hands tightened on her and a growl rumbled through him, "no fair seducing me again. Not when—"

"*Seducing* you?" he nearly shouted in incredulity. "I ravaged you just now." He released her as if she'd burned him, so abruptly she swayed a little before recapturing her balance, and he—seeming to realize his disarray—tucked his cock back in his pants and fastened them firmly. "I don't know what came over me that I practically raped you."

"It's not rape if I consent," she pointed out. "It's just rough sex, and I think I've made it clear I'm an enthusiastic participant there."

"You *didn't* consent," he bit out.

"Did you hear me say no?"

"No, but you wouldn't—"

She stopped him, winding her fingers in his shirt and tugging him close. Seated on the desk like this, she could reach his mouth easily, so she kissed him, hard at first, then softer as he melted under her touch. "I *would* say so. Give me credit for knowing my own mind and body. And *I* know what came over you. That was a major emotional storm, resulting in pressure from a number of truly aggravating sources, fueled in part by an escalation in your magic. You needed an outlet, and I wasn't at all surprised at the one you chose. In fact, I'm glad you trusted me that much."

"*Trusted you?*" he repeated, looking as if he didn't understand the words.

"Trusted me," she affirmed, stroking his cheek. "Your magic is powerful, Gabriel, and you were sorely provoked. Cycling all that fury back through me was an excellent choice. However, pouring it into this storm that's going to wash away all that topsoil and test our tender new levee is *not* a good idea. Plus," she added, "it will keep the proctor from leaving, and all your fracturing of our carefully laid plans will be for naught."

He gazed at her a moment longer, dumbfounded, then glanced at the roof overhead, seeming to just then register the pounding of the rain. "Is that me?"

"I'm pretty sure it is," she told him cheerfully. "The storm escalated along with your sending silver spikes at the proctor."

He winced, stepping back and scrubbing his hands over his face. "I'm so sorry, Nic. I really screwed up everything tonight."

She slipped off the desk and went to pour him a finger of brandy—not great stuff, but better than what they were giving the minions—and pressed the smooth wooden cup into his hands. "You were actually spectacular," she purred, gazing up at him through her lashes. "I was aroused long before you dragged me in here to be ravished, although that part got me going even more."

He grimaced at her. "Nic, you can't be serious."

"I can and am. Drink the brandy. Stop the storm. We can deal with the rest." She waited until he sipped the brandy, wizard-black eyes watching her over the rim. "Your, er, eruption may have not been what we planned, but you've suitably terrified everyone. It was a magnificent display of both power and control. You intimidated even Jadren El-Adrel! That was immensely satisfying to watch."

"We'll have to start over with minions if I frightened everyone away."

"You won't have. You'll see. I'm laying odds you only cleared out the ones here for nefarious reasons. Everyone who sincerely applied to House Phel will stay, because you just demonstrated how well you can defend your house."

"And now the proctor will tell the Convocation everything." He sighed heavily, staring into the empty cup.

She shrugged nonchalantly, one ear on the rain, which lessened with each moment, the thunder receding, and slipped the cup from his hands. "They were going to know anyway. At least this way, if it comes to war, the Convocation will have an idea of what they're up against with you, and—"

He snagged her hand before she could turn away. "With *us*," he corrected.

"And," she continued, "this buys us time to find Selly and make other plans."

He laced their fingers together, gazing at her intently. "Thank you, my heart," he said with soft intensity. "I'm aware that you managed me in there."

She smiled saucily. "As a well-trained familiar should do."

A line formed between his dark brows. "I highly doubt the Convocation Academy taught you how to handle situations like that."

"You'd be surprised." When his frown deepened, she stopped being so flippant. "Remember, my only love, that I am also the first daughter of one of the most powerful houses in the Convocation. My skills and knowledge include a great deal learned in House Elal, as well as at the academy. I know what wizards are like, and Maman had decades of managing Papa, which she did very well, no matter the particular scene you witnessed." Her mood dimmed at the thought of Maman possibly still kept in alternate form. Though Papa would surely need to access her magic, which he could only do with her in human form. Perhaps Maman was only being prevented from corresponding. Nic really needed to finish that letter to Alise, to find out what her sister knew of their mother's well-being.

"I know I'm exceptionally fortunate to have you as Lady Phel," Gabriel said, lifting their joined hands to kiss the back of hers. "Speaking of which, we should move forward with the wedding plans. It will give my mother something to focus on," he added, when Nic opened her mouth to protest, "besides worrying about Selly."

"All right." She smiled, then kissed his hand, too. "As my wizard master wishes!" Then laughed at his irritation. "I'll go oversee the exodus. You stay here, see if you can dry up the road out of here, and maybe clean up this silver. I know I'm covered in it."

He glanced about in dismay, just noticing the silver dusting every surface, including the back of her gown. Brushing at it, he groaned. "If you go out there, everyone will know what we've been doing."

"And won't be surprised," she agreed. "You're far from the first wizard to fuck their familiar senseless after riding a magic wave like that."

"Nic." His voice held flat warning.

"Sorry, I'm a bit giddy still from said fucking." She danced away from him, giving him a seductive glance over her shoulder. "So, unless you *have need of me* again, I'll go ensure that your orders have been duly executed."

He glowered at her. "I'd spank you if I didn't think you'd enjoy it."

"You already did, a little, and you're right—I did enjoy it." She started gathering her skirts as if to pull them up. "You destroyed my panties, so I'm naked under here. Shall I bend over the desk again so you can—"

"*No.*"

"Pity. If you like, I'll limp a little, so they'll know exactly how you—"

"Nic!" he nearly shouted, clenching his hands into fists—and sending her into a fit of giggles.

"I'm going, I'm going." The smile still stretching her face, she reached for the library doors, remembered they were nailed shut. "Oh, dear," she cooed. "I seem to be trapped, still in my wizard's dastardly clutches. Does that mean..." The silver nails flew out, pinging to the floor. "Thank you!" she sang, and slipped out the doors.

THE EXODUS WAS indeed well underway. Though, with the small number of people who'd decided to leave, it hardly merited the grandiose term. Fortunately, Asa and Laryn had efficiently packed the proctor and her things into the carriage, so Nic was spared confronting her old nemesis again.

The dining table had been cleared of dinner, though the silver detritus remained. Pocketing the silver spikes set neatly at the end of the long table, she retrieved the stack of signed NDAs also. Mentally comparing them with the departing parties, she made sure that everyone who'd chosen to remain had indeed signed one, including the familiars. As she reviewed them, she hummed a tune under her breath, her body singingly alive and deliciously sore.

Turned out that intense bout of sex had been exactly what she needed to settle herself in her own skin again. A useful

JEFFE KENNEDY

note for the future, if she could convince Gabriel that she truly
craved that from him.

"Nic?" Quinn Byssan slipped into the otherwise empty
dining hall, her eyes wide, manner full of hesitant curiosity.

"Quinn." Nic smiled at her friend. "How are you and Sage?
No lingering effects from tonight's demonstration, I hope." She
waggled their signed NDAs. "I'm so glad you decided to stay."

"Sage is less certain, but I convinced her. Where else could
we go that will allow me this kind of flexibility? Sage talked to
Lord Phel, you know, about me being able to choose a
husband for myself, from an approved list of candidates," she
added hastily, as if Nic would reprimand her for impertinence.

"He mentioned," Nic replied warmly. "And he approves of
the plan, so we can look into arranging that." *Later. Much later.*
After they handled everything, she reflected ruefully, gazing at
the stack of NDAs in her hand and mentally calculating how
many contracts they still needed to draft versus those already
drafted. And that didn't account for the continuing arrivals.
Plus they needed to check out that workroom before they let
anyone else in there, and deal with Selly, once they found her.
Also: brace for war, get the House Phel product line going, and
plan a wedding. She rubbed her forehead.

"Nic?" Quinn waved a hand, recalling Nic's attention. "Are
you all right?"

"Yes," Nic answered in all sincerity, letting her very real
happiness and satiation show. "It's been a long day, and there's
lots to do is all."

"Well, Sage and I haven't seen or signed the contract yet,
and Sage cautioned me that much depends on Lord Phel's

exact requirements of her, but if we stay—and I hope we do!—then I'm happy to help with the contracts and trademark applications. Sage can only work so many hours before she needs to rest, and I like to keep busy. As Sage mentioned, I was always good at trademark law in the mock trials at Convocation Academy."

"I remember," Nic replied. "You were more than good. You're a champion."

"For a familiar," Quinn said modestly, but clearly pleased.

"The last time I checked," Nic said in a dry tone, "whether or not we can perform magic is irrelevant to our other skills and intelligence."

Quinn wrinkled her nose as she laughed. "What they're saying is true—Lord Phel *has* infected you with his radical ideas."

Nic stilled, a rill of foreboding running chill through her. "Who is saying that?"

"Everyone here," Quinn answered, her smile fading. "At least, the people who've come from the Convocation. That can't be a surprise to you. Unless you've already become so used to Lord Phel's... unusual ideas that you've forgotten just how counter to the Convocation's policy and customs regarding familiars they are."

Perhaps she *had* lost sight of that. Gabriel's grounded conviction in his own notions, that deep certainty in his ideas—a certainty she could wish translated to confidence in his own motivations and feelings—made it easy to get swept up in believing in what he did. "No, I know how 'unusual' his ideas are, and what an unusual wizard he is, full stop. I should ask instead, what is the tenor of those remarks?"

"Hmm." Quinn pulled out a chair, seating herself. "It varies, naturally, from person to person. Reactions range from confusion to interest to the outright certainty that the Convocation will have to move against House Phel." She cocked her head thoughtfully. "Most fall under interested, even optimistic—which includes Sage and me—but we also have none of the wizards who truly regard their familiars as their personal slaves to use as they please. It might be different with them."

"There's a reason we don't have those sorts here," Nic replied with a wide, innocent smile, making Quinn laugh.

"I saw your request to House Byssan and noted your careful wording. Well done on collecting the sorts of wizards who would be intrigued by Lord Phel's radical ideas rather than horrified. And now you've run off the few exceptions."

Nic nodded, unwilling to confess that Gabriel's outburst hadn't been planned.

"The one exception," Quinn said, "is Jadren El-Adrel."

"True." Nic pulled out a chair and sat, too.

Quinn waited, then smiled wryly. "I suppose there are things you can't confide, even in me."

"Let's just say that Jadren is a special case and leave it at that."

"I'll say. Odd that *he* doesn't have a familiar."

"Among a number of oddities." She checked her pile of NDAs to make sure she hadn't dreamed it. She waved Jadren's at Quinn. "But he did sign."

"Will he sign the contract, though?"

"I believe he will." *I am trapped by my mother's machinations as surely as you are, Lord Phel.* "You heard what he said at dinner."

"I did, but..." She shrugged. "I don't always know what to believe."

"I don't know Jadren's story, but I think he says exactly what he means. And doesn't care what people think of it."

"Interesting..." Quinn drew out the word, then sighed when Nic said no more. "So, how about something you *can* confide? What happened when the deliciously virile Lord Phel dragged you off? You said before that he isn't cruel to you, but he looked so furious!"

Nic couldn't help a happy shiver. "Yes, he was. And what happened is exactly what you think."

"I figured that explained the glow. What is it like?" she asked wistfully. "Having all that power and intensity focused on you?"

"It's everything," Nic replied simply. "I am happier and more fulfilled than I ever imagined I could be."

Quinn sighed dreamily. "You two are just like Sylus and Lyndella. The way Lord Phel came to your defense—if he were a fire mage, I believe he would've incinerated the room in his anger. As it was..." She shivered dramatically, eyes bright. "All that icy coldness, that storm! And making silver rain from the air. I could imagine Sylus doing exactly that for Lyndella."

Without the tragic ending, Gabriel's voice cautioned in her mind. "Hopefully I won't end up insane and dying in his arms before he drains the last of my life magic and goes on to wreak vengeance on his enemies, dying in the process," Nic commented.

Quinn giggled and rolled her eyes. "Well, we all know that was just a story. Though their love was indeed epic. I want that, too. And I never dared dream I could have it. Now... I think maybe it's possible. The epic love part, not the Sylus part, as Sage is all the wizard I'll ever need."

"It *is* possible," Nic replied firmly. "If anyone can create a place for everyone to chase their dreams, even familiars, Lord Phel can."

IN THE MORNING, both she and Gabriel awoke early, feeling considerably refreshed—though his mood remained dark, and he was obviously still brooding over the events of the night before. They conferred on the day ahead and decided to check out the workroom before activity in the manse kicked into high gear. She put on the light-green dress she'd worn two days before, biting back a sigh. She'd worked out a rotation with her two day gowns, reserving the silk for dinner, but the cycle had begun to feel like a bit much. There was also the burgundy riding habit, but she felt silly walking around all day in it without going riding.

Gabriel caught her reaction anyway, frowning as he watched her from the bathing chamber chaise as she finished primping. "I thought the Ophiel wizard—Dahlia, right?—was going to make you a full wardrobe."

"She will, but there's a great demand for upholstery for the furniture, as well as bed and bathing linens for our increasing number of denizens."

"I'd argue that you being adequately dressed is higher priority than chair cushions and towels."

"You're sweet, but I disagree. I can wait. Still, it's unfortunate Dahlia doesn't have a familiar, as her magic only stretches so far, but her skill and eye for design absolutely compensates for it."

"Can't she tap a familiar's magic who isn't bonded to her? You said I should be able to tap Selly's magic to release that pressure."

"Why?" she asked, unable to resist poking the sleeping tiger inside her cool water wizard. "Would you like me to share my magic, perhaps with Dahlia, or even Jadren?"

His expression flashed into anger, wizard-black eyes going as hard as obsidian. Recalling Quinn's delighted shivering, Nic reveled in the possessiveness of her wizard. And Gabriel was better than Sylus because—as Gabriel had rightfully pointed out—Sylus was a bit of an asshole to Lyndella, which Gabriel could never be to her. Nic watched him in the mirror as she applied her lip paint and he wrestled with his baser instincts, finally saying in an *almost* neutral voice, "Is that something you want?"

Utterly charmed, she went to him, straddling his lap and planting a long kiss on him, further satisfied when his hands settled on her waist, clasping her tightly. "Silly wizard," she murmured. "I'm bonded to *you*, which means only you have the privilege of accessing my magic, unless I choose to give it to someone else, which I don't. Or unless you command me to. But that would be highly unusual, given the possessive nature of wizards," she teased. "Customarily, only unbonded familiars are shared between wizards."

"Ah," he breathed, drawing her into another kiss. "It's probably terrible that knowing that makes me so happy."

"It's in a wizard's nature to be possessive," she reminded him, threading her fingers through his silken silver-white hair. And perhaps in a familiar's, too, because she wasn't inclined to share her wizard with anyone.

He captured her wrists, tugging them down to her lap and looking her in the eye. "So you said that just to yank my chain?"

"Yes." She fluttered her lashes. "Perhaps you should punish me."

He laughed. "You are incorrigible."

"*You* have lip paint on your mouth," she countered.

She shrieked as he flipped her over, quickly reversing their positions so that she lay beneath him on the chaise, one huge and bulging muscled thigh riding up to part her legs, grinding against her sex as he kissed her with crushing thoroughness. Yielding beneath him, she moaned, writhing in blatant encouragement, dizzy from the sudden passion and lack of breath. Just when she thought she'd have to beg to breathe, he broke the kiss, gazing down at her in smug, masculine satisfaction. His disordered silver curls hung around his striking face, the wayward black lock escaping to hang over one eye.

"Do you want me?" he asked, voice hoarse with desire, his

thigh insistent between her legs.

"Yes," she sighed. "Oh yes, Gabriel, please."

He smiled, giving her a soft kiss. "Too bad." Face breaking into a wicked grin, he leapt up, leaving her bereft. "There's your punishment, naughty familiar."

"Gabriel!"

He only laughed, going to the mirror to wipe off her lip paint. "Just yanking your chain, my heart."

She pushed herself up. "You wrinkled my dress." Steam scented the air, and her dress magically refreshed with Gabriel's easy use of water wizardry, the low-level sort he'd said most of the folk of Meresin could wield. A nifty household trick.

Turning to eye her, he grinned, completely without remorse. "Better fix your lip paint. The workroom awaits." And he strode out of the bathing chamber, whistling merrily.

Nic dutifully repaired her makeup, reordered her hair, and smiled to herself in the mirror. There was more than one way to manage a broody wizard.

THE NORTH WING wasn't completely silent, as a few people were up and about, including a few servants who were delivering linens, hot beverages, and cleaning up empty chambers.

"Where did all these workers come from?" Gabriel asked.

"I mean, I recognize many of them, but how have you rounded up so many to come work in the house?"

"By paying them well," she answered.

"Can we afford that?"

"Depends on how you define 'afford.' It's a pinch, but I figure that by putting coin in the pockets of the people of Meresin, we're creating a pool of money that will find its way back into our coffers as we offer them enticing merchandise to purchase."

He glanced at her with an amused half smile. "I begin to understand why House Elal is so wealthy and powerful—and why people regard Elals warily."

"Like Jadren has any room to talk," she scoffed. "There's a world of irony in an El-Adrel accusing an Elal of guile."

"Are you surprised he stayed?" Gabriel asked quietly. "After his contentiousness last night."

"Not at all. But let's not discuss it here." The far end of the north wing hallway was dim and deserted, but you never knew who might be listening.

Gabriel nodded, saying nothing more. They reached the end of the hall and the set of impressively large and imposing doors that filled the entire wall. Setting down the several lanterns that Nic was really happy she'd remembered they'd need, Gabriel produced the silver key from his pocket. He'd made it from moonlight, following the pattern the house seemed to require, using the Phel traditional magics to unlock the ancient enchantments.

"It will be interesting to see if any wizard can use this key," Nic observed as he inserted it in the lock, "or just you. Or our child," she added. They'd already established the key didn't work for her.

He paused without turning the key in the lock and tipped his head to look at her. "That's an arresting image—our child standing in this spot and unlocking the workroom."

She smiled, too, moved in an unexpected way. "They'll have black hair. Between the two of us, that's inescapable."

"And your green eyes, I hope." He lifted a hand to caress her cheek. "Ready to brave the monsters?"

"I certainly have a nice reserve of magic built up. Though I think if anything was going to try to eat us, it would have the night we blundered in here without light." Just in case, though, she took his hand and opened herself, ready to give him all her magic if necessary.

"Blunder is a good word for it," he agreed, turning the key and pushing the doors open.

Inside was as impenetrably black as that first night, and Nic gamely picked up one lantern, handed it to Gabriel, then took up the other. "So exciting!"

He grunted, sounding not at all excited, taking another step into the gloom. Nic immediately spotted the low bench she'd barked her shins on during their previous visit. It, along with a circle of similar benches, ringed what appeared to be a pit, even blacker than the general gloom of the huge, windowless room. "Is that water in the pit?" she asked, as Gabriel would know.

"Yes. A lot of water." His magic streamed out as he used his water senses to test the pit. "Very deep. I think there are things living in it."

"Given that this was all underwater until recently, it would be more surprising if there wasn't."

"Good point. But this is... something unusual."

She was quiet, letting him concentrate, although her curiosity burned bright, wanting to know what he sensed.

Finally, he shook his head. "I don't know what it is. I can tell it's huge, possibly as big as this house. I can feel it displacing the water, but I can't determine more detail than that. How could a pit this deep and a creature that huge possibly fit inside this space?"

"Magic," Nic answered with a resigned shrug. "Sometimes there's no explaining it.

This almost looks like an arena. Are there family stories about Phel wizards having water-based battles? Magic tournaments, maybe?"

He raised a brow at her, his hair a pale flame in the dimness. "Not that I ever heard, but I can ask Mom if she..." His face fell. "No, I suppose I can't."

"It would be a good excuse to talk to her," Nic prodded. "I know she feels terrible that you overheard what she said. She needs to know that you forgive her."

Gabriel studied Nic for a long moment. "What if I can't forgive her?" he asked quietly.

Her heart ached for him. "Oh, Gabriel. Then you do your best to forget what you cannot forgive. And over time, you might find that the careless words of a fraught moment don't matter as much as the fact that your mother loves you."

"*If* she does."

"Gabriel! Of course she does."

His lips twisted, not quite a smile. "How can anyone love a monster?"

"Are you questioning my taste, integrity, and judgment?" she retorted, not quite annoyed, but close. "Because I love you."

Now he did smile, wistfully. "Yes, but possibly because you, my heart, are also a monster."

She surprised them both by laughing. "This is a legitimate point. You, me, and the swamp monster in yon pit."

Making a face, Gabriel looked back at the pit. "Did you say you decided against recruiting a House Ariel wizard?"

She sighed, mentally rearranging her delicately balanced— more accurately, unbalanced and teetering on the edge of disaster—budget. "I thought having an animal wizard was low priority. I have since moved that up very high on the list. The last thing we need is a rampaging swamp monster."

"I think I can keep it confined to the pit using the water," Gabriel said thoughtfully.

"Oooh, that's a good idea."

"I can just thicken the surface and monitor it. That way I'll know if it's trying to emerge." His magic surged, and the black surface of the water turned less shiny. "Other than this, is there anything else you see to prevent us from opening the work-shop to our minions?"

"Let's do a circuit."

They explored the rest of the room, which was saliently empty of much else. Lots of high workbenches and lower tables for seated studies. The cabinets built into the walls were empty—they checked every one, just in case—and nothing else jumped out at them, figuratively or literally. Not even submerged swamp creatures. She pointed out to Gabriel how each cabinet had a separate lock, so individual wizards could privately store supplies and equipment. They'd had a setup much like it at Convocation Academy. That was, the wizards had. Familiars didn't really need any tools but themselves.

Having finished their assessment, they carried their lanterns out again, Gabriel locking the door and pocketing the key. "If I allow the wizards into the workroom on the condition they stay away from the pit, do you think they'll comply?"

"You're the mighty Lord Phel," she said cheerfully. "They'd better obey you. If they don't, you can send a silver spike through their eye!"

He winced, and she patted his arm. "Too soon?"

"No, I deserved it," he allowed.

"Quinn described you as deliciously virile," she told him, watching out of the side of her eye for his reaction.

To her immense satisfaction, he actually blushed. "I could have lived a long time without knowing that."

Laughing, Nic hooked her arm through the crook of his, hugging herself against his muscled strength. "Apparently everyone was tremendously impressed by your display of power and wizardly rage last night."

"You are going to tease me about this forever, aren't you?"

"Oh, yes. At least, until you do something even juicier."

"Wonderful." He sounded grumpy, but his lips twitched in a reluctant smile. Then he lifted his head, like a hound scenting something interesting on the wind. "Someone's arriving," he told Nic before she could ask. "And—your favorite phrase—you were right. I am getting better at discerning the signatures of the wizards and familiars of our own house from new ones." His brow wrinkled as they entered the main house and turned toward the front doors. He stopped abruptly, alarm rippling through his magic. "Nic..." Looking at her, he hesitated.

"Just tell me."

"The wizard feels like Elal magic."

~ 6 ~

GABRIEL FELT NIC'S magic tense and recoil, withdrawing in apprehension, though she was far too well trained and regally composed to reveal anything in her manner. "An Elal wizard, come to Meresin," she mused. "And they said it could never happen."

Gabriel hugged her arm to him, relieved she could retain a sense of humor. "I think you should go hide in the arcanium. Let me take you there, and I'll deal with our visitors."

She lifted her chin in that obstinate tilt that told him of her refusal even before she spoke. "Absolutely not. I refuse to cower and hide away like a criminal. You've made it clear that you stand behind me as Lady Phel. I'm not undermining that now."

The woman picked the entirely wrong things to be stubborn about. "You could be in danger."

She shrugged that off, squeezing his biceps and fluttering her lashes. "My big, strong wizard will protect me."

If he could. "I would feel better if you were safe in the arcanium."

"I would feel better if I'm at your side, where I belong, in case you need my magic."

"I could make it an order."

She gave him a steady green glare. "You could, but I wouldn't forgive you."

"You like it when I give you orders," he coaxed, lowering his voice to a seductive purr.

"Sexy orders, yes. But unless you plan to strip me naked and chain me up while you stay to do dastardly things to my helpless body, I will *not* be pleased with you."

He grumbled low in his throat, firmly setting aside the enticing image she evoked. "You will be the death of me," he said, resuming the walk to the closed front doors.

"Possibly, but you'll die happy," she chirped, then she lost some of her bravado. "Can you tell... is it Jan?"

The Elal wizard enforcer had nearly captured Nic in Ophiel when they first made landfall. He concentrated. He was getting better at using his wizard senses at a finer level of detail, but he had a long ways to go. The exercises Asa had shown him would be helpful, but they also made his head hurt. Using power in broad sweeps the night before, instead of painstaking and meticulous increments, had been almost a relief.

"I don't think so," he finally answered. "The wizard is recognizably Elal to me, but not someone I've ever met. I feel sure. The magic, though..." Robust and fiery, richly redolent of summer roses and sun-warmed wine. "The magic feels a lot like yours, though definitely belonging to a wizard." And wasn't that interesting that he could discern the difference so decisively now? "But a wizard more like your flavor of magic than your father's."

Nic's Magic faltered infinitesimally. "It couldn't be..." she murmured under her breath. Before he could ask, she asked more loudly. "A lone wizard, no familiar companion?"

"Oddly enough, there are two familiars." He concentrated a bit more. "Neither bonded to the wizard, I'm quite sure."

"You can determine that from this distance?" He'd opened the door for her and stepped out onto the wide front porch behind her, while Nic scanned the long road that circled the lake and ended at the house. Mist rose from the still waters and wafted over the lawn, thick enough to shroud anything beyond a certain distance. "I don't see anyone yet."

"I don't think they're coming up the road," he said, looking off to the orchards lined in their neat rows past the north wing.

"Hmm. That's a bit odd."

"Everything about this is odd." And he didn't much care for it. He took her hand, partly to be ready to access her magic in case of an attack, but also to keep track of where she was—and the better to thrust her behind him, should that be necessary. "But yes, now that you taught me what to look for, I'm much better at discerning the wizard–familiar bond."

"No surprise, as you're—" She broke off, stiffening.

"What?" he demanded, marshalling his moon and water magic, extruding a silver sword for his free hand. He should have made her go to the arcanium.

"A spirit is here," she replied under her breath. "Small, tasked as a scout."

He sensed it now. He'd encountered those spirit spies before, most notably the first time he crossed the Elal border. Pulling mist, he condensed it around the spirit, delineating its cautious exploration of the environs. Sensing his magic—or realizing their presence for the first time—the spirit halted, then vanished. Gabriel cursed quietly.

"Went back to inform its wizard," Nic explained unnecessarily.

"Should I—"

"No, let them come. I think I know who it is, as impossible as it seems."

"Who?"

"I want to see if I'm right first."

He didn't like it, but he trusted Nic implicitly, so he subsided, waiting and scanning the billowing mist concealing and revealing the orchard in turns, seeking to penetrate it with his wizard senses. He discovered little more than what he'd already told Nic, besides one unusual detail. "They're on foot."

"Hmm." Her hand tightened on his, her magic available to him but otherwise firmly contained. She was nervous, not afraid.

Three figures resolved from the mist, one tall and two shorter, one of the shorter ones limping visibly. The tall figure had an arm around the limping one, helping them along. The other figure, who moved wearily, stepped in front of the other two, Elal magic flaring bright as several spirits condensed before the trio, forming a protective phalanx.

"Lord Phel, I presume," the wizard called. A young woman's voice, trying to sound stern, but though her power blazed with impressive strength, a wobble in it betrayed her uncertainty. She also sounded very much like Nic.

Confirming it, Nic caught her breath. "Alise!" she called.

"Alise… Your sister?" Gabriel asked under his breath, and

Nic nodded, her emotions a tumult of excitement and trepidation, joy and … guilt?

Alise took a few steps closer, her two companions staying behind. The spirit guardians manifested swords, an Elal wizard's trick Gabriel had encountered before. As Alise emerged from the denser mist, Gabriel noted her strong familial resemblance to Nic. He'd have guessed her for a sister immediately. If not for being several years younger than Nic, a teenager still, Alise could have passed for her identical twin. With her high Elal forehead, strong nose, and shining, sleekly cut black hair, the young wizard possessed a poise beyond her tender years. He found it somewhat jarring, however, to see wizard-black eyes instead of Nic's striking emerald green.

He used to have the prettiest blue eyes like his father's... his mother's anguished voice echoed in his mind.

"Lord Phel," Alise repeated, tearing her gaze from Nic and focusing on Gabriel, lifting her chin just as Nic would when she'd determined on a course of action and wouldn't be swayed from it. "I demand that you release my sister from your unlawful abduction of her. You will remand her into my custody in the name of House Elal."

"Or?" Gabriel asked, partly amused by the young wizard's temerity. Her magic was strong, and might grow stronger still with maturity, but she was no match for him, even without the massive boost in power Nic provided him. He was also angry, the wizard's instincts Nic liked to tease him about, bristling at the mere suggestion that he'd part with Nic.

"Or suffer the consequences," Alise replied with cool poise.

Beside him, Nic shifted. She wasn't going to interfere, but

she clearly wanted to.

"Nic is my duly bonded familiar," he replied, more gently than he would have, if not for what he sensed from Nic. "She is also my wife, my lover, the mother of our unborn child, and the lady of House Phel. Even if were I to agree to release her into your custody, which I emphatically refuse to do, she wouldn't wish to go."

He risked a glance at Nic, just to make certain, and she smiled warmly at him, her magic curling around him in wine-red, rose-suffused love. All right, then. It would be nice, however, if he could pass one day without someone threatening to take her away from him.

"If that's true," Alise replied in a hard voice, "then why did she bring shame upon House Elal, jeopardizing her entire future, by refusing and attempting to escape you?"

Nic groaned, pressing her lips together and shaking her head.

"You are free to speak up, you know," Gabriel reminded her.

She cast him a startled glance, as if she had indeed forgotten in her ingrained response to a new wizard's presence. "I assume Papa told you that, Alise?" she called.

Alise leveled a look on her sister, expression and magic roiling with conflicting emotions. "Yes. He thought you might have come to me for help, but you didn't, did you?"

That guilt he'd sensed in her flared, but she answered with comparable poise. "No, I didn't want to involve anyone else in my problems, least of all you."

"Why would you be so imprudent?" Alise asked, indignant

and pleading at once. "You had to have a strong reason. And there have been rumors. I heard he put you in an iron collar."

Nic's hand went reflexively to her throat where the hunters' collar had weighed on her, though Asa had long since healed the abrasions and bruises. "You should know better than to credit rumor, Alise," she replied with disdainful amusement. "Especially at Convocation Academy."

"And the rest?" Alise persisted.

"The rest is a long tale best told by a nice fire and over a warm beverage, possibly breakfast," Nic replied. "You and your companions appear to have traveled some distance and under onerous circumstances. I'm interested in hearing your tale as well. Won't you all accept the hospitality of House Phel and be welcome?"

Alise's gaze went to Gabriel, then his sword, and his clasp on his familiar.

Wiser now to the social signals of the Convocation, Gabriel released Nic's hand—after brushing a kiss over the back of it—and sheathed his sword. "I welcome my sister-in-law to House Phel," he confirmed. "And her companions?" He made that a question, as it seemed odd that Alise hadn't introduced them.

Interestingly, she winced, glancing back at them. "As for that..." She gestured them forward, keeping her spirit guardians in place. "I should be transparent before offering insult to House Phel by involving you in a potentially difficult situation."

Nic and Gabriel exchanged an intrigued look as the other two stepped forward. They were also as bedraggled as Alise, the young man tall with penetrating blue eyes and long pale-blond hair tied back. He still had an arm around a lovely, vivacious redhead. Her long curls hung limp and damp, but her eyes remained brightly interested, freckles standing out bright on her pale face.

"This is Han and Iliana," Alise said, indicating first the young man, then the young woman—and interestingly omitting their house affiliations.

"Iliana," Nic said with wariness, tempered by a note of happiness. "I never expected to see you here."

"Hi, Nic," the redhead replied. "It's good to see you again."

"And Han," Nic said, "I remember you, too. Everyone had you pegged to manifest as a wizard at any moment."

The blond young man winced. "That did not turn out as 'everyone' expected."

"We've all left Convocation Academy," Alise put in.

"*Left?*" Nic asked, pouncing on that.

Alise grimaced. "Yes, well… that's also a long story."

"You were the one to caution us that we needed to know the particulars before involving House Phel," Nic reminded her.

Alise glowered, looking very much the annoyed little sister. "I know that," she snapped, then sighed and rubbed her forehead, exactly as Nic often did when feeling overwhelmed.

"We're familiars," Iliana spoke up, then smiled up at the young man. "Well, you've known I'm a familiar for a long time, Nic, but Han is, too." She paused a moment. "And we're in love."

Nic stilled. Even though they were no longer touching,

Gabriel sensed her sudden alarm. "In... *love?*" she repeated incredulously.

"Yes," Han answered, without any sign of shame or guilt. "I only recently manifested as a familiar. We'd hoped I'd be a wizard and could take Iliana as my familiar. I'm a late bloomer," he added glumly, and Gabriel felt for the lad. A young man likely only five or so years younger than himself.

"I repeatedly cautioned you on how unlikely it was that I'd be assigned as your familiar, even if you had turned out a wizard," Iliana broke in, and he kissed her on the forehead before turning back to them.

"As Alise indicated, it's a long story, but... the short version is that circumstances were such that we faced a terrible fate."

"Let's not dance around it," Iliana reproved Han. "They need to know the details of our circumstances. Lord and Lady Phel, the truth is that one of our classmates, Sabrina Sammael, recently manifested as a wizard—and she's always wanted Han. She'd had House Sammael draw up a contract to bond Han to her if he manifested as a familiar. If he manifested as a wizard, she intended to bond me, to force him to be her lover." Iliana retained her poise, but emotion throbbed beneath her words, her eyes bright with unshed tears.

"The contract also ensured that if I became Sabrina's familiar," Han inserted, pale with anger, "Iliana would be given to House Sammael as an unbonded familiar to be used at will— also to ensure my compliance."

Fury burned in Gabriel's gut. He loathed how the Convocation treated familiars at a baseline level, but this was another order of monstrosity. He bore no love for House Sammael—in particular, he hated Sammael's heir, who'd treated Nic so badly—and this only added fuel to his determination to take revenge on them. Clearly cruelty ran in that family, and they deserved to suffer some of the punishment they so gleefully doled out.

"That's ridiculous," Nic burst out. "No house, even House Sammael, can acquire familiars by fiat. There's a process for wizard–familiar matching for exactly that reason."

"House Sammael has ways," Alise said, shaking her head slowly. "I believed Sabrina would do it, which was why I agreed to help them."

"Do tell," Nic replied icily.

"I talked Alise into breaking us out," Iliana inserted, giving Nic a hopeful smile. "I didn't know what to do, so I asked Alise to bring us to you."

Nic was uncharacteristically flabbergasted, staring in what seemed to be very real shock from Alise to Iliana and back again. "To *me*?" she squeaked.

"Because Alise told us about your escape," Iliana said frankly, her gaze going doubtfully to Gabriel and quickly ducking away again. "Or aborted escape? Anyway, we—that is, I, because this was entirely my idea—"

"I went along with it," Han said staunchly.

Iliana beamed at him with the perfect trust of first love. Gabriel nearly groaned at their naivete, and he was the idealist compared to Nic's practicality. Iliana turned back to Nic, speaking earnestly. "We heard that there were people you contacted to, ah…" Her gaze flicked warily to Gabriel.

"You can speak frankly in front of Lord Phel," Nic said in a resigned tone. "I assume that escape route no longer exists?"

Iliana shook her head, glancing at Alise for confirmation. "Papa told me he shut it down," Alise said quietly. "He's in quite the rage, Nic."

Gabriel set a hand on the small of Nic's back, but she only nodded at Alise. "Believe me, I've received that message." Alise smiled back sadly, the sisters sharing a moment of communion. Nic turned back to Iliana and Han. "I'm still unclear on what you think I can do for you."

"We thought you could direct us to an alternate escape route," Iliana replied. "And..." She hesitated, glancing at Gabriel. "Well, we didn't know what your situation was here," she said in a rush, "but with the rumors about you being collared and, um, some of the tales about Lord Phel—no offense intended—we thought you might want to come with us."

Nic gave Gabriel a wary and assessing look, one he returned with a gentle smile. This conversation, at least, didn't set off whatever crazed, wizard-nature jealousy beast that lived inside him. He was secure in the knowledge that Nic no longer wished to escape him.

"I have no desire to go anywhere," Nic told them. "And I'm sorry that we can't help you. My sole opportunity was through that particular operation. If that's gone, then I know of nothing else."

"What about whoever connected you to that operation?" Iliana persisted, undaunted, and Gabriel began to see how this slim, delicate-seeming redhead had orchestrated this plan. "If you give us that contact, perhaps *they* can help us."

Nic stiffened under Gabriel's hand, tension ratcheting to a breaking point. Gabriel knew it had been Nic's—and Alise's—mother who'd helped her, but Nic had sworn him to secrecy, terrified of Lord Elal's potential retribution against his wife and familiar, so completely in his thrall. Nic hadn't spoken very much about her sister, but Gabriel felt certain Nic wouldn't trust Alise with this dangerous information. "I'm sorry," Nic said. "I don't know who it was. It was handled through a series of confidential messages."

Iliana's transparent face crumpled in disappointment. "Is there a way for us to send a similar message?"

"I'm afraid not," Nic replied crisply. "But we wish you well on your journeys. Alise, you are welcome to visit, of course, before you return to Convocation Academy to resume your studies."

"But—" Alise began.

"But nothing," Nic cut her off crisply. "Our father will be angry at your skipping out on your education as it is. Only by going back will you be able to restore yourself in his good graces." She turned to the familiars. "Han and Iliana—I'm sorry, but we cannot give you refuge in House Phel. You have to leave."

Iliana nodded in resignation, but Han looked outraged. "Maybe you didn't notice, Lady Phel," he burst out, "but Iliana has injured her foot and can't walk without support. We've run out of food and water. Our carriage sank in some sort of tarry bog. If you turn us out, we have nowhere to go!"

"No, Han," Iliana said. "Nic is perfectly correct that we

pose a danger to House Phel. She's only protecting her wizard and her house. We can't fault her for that."

"I don't need protecting," Gabriel said easily, and Nic gave him a wide, deep-green glare of warning. He ignored her. "You are all naturally welcome to stay. And we have a Refoel wizard in house. I'll summon him to treat Iliana." He swept a hand at the great front doors of the manse. "Won't you come in?"

After a moment of hesitation, Alise nodded at him, avoiding her sister's gaze, and moved to the other side of Iliana, both of them helping the hobbling girl up the steps of the porch. Gabriel offered Nic his arm, but she pretended she didn't see it, stalking stiffly beside him, her magic red hot and boilingly furious. She wouldn't contradict or countermand him, however, not in front of the others. He should be sorry at this further evidence that she didn't consider herself a true partner in running House Phel, but he was frankly relieved to have a reprieve from her bristling anger.

Also, he knew he was guilty of doing exactly what he was grateful she hadn't done—contradicting and countermanding—but in this case she was flat wrong. He wasn't about to turn away someone in need because of the Convocation's draconian rules on familiars. He might be a monster, but he retained some principles, ones he was willing to fight for. With a mental sigh and a surreptitious glance at Nic, he conceded to himself that a fight was likely exactly what he was going to get.

Nic took over as they stepped into the manse, pulling her gracious highborn lady manners around her like an elegant cloak, all chirpy welcome and solicitousness. She guided them into the library, likely because it was closer than the walk to

Asa's offices in the south wing, and more private than the family dining hall. Along the way, she described some of the history of the manse, pointing out architectural details and describing the ongoing renovation—and also flagged down one of the copious new servants, asking for breakfast in the library and for Wizard Asa to attend them for a minor injury.

If he hadn't been so keenly aware of her magical fury, he'd have thought all was well. Han and Iliana seemed to think so, giving her grateful smiles, but Alise slid her sister a couple of sidelong looks. Sisterly awareness or wizard's instincts? It would be interesting to discover.

If Nic left him in one piece after this.

~ 7 ~

S HE WAS GOING to kill him.

No, death was too easy for naïve and idealistic Gabriel. He wanted to be a hero? Then Nic was going to tear him into tiny pieces and leave him in a suffering heap of pointless nobility. Something for the storybooks.

Nic held on to her temper—and the vertiginous sense of everything they'd worked for dropping away beneath her feet—with all the tenacity of her exquisitely polite upbringing. She refused to show their guests just how upset she was. She revealed none of her inner turmoil, even though, from the moment she'd realized their surprise visitor must be Alise, Nic had been a mess of emotion.

What in the dark arts had possessed Alise to go truant from Convocation Academy? And on top of that exceptionally questionable decision, to help two rogue familiars escape? Inviting the retribution of House Sammael! Sure, Nic had always liked Iliana, who possessed a sweet and sunny nature that had led her to be kind to Nic when few others were after Nic's fall from grace. She knew Han less well, but he always seemed all right, as far as the golden chosen who seemed destined to be powerful wizards ever were.

She sympathized with Han, freshly bruised from losing the dream of being a wizard and relegated to familiar status instead. Convocation knew, she felt for both Han and Iliana with their shitty futures and no power to change that. But those two should've known better than to dream of some kind of true-love outcome where they'd be partnered together. They *did* know better. Even if Han *had* manifested as a wizard, the Convocation likely wouldn't have matched them. Every student at Convocation Academy was aware of that very simple truth.

But Alise... She was Papa's heir. His perfect wizard daughter, gone and absconding from Convocation Academy and fled directly to the black-sheep daughter, already such a disappointment to him. Just contemplating Papa's rage had her feeling sick and sorry.

It made her teeth ache that they'd all been so foolish. Or maybe that was from biting down so hard on the words she wanted to unleash on the lot of them, including her idealistic idiot of a husband, who was enabling them in this doomed escapade. Nic's own foolishness at least had been confined to her fortunes only—well, and Maman's, and look how that had turned out—but it was as if her impulsive flight were a virus. It had sickened her, tainted the lives of many people who were still recovering from that contamination. And now it was spreading.

The Convocation wouldn't fail to notice. And their reprisal would be dire. That wasn't even considering what House Sammael, well known for their brutal vengeance, would do. They'd all come after her, after Alise and her numbskull friends, after everyone in House Phel, and worst of all: they'd destroy Gabriel for this.

Her heart hurt so hard contemplating it that she couldn't seem to take a full breath.

"What have we here?" Asa said, entering the room alone, without Laryn, as Nic had hoped when she'd specified the injury was minor. Even with the NDAs, the fewer people who knew about the *criminals* House Phel was currently harboring, the better. Not that it would save them, but maybe the measures would give her time to think... of something.

Somehow, Nic managed to make the appropriate introductions without sounding crazed, and also discreetly omitted the more dangerous details. Though Asa was no fool. The appearance of an academy-age wizard—no one graduated at Alise's age—in the company of two unbonded familiars was highly suspicious.

But Asa only set to work on Iliana's injured ankle, cheerfully inquiring about how it had happened. She described the treacherous path through the swamps, at least clever enough not to say why the three of them had been trekking through a trackless land far from where they were supposed to be. Han and Alise jumped in to aid in telling the tale, all of them laughing in camaraderie, which made Nic feel small and mean.

She didn't want to hear the story of their adventures. She wanted them out of her home, far away from this fragile thing she and Gabriel had barely started building. Every once in a while, Alise caught Nic watching, her good humor fading as she gave Nic an assessing glance, reminding her painfully of all the unspoken words that crowded between them. Worst of all,

Gabriel stood on the other side of the little group, studying her with wary black eyes, a tinge of damp disappointment to his magic.

Well, fine, then. Let him be disappointed! He was the noble fool here, with his *ideas* about familiars being equal. First trying to court Nic and make her into a partner, then liberating the aged familiar Narlis from the Iblis wizard—an offense that still hadn't been fully settled with House Iblis—and now *this*. This final doom that would put an end to the hope she'd begun to nourish like a tender seedling in an early spring, pretending to herself that the winter storms were over when the worst was yet to come. She couldn't bear it.

"I have things to take care of," Nic declared, drumming up a warm smile that painfully cracked her dry lips. "I'll see to it that you three are given rooms."

"Iliana and I will share, Lady Phel," Han said, politely but firmly. "It will spare you a room for someone else," he added, as if *he* were doing *them* a favor.

Nic inclined her head as graciously as possible, though it felt like her skull might break off at the top of her spine.

"Nic?" Alise said, taking a step toward her, then stopping and wringing her fingers together. "I'd like to have a conversation with you, in private, if possible."

"Of course," Nic replied, head pounding, though she resisted rubbing at the spike that threatened to drive through her temple. "I'll have my secretary add it to my schedule."

Alise nodded in response, biting her lip against something else she clearly wanted to say—which was hopefully not a comment on the absurdity of Nic having a secretary or a schedule. Well, she did have a busy schedule, but hardly a formal or organized one. Or a secretary, for that matter. She turned to go.

Unfortunately, Gabriel came with her, taking her arm in an apparently casual clasp that went straight to the bone. "I wasn't aware you'd engaged a secretary," he said in a quiet and mild tone that didn't fool her for a moment.

Well aware she'd said those words entirely because that was what Maman would've said as Lady Elal, Nic tried to tug her arm away. To no avail. "Don't test me, Gabriel," she hissed under her breath. "I am *not* in the mood."

"No, I can see that." He steered her away from the stairs that led to their suite, where she'd had some idea of collecting herself in peace, and toward the back door instead. They stepped out into the misty landscape, and Gabriel began walking toward the stables.

"Where are we going?" she gritted out. "I have things to do."

"Have your secretary clear your schedule," he suggested.

She growled in frustration, the sound rising to an incoherent shriek inside her head that felt as if it might blast off the top of her skull.

"You need to blow off steam," he replied calmly. Usually his cool silvery magic felt like a balm to her, but it was the last thing she wanted right then.

"I am so…" She had to take a deep breath. "*Angry* with you."

"I noticed. Saddle Vale, please," he called to one of the grooms. Startled, the girl leapt to obey, turned back to bow, then thought better of it halfway as she caught a glimpse of Nic's expression. Her eyes widened, and she dashed off again. "Vale could use some exercise," Gabriel explained. "Though I'm still getting used to having someone saddle him for me instead of doing it myself."

"Am I to run behind?" she asked with heavy sarcasm.

He slid her a warily amused look, black eyes glittering. "You don't have to pick a fight with me. You already have one. We're just not having it with an audience."

"I notice you didn't ask for Salve to be saddled is all."

"I don't trust you not to do something drastic like taking off. We can double up on Vale. He's rested, and we don't need to go far."

The groom brought out Vale, who sidestepped with frisky excitement, tossing his head at the sight of them. Despite her burning rage, fury, and despair, Nic couldn't help smiling at the horse's happiness. Oh, to be that simple and enjoy the moment. Gabriel grasped her by the hips and lifted her onto Vale's back with easy strength, and with such speed that she gasped in surprise. Before she'd come to terms with the rapidly evolving situation, Gabriel had swung up behind her, caging her in the stalwart protection of his big body, and urged Vale into a lunging leap of a gallop that had bits of mud and grass flying up behind them.

The precipitous departure and increasing speed gave her no time to catch her breath or equilibrate. Gabriel leaned low over her, cutting the drag and forcing her to lie low also or be crushed. Vale stretched out, reaching a velocity she'd never experienced with him, which made sense, as both Vale and

Gabriel had been injured in the battle with the hunters just before she met up with them. Now, thanks to healing and rest, both man and horse were back in top form, and they hurtled down a road Nic hadn't yet seen, going flat out so that tears streamed from Nic's eyes from the wind of their passage, Vale's mane stinging her cheeks.

To her surprise, the blistering speed, the feel of the horse's muscles bunching and stretching beneath her, the furious cadence of his all-out gallop, even Gabriel's body against hers as the misty world streamed past them, helped release something in her. That leaden ball of dizzying despair that had congealed in her at the sight of Alise's ill-advised, criminal companions melted ever so slightly.

By the time Gabriel reined up on a hillock, indeed only a short time later, she felt a little bit less like she might shatter. He swung down, then offered hands up to her, expression composed but eyes dark with a challenge. No doubt if she was huffy and refused, he'd just pull her down. She braced herself on his forearms and let him lift her by the waist and set her on her feet.

He stepped back a careful distance, as if she were an improperly balanced fire incantation that could erupt if jostled. "You were saying?" he inquired. When she stared blankly at him, thoroughly disoriented by his unusual behavior, he raised one dark brow. "You are so angry at me..."

He'd employed a dramatically unfair tactic. Somewhere in that headlong race to nowhere, she'd lost the fiery impetus to rake him over the coals for his idealistic nonsense and shortsightedness. Raking her fingers through her hair, she found it damp with condensed mist, the low-lying area below filled with fog, like a shifting grey sea. "Why here?" she asked.

"You'll see when the sun burns through," he replied. "And this is far enough away from everyone that you can yell at me and vent whatever has you wrapped around your own axel without anyone overhearing you."

She gaped at him with no idea where to start with that. "Wrapped around my own axel? What does that even mean?"

Folding his arms, he frowned at her. "The metaphor is obvious."

She set her teeth. "It is the *wrong* metaphor, Gabriel. What I am is trapped in the back of a runaway wagon, careening off a cliff, and you're urging the elemental on and laughing as you do it."

His lips twitched in a quickly suppressed smirk—which was a good thing, as she couldn't have vouched for her behavior if he'd displayed actual amusement at that. "Why is letting those three stay so terrible?"

"*Now* you ask? After you countermanded me?" She grasped for words, sputtered, then turned her back on him, clenched her fists by her sides, and let out a bloodcurdling shriek at the unoffending fog. Vale snorted, lifting his head from grazing, long grass draping from his muzzle as he eyed her.

"Feel better?" Gabriel asked.

"No!" she shouted, whirling on him and advancing.

He stood his ground, imperturbable. "Are you angry because I countermanded you or because I did it because I decided you were wrong?"

"Both! And I am *not* wrong about this. Letting Han and

Iliana stay was the stupidest thing you've ever done. Worse than abducting Narlis by several orders of magnitude."

"I don't regret liberating Narlis."

"Just because the results weren't an utter disaster—and we don't know that it still won't come home to roost like a Ratsiel courier with bad news and a wait-for-reply command—doesn't mean it was a good idea."

"Your sister brought Han and Iliana to us. Alise knows what she's doing."

"Alise is a *child*."

"She's only a few years younger than you are."

"She's been spoilt and protected and she has no idea what kinds of consequences she's facing."

"Funny," he retorted, "that's almost word for word what the Convocation proctor said about *you*."

"And she was right!" Nic hurled back at him. "I *didn't* know. I was stupid and naïve and selfish and foolish and—"

"No, you weren't. Stop saying those things," he bit out.

He didn't understand, and Nic didn't know how to get it through his stubborn head. Changing tone and tack, she tried to explain rationally. Alise wasn't the point here. "Han and Iliana are valuable familiars who have gone rogue. House Phel is now harboring valuable stolen property, and I can promise you that House Sammael will not be as easy to deal with as Iblis. You just made a powerful, perhaps devastating, enemy."

"House Sammael was already our enemy. This is just one more offense to add to their ledger."

"They better not be our enemy, because we cannot stand against their might. And now you've baited them for no better reason than, what, *sympathy*?" She sneered the word.

His eyes and expression hardened. "Han and Iliana are human beings, Nic, not property. And they are people being hunted for the 'crime' of daring to choose who they love and what kind of life they want to have. I'd think that *you*, of all people, would understand and, yes, *sympathize* with that."

"Well, you would be wrong," she hissed. "I have zero sympathy for fools. And idealists."

"If we turn them away," he persisted, "they could die out there, or worse. They don't know the dangers of our wet-lands—which, I might point out, you don't either."

"You're right, I don't," she snapped, "but what I *do* know is the Convocation and the serious consequences those two face for running away like that. Worse, they're like the dog that encounters a bear and comes running to you for safety—with a raging grizzly on its tail. The Convocation will unleash fury like you've never seen on House Phel when they discover this. That's if House Sammael doesn't destroy us first—*and* take Han and Iliana anyway."

"Let them try," he snapped. "No society should allow spoiled teenagers to weaponize social status to the extent that they can ruin people's lives."

"Teenagers specialize in weaponizing social status to ruin people's lives," she retorted. "It's all a matter of scale."

"Don't minimize this as a matter of scale," he said, warning in his tone.

"Fine. I won't. Just let me point out—as the person you specifically sought out to help you navigate the social web that is the Convocation—that we are stacking up more houses, very powerful ones, as enemies of House Phel, than we are allies."

"So be it," he nearly growled. "I wouldn't have them as allies."

"Are you sure? Because you cannot dismiss an entire house, which may consist of thousands of people, based only on the behavior of a few individuals. This year's head of house may be gone next year, and might become your much-needed ally. You think you can defy the entire Convocation and win, because you haven't been crushed yet, but that only means the forces are marshalling outside of your awareness. It could be that by the time you are aware, it will be too late."

"I am not afraid of the Convocation," he gritted out. "Or Sammael."

"You should be!"

"They all are tyrants perpetuating a destructive society that ruthlessly suppresses the rights of human beings!" he roared back. "I refuse to humbly bow to their oppression, or worse, become exactly like them by enforcing their corrupt laws because I'm too afraid to stand up for what's right."

"Then you're the biggest fool of all," she shouted back, fists clenched in impotent rage, wanting to beat them against his chest and knowing it would be like hurling herself against a wall. "Because they will *crush* you. And you don't understand: This is all *my* fault! Because of me, all of these people will suffer and maybe die. My friend Iliana, who never hurt anyone, my sister, the people we've gathered here, your parents, your sister, *you*." By the time she got to the last word, she practically choked on it, a sob escaping with it.

She tried to grab it back. Tried to catch her breath and couldn't. She burst into a torrent of tears.

"Oh, my heart," Gabriel said, reaching her in one stride and sweeping her into his arms. He carried her over to a low wall and sat, cuddling her against him. "Don't do this to yourself. None of any of this is your fault."

"It is," she insisted through her tears. "You heard them. They learned about me escaping, so they thought they could do it, too. If I hadn't been so irresponsible, if I'd simply sucked it up and performed my duty as I'd been trained to do, then they, you, your family, would all be safe. Instead, I've brought—" With horror she realized *she* was the dog leading a raging grizzly to ravage everyone and everything she cared about.

He stopped her words with a kiss, cupping the back of her head with one big hand and kissing her breathless. Which didn't take much, as the flood of tears had already nearly drowned her. Still holding her close, Gabriel showered kisses over her face, murmuring soothing words, embracing her with ferocity, as if she were the fragile seedling now and he could somehow shelter her from any storm that came their way. She knew he couldn't—especially against the might of the Convocation and cruel House Sammael—but, perversely, in that moment, it felt as if he could. As if, if she stayed like this forever, everything would be fine.

"None of this is your fault," he murmured, and she realized he'd been repeating that same phrase, patiently wearing her down until she heard and understood. And, of course, he believed that, but he believed all sorts of noble things that simply weren't true.

"You're wrong," she gasped, still out of breath from the fury, the grief, and his kisses. "I kicked over a lantern out of a fit of pique and set the world on fire."

He laughed a little, then pulled back to study her face, wiping away her tears with his thumbs. "Everyone has a breaking point. Have you ever considered that you are a hero? You dared to imagine a better life for yourself than the cage they tried to cram you into, and because you had that courage, others are now seeing a way to do the same."

"No," she answered, miserable and embarrassed and horrified at once. "I was selfish. I ran because I was afraid. And now I've perhaps permanently harmed Maman, jeopardized Alise's future, and will likely destroy you and your house along with it. You should despise me." Her heart throbbed with the cold knowledge—and the bone-deep awareness of how much she'd come to depend on his love. She couldn't live if he came to hate her.

"And yet I love you," he replied, kissing her, drawing her into a deeper, sweeter caress of lips. "I find you incredibly admirable, and so do your sister and your friends. I saw the way they looked at you with hope, believing that you can help them."

"Wait until you see their faces when they discover the truth—that I can't do anything for them."

"You already did. You gave them safe haven."

She laughed bitterly. "No, *you* did that, oblivious to the fact that I was trying to protect you and House Phel."

"I wasn't oblivious." He produced an angelic smile. "I

simply ignored you and did what I knew you'd want if you hadn't been afraid in the moment."

"I'm *still* afraid. And my course of action was the smart one, the practical choice."

He tapped her on the nose. "You would've regretted it. If you'd sent them off again, you wouldn't have forgiven yourself for it."

"I might have," she muttered, unwilling to concede that he was right. "You don't know me that well."

"Keep telling yourself that," he replied with warm affection. "I know you considerably better than you want me to."

He always had, even from that first game he'd played with her in her tower room, finding ways to sneak past her careful defenses, extracting personal details from her like a spy on a critical mission of grave political import. "Gabriel..." She shook her head, her temples throbbing. "This is truly a fight we can't win. What are we going to do?"

"At least you're back to considering courses of action rather than stewing in despair," he noted in satisfaction.

"Are you managing me?"

"How am I doing?" He smiled guilelessly into the face of her suspicion.

She considered lying. Reconsidered. The dread and despair had dissipated. "Remarkably well, actually."

"Glad to hear it. I'm learning from the best, you know. You talk me down from wizardly eruptions, and I haul you out of the bog of negative thinking. We make a good team."

"And all this time I thought I was the fire to your water— that I'd be pushing you while you calmed me down."

His smile widened with genuine delight. "We do that, too. I love that you've been thinking of us as a team also."

Ugh. Now she was giving him ideas. "I haven't been—"

He stopped her with a finger pressed to her lips. "Don't ruin it," he told her sternly.

She smiled, kissed his finger, and purred, "Yes, wizard."

His expression hardened with desire, even as he shook his head slightly, sighing. "I think you will be my doom, though not in the way you mean."

That sobered her. "We should discuss plans. We'll have to—"

"Not yet." He tugged at her lower lip with the finger resting there. "I want you to see something."

She waggled her brows at him. "I've already seen it, though I agree it's worth multiple viewings."

Laughing, he turned her in his lap so she sat with her back against his chest. The sun was burning through the fog, making everything brighter, though still shrouded. "Not that, either," he said with mock reproach. "I'm not at all clear on how you can go from murderously angry to heartbroken to flirtatious in such a short time."

"I'm just naturally talented," she informed him loftily. "And I wasn't going to murder you. Just chop you into miserable pieces."

"Wouldn't that have the same effect?"

"Not if done correctly. I have *ways*."

"I'll keep that in mind."

"Wise of you. Meanwhile, why am I gazing at a sea of fog?"

"You'll see," he murmured in her ear, taking the opportunity to trace the shell of it with his tongue, sending delightful shivers through her. His hands spanned her waist, pressing her back against him, slowly smoothing upwards to caress her breasts over her gown with teasingly light touches, too fleeting to satisfy.

"Are we having sex?" she asked, feeling like she needed to know. He'd gotten far too adept at teasing her and leaving her hanging, all in the ostensible name of building up her magic and keeping her healthy.

"Even in Meresin this is known as fooling around," he replied, lips finding the pulse point under her ear and nuzzling there with erotic effect.

"That's a no," she decided on a wistful sigh. The knowledge didn't do any good. It wasn't as if she had it in her to put a stop to his caresses, nor could she force herself not to react. The desire washed over her, sweet and lazily warm in the aftermath of her tirade and subsequent crying jag. "I wonder if it's partly the pregnancy," she said aloud as it occurred to her.

"That we're not having sex? I can promise it's because the fog is clearing, and at any moment, we'll be clearly on display to anyone who cares to look."

"No, that I'm so emotional. I never used to be like this."

His hands stilled, then he wrapped her in his arms, leaning his cheek against her hair. "Or it could be that you've been living through extraordinary changes. We both have. Unless I can blame the pregnancy for last night?" he added with a hopeful note, as if excited by the possibility.

She giggled. "You are the great and powerful wizard Phel.

You can do as you like and no one will question it."

"Except those things the Convocation doesn't like," he reminded her.

"True." She sighed, feeling safe in his arms and knowing it for an illusion. "Gabriel, we should discuss the probability that my father will arrive to retrieve Alise, in force. That's likely to happen first, and—"

"Shh." He kissed her cheek. "No war planning yet. I want this moment with you. Watch." He gestured over the sea of fog, glittering and billowing in soft blues and ivory as the sun rose over the trees. A chorus of birdsong rose in greeting, the air suddenly filled with their music and the scent of rain-washed vegetation. Tendrils of Gabriel's magic stirred the mist, encouraging it to stream away.

Revealing a meadow of deep crimson blossoms.

Nic gasped as the flowers stirred, lifting their petals to the sunlight in an almost audible susurrus of movement. The color stood out vividly, almost shockingly, against the misty green of the shallow valley and the rounded hills surrounding it.

"Blood poppies," Gabriel murmured, nuzzling her cheek. "I learned yesterday that they had begun to bloom. Your lips have always reminded me of them."

Her heart shivered at the romance of that. "I don't deserve you," she whispered, wishing desperately that it was other-wise.

"Funny, I often think the same thing."

She turned sideways, facing him, searching his face. He kissed her, lingering over it. "Blood poppies," he whispered against her mouth. Then he lifted his head. "I may not deserve you, but I love you."

"I love you, too, Gabriel," she replied in a hush. "So much I think it might break me apart sometimes. I want to deserve you, too."

His lips curved in a crooked smile. "That sounds like a good goal for our marriage. Let's spend our lives trying to deserve each other."

She had to laugh. "Shall we put it in the wedding vows?"

"Yes," he answered, then kissed her again, with such leisurely thoroughness that she forgot everything for a while.

~ 8 ~

B Y THE TIME they returned to the manse, several more groups of applicants had arrived. Some were hoping to serve House Phel as junior wizards, and a few were new graduates from Convocation Academy, responding to their call for apprentice wizards with measurable MP scores in water magic. It would be interesting to see the results once Convocation Academy began measuring moon magic, too.

Of course, once the Convocation, and Houses Elal and Sammael, were done with them, they wouldn't be seeing anything at all. But Gabriel deferred their planning conversation yet again, saying they should deal with the onslaught of business, and she didn't have it in her to break their restored harmony by insisting. Also, the more minions they had, the more people to fight for House Phel, should it come to that. And if they were destroyed, at least she wouldn't have to make payroll. Bracing thought.

A virtual army of Ratsiel couriers had also arrived, delivering correspondence of varying importance. Nic volunteered to handle the correspondence while Gabriel interviewed the hopefuls. Handing him a stack of blank NDAs, she reminded Gabriel to get them to sign first. She promised to send more once she'd gotten them copied. She really needed that copying gremlin or—perhaps there'd been truth in the lie—a secretary. She and Gabriel could share someone, if they could find a person with the requisite skills. It wasn't standard practice for the lord and lady of a High House to share a secretary, but— given how Gabriel just loved to share equally with her—it would likely work for them. At least to begin with. Quinn Byssan had offered her help, of course, but her first allegiance and priority would have to go to assisting her wizard.

Gabriel grimaced at the prospect of dealing with more people, but he agreed to the plan, also acceding to her reminder that everyone needed to sign contracts that day or be gone. She soothed him with the prospect of being able to rage and kick out the contract-hesitant, then left the library to him so he could have the privacy for his conversations. Since the sky remained blissfully clear and the sun had continued to warm the day to a delightfully balmy temperature, she carried the stack of correspondence with her up to the balcony sitting area off the master suite.

And she sent for her sister. Along with a carafe of wine. Though it wasn't yet noon, she figured they'd need it. At least this one thing Nic could attempt to resolve.

Alise arrived quickly enough that Nic figured her sister had been awaiting the summons. Well, that and Alise likely didn't have much else to do. Alise meandered through the suite, making soft comments to the page who led her out to the balcony, then stood awkwardly a moment, nodding a cautious hello.

Nic gestured to the other rocking chair. "Please, sit. Wine?"

Alise sat, perching on the edge of her chair warily, and accepted the glass Nic poured. "This is lovely," Alise said, gesturing at the view of the river, the low, lush hills beyond. "In fact, Lord Phel seems to have ensconced you in the best part of the house." She didn't quite make it a question, but Nic set aside the stack of correspondence—along with her supreme irritation that House Iblis had counter-offered yet again, further stalling the resolution of the Narlis problem—and lifted her own glass in a toast.

"To family," Nic offered, rather amused by the suspicious glimmer in Alise's dark eyes. "It's not Elal wine," she said by way of apology when Alise pursed her lips at the taste, giving the glass a dubious look. "And yes, this is the core part of the house that remained standing even after the family abandoned it. We've made more progress on this section, and Gabriel— Lord Phel, that is—was concerned that I be housed in comfort, if not in Elal style."

"And are iron collars de rigueur for House Phel?" Alise bit out. "Because I know that's not Elal style by any stretch."

"How did you even hear about that?" Nic demanded, half in irritation and half in resignation for the ways of the Convocation. "I think maybe five people saw me wearing that cursed collar."

"Then he *did* put you in one," Alise pounced on that morsel of information, expression hard. In that moment, she looked just like Papa, full of righteous indignation, Elal magic sparkling in the air around her.

Despite her frustration, Nic's heart warmed. Apparently, Alise cared about her, acting out of that concern, even though

Nic hadn't managed that apology yet. "No," she replied firmly. "Gabriel abhors collars of all kinds. Here is the truth, though I am asking your discretion in sharing this information." Her gaze strayed to the NDA template she needed to copy over, knowing that she should ask Alise to sign it but somehow unwilling to risk the tentative peace between them by broaching the topic. Besides, where their father was concerned, his might would trump any NDA.

"When I escaped, the Convocation sent hunters after me." She held up a hand when Alise frowned, opening her mouth. "No, I'd never heard of them either, but the people on the escape conduit who helped me had. Though they'd never seen a hunter until the creatures came after me. The hunters aren't visible to anyone without magic, but they are physical beings, after a fashion. They're clearly a combination of Ariel animal magic and Tadkiel justice-seeking. Perhaps some Hanneil psychic manipulation is in there, too." And Sammael's cruel punishment, she wondered.

"That is very disturbing." Alise looked both stricken and intrigued. "I wonder why this is such a secret?"

Nic snorted. "Aside from the fact that wizards are paranoid and pathological about keeping secrets, even if there's no good reason?"

"There is that," Alise admitted with a wry smile.

"I only know that the hunters cannot be killed by physical means, only magical, and they regrow entirely from small pieces. They have rudimentary intelligence, enough to pursue a task with single-minded relentlessness, and some of them can even speak. They can employ canned enchantments. They tracked me all the way to Wartson, captured me, and put that iron collar and chain on me in order to take me back to Convocation Center for punishment and retraining."

Alise stared at her, face pale, her shock and horror apparent in the very stillness of her body. "But what happened then?" she finally asked.

Nic shrugged for the force of nature that was her wizard. "Gabriel happened. He also tracked me, then fought off and destroyed the hunters. After we returned to Convocation land, Gabriel hired an Iblis wizard to remove the collar, and he brought me home to Meresin rather than turning me over to the Convocation or to Papa's wizard enforcer, who..." The realization struck her. "Jan."

"Disgusting *Jan* found you?" Alise made a face.

"Yes, he and Daniel found me at an inn right when we arrived. I'll bet he's the one who told you about the collar."

Alise shrugged a little, a mirror of Nic's. "He told Papa, anyway, who contacted me. If he hadn't, I wouldn't have known about any of this." She lifted her chin, meeting Nic's gaze, accusation in her wizard-black eyes. "You could have trusted me to help you, Nic. I know we haven't always been close, especially in the last few years, but you couldn't have thought that I would have turned my back on you. Or turned you in."

Shaking her head, Nic picked up the box holding her correspondence and blank stationery, found the letter she'd started to Alise, and handed it over.

Clearly bemused, Alise took it and read the bare two lines, the second hanging in eternal forlorn inadequacy. She lifted her gaze to Nic's. "Forgive you for what?"

"For not writing to you before this," Nic answered. "I should have told you what was going on, should have trusted you, and I'm sorry I didn't. But also for everything else." She ticked them off on her fingers. "I haven't been a good sister to you. I know I was insufferable when we were growing up. I was unkind when I banned you from our company when my friends visited. I wasn't kind to you for our whole lives, really! I was so self-involved and snooty about being Papa's heir, so full of hubris. And then, when I discovered I was a familiar, I cut you off. Because I was ashamed of myself, but that wasn't fair to you. I never congratulated you on your wizard status, which is unforgivable. I really am happy for you, by the way, and I think you'll be an amazing Lady Elal. But I don't blame you for being angry at me, and I don't expect you to forgive me for any of it."

Alise narrowed her eyes. "What about the time you threw my doll in the fireplace?"

Nic groaned, rubbing her forehead. She'd forgotten that one. The House Beatrix doll could blink its eyes, cry, say a few words, and actually pee, which Nic had found disgusting, especially after Alise left it, diaperless, on Nic's pillow one evening. In a fit of pique, Nic had thrown the wretched thing on the fire, where it proceeded to scream with unnerving realism. Alise had fished the poor doll out of the fire and swathed its bald head in bandages borrowed from their in-house Refoel wizard. Only three years old, Alise had been utterly despondent, carrying the burnt carcass around ceaselessly. Unfortunately, the fire had also damaged the magic, so the doll only made horrible slurring noises. Maybe Nic had blocked out the memory of that particularly grisly event.

"I am *so* sorry about your doll," Nic said, shaking her head at the memory. "That was cruel and intolerant of me."

Alise burst out laughing. In fact, she laughed so hard, she had to put down her wine and hold her ribs. She laughed until tears squeezed out of the corners of her eyes, and she was breathless, but every time she seemed to be getting a hold of herself, she took a look at Nic's face and started laughing again. It got to the point that Nic took up her quill and began copying the NDA while she waited, just for something to do.

"Nic," Alise finally said on a gasp, pointing a wobbly finger at her. "You were *seven*. I think you get dispensation for being a child. I'm sure I was equally as terrible to you. I know Nander drove *me* batty with his pranks."

That wasn't what Nic had expected, and the anticlimactic response left her feeling oddly deflated. "Even so," she replied, sounding stiff to her own ears, "the apologies stand. For that and for everything else."

"Nic…" Alise threw up her hands, then huffed in exasperation. She held up the unfinished letter, produced a fire elemental, and set it ablaze, the ashes wafting away on the balmy breeze.

"Nice trick," Nic said, squelching the insidious envy. How she longed to be able to use her Elal magic, rather than simply pass it along to Gabriel.

Alise looked briefly abashed, then straightened. "That's what it is. A bit of a trick. That wasn't my point—I wanted to show how apologies are like ash, to be blown away on the wind—but it's a good one for this moment. I'm an adequate wizard, and I'm getting better, especially at my technical skills, but we both know my magic is *nothing* compared to yours. More, I don't have half your smarts and savvy. I shouldn't be Papa's heir. *You* should be. You're the one who should be Lady Elal, and Papa's a fool to have cast you aside. Also, I don't need or want your apologies, so keep any further whining about them to yourself, please."

Nic gaped at her sister, completely flummoxed. "I will never be the head of House Elal. No familiar can be."

Alise waved that off as inconsequential. "Yes, yes. I know that. You know that. Everyone in the freaking Convocation knows that—but do you ever think about how stupid that is? All the Convocation houses being led only by the most powerful wizards the family can produce, as if magical potential gives you *any* ability to run a business, which it emphatically does not. No wonder our high and lower-tier houses are forever foundering, being relegated to obscurity. Just imagine if the houses chose the most business-minded and savvy person to head the house!"

"Even a familiar?" Nic asked, her head spinning a bit. She'd never imagined Alise harbored such radical ideas.

"Even a commoner!" Alise fired back, face alight with enthusiasm. "Magic doesn't make you intelligent or competent. Why can't people with MP scores below the almighty 3.0 hold positions of power?"

"Because the wizards don't like it," Nic answered reflexively.

"Exactly. Because they're power-hungry megalomaniacs. And we just let them control the whole world!"

"Well, we *let* them because otherwise they'd kill us all," Nic replied drily.

"It's not right, Nic," Alise insisted. "No one should hold so much power, and for all the wrong reasons. They become consumed with battling each other rather than working for any kind of common good. It's as if we put feral bulls in charge when we know they only want to rut and ram horns with each other."

"I had no idea you were such a rebel."

"Back at you," Alise retorted with raised brows. "*You* were always the good girl, Papa's pet, so determined to be the perfect student and perfect everything. I'm frankly amazed—and impressed—that you had it in you to try to escape Lord Phel's claim."

"Don't be impressed. I failed miserably."

Alise studied her. "I'll still help you," she said in a lowered voice. "I'm not a powerful wizard by any stretch, but I'm competent and getting better. We can run away, back to Wartson, if you like. I can tap your magic to keep you sane. Han and Iliana would come with us. We could begin something new there. A magical community without the Convocation rules."

"Is that why you helped them?" Nic asked, genuinely still unable to wrap her mind around it.

Alise took up her wine and studied it without drinking. "In part? I'm not sure why I did, except that I really loathe Sabrina Sammael and couldn't stand by while she hurt my friends."

"You *could* have," Nic suggested gently. "No one would've held it against you."

"I would've held it against me. Iliana asked, and I hadn't been a good friend to her since I became a wizard. I didn't like who I was becoming. I hate what it does to us, you know? When we were young uncats, we could all be friends, but then as, one by one, everyone was categorized as wizard or familiar, it's like we became something... else. Only our magical roles and no longer people. Monsters instead of humans, particularly the wizards."

"You sound like Gabriel," Nic commented with a sigh. Apparently this kind of thinking was as contagious as a new virus.

"Do I?" Alise sat back, easing into a more comfortable posture in the rocking chair and cradling her wineglass in her hands as she studied Nic with canny black eyes. "You almost sound as if you like him."

She sounded so dubious that Nic laughed, then grimaced ruefully. "I do like him. I'm in love with him. I wouldn't leave him even if I thought there was a feasible way to do so."

"Just like Maman," Alise replied softly, regret in her voice. "You're Fascinated by him, aren't you?"

Arrested, Nic didn't know how to answer at first. "What makes you think that Fascination is real?"

Alise snorted. "Oh, come on, Nic! We grew up in the same house—when we weren't away at school, of course—and we both saw how Papa ruled Maman and she just smiled and took it, never going against him in the least little way. Convocation Academy might say there's no scientific basis for Fascination, but nothing else explains the way she adores him. You had to have seen that for yourself."

Nic had seen, but much too late. Clearly Alise had paid more and better attention than Nic had. "I agree, but I didn't realize it until just recently."

"Well, you always were Papa's favorite," Alise replied with a resigned sigh. "No reason you would have noticed. But I always hated that Maman never stood up to him, not even for us." She had a bitterness to her voice that surprised Nic.

"She did, though," Nic said quietly, reflexively looking around for listeners, though she knew they were alone. "You say I can trust you. If I share a secret, will you keep it?"

"Yes," Alise replied immediately, surprising Nic again that she didn't ask to know the nature of the secret first. "I'll swear by whatever you ask me to."

"Not necessary," Nic replied with a smile, realizing that she could have asked Alise to sign the NDA, and that now she didn't need to. Her sister. "Maman is the one who helped me escape."

Alise stared, mouth working silently. Then she sighed and dropped her face into her hands. "Now I understand why you were so firm about not giving that information to Iliana and Han." She lifted her face again, expression bleak. "Does Papa know?"

"Maybe?" Nic took a breath. "Alise, have you heard from Maman at all lately?"

Mutely, Alise shook her head. "I thought it was odd Maman didn't include a note in Papa's missives about you."

"When Gabriel came to collect me at House Elal, he witnessed Papa forcing Maman into alternate form. I'm terribly afraid she's been a cat since then."

Alise blanched, evincing the same horror Nic felt at the prospect of being trapped in animal form—and animal thinking—for so long. "If you think that's the case, why haven't you done anything about it?" she demanded. "This is Maman you're talking about!"

"I *know* that!" Nic fired back. "And what, exactly, do you think I could do? I'm not going to ride up to House Elal and force Papa to return Maman to human form. I couldn't do that before I was persona non grata to him. Or hasn't it occurred to you that I betrayed him and shamed our house? Papa will never forgive me, much less listen to my pleadings."

Alise had paled, her magic thin and transparent. "And now I've done the same. Oh, Nic—what have we done to Maman?"

Nic shook her head, then laughed without humor. "Perhaps Nander can do something, then."

"He'd have to drag his head out of his ass first," Alise replied with a snicker, and they shared a smile, a real one. Despite the gravity of the conversation, Nic savored the harmony with her sister.

"Well, one predictable result of you coming to House Phel is that Papa will send someone to retrieve you. When they're repulsed, he'll eventually have to come himself."

Alise caught her breath, a queer look of hope and trepidation combined on her face. "Will Lord Phel do that for me?"

Nic nearly rolled her eyes, deciding against explaining how eager Gabriel would be to defend Alise from their father. "He would. More, he can. He's the most powerful wizard I've ever been privileged to know, and no fan of our father."

"Interesting." Alise nodded to herself. "I've already been hearing tales of his displays of magic. He's not your typical Convocation wizard by any stretch, is he?"

"Not even close," Nic answered with emphasis.

"And you're pregnant," Alise said, dipping her chin toward Nic's flat belly.

"Yes." Nic laid a hand there, imagining the child she and Gabriel would have, the idea thrilling and effervescent. If they all survived for her to give birth.

"You're happy," Alise noted softly. "I wouldn't have believed it if I hadn't seen it for myself."

"I *am* happy," Nic replied, allowing herself to embrace that truth. Despite everything, she was happier than she'd been in her entire life. Yes, everything was more difficult, but she felt loved and fulfilled in a way she'd never before attained—and might not have, had things not worked out the way they had. "At first I thought what I felt for Gabriel was Fascination, which terrified me and is part of why I tried to escape, but now I wonder if I didn't start to fall in love with him from the beginning. Which, to be frank, was also terrifying."

"I can understand that," Alise said fervently and without irony. "Is he worth it, Nic?"

Nic understood what Alise was asking. "More than. I will be happier and able to do more as Lady Phel, even as a familiar, than I would have thought to do as Lady Elal."

Alise nodded as if that decided her. "Then I'm staying with you. Nander can be Papa's heir."

"You—I—what?" Nic stammered, and Alise laughed.

"I was serious when I said I never wanted it. I do *not* want to be the head of House Elal. Maybe that's part of why I agreed to help Han and Iliana." She chewed her lip pensively. "Maybe, in my own way, I was running away, too."

Nic wasn't sure what to say to that.

"Besides," Alise ventured, "I notice you don't have an Elal wizard on your roster yet, and there is a serious dearth of house elementals and useful spirits. The lighting, forgive me for saying, is terrible. And how do you even dust this enormous place without earth elementals?"

Alise so perfectly echoed Nic's own dismay that she laughed. "So far it's the damp that's the real problem. Did you know that most of the people of Meresin are low-level water wizards? Their MP scores are too low for Convocation standards, but they have enough magic to survive and flourish here."

"That's interesting," Alise replied, sounding confused about Nic's point, which was fair. Nic was indeed deflecting giving a definitive answer.

"I've been dying for Elal magic," Nic admitted. "It's been a bit of an issue since Gabriel refuses to deal with Papa or any subsidiary of House Elal, and that was before Papa reneged on my dowry, so—"

"Wait." Alise held up a hand, eyes wide. "Papa refused to send Lord Phel your dowry?"

"And my trousseau." Nic grimaced. "Which, yes, is my fault for absconding before the wedding, but everything I have is what Gabriel has given me, which doesn't sit well."

"No," Alise murmured, "it wouldn't with anyone, least of

all you. Still, that's not legal. The contract terms set in the Betrothal Trials are set by the Convocation. House Phel has a legitimate grievance with House Elal for contract violation."

"But under the circumstances, will the Convocation even listen to House Phel's complaint?" Nic countered. "Gabriel refused to turn me over to the Convocation proctor. Doesn't that put House Phel on tricky ground to approach the council?"

"It's an interesting legal question," Alise mused. "I notice that Wizard Ratisbon is on your roster now, along with Asa Refoel and Quinn Byssan." She smiled briefly. "I know you and Quinn were always close. It's good she's here—and not only because those three have their portraits in the trophy hall at Convocation Academy for debate team and mock trial championships. They ought to be helpful in sorting the legalities. Quite the assembly of talent you and Lord Phel have accumulated already."

"You've been busy gathering intelligence," Nic noted with some surprise. "Quickly, too."

Alise flicked her fingers, and several higher-level spirits appeared, hovering in the air around her. "I may not have your power, but it turns out using spirits to spy is something I'm decently good at." She smiled thinly. "Knowledge is power, yes? I wanted to be able to make my case for a contract with House Phel."

"A contract, here?" Nic echoed in astonishment. "But you haven't graduated from the Academy yet."

"The only reason to graduate is to get a good house contract or to please Papa. Both are moot points now. Also, now that I've crossed Sabrina Sammael, her cadre of bullies will make my life miserable. Please don't make me go back."

Nic considered it, knowing Alise was right about Sabrina, if nothing else. "Papa will lose his mind if we do this."

"At this point, given how Papa has dealt with you, that's sounding like a bonus."

Nic considered, wishing she could consult with Gabriel, knowing that he'd tell her the choice was hers. "Your wizardry would be welcome," Nic began, then hesitated.

"But?" Alise waited, expression bland and spine rigid. "You might as well spit it out, Nic. Let's not dance around each other anymore. If you don't want me here, I understand and will abide by that."

"It's not that," Nic assured her hastily, burying the uncomfortable stab of guilt that she kind of *didn't* want her brilliant wizard sister around dazzling everyone. The time for sibling competition was over.

Alise was watching her carefully. "Then what is it?"

With a sigh, Nic handed Alise her last blank NDA. "This is not because I don't trust you," she said as Alise studied the document with climbing eyebrows. "We're asking everyone to sign them before we discuss the contract to the house."

"Bold," Alise murmured as she read. Without looking up, she held out a hand for Nic's quill, signing with a flourish. "I assume Han and Iliana will be asked to sign, too?"

"Yes, as soon as I copy over some more. Beyond that, now that you've signed this..." She waved the document in the air, determined to keep it safe until Gabriel could seal the promise magically. "I can tell you that Han and Iliana will be asked to sign contracts also."

Alise sat back, taking up her glass again. "I don't have to tell you that a familiar's signature on a contract isn't legally binding in the Convocation."

"No, though it might be helpful to have someone besides me explaining that to Gabriel," Nic replied drily.

"Aha," Alise breathed, clearly thinking that through. "Now I understand."

"What's that?"

"It's not that you're in love with Lord Phel—though I don't doubt that you are—but he's a radical. An outsider. He's making you his equal partner in this enterprise. That much was clear already, that your input and opinion matters."

"I don't see how that was clear when he obviously over-ruled me about you all staying," Nic muttered, still annoyed by that, even though they'd made up.

Alise grinned broadly. "See? Just the fact that you were, and still are a bit—unless I miss my guess—annoyed that he overruled you demonstrates that you're not used to that. In point of fact, you were smart to turn us away, and I can see why you're worried that Lord Phel chose to take us in. While I'm selfishly glad for his soft-hearted decision, I can see that you have to be the one to hold his feet to the fire regarding truths of life in the Convocation."

"You're not wrong," Nic replied with resignation.

"But what you two are doing here is important," Alise continued. "I realize now that we don't have to run away to establish the community I described."

"We don't?"

"No, because you're already doing it."

Nic considered that with some astonishment and considerable consternation.

Alise smiled blissfully at her. "How do you suppose a pair of rebels like us emerged from the same family, particularly ours?"

"It's a fine question," Nic answered faintly. All along, she'd blamed Gabriel for this, but more and more it seemed she'd played a larger role than she'd realized in positioning House Phel against the Convocation. And now it seemed that perhaps Maman had, too, by helping her. "You know, if the Convocation had simply let me go, they wouldn't be facing this now."

"Yes, well, the Convocation has never been smart about picking their enemies."

"Not that we're much of an enemy. More like a biting gnat who will be easily swatted."

"I don't know... We shall see!" Alise's smile turned sunny. "Let me get to work. I don't have a familiar, obviously, but I've got a fair reserve of magic. Where's your list of needs? I know you have one."

"Am I that predictable?" Nic asked, somewhat chagrined that she apparently was. She shuffled through her papers and found the list of unfulfilled vendor needs, pulling out her wishlist of Elal conveniences, ranked according to priority. Another sheet wafted out from the unruly pile, and Alise deftly caught it, reading with a raised eyebrow.

"Wedding plans?" she said with considerable surprise.

Nic snatched it back. "It's important to Gabriel."

"He really is soft-hearted under all that broody glowering,

isn't he?"

"Yes," Nic agreed, both ruefully and with affection. "He is. We're telling his family that it's a second ceremony, so they can witness and participate. His mother and I have been making plans." And who knew where those plans stood now that Daisy was so angry with them both? Nic would have to sort that out. "His family doesn't know I tried to run away," she added, a note of pleading in her voice. She didn't want to ask Alise to lie for her, but...

"Your secret is safe with me," Alise promised. "No reason for commoners to be dragged into Convocation politics. I'll get started on your list."

"But you haven't signed a contract yet."

Alise's wizard-black eyes unfocused a moment. "Lord Phel still has a considerable queue for interviews. I'll wait my turn. Meanwhile, I'll handle some of your wishes for your bathing chamber. Consider it a wedding gift." Alise winked and stood to go.

"Alise?" Nic said, impulsively holding out a hand. Alise's slim, cool fingers slid smoothly into her hand, and Nic squeezed it lightly. "I am really happy that you're here."

"Let's aim to keep it that way," Alise replied.

~ 9 ~

I F HE HAD to listen to one more wizard brag about their impressive MP scores, core competencies, and overweening ambitions, Gabriel would set his hair on fire. Better than losing control of his water and moon magic, anyway. Though it probably wouldn't help his headache.

At least he'd finally completed his assignment, having dispensed with the hopefuls for the day. Everyone had either signed or departed, which should satisfy Nic's sense of order. Putting the House Phel seal to the last petitioner's contract, he set it with moon magic, deliberately practicing a delicate touch. He had to admit that Asa was a decent teacher. He might even be growing to like the Refoel wizard, as unlikely as that had seemed even a few days ago.

Wondering what Nic was doing—and if he could drum up an excuse to spend some time with her—he pushed to his feet, then halted at the knock on the library doors. With a sigh for missed opportunities, since Nic wouldn't have knocked, he bade whoever it was to enter.

To his surprise, his father edged through the doors, hat in hand so his balding pate gleamed in the sunlight from the big windows. GF looked around at the great room, considerably improved since the last time he'd been inside, and whistled low and long. "This place is looking downright elegant," his father noted. "Hard to believe it was sunk hip deep in marsh water not long ago. And look at you, like a fine lord of the Convocation behind your big fancy desk."

Though his father didn't speak the words with recrimination, Gabriel nevertheless felt the bite of them. "Dad," he said by way of greeting as he came around said big fancy desk, unwilling to let the thing stand between them. "I'm glad you're here. Care for a glass of brandy?" Gabriel gestured to the chairs by the fire, which remained unlit with the balmy weather.

"In the middle of the day?" His father's bushy brows rose in disdain. "Eesh, no. I still have work yet to do. We're clearing the east field." He nodded to himself. "Getting it ready to plant. Did you see the blood poppies are in bloom?"

"I did." Gabriel tucked his hands in his trouser pockets, leaning back against the desk and crossing his ankles. He didn't care for how his father still stood there like another petitioner, but he'd already put his foot in it by suggesting brandy, and he couldn't think of another excuse for them to sit down. "I took Nic there this morning to see them."

"Good. They're your mother's favorites, too." GF squinched up his face in thought. "Couldn't budge her out of the cottage to see them, though."

Ah, thus the reason for this visit. "I'm sorry to hear she's in distress," he replied evenly.

"Are you? Then why haven't you been by to apologize?"

Gabriel felt his mouth fall open but seemed to be unable to

do anything about it in his shock. "Me... apologize?" he sputtered. "She's the one who—"

"Aye, I know, I know. She said some things she shouldn't have. She was fair upset at the time, you know."

"I noticed," Gabriel bit out.

"She didn't mean it, son."

"I think she did." He raked his hands through his hair. Setting it on fire would've been better than this conversation. "I am... aware that I am not the son either of you hoped for."

"Hoped for?" His father squinted in puzzlement. "You'll be a father before long, so you'll see how it is. For your children, you just hope for them to be happy. I've been sorry for the wizardry, and that it took you so sudden and hard, with no one to guide you, but only because it made you so miserable. It's good—we're both glad to see it—that you have Nic now and that she's making you happy."

Gabriel nodded, agreeing, but uncertain where to go with this. "Dad... the things Mom said to Nic, they—"

His father held up a hand to stop him. "I know. She told me, and she feels terrible about it."

Gabriel bit back saying that she should feel terrible. "Then why am I the one who's supposed to apologize?"

"Because she can't, and won't. She's caught up in feeling guilty. Worried to death about what will become of Selly now. You know, your mother has always blamed herself for Selly turning out off kilter. And she blames herself for your troubles. She knows the magic comes down from her side of the family."

"Nic thinks it had to be both of you. Recessive traits combining in a happy reemergence of the old powerful magic of the family."

His father scratched his chin. "Well, could be. I suppose she'd know. That sort of thing isn't our expertise, unless it's livestock or orchards."

"I suspect the principles are the same."

"Could be, could be," his father acknowledged. "Come by the house after supper tonight. Apologize so your mother can save face. Let her make it up to you. Don't let this fester."

With a sigh, Gabriel nodded agreement. "Nic would like to ask Mom about family gossip regarding the fall of the house and some other things. And maybe by then we'll have retrieved Selly."

Another knock came on the library doors. His father stuck his hat on his head. "I'll get out of your way, as I know you're a busy man." He paused as he turned to go. "It's a fine-looking desk. I didn't mean anything by it, calling it big and fancy."

Gabriel smiled. "I know, Dad." Just as he knew the changes to the house and to his son made the man uncomfortable. But there was no going back. If he'd learned anything from Nic, it was the impracticality of regretting and longing for the past.

His father smiled back, nodding, and opened the library doors, admitting Jadren El-Adrel. "Guess you're next in seeing his lordship." GF cackled at his own joke, one Gabriel would find painful if Jadren didn't look so offended. The pompous High House scion deserved to be unsettled.

Gabriel waited until Jadren closed the doors, then he gestured to the pair of armchairs yet again. "Brandy?"

"Yes, thank you," Jadren agreed. Though he made a face

when Gabriel handed him the snifter. "You know, Phel, if you want to compete with the High Houses, you're going to have to up the quality of your liquor offerings."

"If only in that arena," Gabriel replied, lifting his own snifter in an air toast, "you and Nic are in agreement."

"q9" Jadren said, making it sound as if he was only agreeing with something Gabriel had observed.

Gabriel set his teeth, refusing to be baited. "Is there a reason for this visit? I do have work."

Jadren nodded easily. "I signed your contract."

"I noticed."

"Regardless of it being highly irregular."

Gabriel said nothing.

"Even though I didn't need to, given that my mother ensured you can't kick me out."

Gabriel only raised a brow.

Jadren bit out an impatient sigh. "I dislike cooling my heels and doing nothing. May I have entrée to the workshop space, Lord Phel?"

Oh, that. "Yes," he answered easily, resisting the urge to smile at Jadren's obvious irritation that he'd been made into a supplicant. Gabriel fished out the key and handed it to Jadren. "Let me know if your wizardry is insufficient to use this in the lock," he said, adding a tone of sympathy just to ruffle the arrogant wizard's feathers. "And stay clear of the water-filled pit. No one is to approach it without my express permission. I've warded it to prevent any accidental incursions."

Jadren grunted, examining the silver key. "You made this, I take it?"

"For internal use only," Gabriel replied, watching the other wizard carefully. "I understand the lock itself is centuries into common domain."

Snorting softly, Jadren eyed him, turning the key in his fingers. "Your familiar is at least redressing some of the lacunae in your understanding of Convocation trademark law. But I'm not here to report your enchanted artifact transgressions to my esteemed mother, if that's your concern."

"My concern is that I don't know why you *are* here," Gabriel said softly.

Jadren flashed a quick grin. "I am a wizard of mystery." He held up the key. "You made this from moon magic?"

"From moonlight," Gabriel conceded, figuring the other wizard knew plenty about him already. If the NDA and contract didn't muzzle him, nothing would. "Moonlight solidifies as silver," he added, refraining from saying that he didn't know why.

"There are rumors, you know," Jadren said thoughtfully, holding the key up to the light, "that sun magic wizards can make it into gold. I never credited those stories." When Gabriel didn't reply, Jadren huffed without humor. "After all, why bother selling products if you can simply make your own gold?"

Gabriel recognized the question in there. "The silver persists, and it passes muster as real silver, but the magic spend is considerable."

"Not for a wizard with access to the most powerful familiar known to exist."

Smiling thinly, Gabriel didn't say he had no intention of

draining Nic to line his pockets. They had other ways of enriching House Phel.

Jadren dipped his chin and pocketed the key. "This ever-replenishing water flask—got a sample?"

Going to his big fancy desk, Gabriel opened a drawer and retrieved the flask. It was his only one, but he could always make another, Convocation trademark law notwithstanding. He and Vale wouldn't be traveling anytime soon.

Jadren took it, examining it much as he had with the key. Focusing his wizard senses, Gabriel could determine that the man was using wizardry to analyze the flask, but not exactly what kind of magic Jadren used. Interesting, given Jadren's missing MP scorecard. Oblivious to Gabriel's scrutiny—or studiously ignoring it—Jadren unstoppered the flask. "Not a very sophisticated mechanism," he noted.

"Isn't that your department?" Gabriel inquired blandly.

"Fortunately for you, yes." Jadren sniffed the contents. Pouring some water onto his palm, he tasted it, brows climbing in what might be appreciation. "It's pure?"

"Naturally."

"Is that difficult?"

"Not for me."

"Hmph." Jadren sounded dubious. "How difficult for these wide-eyed, dewy freshwater wizards you're signing up for classes?"

"That remains to be seen," Gabriel allowed. That would be the real trick in attempting to teach these students Nic had wanted. He hardly knew how he did the magic himself; he had no idea how he'd teach someone else.

Jadren went to the window, nudged it farther ajar, and upended the flask. Water flowed out, then stopped. Frowning, Jadren glanced at Gabriel. "Turn it upright again," Gabriel told him.

Doing so, Jadren made a sound of interest to find the flask full again. He emptied it several times, testing the effect. "Why do it that way?" he asked. "Why have it empty and replenish, rather than an unending stream?"

It had made sense at the time, though Gabriel didn't want to admit he hadn't considered doing it any other way. Inspiration struck him. "As you noted, my stopper mechanism is primitive. I didn't care to risk a flask that, if accidentally spilt, would produce an unending flood."

"Hmm. There is that, though—again, a better closing could prevent that. What's the mechanism for triggering the refill?"

Gabriel didn't know, and Jadren pointed a finger at him knowingly. "Ha! That's what you get for going on instinct. Still, this is impressive for making it up as you go along. I can make it better. Is there a way to make the water colder or hotter?"

"I always handled that aspect for myself."

"Well, you would, wouldn't you? But in designing a product line, we want to think about what even a commoner would like to be able to do with it. I can see that being a feature people would want. We could charge more for extras like adjustable water temperature—have the basic model, then some with bells and whistles."

"Sounds good," Gabriel allowed, somewhat bemused by

the other wizard's didactic attitude, but not actually offended. Jadren's approach was solid, anyway. "Nic mentioned she encountered a healer in—" Oops, he'd almost mentioned that Nic had made it all the way to Wartson and beyond. "At one point," he corrected, hoping the cover was smooth enough, "who had a vase with a water elemental that made water placed in it continually pure, sufficient to disinfect wounds and so forth. Is that a variation we could consider?"

Jadren tugged on his lip thoughtfully. "We'd have to dance around the Refoel license, but as long as the water didn't actually heal anyone, we should be safe there. House Elal has a monopoly on water elementals, but not water, full stop. I'll give it some thought." He turned to go, taking the flask with him, then turned back. "Where did your familiar encounter this healer? I can't imagine a House Refoel wizard needing such a device."

"I'll have to ask her," Gabriel replied breezily, taking up a missive from his desk and pretending to study it. Nonchalantly, he glanced up, as if surprised to find Jadren still standing there. "Was there anything else?"

"No, Lord Phel." Jadren smiled easily, a glint in his black eyes. "I'll let you know if the key doesn't work. It would be a shame if we had to trot you down to the north wing every time we needed to go in and out." He made it sound like not a shame at all. "Stay away from the pit, you say?"

"You'll know it when you see it."

"Good to know. What's in it?"

"House Phel proprietary information, I'm afraid," he answered coolly. It wasn't a lie: someone in House Phel had installed the creature there, knew why, and what it was.

"Ah." Jadren's smile widened as he saw right through Gabriel's prevarication. "I'm sure you'll tell us once you figure it out. Nothing like the ancient monsters lurking in these mazes our ancestors saw fit to build. You should see House El-Adrel some time. Layers upon layers of mechanisms. Entire wings disappear for years, sometimes with unfortunate non-wizards trapped within and unable to extricate themselves."

"How disconcerting," Gabriel observed, quite sure he did not want to see that for himself.

Jadren's smile faded. "You have no idea." He tossed off a jaunty salute. "I shall report."

"Jadren," Gabriel called on impulse as Jadren opened the door to leave. He waited for the man to turn back. "Would your work be aided by the assistance of a familiar's magic?" He couldn't quite believe himself that he offered, but he also seemed to find himself awash in unbonded familiars who'd need their magic tapped. Clearly Nic's practicality was rubbing off on him.

Jadren turned back slowly, all hint of amusement fled. "I am not interested in bonding a familiar, Lord Phel."

How fascinating. And how fabulously unlikely it was that the spy fastened upon him by High House El-Adrel via extortion was the sole other wizard he'd encountered totally uninterested in bonding a familiar. Or was he? "I didn't offer that," Gabriel replied loftily, pleased when the arrogant man winced ever so slightly, caught neatly by his own confession. "I understand a wizard can tap an unbonded familiar's magic. I might be able to provide that resource if it would be helpful to you."

If anything, Jadren's scowl blackened. "Are you implying I lack sufficient power to conduct my work, Lord Phel?"

"No," Gabriel answered calmly, unwilling to antagonize the man, as much as he enjoyed poking at his pomposity. "I'm simply—"

"Because there is more to wizardry than brute power," Jadren interrupted. "The meticulous application of skill, creativity, and intelligence can do more than wild displays of raw power that dazzle but produce nothing more than very loud storms and frightening special effects."

Ah, well, Gabriel reflected to himself, *poke a mad dog and expect to be bitten.* Besides, Jadren's accusation was fair enough. "The offer is there," he said with a shrug, as if it didn't matter to him. "I may have familiars in need of having their magic tapped. It occurred to me that we might as well put that magic toward the good of House Phel and the development of our promising new product line." Listen to him. He sounded just like Nic. The thought amused him greatly, and he wondered again where she was and what she was up to. Amazing how he'd gotten so he missed her desperately after only a few hours deprived of her company.

"Like your sister?" Jadren asked silkily, stalking back toward Gabriel.

The volley hitting its target, Gabriel stiffened. "Selly is not in residence at the moment," he bit out, realizing as he said it how absurd that sounded.

Jadren snickered. "Oh, I know. I was standing there when she scampered off like a wild goat escaping over the eaves like she was leaping into the mountains. Quite feral, your sister. Not at all the elegant lady of House Phel that one might expect."

Gabriel viciously reined back the urge to throttle the snide words in the man's throat. The worst part was, they weren't lies. He recovered enough cool to realize the layers of insult in Jadren's attack. House Phel obviously fell far below the elegant standards of the Convocation High Houses. Even were Selly perfectly sane and healthy, she wouldn't meet the standards of a snob like a scion of House El-Adrel. Deciding the better part of wisdom lay in not taking the wizard's bait, Gabriel faked a yawn. "The offer remains, Wizard Jadren. If you need to avail yourself of a familiar's magic, I can potentially arrange that for you."

"I won't need it," Jadren bit out on a low growl. "Certainly not for such a simple task."

"I imagine the results of your work will be the deciding factor," Gabriel observed coolly.

"Then I best get to it." Jadren bowed, making a mockery of the gesture. "If I may be excused, Lord Phel?"

"Go, go." Gabriel waved him on, waited for him to turn and nearly exit before he called after him once more. "Do try to work the lock without my help, if you're able."

Jadren slammed the door shut behind him without comment. Gabriel chuckled at his own joke, though his amusement faded immediately into a deep sense of weariness. Sometimes this endless circling felt like an exercise in futility. Making himself face the list of tasks, he looked to see what he most needed to focus on next. To his relief, a knock on the door saved him. Even better, when he called for the person to enter and it turned out to be Nic in all her fiery radiance and nourishing rose-red vivaciousness, he felt a true reprieve. He opened his arms to her, and she set down her things, coming to him eagerly, a warm smile on her face.

Enfolding her in an embrace, he held her against him, inhaling her scent and savoring the vitality of her magic. He sipped at it, just the tiniest bit, more to taste her than anything, and she hugged him tighter, arms around his waist and cheek pressed to his chest. His world righted, steadied, and all the reasons he did any of this returned to him.

Finally, Nic loosened in his grasp enough to tip her face up to his. "Bad morning?"

"Endless," he answered, then kissed her lightly. "I missed you."

She smiled, green eyes sparkling with affection and humor. "It's only been a few hours."

"Endless," he repeated. "But better now that you're here. I'm hopeful time will resume it's normal pace and cease crawling like honey in a cold snap."

"You and your farmer's metaphors." She laughed softly and kissed him, then disentangled herself. "So, I did a thing. Without consulting you."

Intrigued, he leaned back against his desk and crossed his ankles, watching her move gracefully to retrieve her box of papers and set them on her desk, efficiently ordering them into piles. "Is that why you knocked?"

She sniffed. "I was being polite."

"You don't have to knock."

She rolled her eyes. "Fine."

"You also don't need to consult me about whatever thing you did."

"I know that's what you intend, which is why I did it." She took a deep breath and met his gaze. "It still feels… wrong."

"That's Convocation conditioning speaking."

"I know, I know." She waved a hand in irritation. "But sometimes it speaks really loudly. Anyway, I agreed to let Alise stay on, as a wizard of Elal magic, pending her signing the contract with you."

Gabriel felt his eyebrows climbing in surprise. "I didn't expect that."

She studied him. "Are you annoyed? I left room for you to back out of the agreement. Alise signed the NDA." Nic held up the document in demonstration, bringing it to him. "And she knows she has to pass muster with you first."

"I'm not annoyed." Gabriel took the NDA without reading and tossed it onto one of his own piles, then caught Nic's hand, cupping it in his as he searched her face. "It's a fair change, however, since a few hours ago when you wanted to send her straight back to the academy."

"Yes, well, we talked. And I'm frankly as surprised as you are, but she asked to stay and made a good argument for it. I didn't want to refuse her, especially as we could absolutely use Elal wizardry, and the odds of obtaining that assistance from any other avenue looks decidedly grim. It was really the most practical decision."

Gabriel nodded, managing to squelch a smile at her raft of excuses. Nic would probably forever cast her decisions as practical, even when—or perhaps especially when—they came from the depths of the very soft heart she liked to pretend she didn't have. "I'm sure the decision is eminently practical," he replied, adding quickly when she narrowed her eyes at him. "And your sister is, of course, welcome here as long as she likes, even without an interview. She's family."

She sighed, heartfelt, shaking her head. "I knew that's what you'd say. She wants to help with the wedding."

"Even better. It's good for you to have your family with you, Nic. I would never go against that."

"My soft-hearted wizard." She laid her free hand against his cheek, then she patted it, just shy of stinging enough to be a slap. "But you *will* interview her. Ask her the hard questions."

He considered that. "Clearly you know Convocation etiquette far better than I, but I'm wondering—is it not a problem that Alise is your father's heir?"

Nic sighed, tugging her hand away to pace, the lighter gown swirling with the vigor of her movements. "Oh no, it absolutely *is* a problem. A huge problem. Alise says she doesn't want it, which … obviously that's not a sentiment I understand."

"Does her accepting a contract with another house preclude her from becoming Lady Elal in time?"

Nic wagged a finger at him. "Good question, and no, it wouldn't. Not typically anyway. The naming and training of heirs isn't a standardized process across the Convocation. Each house—indeed, each house head—handles it as they prefer, frequently changing their minds according to whim. Very often presumptive heirs and secondary candidates will be sent to other houses on limited contracts, so the wizards can learn various kinds of expertise, along with a variety of ways of doing business and in order to gain a certain intimacy with the other houses."

"Ah." That's what he'd suspected. "More spying."

Nic held up her hands. "The Convocation runs on spying."

"I thought that was gossip."

"Same thing, really."

She had a point.

"In this case, however," Nic continued, expression somber, "we have to face two grim possibilities. Either Alise is, as she claims, operating without our father's knowledge and permission, which is never a good thing, even if we weren't already at cross-purposes with House Elal. If we aren't at war with Elal already, this will seal it. Gabriel, we have to make plans for what happens when they, or the Convocation, or House Sammael—or all at once—come after us."

"I do have a plan," he replied. "I'll handle whatever they throw at us."

She groaned in frustration. "That does *not* count as a plan!"

He considered whether to tell her that he, in fact, hoped they'd come to him. That he welcomed the opportunity to do more than piss on Elal lands and steal Elal's favored daughter. Never in his wildest dreams of vengeance had he imagined winning two of Elal's heirs to his own house. He'd never quite found the words to explain his vendetta against Elal to Nic, and the reasons for it. He'd hoped time would bring her to his side, which indeed it seemed to be doing. "I'm not afraid of House Elal, or House Sammael, or the Convocation," he told her instead. "I refuse to cower before their blustering."

"You should be," Nic replied without venom. "It's far more than blustering."

"You keep telling me that I'm powerful and unpredictable, that the Convocation has no idea what they're dealing with in me," he argued. "You also urge me to have confidence in my wizardry and what I can accomplish. Therefore, I think you should trust me to protect you and everyone in House Phel."

She gazed at him with a long, contemplative stare. "You never do anything by halves, do you, Gabriel? I wanted you confident, yes, not overcome with hubris."

"You're only just now realizing the level of my hubris?" he teased, but she didn't smile. "Nic," he said more seriously, "I knew when I set out to reestablish House Phel that I would be fighting an uphill battle. I've reached higher than I imagined possible in the beginning. This is yet another ledge, and I'm stronger than I ever was because I have you and everything you've helped me build."

"It could be an illusion," she warned. "They may have let you climb this high so that, when you fall, it will destroy you completely."

"Or it could be that I'm stronger and more persistent than they imagined, and I cannot be stopped." He grinned at her, and she sighed, throwing up her hands.

"I can't seem to knock sense into your thick head, so I've stopped trying."

"I hadn't noticed."

"Ha to that." She stopped pacing, standing by the windows and gazing out, the bright spring sunlight gilding her lovingly.

"Back to our most immediate problem: Alise. The other possibility we must consider is that Alise's entire tale is a lie. She could be deceiving us, luring us in with her 'rogue' familiars." She spun, using her fingers to bracket the word "rogue" with strong doubt. "It's the perfect trap. The Convocation knows you're sentimental about the rights of familiars. Alise is my sister, Iliana my friend. What better way to slide inside our defenses?"

"To accomplish what?"

"Destroy us from within," Nic answered, doom in her voice that was only partially in humor. Very real fear haunted her eyes. "Knock you off that mountain and send you and House Phel back into the abyss."

He went to her, lifting her to sit on the window ledge, wide and now cushioned with bright pillows that complemented the other upholstery in the library. Standing before her, he smoothed his hands over the narrow curve of her waist, the seductive flare of her hips. "And here I thought I'd plumbed the depths of your cynicism."

She looped her hands loosely around his neck, caressing the nape so he shivered. Essaying a smile, she purred seductively, "You're welcome to plumb my depths anytime."

"Are you serious about this?" he asked. Then hastily added, lest she interpret his words the wrong way, "Do you truly believe Alise being here could be an elaborate trap?"

"It would be an exceedingly clever and effective one," she pointed out. "Elals are known for their guile, after all."

"Or you're being excessively paranoid."

"Or rightfully suspicious," she retorted darkly. "And if

you'd spent the time in the Convocation that I have, you'd know it was well-earned."

"I have no doubt that's true," he allowed. He studied her brilliant green eyes, sifting through her magic and the core-deep sense of her. "But if you believe that, why did you agree to accept Alise into our household?"

Her lush mouth twisted ruefully. "I was hoping you'd tell me. Am I being an idealistic fool?"

"You've come to the right person to ask about that," he murmured, easing closer to her. Welcoming him in, she parted her thighs to bring him near, looping her ankles around his hips, much as she'd done with her hands about his neck. He couldn't help reaching down to trail his fingers along the smooth skin her raised skirts revealed. "I am an expert in idealistic foolishness."

"I know," she murmured, tipping her head back in lascivious invitation, her lips parting as invitingly as her thighs. "I love that about you, Gabriel."

"Do you?" he mused, brushing his lips over hers, tempted to take all that she offered. "I thought you wanted to murder me for it this morning."

"That, too," she acknowledged. "Imagine my confusion."

"How can I help?" he asked, trailing his lips along her swanlike throat, succumbing to temptation and sliding his hand up to her core, so very hot and wet.

She shivered at his touch. "You're doing it. I need you, Gabriel."

"Then who am I to refuse my heart when she asks so—"

A knock on the library doors interrupted them, Nic groaning in frustration. "Don't answer."

"The doors aren't locked."

"Then lock them," she replied with meaningfully arched brows.

Ah, right. "Later," he called out to whoever it was, aware of how sexually hoarse his voice sounded as he summoned silver nails to seal the doors.

"Lord Phel!" Asa's voice sounded both urgent and amused. "I'm sorry to disturb you, but you're urgently needed in the wizard's workshop." He paused. "There's some sort of monster on the loose."

~ 10 ~

"J ADREN," GABRIEL GROWLED, stepping away from her and tugging down her skirts as he did. Nic allowed herself to whimper a little at the loss. "On my way," he called to Asa. Taking her by the waist in his big hands, and *not* how she'd been fantasizing he would, he lifted her off the window seat and set her on her feet. "Will you come with me, in case I need your help?"

"Of course," she replied without hesitation, giving him her hand and not reminding him that he didn't need to ask. Gabriel *did* need to ask, for his own sake, and she was learning to respect that. "Dare I ask what this has to do with Jadren?"

Holding firmly to her hand, Gabriel strode across the library. "I gave him the key to the workshop not a quarter of an hour ago—and expressly warned him away from the pit." He yanked the door open to a worried-looking Asa, Laryn at his side. "Why are *you* the messenger?" he demanded of the Refoel wizard.

"I'm told there are injuries," Asa answered, hastening to catch up, as Gabriel hadn't paused in his angry strides. "But the door is locked and no one can get in."

"How did he get a message out, then?" Nic asked over her

shoulder, as Gabriel still had ahold of her hand, pulling her along beside him.

"He'd taken a few apprentice wizards inside with him," Asa explained, "and sent one out to fetch me."

"Idiots," Gabriel snarled, circumnavigating the long table in the dining hall and charging through the adjoining receiving room to pass through the open door to the arcade. "Disobedient fool."

Nic took a depth breath—partly because she needed it with Gabriel rushing her along, her shorter legs no match for his stride—and partly to enjoy the sweet, spring-fresh, and sun-warmed air streaming through the gracious arched open windows of the arcade. She was glad she and Sage had decided not to glass these windows in yet. The glass wizard had pointed out that the deep outer eaves of the windows seemed to be designed to shelter the interior from all but the worst downpours, and that the parquet floors made from the water-resistant tectona trees should withstand damp. In point of fact, they already had survived full immersion, being underwater for decades until just recently. That they'd recovered fully was partially Gabriel's wizardry at work, but some might be from enchantments embedded in the architecture by his Phel ancestors.

Regardless, the lovely arcade deserved to be open to the elements. They could always glass it in come autumn, if necessary. If they survived that long. Still, it occurred to her to ask Gabriel, "Does it ever snow here?"

He glanced at her with consuming irritation. "What does that have to do with rampaging swamp monsters?"

"We don't know that it's a swamp monster," she pointed out pedantically.

"I should've sensed that the water surface had been disrupted," he growled under his breath.

"You were preoccupied," she pointed out with a sweet smile, rewarded by a magical caress from him. "And you need to calm down. Be Lord Phel, in control of everything. You can be justifiably angry, but not panicked. Your minions will look to you," she added hastily under her breath as they passed from the sunny arcade into the mirror receiving room of the north wing.

Sure enough, most of the junior wizards, new apprentices, and assorted familiars were gathered in the unfinished, echoing hall they intended to make into a gathering space and study area. Han and Iliana stood nearby, hand in hand. An air of frantic excitement greeted them, one junior wizard sitting on a table, bleeding through what looked like a hastily tied bandage. Costa, Wolfgang Ratisbon's familiar, looked up from bandaging another young wizard Nic didn't recognize. "The bleeding has slowed, Healer Asa. I believe you're all right to defer treatment for now, but my first-aid skills are basic ones."

"Check that he's correct, would you?" Asa asked Laryn, and Nic marked that the Refoel healer asked it of his familiar when he would've ordered without thought only days before. "Then join me in the workshop."

"Everyone else stay here," Gabriel ordered. "You..." He pointed at the bleeding apprentice, who blanched visibly. "How many people are in there?"

"Five, Lord Phel." The apprentice swallowed hard. "We

talked Wizard Jadren into letting us accompany him. We didn't mean to—"

"Later," Gabriel bit out.

Alise came running into the room. "Can I help?"

"We could use her help," Nic told him with quiet urgency before he could turn her away. "And Iliana's."

Gabriel quirked a brow at her but told Alise and Iliana to come along, doing an admirable job of making it sound like his idea. Han followed Iliana. Since he wore his sword and Gabriel didn't mark the young familiar's disobedience, Nic said nothing. By the fiercely determined expression on Han's face, it would be impossible to keep him from defending his lover. Nic allowed herself a mental eyeroll for that.

"Why Iliana?" Gabriel asked under his breath. He clearly had misgivings about bringing the delicate, bright-eyed redhead into a potential battle. They charged down the long hall, a small parade of herself and Gabriel, followed by Alise and Asa, Han and Iliana bringing up the rear. Light and shadow flashed with the speed of their near run as they passed doors, both open and closed, that gave onto the various living spaces of the ground floor of the north wing. Most of the open ones showed rooms in their original dilapidated, barren state, their windows not yet glassed in.

"Stop thinking of people in terms of the manual chop-chop method," Nic retorted. "You saw her MP scorecard."

"I'm still not good at deciphering those things."

Nic decided that meant he'd barely glanced at it. "She's very strong in Ariel magic, much more so than I am. Her magic will be useful to have when attempting control an unknown rampaging beast."

"Even if she's not a wizard?"

"Even so. Think of yourself as a warrior pulling the correct weapon to hand. Sometimes you need a sword. Sometimes you need a long bow."

"I don't know how to use a long bow," he muttered.

"A crossbow, then. Any idiot can use one of those."

"Happy to be the idiot you require."

She didn't retort as they'd reached the end of the long hall. The door was sealed, as reported. Nic was aware of Alise and Asa watching closely as Gabriel manifested a new silver key out of moonlight. He was getting faster and more efficient, barely drawing on her magic. She suspected he wouldn't have used her magic at all if he weren't concerned about what they'd find within—and what he'd have to do to stop it.

"Brace yourselves," he told them brusquely.

As soon as the door opened, noise flooded out, along with a wave of algae-smelling water. Their small group of rescuers shouted and shrieked in surprise—all except for Gabriel, who stood splay-legged and strong, supporting her against the current. He'd no doubt felt the water on the other side of the door. They would have to discuss how implementing greater detail into his warnings would be more useful.

She wondered why Gabriel hadn't used his magic to contain the water, but it quickly became clear that the waves were periodic, with a new one rushing toward them from the pit. This one Gabriel stopped, parting the wave with a raised hand and sending it curving back to the pit. With the recession of the flood, several people within the room flopped to the stone floor like so many stranded fish, gasping and scrabbling to get up. One man seemed to be bleeding copiously from multiple… bite wounds? If so, from very large teeth. Jadren stood atop a tall workbench, not dry, but apparently uninjured, employing some sort of artifact that looked to be a shield with moving spikes.

Another woman faced the pit, summoning some kind of magic to deal with an immense tentacle waving from the pit. Another tentacle shot out of the water, slamming down where she'd been a moment before she rolled away. Fanglike spikes screeched as they dragged against the stone floor. Nic grabbed Gabriel's upper arm with her free hand, digging in. "Don't kill it," she urged.

His wizard-black eyes glittered like knife-edged obsidian as he glanced at her. "I don't plan to. You! Get back from the pit."

The woman flashed a pale, startled look at them but obeyed, scrabbling back. As soon as she did, the water all around rose in a column, creating a clear pillar all the way to the dim ceiling towering overhead, the tentacles flailing within but unable to penetrate, as if walled in by thick glass. Nic had seen this trick of Gabriel's before, but the others gasped in wonder. It was truly a sight to behold, the creature rising within as if captured for their observation.

"I have it contained," Gabriel informed them unnecessarily, "and can hold it for a while." Nic figured it would be much longer than "a while," as Gabriel was barely drawing on her magic, but he was smart to preserve the sense of urgency. "We have time to develop a solution."

"Lord Phel, the injured?" Asa asked urgently.

"Go." Gabriel jerked his head at Jadren. "Get down and protect them, just in case."

Jadren snarled something incomprehensible but also obeyed, leaping to the floor and taking up position with his shield.

"Can you make use of Iliana's Ariel magic?" Gabriel asked Alise, who nodded, holding out a hand to the redhead. "Good. Guard them," he told Han. The blond man nodded grimly, face clear and set as he raised his sword, stepping between the women and the creature.

"I'm looking for ideas," Gabriel said to the lot of them. "Ideally I'd like to communicate with the creature. Calm it down and assure it we mean no harm. Can Ariel magic do that?"

"An Ariel wizard could," Iliana replied doubtfully. "But we'd need someone skilled in working with monsters. Very different minds. It's a niche expertise."

"I think it's awfully judgmental of you to call our new friend a monster," Han teased her.

"I may not be a wizard," she retorted tartly, "but I have enough magic to know our new friend is no natural creature. It was created."

Gabriel looked at her curiously. "How can you tell?"

She shrugged, blushing lightly. "I know animals."

"Hmm." Gabriel's gaze wandered to Nic, speculation in it, and she suspected he was thinking of the hunters and how to use this skill of Iliana's. "Ultimately, I was hoping to relocate the creature once we discovered its natural habitat, but…"

"You thought to slip it into the Dubglass River and send it

swimming off to Sammael to plague our neighbors?" Nic asked with raised brows.

"The fantasy may have occurred to me," Gabriel murmured. Beyond him, the fanged tentacles thrashed soundlessly. "Regardless of next steps," he said to everyone, "we need to calm the beast. Ideas?"

"I can send a spirit infused with Ariel magic, maybe," Alise said. "I've never done anything like it before, though."

"Your MP scores in psychic magic are high," Nic reminded her sister. "Han's Hanneil magic could be useful there, for psychic communication, depending on the creature's intelligence."

"You're welcome to it," Han said, staring at the tentacles flailing in the column with such a bleak and bitter expression that Nic nearly reached out to him. He was still in the early days of reconciling himself to his inability to use his own, powerful magic.

Alise was shaking her head. "I've never trained in Hanneil techniques. Only in Elal-licensed wizardry."

"Long bows and crossbows," Gabriel muttered.

Nic was frankly taken aback by Alise's revelation. Of course, once wizards had contracted with a house, they were bound to that house's license and forbidden from using other kinds of magic for profit. But profit was the key concept there. Most wizards dabbled in other magics as a hobby—and as insurance against the future. One never knew when a wizard might be fired from their contract. Wizards could have uncertain tempers and, as Alise had noted, the heads of houses the most temperamental of all. Also, houses occasionally lost their status, their licenses reclaimed by the Convocation or redistributed. The Convocation could be savage to those who didn't come out on top.

The wise always had backup proficiencies.

"You didn't take any other electives?" Nic asked, aghast.

"Papa wouldn't let me," Alise hissed in agitation. "Not after you wasted—" She bit down on the words, but not before Nic caught her meaning. Not after Nic wasted all that time and tuition money on wizardry classes she'd never use.

"Try the Ariel-infused spirit," Gabriel told Alise with gentle compassion that surprised Nic. He smiled reassuringly at her sister. "We encourage innovation here at House Phel."

"And violation of trademark licenses, too," Jadren called from nearby.

Gabriel cast the El-Adrel wizard a slight smile. "Consider this effort an amateur training exercise. No one is profiting, and the result won't leave the grounds."

He was learning. Catching her approving smile, Gabriel winked. "Go ahead, Wizard Alise. Take your time and see what you can do."

Nic rearranged her thoughts as she watched the mesmerizing dance of the tentacles in the water. Gabriel was mentoring her sister. It shouldn't come as such a shock—Nic had been the one to tell Gabriel he needed to train the younger wizards to win their loyalty—she just somehow hadn't expected him to take the assignment so seriously, and to begin with her own sister. She'd meant for him to teach water and moon magic, but she could see now that Gabriel, in his inimitable, iconoclastic way, was instructing the Convocation-trained students in taking on his perspective.

They'd end up with a raft of rogue wizards and unbonded familiars choosing who to give magic to at this rate, all according to Gabriel's diabolical plan. She rubbed the ache at her temple. She should've predicted this.

Alise, standing on Gabriel's other side, was frowning in concentration. At Gabriel's suggestion, she'd summoned a water elemental and was giving it simple instructions laced with Iliana's Ariel magic.

"That looks right to me," Gabriel said to Alise, seeing something there with his wizard senses that Nic couldn't.

"Do you think so?" Alise asked, uncertainty and shy hope in her expression as she gazed up at Gabriel.

Nic ruthlessly suppressed the stab of jealousy. She really needed to get past this, but she didn't know how to not feel it at all. Gabriel was *hers*, a fierce part of herself snarled. Perhaps it wasn't only in the nature of wizards to be possessive.

"I do think so," Gabriel said with a nod. "And it won't hurt to try. Go ahead and send the elemental into the water column."

The elemental cruised to the column eagerly, drawn by such a large volume of its native element. It bounced off.

"I can't penetrate your water magic," Alise said in considerable surprise.

"Hmm." Gabriel considered the problem. "How big of an opening do you need?"

"A pinprick," she assured him. "Make one, and the elemental will find it."

"Done."

The elemental disappeared, and Nic wrestled the invidious and ugly feeling of being left out of their easy wizardly camaraderie.

"Anything?" Gabriel asked Alise as they all studied the thrashing tentacles. Did they seem less agitated?

"An elemental doesn't have a lot of intelligence," Alise murmured, gaze unfocused. "I maybe should have tried a more complex... ah. Wait a moment."

The thrashing *had* decreased incrementally.

"Can you determine anything about the creature?" Gabriel asked quietly.

"No." Alise sounded disappointed. "I'll keep trying, but so far all I can determine is that the elemental has made contact and that it's happy in there."

"Keep concentrating," Gabriel coached her. "I can see what you're doing. Try something else, something new."

Alise grunted softly. "I can tell you that the elemental seems to really enjoy the water."

"Nothing finer than House Phel water," Nic murmured.

"Good tagline," Jadren said from right behind her, making her jump. "We'll use it in the ad campaign for the higher-end ever-replenishing flasks. Should it be spelled with a P-H? Nothing *phiner*—or is that too cute?"

Gabriel scowled at the El-Adrel wizard. "I thought I told you to guard Asa and the patients."

"Did. Done. They've all gone off to the infirmary."

Nic realized that was true. While they'd all been so focused on taming the sea monster, everyone else had cleared out. Jadren stepped forward with a jaunty grin, surveying their group with considerable interest. Nic groaned internally. "Is now a good time to ask when and where you acquired two more unbonded familiars along with the House Elal heir?"

"No," Gabriel bit out.

"Now I understand why you offered me a familiar," Jadren continued, leering at Iliana. "That's a tasty morsel there."

Iliana flushed but otherwise ignored him.

"I offered you access to a familiar's magic, subject to their agreement," Gabriel returned evenly, "much as Wizard Alise is utilizing. And you are a distraction. Get back to work. Later, you can explain how this happened."

"It wasn't my fault that—"

"Later," Gabriel repeated, cutting him off. "All I require of you now is silence."

Jadren stalked away and busied himself on the other side of the room—making very little noise. Nic smirked to herself with pride at her wizard's ability to command. Gabriel caught her eyes and lifted his to the ceiling ever so slightly in exasperation, a shining tendril of moonlight sliding through their connection to caress her with affection. With a start, she realized he'd likely sensed her turmoil and shameful jealousy, which only made her feel worse about it. The affectionate tendril tightened, a sense of cold silver chains caressing the inside of her skin making her shiver, this time with need. She risked a glance at Gabriel, finding him watching her with hot black eyes.

Yes, they would always have that between them. She managed a smile for him. He'd been right in saying that it had been easier when it was only the two of them.

"I can't sense anything," Alise ground out, her frustration clear.

"I can," Iliana said, with considerable surprise. "I mean…" She flushed a deep pink that made her fawn-colored freckles stand out as everyone focused intense attention on her. "I can't do anything to communicate with the creature, but I must be feeling this through Alise's wizardry. I can sense how it's feeling, and some of its thoughts."

"Excellent," Gabriel approved, oblivious to how unusual a moment this was. "What can you tell us about it?"

"It was sleeping," Iliana said slowly, her brows knitting. "Hibernating for a very long time, deep in the mud. Then a huge wave of magic hit and awakened it. Only a few days ago?" she made it into a question.

Nic exchanged rueful looks with Gabriel. "That makes absolute sense," she reassured Iliana. "Can you find out any more than that—why it was here in the first place, where it came from?"

"Maybe with time. Right now it's too agitated. And hungry."

"Hungry?" Gabriel echoed with consternation. Of course her nurturing wizard would be worried about feeding his captive monster that just nearly killed a few people. "Can you tell what it wants to eat?"

"Fish, I think."

"If it will go back into its pool, we'll bring it fish," Gabriel promised. "Can you convey that?"

Alise and Iliana both shrugged in bemusement, then focused on the column of water. The tentacles stilled, then gradually—perhaps sullenly, if Nic wanted to read into its body language, and perhaps via her own native Ariel magic—withdrew beneath the level of the floor. Gabriel drew on her magic again, creating a seal over the top of the column as he slowly lowered it until the surface of the pond once again lay smooth and undisturbed well below the surrounding rim.

"It wants the cover off," Iliana whispered. "Or it can't breathe. That's why it was upset."

There was one answer.

Gabriel removed the last of the confining magic, his hand tense in hers as they braced for retaliation. But the water lay clear and still. They let out a relieved breath as one. "That was good work, people," Gabriel said with a smile. "I'm proud to have you as part of House Phel."

They all beamed with pleasure, almost preening under Gabriel's approval. It was nice to know she wasn't the only one lethally vulnerable to the wizard's charm.

"Lord Phel?" Iliana asked shyly. "May I keep trying to listen to the monster?"

Gabriel's gaze flicked to Han. "I assume you'd be willing to stand guard and protect Iliana?"

"Yes, sir, Lord Phel." Han even bowed, he was so pleased by the request.

"Then I'd very much appreciate if you would do so," Gabriel told Iliana. "So long as Han is available to guard you."

"Yes, Lord Phel," Iliana agreed with enthusiasm. "I'd like to rest first, but perhaps we could try this afternoon?"

"Perfect," Gabriel replied. "And," he said, raising his voice, "Han can ensure that no one else approaches the pool. I'll arrange for a guard rotation for when you two aren't here, to prevent further *incidents*."

"I told you," Jadren called from across the room. "It wasn't me. I only—"

He at least had the sense to stop talking when Gabriel raised a hand. Gabriel looked at Nic. "I'll stay to discuss with Jadren. I don't think I'll need you, and I assume you have a long list of things to do."

Sadly true. "I'll see you at dinner?"

"Hopefully beforehand," he murmured, gaze still warm. He'd begun a habit of lounging on the bathing chamber chaise to watch her bathe and change for dinner, which pleased her no end. As their increasingly busy days took them in different directions, that time had become a quiet moment to catch up with each other. "I may have need of you in the arcanium tonight as well, familiar," he added, black eyes hooded.

That did it. She flushed hot with new and returning desire, so much so that she couldn't continue to meet his gaze and keep herself together—and restrain herself from kneeling at his feet right then and there. Not something they needed an audience for. "Of course, wizard," she murmured in reply, savoring the answering leap of desire from him.

He lifted their joined hands and kissed the back of hers, his lips cool, the covert flick of his tongue hot. "I'll check in with Asa, see how his patients are," she said, instead of the several other ardent phrases crowding her lips.

"Thank you," he said—and she understood it was the same for him.

With a sigh, he released her, turning resolutely toward

Jadren.

"May I stay, Lord Phel?" Han asked. "It might be helpful for me to know what went wrong."

Gabriel considered him, then rested a hand on the younger man's shoulder. "I could use your insight, yes."

Iliana and Alise flanked Nic as she left the workshop, though neither of them said anything until the door had closed, and locked, behind them. Then both spoke at once, gushingly.

"Nic," Iliana nearly squealed, "he is so dreamy!"

"He is *so* in love with you!" Alise exclaimed at the same time.

They leaned around Nic, exchanging grins, complete with waggling brows. Nic actually felt herself blushing. "Not so loud," she hissed at them.

"That is," Alise continued cheerfully, not the least bit more quietly, "you told me that you were in love with him, and that it might be the Fascination, but you did *not* mention that Lord Phel is head over heels in love with you and that he looks at you like you're a big creamy dessert he'd like to lap up in a thousand tiny licks."

"*Alise*," Nic moaned, tempted to clap her hands over her ears in mortification. It did not help that Gabriel *had* licked her all over, in exactly that meticulous fashion, as if he savored every taste.

"You are so lucky, Nic," Iliana said fervently. "I don't mean to embarrass you. I just want you to know that, well—it isn't luck. Having all of this, with a wizard like that..." She sighed wistfully. "It's exactly what you deserve. I'm not at all surprised that you, of all people, landed on your feet. You and Lord Phel are a modern-day Lyndella and Sylus. It's *so* romantic."

"Except their story ended tragically," Nic pointed out, feeling very like Gabriel in that moment with his sour take on that epic tale.

Iliana shrugged that off. "I'd do Sylus anyway, even knowing that. Don't tell Han. So, tell me," she said, switching topics rapidly, "is the 'meet me in the arcanium' line code for—"

A door opened, Quinn Byssan popping her head out. "I thought I—Iliana! I heard you were here." She hugged the redhead, both of them making happy noises of reunion.

"And…" Quinn remembered herself and inclined her head. "Wizard Alise. Forgive me for not greeting you properly."

Beside Nic, Alise stiffened unhappily. "You don't have to be formal with me, Quinn. It's good to see you again."

"Thank you… Alise." Quinn looked uncomfortable.

"I seem to recall a time when you were visiting House Elal, and you called me a snot-nosed thief," Alise remarked, pretending to think.

It was Quinn's turn to blush in mortification. "I am *so* sorry for that. I—"

"You could've called me worse, and it would've been true." Alise grinned. "But, for the record, it was Nander who stole your grooming imp and replaced it with an earth elemental, not me."

Quinn's embarrassment turned to outrage. "That little shit! Do you know how—" She stopped herself, realizing that "little shit" was also a wizard now.

Alise burst out laughing. "Nander *is* a little shit, unfortu-nately. Maybe he'll mature someday, but..." She and Nic exchanged glances, processing that the little shit might become Lord Elal. Nander wasn't an idiot, but he did have a mean streak. Having the power of running a house on top of being a wizard wasn't likely to do his character any favors.

Quinn ventured a smile, holding out a hand. "Fresh start?"

Alise bypassed the hand and hugged her. "Sister minions of House Phel," she declared. "We were just grilling Nic about her sex life, want to join us?"

"Oooh, yes!" Quinn exclaimed, even as Nic declared they were doing no such thing.

"I've got a gorgeous suite on the top floor," Alise said. "How about we impose on Lady Phel to order up some lunch, and we can all catch up." She looped her arm through Quinn's, steering them toward the stairs to the third floor and ignoring Nic's protests. "I understand you did the windows? They're lovely."

"I only supplied the magic," Quinn said modestly. "My sister, Sage, is my wizard, and she does all the work, but she does have exquisite technique."

"Now, now," Alise reproved. "I'm learning that in House Phel we are exploring what familiars bring to the equation. Be proud of your magic."

"I really *do* have things to do," Nic grumbled to Iliana as they found themselves trailing behind.

Iliana smiled sympathetically. "You can take time to eat lunch, Lady Phel. The babe needs it, even if you don't feel it. I'm sure Healer Asa would say the same."

"Asa," Nic echoed, remembering. "I promised I'd check on the patients."

Iliana caught her arm. "Please don't go yet. I'm sure Wizard Asa has the situation well in hand, and it would be really lovely to spend an hour chatting with girlfriends, you know? Like we used to do, before everyone… moved on."

She sounded so wistful that Nic agreed. Besides, Alise and Quinn's conversation had reminded Nic sharply of those long-ago days, when they'd been neither wizard nor familiar, only students together in magic, and her friends had come to stay at House Elal during school breaks. Those had been carefree days that she hadn't realized she'd missed until this moment. It was a bittersweet kind of missing, the softer variety of regret, the sort that got drowned out by the flood of greater miseries.

But on this sunny spring day, against all odds, here they were, all together. A lunch with her friends suddenly sounded like the absolutely perfect thing. "All right," she conceded. "But we are *not* discussing my sex life."

"Mm-hmm." Iliana's brown eyes sparkled with such mischief that Nic knew she was in trouble. "I also understand we have a wedding to plan!"

"How did you—*Alise.*"

Alise glanced over her shoulder, eyes wide in feigned innocence. "Was it a secret? If so, I have to warn you that people will find out eventually, especially once we send out invitations. Big society weddings are difficult to hide." She smirked at her own wit.

"Ha-ha." Nic decided to confide in them, this unexpected, unlooked-for group of female friends. "It just feels really strange, you know, to plan to invite a bunch of people to a wedding at the same time that we're strategizing how to keep our vengeful enemies from arriving to attack."

They were all quiet a moment, ascending the final flight of stairs.

"It's life, isn't it?" Iliana finally said. "You plan for the best and prepare for the worst. That's all we can do. I thought I was going to be Sabrina Sammael's plaything by this time, having to watch her bond Han as her familiar, helpless to stop her from tormenting us both. But here I am, lunching with Lady Phel." She flashed Nic a brilliant smile. "And Han is my love and my lover, as I never dared hope for. We have a room of our own and a place where we can be useful."

"Except it might not last," Nic warned her, feeling—as always—that she needed to be the practical one amidst this group of dreamers.

"I don't need a guarantee of the future to be happy right now," Iliana insisted quietly. "Now can be enough."

Nic smiled at her. She'd always liked this about Iliana, her determined sweetness and good nature. In fact, she liked all of these women, and it was really lovely to have friends again. If only it could last… But Iliana was right: now could be enough.

~ II ~

GABRIEL WAS JUST about to go look for Nic when she swept into their rooms in a flurry of swirling skirts and rolling eyes. "Ugh!" she exclaimed in disgust. "I can't believe I'm running late yet again. One day, I swear, I'll won't be in a rush to change for dinner."

"We have time," Gabriel told her, watching with interest as she shed her gown and underthings, leaving a trail behind her as she raced for the bathing chamber. He followed her in at a more leisurely pace, settling himself on the chaise. He'd already bathed and dressed. He'd begun to like this transition to mark the end of the day, much as he'd initially protested the need for it. Farmers tended to bathe in the evening anyway, to rid themselves of the day's accumulated dirt, but not to attend a fancy dinner. "There seem to be a few improvements in here, I noticed."

"Towel-warming fire elementals! Bless Alise." Naked, Nic set loose a water elemental to clean her body while she set the grooming imp to do her hair. "I'd rather have a bath, but there's nothing like water-elemental clean." She leveled a look at him in the mirror. "What's bothering you?"

It amazed him that she could pick up on his mood so

quickly. "Am I being spiky?"

"No—damp and gloomy. Your mother?"

"Got it in one. Dad asked me to come by after supper and apologize to her."

She met his gaze as she applied her makeup. "So you have to be the peacemaker since she won't."

"Apparently."

Shrugging, as if unsurprised by the counterintuitive logic, she rolled her gorgeous eyes, then began shimmying into the lingerie she'd grabbed from her wardrobe. "I'll go with you, of course."

"Thank you."

"All part of the job," she declared with a cheeky smile. "I take the care and feeding of my wizard very seriously. Besides, I want to ask Daisy some questions about House Phel's history."

"I mentioned that to my dad. It will be the ostensible reason for our visit."

She turned to face him, dazzlingly sexy in her lacy lingerie, narrowing her gaze in accusation. "So, you already assumed I'd go with you."

"I did," he admitted, and she smiled with genuine warmth.

"Good. It was the right assumption. Now I need to find a dress to wear, not like it will be a difficult decision. Let's see… Oh! I'll wear the one I didn't wear last night!"

She started to march out of the bathing chamber, but he caught her around the waist, pulling her back against him. She smelled of red wine and roses, her physical scent intertwined with her magic, and he nuzzled her dark curls, then turned her to face him. "Truly," he said, "I appreciate your support in this."

"Families." She infused a world of emotion into that one word.

"Indeed. Speaking of, how are you getting along with Alise?"

"Surprisingly well." A flurry of expressions crossed her face, along with a blizzard of emotional notes within her magic.

"You don't have to be jealous of her," he said, feeling that he should address it. "I'm friendly with her only because of you."

"I know." Her lush mouth twisted ruefully. "I don't like being jealous, but apparently I'm not as evolved as I'd like to be."

"So say we all."

They stood there a moment longer, sharing the unspoken understanding. "I really should get dressed," she finally said.

"Or we could stay here, hide in our room, and let the rest of them go plow without us," he suggested. "You could have your bath. We could have sex. Perhaps combine the two."

"Now you sound like me." She kissed him, but fleetingly, as she immediately tugged herself out of his grasp. "As tempting as that is, we should make an appearance. A calm dinner to contrast with last night's display of might and to reinforce your calm leadership through today's developments is what your household will need."

"*Our* household," he corrected automatically, following her out to the bedroom and the wardrobe where she kept her gowns. Tucking his hands in his pockets, he awaited her reaction. She deserved a happy surprise for once.

She flung open the doors, reached in, then stopped. Whirled around. "Gabriel!"

He grinned in the face of her astonished delight. "Sometime between arguing with Jadren and firing wizards, I managed to squeeze in cornering Wizard Dahlia into making you some new gowns."

She whirled around again, touching the different fabrics with reverence. "Oh, you didn't have to do this. It really wasn't a high priority. I shouldn't have made snotty remarks about my dearth of gowns."

He went to her, stroking light fingers down her arms. "The care and feeding of familiars," he reminded her softly. "You told me from the beginning that you were high maintenance, so I'm acting accordingly."

She craned her neck to look up at him in chagrin. "I hope I'm not, *really*. Probably that's another way in which I need to evolve."

"If you were, *really*," he returned, gravely mimicking her, "it wouldn't be nearly so fun to give you presents. Now pick one out and get dressed, or I won't be responsible for my actions." He smacked her nearly naked bottom lightly, pleased by her gasp and the immediate heating of her magic.

"That's not exactly a threat," she taunted as he removed himself a safe distance from the temptation she represented.

"Hmm. Good point. How about: pick one out and get dressed or no arcanium sex after we get home?"

"That will do it," she agreed cheerfully, immediately selecting a gown.

THEY RODE THE horses to his parents' cottage, Vale and Salve pleased for the outing in the balmy evening, dark as it was, the days still short. Gabriel had barely dismounted, turning to help Nic down, when his mother burst out of the illuminated doorway. "Did you find Selly?" she demanded breathlessly.

"Not yet," he answered, irritated by both his failure to bring Selly home and that she was his mother's first concern. Nic squeezed his arm in sympathy, then breezed over to his mother, kissing her cheek.

"We brought you some ginger cake," she said, pressing the package into Daisy's hands, then putting an arm around her to steer her into the cottage. "We had so much left over from dinner, and it's best fresh, you know."

His father rose from his chair by the fire where he nursed a cup of tea, holding out a hand to shake, then pulling Gabriel into back-pounding embrace. "Thank you," he murmured in Gabriel's ear.

"GF, do you want cake?" Nic asked brightly.

"I do," his father answered. "And I'll show you how to make my special whiskey sauce to put on it."

"I can do that," Daisy inserted, moving to do so.

"Nothing doing," GF declared, affectionately nudging her aside and pointing Nic to the kitchen. "It's my secret recipe that I'm sharing with my daughter-in-law. No spies allowed."

"Oh, *you*," Daisy fumed, wringing her hands in her apron and looking everywhere but at Gabriel while the other two left them alone in the sitting room. The discomfort between them thickened.

Gabriel could see how this would be up to him. "I'm sorry, Mom," he offered.

Her startled gaze flew to his. "Whatever for?"

"I should have talked to you right away. I know that all of this has been hard on you. I don't—" His voice caught on the emotion, and he had to take a breath. "I don't blame you for hating all the ways things have changed."

Tears filled her eyes. "I don't. Not really. I didn't mean those things I said."

"It's all right if you did mean them," he said gently. "I know I've changed, that you never wanted a wizard for a son. Or a familiar for a daughter."

She wiped away the tears as they spilled over. "I just... I thought our lives would be different. Simpler. It would've been enough for me."

"For me, too," he told her, waiting for her to see the honesty in his gaze. "But my mother always told me we have to take whatever life throws at us and make the best of it."

She laughed, a watery sound. "I did always say that, didn't I? Who knew you listened to anything I said, though!"

"I listened, Mom," he said. "I still do." He opened his arms to her, hoping she'd take him up on the offer of a hug.

To his relief, she moved into his arms, hugging him tightly. "I *am* proud of you, Gabriel," she said softly. "And Nic is right:

you are still all those things I've always loved about you, no matter the color of your hair or eyes."

His heart thawed from the tense fist it had hardened into ever since he overheard her words to Nic. "You don't have to be afraid of me."

"Oh, I know that." She pulled away. "But you will bring Selly home?"

"We're working on it."

"And you will make her normal again?"

He winced internally over the word "normal" but let it go. "We have a lot of people with the expertise to help her. And I'll do everything in my power to do what's needed."

"All right, then." His mother tucked her arm in his. "Let's have some cake."

UNFORTUNATELY, ARCANIUM SEX was not to be. By the time Daisy finished regaling them with tales she'd heard as a child about House Phel's former glory, it had grown quite late. Also, Nic was no fool, and she could easily fill in the blanks in Daisy's stories, just as Gabriel half feared, half hoped she would. At least the time of reckoning had come.

Nic was quiet on the ride home, and Gabriel waited tensely for her inevitable questions. She was too poised, too well trained to have revealed anything to his parents, but he'd watched her put the puzzle pieces together, seen the occasional accusing glint in her gaze as she glanced at him speculative-ly, before hiding her eyes behind the lush fringe of her dark lashes.

"You suspect House Elal was behind the fall of House Phel," she said finally, her tone neutral.

He'd lit their path with some moonlight, but it wasn't enough to show her expression. Relieved that the topic was at last out in the open, he let out a breath. "Yes."

"And you've thought so for a long time," she clarified.

"I'd heard the stories people passed around, about the old days," he said, by way of explanation. "When I began reading the books on magic in the library, trying to learn all I could, I began to see a pattern, details from those tall tales aligning with the information about the magic specialties of various houses. Elal matched perfectly."

"Ghosts, demons, and goblins plaguing the countryside. It does fit," Nic murmured. "Is that why you wanted me to hear it for myself?"

He should've known her agile mind would put that to-gether, too. "In part," he admitted. He didn't add that the other part was that he'd been too much of a coward to come out and tell her. "You know these things better than I do. I knew that I could've come to the wrong conclusion, so I wanted to discover if you'd see the same pattern without me leading you in that direction." That sounded good, even if it wasn't all of it.

"Is that why you risked everything to try for me in the Betrothal Trials?" she asked with deadly neutrality. "You wanted revenge against House Elal."

He wanted to tell her she was wrong. He also wouldn't lie to her. "In the beginning, yes. There was a symmetry to it I couldn't resist."

"Understandable." She said nothing more.

Cursing under his breath, he stopped Vale, swung down, then caught Salve's bridle. "Will you come down and talk to me?"

She regarded him, eyes shadowed. He thought she might refuse, might point out in her acerbic way that they were already talking, but she finally nodded, holding out her hands for him to lift her down. Once he set her on her feet, he held her by the waist for a long moment, then brushed a hand over her cheek, tangling his fingers in the curls at her temple. She'd looked so right, so perfect at his parents' old kitchen table, eating cake and teasing his dad about his secret recipe. He knew she'd repeatedly told him she wouldn't—couldn't—leave him, but he couldn't escape the sinking fear that he'd destroyed everything. She might be compelled to stay with him, but nothing could make her love him if she didn't.

"Remember the miniature?" he asked her.

She nodded. "You carried it with you when you came to House Elal to claim me, and after, when you chased me."

"I carried it all the time," he corrected. "Yes, you caught my attention because you were an Elal, and I suspected Elal of being my house's enemy. I knew very little about the Convocation then. I needed a familiar, I'd been told, if I wanted to accomplish anything. You were available, powerful, beautiful..."

"And an Elal," she finished for him, unmoved. "I understand."

"I don't know that you do. It was more than that. I used to study your miniature, convinced that I saw something in your image that spoke of a connection between us. I wanted that more than I wanted the rest of it. Even more so when I finally met you."

She regarded him gravely. "You don't have to justify any of it, Gabriel. Ours was never a romance. We both knew the terms of engagement from the beginning."

"I never thought of you as the enemy." He wasn't sure what to say to make things right.

With a soft laugh, she cupped his cheek, scratching lightly with her nails. "Conversely, I was convinced you *were* my enemy. I fled from the prospect of marrying you for that very reason. Do you hold that against me?"

"No. I never did," he answered softly. "I only ever wanted to understand. What you said about House Sammael? It's important to remember. You cannot dismiss an entire house based only on the behavior of a few individuals. Especially the actions of those long dead."

Her eyes gleamed in the shadows, moonlight silvering her dark hair. "Or even those still living."

He caught his breath. "Do you think Elal still conspires against House Phel?"

She breathed a laugh. "Darling, Elal conspires against everyone all the time. Wizard Jadren isn't wrong about Elal guile." Chewing her full bottom lip, she considered. "But against House Phel specifically, still, after all this time? I don't know." She rubbed her temple. "I really don't know. I'll have to think about it."

"Not tonight," he suggested, brushing her fingers from her temple and placing a kiss there. "You need to rest."

"I am tired," she admitted, and he knew that she must be exhausted, that she didn't protest at all.

Still, he paused before lifting her onto Salve's back again. "Am I forgiven?"

"Gabriel." She lifted onto her toes, leaning into him and brushing his lips with hers, roses and wine twining through his senses. "No forgiveness is necessary. You are far from the first wizard to acquire a familiar from a rival house in order to score against them. It's standard Convocation cold warfare."

He slid his hands up and down her back. "Somehow that doesn't ease my conscience."

Eyes sparkling with amusement at his expense, she kissed him again. "No, because you want to believe you're above such things."

"That doesn't make me feel any better either."

"Do you want me to make you feel better about this?" She asked the question earnestly, not teasing at all.

He considered the question seriously. "No. I suppose not."

"That's what I thought." She kissed him a third time, lingeringly. "We all have our flaws, and being flawed doesn't make you a monster. It means you're only human," she whispered against his lips. "Now let's go home."

He lifted her into the saddle, and she caught his hand, speaking quietly, as if they could be overheard. "You should keep in mind—Elal magic doesn't account for everything in those stories. They wouldn't have been working alone."

"That thought occurred to me, also."

And an uncomfortable thought it was, too.

Nic still looked weary in the morning, shadows under her eyes, which sparkled a bit less than usual. Fortunately he'd barely drawn on her magic the day before when dealing with the pit creature, but she still hadn't recovered completely from taking alternate form so many times in a row. He also suspected the pregnancy was taking more out of her than she wanted to admit, though he was loathe to suggest that to her.

He studied her closely as they debated over breakfast when exactly to have the wedding—a topic his mother had brought up several times. He was all for as soon as possible while she continued to worry about spending time and energy on frivolous efforts instead of on the war she feared so much.

"Even this conversation is a waste of time," she declared, throwing down her napkin and dropping her face in her hands. "We should be discussing what we'll do when the combined might of our enemies drops on our heads. Not to mention the Convocation."

He was also loath to suggest that their situation might feel more overwhelming to her because she was tired and that, if she'd take a day of rest, it would be good for her. "I do have good news," he told her. "I meant to tell you last night but forgot. Iblis accepted yesterday's counter-offer for Narlis. That, at least, is done with." He decided against mentioning that it had all come out fine, despite Nic's dour predictions.

Indeed, she dropped her hands and narrowed her eyes. "Just like that?"

"They sent a signed agreement yesterday."

She tapped her nails on the table. "What was the final amount?"

"Worth it. I thought you'd be happy to have one less potential enemy to worry about."

"The number, Gabriel."

He should've known she'd insist. She'd find it in the house accounts, anyway, so he told her the figure, bracing himself.

"You went *up*?" she asked in disbelief.

"I was tired of haggling," he replied defensively. "It's still far less than their original demand."

She rolled her eyes. "Oh, well, now I feel so much—"

A knocking on the doors to their rooms interrupted her, and they turned as one to glare at the offending sound. "Why did you want to bring more people into the house again?" he asked with considerable irritation.

"I can't recall. Clearly I was not in my right mind," she answered drily as he got up to manually unlock the door. Despite the reconciliation with House Iblis, he doubted there would be magical locks in their future.

He opened the door to find one of the student wizards outside. Her eyes were large in a pale face. *What now?*

"Lord Phel." She bowed. "Lady Phel." She bowed again as Nic came to his side. "I've been sent by Wizard Asa to inform you that Lady Seliah has been retrieved and is in the infirmary.

He asks that you both come at once."

Selly. In the infirmary. Was she injured? Surely she wasn't... dead.

"You go," Nic said, her decisive tone cutting through his rising panic. "I'll send for your parents and will be right behind you."

He focused on her. His parents, yes. They would want to know. "Thank you."

"Go," she said firmly.

He went, running down the big stairs in great strides, turning to the south wing and racing to the space that, instead of the ballroom in the mirroring north wing, had been subdivided into offices for the various in-house wizards. Asa had been the first to claim his space—a smaller set of interconnected rooms for him to see patients, along with a larger room to serve as an infirmary—but he wasn't the last. Other wizards, including Alise, he noted as he ran past, already had their names on office doors.

The outer rooms of Asa's offices were empty, though with more furniture than when he'd been there a few days before. They were more than filled, however, with Selly's familiar screaming. He raced through to the infirmary. The room bordered the back of the house, the same view as their bedroom balcony, with a view of the long lawn that sloped to the river. Recently the lawn had been submerged, along with the rest of the south wing, but a few days of sunshine had the grasses growing tall outside the long row of windows admitting the bright morning sunlight.

Two of the injured from the encounter with the swamp

monster were ensconced in beds along one wall, sitting up and watching the scene with great interest. They blanched when they saw him, avoiding his gaze. He'd fired the two wizards who'd just had to poke the pit, and everyone else involved, especially and including Jadren, had been thoroughly reprimanded. He had no time for them, however, his gaze entirely on a bed near the windows, where a thrashing and shrieking Selly fought Asa, Laryn, and Rat. They were attempting to tie her to the bed frame, with little success. Despite the odds and Selly's too-thin, bony frame, she was gaining on them, fighting with near supernatural strength.

Grimly, Gabriel wondered how the Convocation subdued such wildness. House Hanneil psychic control? He didn't want to know. He reached Selly, taking her thrashing head forcibly in his hands, holding her still and making her look at him. "Selly," he said loudly enough for her to hear, but keeping his tone calming. "Seliah, it's me. Shh. You're safe. You're home." His voice broke a little on the word "home."

Selly stared at him with feral eyes that held no recognition. Her long hair snarled and caked with mud, she was filthy and emaciated, looking bonier than even two days before. Screaming as if he were a monster, she shrank away, trying to escape him, fighting even harder.

"She needs to be contained for me to work on her," Asa told him in clipped tones as he held down one wrist. Laryn was fighting to contain the other hand, while Rat sat on Selly's frantically kicking legs, the slight man bouncing with her furious gyrations. "She's dangerously dehydrated, on top of being malnourished. We need to get some water and broth in her."

With deep regret, Gabriel did something he never imagined doing to his sister. Ruthlessly drawing on his native magic, he extruded chains from moon magic, growing them like living vines to snake around the wrist Asa held, tightening to drag Selly's hand down flat by her side. Selly howled in outrage, yanking her unchained wrist from Laryn's grip and punching the woman smartly on the cheek. Laryn reeled back but didn't fall. Gabriel whipped a chain around that wrist, too, restraining Selly on that side. In another moment, he had her ankles chained also, Rat climbing off wearily with a nod of gratitude.

Asa was at Selly's head, speaking to her, though she screamed even more loudly now that she was constrained. "Can you put her unconscious?" Gabriel shouted to Asa. The last thing he needed was his mother arriving to witness this horrible scene.

Meeting Gabriel's gaze, Asa nodded, his dark face grave. "I don't like to resort to that, but..." He laid a hand on Selly's forehead, having to grip firmly to keep her from shaking him off, and held out the other for Laryn. She obeyed readily, her magic flowing into the healer wizard in a bright stream.

Selly went limp, the sudden silence almost a shock. Gabriel hastily erased the evidence of what he'd done, withdrawing the silver chains, looping them into a coil and pocketing them.

"Are you all right?" Asa asked Laryn with concern.

She fingered her swelling cheek but nodded. "Save some healing for me," she told him, "but I'll live."

"Always," he said, smiling with an affection Gabriel had

never seen his familiar return, though Asa seemed blissfully unaware of it. "Would you get the bindings? We'll need to strap her down securely but comfortably, just in case."

She hastened off to retrieve the supplies, and Asa turned his attention to Gabriel. "I won't be able to do much without her awake. The most important step we can take is to begin to drain her magic. She has to be conscious for that."

"Just as a wizard can't tap a familiar's magic while they're in alternate form." Gabriel recalled Nic explaining that. A natural protective measure, perhaps, or some of these Convocation wizards wouldn't bother with the annoyance of having their magic reservoirs be walking and talking human beings.

"Exactly." Asa had his hands splayed, moving them through the air over Selly's prone form, his magic sifting down and into her. "For the time being, however, I can address the effects of dehydration and malnutrition, and attempt to calm her mind so that when we wake her, you can begin to tap her magic."

"Me?" Even though Nic had assured him that the process didn't have to be sexual as it was between them, the thought of taking his own sister's magic didn't sit well with him. "Can't you do it?" he asked hopefully.

"No, Lord Phel. I really can't. I'm not a powerful enough wizard to manage the huge pressure of magic trapped in Selly here." He smoothed the hair back from Selly's forehead, his face filled with compassion. "Poor girl is bursting at the seams with magic. That first tapping will be incredibly volatile. I advise that you have me here to help in case it's too much for even you."

"All right, do what you can for now," Gabriel replied, stepping away as Laryn returned with the straps.

Rat stood nearby, looking worried. Also filthy, scratched, and considerably worse off than he'd been a few days before. "Lord Phel," he said, "I am beyond sorry for this scene. I just—"

Gabriel clapped him on the shoulder. "No apologies. I asked you to do what needed to be done and you did. I'm frankly astonished you managed to bring her in at all."

"Me too," Rat admitted. "It were a near thing, too. That gel... I'm afraid her mind is plumb gone. Not once did she know me like she used to."

He sounded so wrecked that Gabriel contained his own distressed reaction. "How did you manage it?"

"Dirty trick," Rat admitted. "Never woulda worked if she'd been her usual wily self. I set a snare for her. Was all I could do to tie her up, even snared like that. Had to carry her all the way. Kicking, fighting, screaming like I meant to murder her." He scrubbed a hand over his face, clearly exhausted. "I think I'll go sleep now—haven't in two days—now that she's in good hands."

"Stay," Gabriel urged. "Take one of these beds, and Wizard Asa will take a look at you once he's done with Selly."

Rat eyed the unconscious woman askance, shaking his head rapidly. "If it's all the same, Lord Phel, I'll skip the magicking."

Gabriel nearly protested that it wasn't what Rat feared but decided against it. Most of the folk of Meresin were unused to magic, and there would be time to bring them around to the positive benefits. "Come back if you need anything at all," he urged instead. "Maybe eat something before you sleep, too." He dug a handful of coins from his pocket.

Rat gave the coins an equally suspicious glare. "That's far too much, Lord Phel. And where's a fellow like me to spend that sort of coin, anyhow?"

Again, not the time to explain Nic's grand plans to bring in opportunities for people to spend coin they earned, to purchase conveniences to improve their lives. "Stop by the kitchen, then, and help yourself to all the food you like—take it with you. And, Rat..." He put a hand on the man's shoulder, drawing his miserable gaze. "You did well. I know it may not feel like it, but we can help Selly now that she's here. Something we couldn't do with her out there."

Rat nodded. "I know it, and I don't. Not to disagree with you, Lord Phel, but these measures..." He glanced again at Selly, now bound to the bed, Asa's magic shimmering brightly to Gabriel's wizard senses. He had no idea what Rat saw. "Well, I wonder if she wouldn't have been better off left alone. She was happy in a way, out in the wilds. Is this really an improvement?"

"It will be," Gabriel averred, hoping he was speaking the truth.

Rat nodded again, clearly unconvinced, then wiped a hand over his face. "I'll get that food and sleep. It will no doubt make a considerable difference in my attitude." With that, he turned and left.

Gabriel had barely a moment to take a breath and attempt to regain his equanimity when his parents came barreling in, both looking as if they expected the worst, Nic following behind with an apologetic expression.

"Selly!" his mother cried, rushing toward the bed. Gabriel caught her before she could disrupt Asa's work. Daisy fought him in a burst of fury, reminding him of wrestling Selly just now.

"Mom." He held her firmly, as gently as possible. "You have to calm down."

"Don't you tell *me* to calm down, boyo," she shouted. "I changed your diapers."

"Daisy." His father was there, extracting his mother from his hold. "Trust Gabriel. They're only doing what's best for Selly."

"What is that man doing to her?" Daisy demanded on a sob.

Nic slipped up next to him, taking his hand, her magic flowing into him like a heady draught of wine, soothing as a summer afternoon redolent of roses. Her presence steadied him as nothing else seemed to, making what felt impossible to handle only seconds ago suddenly within grasp.

"That's Wizard Asa," he told his mother. "You met Asa. He's a healer. He's helping Selly. You can't disrupt him now."

His mother collapsed into tears, but his father gave him a nod of support. "Give him a moment, Daisy, and we can see our girl."

"What's wrong with her?" Daisy demanded.

Gabriel wasn't sure how to answer that question—one she should already know the answer to, as he'd explained it before—without upsetting her further. During his moment of hesitation, Daisy pulled herself together, extracting herself from her husband's arms and facing Gabriel with a stalwart stare and a spine of steel. "It's the being a familiar thing." Her gaze slid uneasily to Nic and back again.

"Yes," he replied. "That's what has made her so crazed all these years. And she's suffered from running wild, so Asa is helping her body recover from that. Then I can take steps to release the pent-up magic that's been clouding her mind."

"Pent up, eh?" his father repeated. "Like dammed pond gone stagnant."

"Just like that," Gabriel answered with considerable relief. "I have to release the old water, so fresh can flow in."

"And then she'll be back to her old self?" his mother asked, making it sound like she expected nothing less.

Nic squeezed his hand. Warning? Support? He wasn't sure. Asa and Nic had both warned him about permanent damage. "We'll do everything in our power to make it so."

"But you don't *know*," his mother persisted. "You can't promise."

He was tempted to promise. To say whatever would make everything right again. But no mere words could ensure that. He could only forge ahead, do his best, and hope that all would be well. "I can't promise," he admitted, "because we don't know."

Nic squeezed his hand again, her magic warm, and he knew that she, at least, approved of his answer. His mother's chin wobbled slightly before she set it, then dipped it in acknowledgment. "Thank you for your honesty."

He nearly protested that he'd never been anything less

than honest with her, but that wasn't precisely true. What a difficult line to walk when you were trying to protect people, especially those you loved. "I only want what's best for all of us." And why did that seem to be such a difficult place to find?

She softened. "I know. None of this is your fault. You'll see when your child is born... Sometimes being a parent isn't a rational thing."

As Gabriel already didn't feel fully rational, he could only imagine what adding a child to the equation would do to him. He supposed he had time—well, seven and a half months?—to work himself up to it. Glancing down at Nic, he found her watching him with mingled compassion and amusement, her emerald-green gaze steady. At least they would be in that particular exercise in insanity together.

"Lord Phel?" Asa called. "Your sister is awake. You all can come see her now."

Gabriel only hoped she'd be somewhat sane.

~ 12 ~

NIC WAS KEENLY aware of Gabriel's reticence, his water magic damp with dread and sluggish as slush, the moon magic dark. "Asa wouldn't call us over if she's in a state that would panic your parents," she whispered, and he nodded, tightening his grip on her hand.

As one, they moved to Selly's bedside, though Gabriel's parents took the lead. After an initial kerfuffle where they protested her being strapped down—answered crisply by Gabriel that he was *not* risking losing her again, especially as this time she might not survive the experience—they settled into soothing and petting her. Selly wasn't articulate, but she seemed to recognize them, and she appeared to be relatively peaceful, blinking with vague amber-brown eyes at her parents.

"Was it bad?" Nic murmured for his ears only. When he glanced at her, she gave him a sympathetic smile. "Your magic is all muddy."

His eyes were like black stones, and he pulled her into his arms, wrapping her up tight, his magic enfolding her also. "Thank you for being here," he whispered in her ear. "Yes, it was bad."

She pressed into him, meeting his magic with hers, to warm and brighten his cold, shadowed places, pushing up to her toes to better fit herself against him. "It will be better now. You're doing the right thing."

"Keep telling me that," he muttered back.

"You're doing the right thing."

He laughed hoarsely, pulling back just enough to caress her cheek. The magic thrummed intense between them, hot with mutual yearning. "What would I do without you?"

"You'll never have to find out."

"Good, because sometimes I feel I'd destroy all the world if something happened to you."

"Just like Sylus," she whispered. "My fierce wizard."

He didn't laugh. Instead his magic spiked, and he captured her mouth with his, heedless of the company they kept, kissing her with rare ferocity—at least in public—that nearly bruised. As suddenly as he'd taken her mouth, he released her lips, though he still held her close, their faces a breath apart. "I finally understand that bastard, but you're no helpless Lyndella."

She kissed him then, with all the gentleness that mirrored his desperation. "I love you more than she ever loved Sylus— because you love me for me."

Groaning deep in his throat, he kissed her again, almost beseeching this time, and she answered his need as best she could. Asa cleared his throat, and Nic reluctantly extricated herself.

"Apologies, Lord and Lady Phel," Asa said quietly, "but our window of opportunity is narrow."

Nic looked to Gabriel for explanation.

"Asa wants me to tap Selly's magic as soon as possible." Gabriel frowned. "He seems to think the first tap will have considerable backlash and that I should be the one to do it."

Asa met Nic's gaze somberly, his wizard-black eyes more serious than she'd ever seen them. She'd never heard of a familiar who'd gone this long without having their magic released, but she wasn't surprised that there could be issues like he described.

"You're the most powerful wizard I've ever met," she reassured Gabriel. "And you have affinity for Selly's magic, and for her as your sister. You'll do well."

Gabriel didn't look convinced. "I suppose I need to move my parents along, then." Letting go of Nic, he went over to join the group by the bed, fortuitously leaving Nic alone with Asa.

"Just how dangerous is this?" she demanded once Gabriel was out of earshot.

Asa didn't blink at her aggressiveness. "Dangerous," he acknowledged. "Under other circumstances, I'd insist she be given into the immediate care of the Convocation. They have the expertise to release stagnant magic of this scale. And they have Hanneil wizards who can heal Selly's mind, if it can be healed at all.

"Alternatively, I'd point out the risk/benefit scenario here: Is it worth risking Lord Phel to save someone who perhaps cannot be saved?"

Nic's gut chilled. "But under these circumstances?"

"Do you think Lord Phel would be amenable to either of

those arguments?"

No. No, he wouldn't be. He'd risk himself to save Selly. With a heartfelt sigh, she realized she'd placed a hand over her belly. Would she be raising this child alone? When she'd contemplated the prospect once before, it had seemed daunting but doable, the price she'd pay for freedom. The baby had also seemed considerably less real. Now...

Now that she'd had this time with Gabriel, he'd somehow become the center of her life. And it wasn't the Fascination, or not only the Fascination. Deep in her bones, she wondered if *she* would survive losing him.

"Nic?" Asa asked, looking concerned. "Is all well with the pregnancy?"

"You tell me," she shot back, then shook her head. "I apologize. That was uncalled for. I'm just realizing I don't want to raise this child alone."

"You won't have to," Asa promised. "You have all of House Phel. And, as Lady Phel, mother of the sole possible heir to the house, you can always opt to bond to a new wizard, one of *your* choosing this time." He smiled in what he likely thought was a reassuring manner, quickly fading in light of whatever he saw in her face.

"You don't understand," she told Asa emphatically, trying to restrain her anger. "I *love* Gabriel."

He relaxed and actually patted her arm. "Of course you do. It's in a familiar's nature, and in the nature of the bonding, for you to feel that way. But there are other wizards in the world."

She shook off his hand with enough force that he reeled back, shocked. "I like you, Asa," she said in a harsh whisper she hoped wouldn't carry. "We've always been friends, so I hope you'll take this question in the right way. Do you think Laryn loves you?"

Blinking, he actually looked to Laryn, who stood brooding by the window, waiting to be called on again. "Laryn is my familiar. We're bonded. And we're having a child, also, as you know," he said, as if that answered anything.

Nic couldn't help laughing. "Do you even hear yourself? That doesn't answer my question."

Asa stiffened, clearly offended. "You know as well as I do, Lady Phel, that the wizard–familiar relationship isn't based on something as transient and subject to whimsy as love. It's a working relationship, not a romantic one, which makes it all the stronger."

"No wonder you don't understand what I'm telling you," she replied with sincere pity, though she was acutely aware of her turnabout. She'd spent a great deal more time with Gabriel and his radical ideas than anyone else, so she shouldn't expect others steeped in Convocation brainwashing—as Gabriel had once accused her of being—to automatically open their own minds. "Give it some thought," she suggested. "Remember, you'll be joined until one of you dies, raising at least one child together. Consider what your life might be like if you two developed at least an affection for each other, as opposed to not."

"I'm terribly fond of Laryn," he protested. "I take very good care of her."

"That's lovely. How does she feel about you?" Nic was afraid she knew the answer, and that she was sowing seeds of discord by pushing this. Still, she looked over to Gabriel, standing back slightly as his parents spoke softly with Selly. He'd want her to point these things out.

Asa looked at Laryn again, considering. "I assume she's fond of me also." But his voice held a note of uncertainty.

"But not that she loves you?" Nic persisted.

Asa frowned. "As I said, the wizard–familiar relationship isn't—"

"Yes, yes, I know," Nic interrupted, brushing that absurd argument away. "You also told me that the reason I think I love Gabriel is because it's in a familiar's nature, and in the nature of the bonding, for me to feel that way. How can both be equally true?"

Asa's frown deepened. "I'm sure there's a logical fallacy in your argument."

"When you find it, let me know."

"Wait." Asa stopped her as she went to move past him. "Why are you concerned? I was under the impression that you and Laryn were not particular friends."

That was true. Indeed, Laryn glanced over just then, expression set in smoldering dislike. Or, perhaps, in general unhappiness. Who knew how much of Laryn's resentments sprang from her own misery, simply latching on to those who seemed to have it better than she did? Though Nic had to concede that she did have it better than Laryn. She'd been fantastically lucky in finding Gabriel—or, rather, in him finding her. She could be generous enough to wish that for everyone, even the people who hated her. "I don't have to be particular friends with Laryn to wish her well," she explained to Asa.

"And it seems to me that she's not happy."

"She has a serious nature," Asa explained, then paused. "And the pregnancy affects her emotional state, as you've experienced."

Nic raised a brow and waited.

"All right, she also wasn't happy about leaving Convocation Center," Asa allowed. "She's too diligent in her duties to complain, but I knew she enjoyed the whirl of the city and society there. I think she could learn to like it here, though, and I had to take the opportunity presented to me. It's good for both of us. I wouldn't have gotten a position this good, so high up in the hierarchy of a new potential High House this quickly anywhere else."

"Did you discuss that with her?"

"She understands. Laryn knows how the Convocation works as well as either of us."

Nic restrained a sigh. "That's not the same as including her in the decision, Asa."

Asa studied her, his keen intelligence evident as he sorted and rearranged his thoughts. "And you think that, if I include her in decisions, it will encourage her affection for me?"

"I think that, if you treat her like a thinking, feeling human being who has an equal say in your lives that it will, if not encourage her affection for you, at least mitigate resentment that will build to utterly destroy it."

Asa looked vaguely green. Clearing his throat, he said. "This brave new world of yours and Lord Phel's is not an entirely comfortable one."

"And you're saying the Convocation is?" Before he could

answer, she pressed. "Or is it that the Convocation is comfortable for *you*?"

He clearly didn't like that, his posture going rigid as he gave her a formal bow. "Lady Phel. I'll be at your service when you and Lord Phel are ready. It needs to be soon, while she's still calm."

He strode off with a stiff gait—but he did go to Laryn, at least, saying something to her that had a surprised look lighting her face. Nic turned away, giving them that much privacy, and went to Gabriel's side. In deep conversation with his parents, he enfolded her under his arm, an absentminded gesture of welcome that meant everything. "You can't be here," he was saying. By the tone of his voice, it wasn't the first time, either. "We're moving out the other patients and will be warding the room. We can't risk anyone being hurt by the magical backlash."

"I don't even understand what that means," Daisy argued.

"Think of it like removing a lid from a pressure cooker left too long on the fire," Nic suggested impulsively. She'd spotted the old-fashioned, manually locking pressure cooker in their kitchen. "To release the steam, someone has to carefully unlock that lid. But you can't have people standing around watching because they might get scalded."

The pair of them studied her shrewdly. "Or the whole thing blows," GF observed astutely, "hitting everyone with shards of metal."

He wasn't wrong.

"In this case, Dad," Gabriel put in, "we cannot simply turn off the flame. I can do this. And afterward, you can both visit

Selly as much as you like."

They didn't like it, but they gave in eventually and allowed themselves to be shepherded out. Laryn was overseeing the temporary removal of the other patients—who seemed disappointed to be missing the show—and Asa beckoned to Gabriel and her from a short distance away.

"I'll remain, Lord Phel," he said, avoiding Nic's eye, "so I can be ready to assist in case of trouble. Laryn, too," he added as an afterthought, finally sliding a glance Nic's way. "I suggest that Lady Phel remain also, in case you have need of her."

"Not if it's dangerous," Gabriel replied firmly. "Nic's safety is a priority."

"It's dangerous for you," Nic retorted. "If I can mitigate that in any way, then I will. I'm staying," she insisted, staring Gabriel down when he went to argue. He held her gaze for a long, fraught moment, wizard-black eyes glittering, and she knew he was considering exerting his power over her, to compel her to obey.

But even to protect her, he wouldn't do it. Instead he laid a hand on her cheek, magic sizzling silver in it. "Remember what I said about destroying the world," he told her.

"That no one person is worth that," she retorted with a saucy smile. "Check."

He scowled at her, running a thumb over her lower lip before turning to Asa, who watched them thoughtfully. "What do I need to do?"

HE WAS FRANKLY nervous. Nervous as he hadn't been about working any kind of wizardry, saving some of the experimentation with Nic. Even with her, and being concerned about hurting her, he'd been swept up in the powerful erotic connection between them, forgetting to think and worry after a while—as Nic was always urging him to do. *Follow your wizard's intuition*, her voice whispered in his mind.

Funny that. When he'd been only a few years younger, less experienced, and considerably more foolish, he'd been cavalier, even reckless, about trying out various magics. Of course, he'd also managed to accidentally turn most of his hair silver in his bumbling. Ironically, however, now that he'd learned so much, first on his own, then from Nic and from Asa, and had refined his control and technique by leaps and bounds, he was far more afraid of the consequences than he'd ever been. Apparently experience made you less confident in your expertise.

"What do I do?" he asked Asa, smoothing his hand over Selly's brow. She gazed at him with bleary, trusting amber eyes, looking fragile and so very young with her face pale and her black hair spilling over the pillow. A montage of scenes flashed through his mind of Selly at various ages. All tangled black hair and big brown eyes in a tiny face as she waded on stick-thin legs in the pond, catching frogs with him. Those same amber eyes filling with tears at some frustration, then lighting with laughter when he agreed to swing her through the air by one hand and one foot, making her fly like the bird she'd always wanted to be. Perhaps that could be a happy outcome—if she regained her health and sanity, Selly could perhaps have an alternate form that would let her truly fly.

Though if she had to bond to a wizard... He shook off the immediate rage at that prospect, making himself listen to Asa's instructions.

"We've all had our magic tapped since we were children," Asa was explaining, "so, when we manifest as wizards, we know what that feels like in general. It's not much of a leap to reverse the process. But I imagine no one ever tapped your magic, so you don't know how it feels. Therefore—"

"Wait," Gabriel interrupted. "Wizards can be tapped for magic, too? Just like familiars?"

Asa's brows drew together. "Well, a wizard doesn't have to be tapped. We can use our own magic."

"But they *can* be tapped," Gabriel persisted.

"Before we manifest as wizard or familiar, we are all un-categorized," Asa said. "Uncats, we call them at Convocation Academy, and it's considered healthy to tap that magic regularly."

"Also, why leave all that magic unused?" Nic put in sardonically, surprising him. Usually she said nothing unless spoken to when she was playing obedient familiar in company. She met his gaze with an opaque glitter to her eyes. She was worried about him, so he gave her a reassuring smile—which she met with rolled eyes.

"But there's no reason a wizard couldn't tap another wizard's magic," Gabriel said to Asa. "I could, for example, tap your magic and use it."

Asa stiffened, clearly outraged. "It would be a kind of rape," he retorted. "An extreme violence against another wizard."

"Then why isn't it a kind of rape and extreme violence to tap a familiar's magic?" Gabriel demanded.

"Because familiars are willing!" Asa retorted.

"Are they?"

"Yes, because they need us." Asa gestured angrily at Selly. "You may be a stubborn iconoclast, Lord Phel, but even you cannot deny this extremely distressing example of the ravages of untapped magic."

"I cannot." Gabriel smoothed Selly's forehead again. "But I'm putting to you that a person needing something so desperately that it puts them in your power is not exactly the definition of willingness."

Asa glared at Nic, making Gabriel wonder what had transpired between them. "The pair of you..." He didn't finish, shaking his head.

"Indeed," Jadren drawled. "Quite the baby rebellion brewing in House Phel."

Gabriel should've been aware of the El-Adrel wizard's arrival. Would've been, if he hadn't been so caught up in fretting over Selly. He should've put up the wards already. "Did I summon you?" he asked Jadren drily, not bothering to temper his tone. Sometimes Nic's advice to play arrogant and brooding wizard-lord came in handy.

Jadren, however, remained undaunted, grinning cheekily at him. "A little birdie told me there was interesting wizarding afoot." He stepped up on Selly's other side, studying her with interest. "I'm here to learn, aren't I? So here I am."

"Fine," Gabriel said, surprising everyone, including himself. He'd agreed before he knew he was going to say the words. That wizard's intuition, perhaps. He pointed a stern finger at Jadren to make up for it, allowing a bit of sharp silver magic to leak through. "Be seen, not heard or felt."

Jadren bowed low, managing to make it supremely sarcastic. "As you say, Lord Phel."

"Shall we focus on the task at hand?" Asa inquired with silky irritation. "Before I have to resort to sterner measures to keep our patient sedated?"

"Show me what to do," Gabriel ordered, not about to apologize to the healer for the delay—or for challenging his horrible Convocation attitudes. He glanced at Jadren. "Are you able to establish wards?"

Jadren raised a brow. "A first-year wizard can put up wards."

"Then make yourself useful and ward the room."

Asa had him sit beside Selly, placing one hand on her forehead and the other over her heart, Nic behind him with her hands on his shoulders. She always claimed she couldn't send her magic into him, that he had to pull it, but he felt a steady flow from her, bloodred fire, rose-red love that steadied and filled him.

"You know how to tap Lady Phel's magic," Asa said, fully in neutral professional mode again. "But she is a highly trained and talented familiar. Tapping Selly's magic will be like and unlike that. The process is fundamentally the same, but she doesn't know how to yield to you. She may fight you."

So much for familiars being naturally willing. But he restrained the words, as they truly didn't have time for another argument. "Noted," he said instead.

"You'll have to assert your control over her," Asa continued. "Your magic will function as the reins. Do not let her magic run away with you."

Amusement flickered through the connection to Nic, and he swore he caught from her a visceral memory of them racing at breakneck speed on Vale's back. His own mind went to the arcanium and the sorts of control they'd been practicing. So difficult to separate those erotic games from this painfully real extremity. "Understood."

"Proceed at your own pace, then."

In Gabriel's peripheral vision, Asa took Laryn's hand and moved to the foot of the bed—several paces back from it. Gabriel glanced at Jadren. "Wards established, Lord Phel," he reported, dashing off a faux salute.

Gabriel tested the wards with his own senses, finding them solid. Impressively so. "You might want to move a safe distance away."

Jadren bared his teeth in a not-grin. "I'm fine where I am."

Not Gabriel's problem, then, if Jadren got caught in some backlash. It might even serendipitously free them of the albatross of the El-Adrel wizard's presence in their house. He took a deep breath, calming and centering himself, clearing his mind of all else.

Well... as best he could. Various worries continued to flit into his mind like disturbed bats, inserting themselves like snatches of overheard conversation, tugging at his attention.

"Think about the arcanium," Nic whispered in his ear, brushing the shell of it with her soft lips. "When all is calm and silent, moonlight filtering through still water. How it feels when all the world falls away and it's only the two of us."

He did as she suggested, surprised to find that the image she evoked could be as restful as it was erotic. He had so many conflicting feelings about the arcanium, and his monstrous ancestors who'd built it, that it hadn't occurred to him that one of those emotions was deep pleasure, even love. Nic was right: when it was only the two of them in that bubble of moonlight and water magic, when nothing else could intrude, that had become his ideal of perfect peace.

Taking action before he lost that bubble of silver stillness, he reached for Selly's magic, sipping ever so lightly, like the lightest draw on Nic's magic. Nothing. No channel opened with generous abundance. It was like taking a drink from a rock, his wizard senses snapping back bruised and stinging from the attempt. He tried again, pulling harder—and again rebounded. This time it was more like biting into an unripe fruit, the rind tough and unforgiving, the taste sour.

Beneath it, though, Selly's magic, so like his own, water and moonlight, tumbled together with keening pressure. Honing his magic into a mental version of a silver spike, he jammed it through the rind of her resistance.

And broke through.

Her magic roared over him, a tidal wave of water both stagnant and churning, like the raging sea that had nearly decimated their barge on the Wartson coast. He choked on it,

JEFFE KENNEDY

the foulness filling his lungs, drowning him and sucking him ever deeper. Flailing helplessly under the rancid onslaught, he suddenly remembered falling into a peat bog as a child. The plummeting panic of that first missed step, the desperate need to breathe as the stink filled his ears, mouth, and nose, even his eyes. The chill fear of death.

Only this time, he'd take Selly with him. The certainty came bone deep. *You'll have to assert your control. Do not let her magic run away with you.*

He groped for the reins, for some semblance of control, finding nothing. Only dankness and an unsettling lack of any foundation. This was Selly's magic, and her mind, a whirling cacophony of lightless, airless nothingness. If he didn't find something to hold on to, a sense of the real world, they'd drown here together, trapped in this wild magic that held no mercy for them.

Then, something. A light permeating the tenebrous depths. Warm and rosy, the light filtered through, showing him a pathway. Not moonlight, but liquid heat, like a summer afternoon in a rose garden, red grapes bursting with juice, the embrace of family and the sweetness of safety. And Nic, holding out her arms to him in welcome, a sensual smile on her lush lips, a sparkle of mischief in her emerald-green eyes.

He stepped into the circle of her arms, bringing Selly with him. She held on to his hand, no more than a child, gazing up at him with trust that he'd lead her out of the trackless wilderness her mind had become. Firming his grip on her, he encircled her magic with his, taking it in.

It was like chugging sour wine, the volume choking him,

the flavor foul enough to sicken. But he kept on, determined to siphon as much of this vile flood from her as possible. Like repairing the levee: first he must drain the water so they could see to work, to set the cement.

Still, the torrent flowed, unending. He barely retained control, his mental muscles straining, fraying, then snapping under the stress. With that same sensation of falling, he lost his grip entirely, dropping into the morass of chaotic nothing.

~ 13 ~

NIC FELT IT the moment Gabriel snapped.

He'd been doing so well—astonishingly well, given the sheer enormity of the pressurized magic erupting from Selly—but even the most powerful wizard had their limits, and Gabriel hit his with crashing finality. His mental presence vanished like a quenched flame. He sagged into unconsciousness, slipping from her grip, his big body tumbling boneless to the floor despite her effort to hold on to him.

As she fell to the floor beside him, calling his name, reaching for him along their bond, magic gusted around them, formless and without boundary. In it, she sensed moonlight and water, fiercely pulling at each other, and scents of the swamps and marshes, the wild things clawing for survival.

She patted Gabriel's cheeks, his dusky skin sickly pale. "Gabriel," she urged. "We need you."

Dimly she was aware of Asa and Jadren shouting. Then Laryn's stern face was before her, Laryn gripping her arm hard enough to bruise bone. "Lady Phel!" she yelled above the magical din. "Snap to! We need you."

"Gabriel needs me," Nic gasped, utterly shattered by the gaping abyss where Gabriel's magic had been, as if he'd

226

infiltrated even the marrow of her bones and then been brutally ripped out again.

Laryn slapped her, not hard, but shockingly sharp. Nic gaped, then growled in rage. That was it, she'd show this bitch once and for all that—

"Get a grip," Laryn shouted, shaking her by the shoulders. "Selly's magic is raging wild, venting through Lord Phel without control. Jadren is offering to take over, but he needs your permission."

"Fine," Nic bit out, returning her attention to Gabriel's too-pale, sunken face.

"*You* have to tell him," Laryn ordered, dragging Nic to her feet. Asa crouched at the foot of the bed, hands gripping Selly's ankles, his head bowed in concentration—or to stay clear of the buffeting winds of Selly's magic. Liberated through the conduit Gabriel had created, her magic lashed like a coastal storm, full of icy water and bits of solidified moonlight that stung her exposed skin. Jadren glared at her, wizard-black eyes accusing, as he bent over Selly in a protective posture, his hands hovering over her.

Nic nodded at him, gesturing for him to go ahead, but he shook his head in emphatic negation. What in the Convocation? "He needs your help," Laryn shouted in Nic's ear. "Go to him. I'll stay with Lord Phel."

Nic nearly told the woman not to lay a hand on Gabriel, but that was foolish. Laryn was resentful and stubborn—and no friend of Nic's—but she wasn't actively malicious. She had a duty to assist her wizard, and Asa no doubt expected her to do this sort of thing. Making her way around Gabriel's prone form, head down against the fierce storm of magic, Nic clawed her way to Jadren's side. "You have my permission," she shouted.

He held out a hand. "I need your magic."

She stared at the proffered hand as if he held a venomous snake. *No.*

"If I'm not strong enough on my own, without your help, I'm going down like Phel, and you'll never get either of them back. Help me, curse you."

It made sense, but every instinct in her revolted at the idea. Her magic belonged to Gabriel, not this other wizard. Jadren stared her down, a taunting challenge in his expression, as if he knew full well how much she hated this. Feeling as if she'd stripped naked and spread her legs for him, she laid her hand in Jadren's and offered up her magic.

He grunted, yanking at her hand. "Come on, Lady Phel. You're clenched tighter than your father's fist on his fortune. Work with me."

Somewhat taken aback that he hadn't been able to simply take, she concentrated on truly opening. It took some doing, but the channels that had apparently attuned themselves only to Gabriel gradually opened, and her magic responded to Jadren's oddly mechanical pull. He let out a long breath, relaxing his death grip on her, and exerted his magic.

The shift was immediate. The storm diminished considerably at first, then vanished with deafening suddenness, leaving her senses—physical and magical—raw and burning. Bits of silver rained to the wet floor. But Jadren continued to pull on her magic.

He was deft enough, and not greedy. Still she had to fight herself to keep that channel open, to resist the urge to thrust him away. She hadn't had another wizard's touch inside her since the night she met Gabriel, and the violation shook her deeply. That, on top of the aching absence of Gabriel's vibrant presence, left her feeling sick and simultaneously invaded and isolated.

She sank to the floor beside Jadren, resting her forehead against the bed, one of the straps confining Selly scratching her cheek, only her hand upraised in Jadren's grip.

And then he released her, the sudden cessation of magical connection and his supporting hand sending her reeling. Jadren collapsed over Selly, breathing as if he'd fought a pitched battle. Nic looked around, seeing Asa at Gabriel's side now, drawing heavily on Laryn by her pained expression. Nic herself felt wrung dry, limp as a wrung out washcloth, but she needed to get to Gabriel. It also seemed that it would be as easy to circumnavigate the Convocation as to make her way around the bed. But an Elal didn't give up without a fight.

Nor did a Phel.

She made herself move, feeling her bones creak in protest, her muscles tight as dried sinew, protesting with shrill alarm. Jadren breathed a laugh. "Now I know why he's so obsessed with you, Lady Familiar. Your magic is more intoxicating than the finest wine I've ever drunk."

Nic nearly snapped that she wasn't his to drink, but she was too tired. In the end, she crawled on hands and knees to Gabriel's side. Was his color slightly better—or was that wishful thinking? She took his limp hand in hers, seeking his silvery cool presence, breathing him into her airless spaces. *Nothing.* She'd found him before, when he was lost in the onslaught of Selly's magic. Or, rather, she'd made herself as big and bright as possible and he'd found and followed her out, but now... Nothing.

He was alive, but what if his body was an empty husk? She'd heard tales of wizards burning themselves out, expending so much magic that their life force went with it, leaving nothing but a mortal shell behind. Sylus had done that, giving everything to avenge Lyndella. But she'd been dead and he'd had nothing left to lose. And Sylus hadn't had his familiar anymore, confined to drawing only on his own magic.

Wishing she hadn't given up so much of her magic to Jadren's efforts, Nic tried offering her magic to Gabriel. If only there were a way for her to inject it into him.

"Don't," Asa said wearily, lifting his face, complexion gray with exhaustion. "You're tapped out, Nic. You give up any more magic and you'll be risking your life, and the baby's. You, too, Laryn. That's enough for now." He shook off her touch, leaning away, and she opened her eyes, giving him an inscrutable look.

"But Gabriel..." Nic protested, staring into his beloved face, the cheeks gaunt, shadowed eyes sunken in his skull, as if the precipitous draining of magic had emptied his flesh as well.

"I've done all I can do for the moment," Asa said, listing with exhaustion. "We need to move him to a bed. Once we've recovered somewhat, I can work on him some more."

How bitterly ironic that a flood of uncontrolled magic had nearly killed them all, and now they couldn't recover for want of magic. "What about other familiars?" Nic asked.

Laryn's eyes flew wide, her lip curling in a silent snarl. Nic ignored her. She'd given her own magic to Jadren; Laryn could share her wizard. Asa was frowning. "The unbonded familiars Alise brought?"

"Yes." Or bonded ones, Nic didn't care at this point. "Let's round up every unbonded familiar in House Phel. Do you have the strength to use them?"

Asa's expression wavered—and Laryn glared hot daggers at Nic—but he straightened and nodded. "I need some food first, and we need to get him into a bed."

"I'll take care of that," she replied, forcing herself to her feet, despite the aches in every pore. Jadren appeared to have fallen asleep, or passed out, over Selly's prone form. Selly herself was sleeping, looking more peaceful than Nic had ever seen her. Nic made it to the infirmary doors by concentrating on putting one foot in front of the other. Fortunately, Jadren's wards had collapsed with his consciousness, and she was able to manually unbolt the doors.

Outside, GF and Daisy sprang to their feet with anxious expressions. Of course they hadn't gone home. "Nic!" Daisy exclaimed. "You look awful. Let me help you."

Nic couldn't even manage a sarcastic reply. GF put his arm around her, his strength and bulk so like Gabriel's she wanted to cry. "I've got the gel," he said gruffly.

"Are they…" Daisy didn't finish, trying to peer around Nic, eyes narrowed as if afraid of what she might see.

"They're both alive," Nic managed to say, her ribs protesting the draw of breath. "But we need help. Brawn to move

Gabriel to a bed. And I need unbonded familiars—Han and Iliana."

"What about Narlis?" GF asked, surprising her. He frowned at Nic's blank face. "Didn't you say she's an unbonded familiar, too?"

Yes. An aged one, her magic weak, but they could use all the help they could get. GF nodded at her. "I'll fetch Narlis and send brawn. Daisy, my love, you find this Han and Iliana."

"But—" Daisy protested, straining toward the infirmary.

"You can help the kids more right now by getting them what they need," GF told her.

"Food, too," Nic remembered.

"Let me help you sit," GF said kindly. "You're weaving on your feet. We'll be back soonest."

He sat her on a chair probably intended for patients to wait in, and Nic stared numbly at the blank wall, unable to do more than that. She really wanted to go back to Gabriel, but apparently the chair had developed magnetic properties, sucking her down and practically inside of it. Alise found her there soon after, crouching before Nic and taking her hands as a stream of people rushed inside, carrying food and drink. Iliana ran past, also, the redhead flashing her a reassuring smile. They would help. Bless them all.

After a while, Nic became aware that Alise was talking to her, low and quiet. Telling her some bit of gossip from Convocation Academy about people Nic was certain she didn't know.

"Why are you telling me about Cordelia Calliope's wardrobe malfunction?" she finally asked.

Alise grinned, climbing to sit beside Nic. "Because I knew when you asked me that it would mean you were back inside your head." Alise stroked Nic's hair, concern in her wizard-black eyes. "You frightened me. You're drained dry, honey."

"Gabriel," Nic said, leaping to her feet. Or, at least, in her mind she did. Her body stubbornly failed to obey her intention and Alise restrained her easily.

"There's nothing more you can do for him," Alise said, then her eyes flew wide at Nic's choked gasp. "No! I mean, he's alive. But you're tapped out and other people are working on him. You've already done everything."

"Selly?"

"Also alive, being hovered over. Jadren is like a felled tree. Laryn is completely tapped out and sleeping. It's like the aftermath of an epic magic battle in there. Actually, of them all, I think Selly is in the best shape."

Nic tried to smile, but her face felt too numb for it. GF arrived, moving slowly as Narlis crept alongside him, her arm through his. Narlis beamed, her wrinkled face lighting with it. "Hello Nic," she said—a bit of a shock as Nic hadn't been sure Narlis knew her name. "Where's my good boy?"

"Inside," Nic managed.

"I walked as fast as I could," Narlis confided, and GF raised his eyes to the sky.

"She wouldn't let me carry her."

"I'm old," Narlis scolded him, "not decrepit. Now take me to my boy."

"Would you help me inside, too?" Nic asked Alise in their wake.

"Nic, maybe you should—"

"Please." Nic didn't have the energy to beg, but Alise took a long look at her and stood, a resigned set to her shoulders as she helped Nic to her feet. "Come on. Though if this is how love makes people behave, I want none of it." She moved slowly, arm around Nic's waist, and Nic felt much like Narlis, shuffling her feet and leaning heavily on her sister.

They'd gotten Gabriel into a bed—one hardly adequate for his big frame, and Nic wished she'd told them to move him to their own bed. Asa glanced up. He looked less grey, but his face was set with lines of strain. Iliana sat in a chair beside his, her hand on Asa's shoulder, her expression distant, while Han hovered protectively behind her. No sign of Laryn anywhere. Perhaps she'd gone to their room to sleep it off. "Put her in that bed over there," Asa instructed Alise, returning his attention to Gabriel.

"No," Nic said.

Daisy and GF, on the other side of Gabriel's bed, gave her worried looks. Behind them, Narlis sat at Selly's bedside, patting her hands. They'd removed the straps and Nic idly wondered if that was a good idea. Not that she had energy to argue about it.

"You need to be in bed," Daisy said, "for the baby, if nothing else."

"Bring a bed over, then," she gritted out, really hoping they'd obey. If she had to stand much longer, even with Alise's sturdy support, she might soon fall over. *Like a felled tree.*

Asa gave her a weary look. "You can't do anything for him right now."

"I can be here."

"I'll get her a bed," GF said. He winked at Nic. "Or, rather, I'll get the brawn to do it. Jake, Mike! Grab that bed and carry it over here."

With impressive speed, a bed was wedged up against Gabriel's, and Nic sank down onto it. She was able to roll onto her side, scooting close to her wizard so she could interlace her fingers with his, clasping his hand between hers.

And the world fell away.

SHE WOKE TO moonlit darkness and silence broken only by the muffled breathing of sleepers. For a long, disoriented moment, she struggled to parse where she was. She needed to pee quite desperately, and she had no idea where to go to take care of that. Then she became aware of Gabriel's hand clasped in both of hers.

Gabriel.

With a sharp intake of breath, she remembered everything. They were in Asa's infirmary at House Phel. And Gabriel... Nic levered herself up on one elbow, her body as stiff as if she hadn't moved in days, the blanket someone had thoughtfully covered her with sliding down. She really hoped that it was only that it had been half a day since she passed out, not a full day or more.

Gabriel lay on his back, looking less gaunt—though that

could be the moonlight, lovingly silvering his hair, making the pale shades of it almost luminous, save for that single black streak, like a reminder of darkest night amid the illumination. She still couldn't feel *him*, though. No magic. No answering tug along their bond. No Gabriel.

Scooting closer, she laid her head on his shoulder, nestling into the divot there that usually welcomed her in. It was all wrong without his arm around her, and she wept silently, letting the tears trail down her cheeks to dampen his shirt. She was all alone, and she didn't know what to do.

Soon enough, however, her body answered that question with renewed urgency. At least now she could recall where the relief room was. Moving through the silvery moonlight filling the room, she felt like a ghost, silently passing the beds. There was Selly, and Jadren, and even Asa, sprawled face down, as if he'd collapsed there. Perhaps he had—and it made her hopeful that it was night of the same day, particularly as he wore the same clothes.

She wondered, however, that no one had made him more comfortable. Had Laryn simply gone to their rooms and abandoned him? They might not have a loving partnership, but most familiars were too well trained in seeing to the comfort of their wizards for this kind of neglect. So, after she blessedly relieved herself—sending a mental thank-you to Alise, who must've been the one to install a fire elemental in the little bathing chamber, one that courteously brightened when she entered, dimming again when she left—she stopped at Asa's bed.

She removed his boots, then eased him into a less crooked

pose, his head more firmly on the pillow, and she covered him with a blanket that had been left folded at the foot of the bed. While she was at it, she checked on Selly, too, and even Jadren. The latter lay on his back, arms and legs splayed in masculine abandon as he snored heartily. What had possessed him to help with Selly? Nic studied Jadren's hawkish profile, remembering with distaste the feel of him sucking away her magic. It had been the right thing to do, and Jadren had been able to stop the flood of Selly's magic. Who knew where they'd be if he hadn't?

Jadren's snores choked to a stop, and his eyes flew open, fastening on her, glittering black even in the dimness. "Mooning over me now, Lady Phel?" he taunted in a hoarse voice. "I know my wizardry can be powerfully attractive."

She nearly retorted in kind, still unsettled by his earlier remark. *No wonder he's obsessed with you.* But she bit her tongue, aware for the first time of a hint of vulnerability under Jadren's bravado. "Why did you do it?" she asked.

He stretched. "Couldn't have yon sweet Seliah sinking House Phel into the swamp again when I'm on the verge of creating a *very* profitable product."

He sounded insouciant and arrogant, but there was something more. "Well, thank you," she said. "I suspect we owe you our lives, Wizard Jadren."

"Oh, I'm sure you do." He smirked at her. "Ah... Nic," he said, as she turned to go, using her name for the first time. "May I call you that?"

She hesitated, then nodded. It couldn't hurt anything. And she was intrigued by his uncharacteristically humble manner.

"I'm sorry for what I said earlier," he told her, pushing up onto his elbows, the moonlight revealing the sincerity of his expression, his auburn hair nearly black. "It was out of line and... truly obnoxious. I have no defense except that..." He shook his head. "Your magic is truly heady stuff. Between your potent magic and Selly's compressed power, I'm afraid I lost my wits. Still, I'd rather not face Lord Phel's wrath over my loose tongue. It's your call—and I know you owe me nothing—but I'm asking you not to mention my indiscretion when he wakes."

Involuntarily, Nic looked over to the still form of Gabriel. "*If* he wakes up."

"Oh, he will." Jadren grinned at her, teeth white as he bared them. "That silver bastard is too stubborn and powerful not to pull through this. Mark my words."

"I will," she promised. "And I don't see why he needs to know something that will make him want to kill you more than he already does." She simpered and walked away, Jadren breathing a laugh behind her.

As she settled back in her place next to Gabriel and arranged the blanket over them both, she mused over the exchange. Perhaps a human heart lurked inside Jadren's carelessly cool exterior. Maybe not. But one thing she was sure of: There was no way Jadren had risked his life for a profitable product line. He'd done it for an entirely different reason, and she suspected she knew what it was.

WHEN NIC WOKE again, misty morning light sifted through the infirmary, along with the noise of soft conversation and the louder clatter of dishes. Gabriel lay beside her, still asleep or unconscious, no glimmer of magic to indicate he was anywhere closer to reviving. Asa appeared on the other side of Gabriel, giving her a broad healer's smile. "Good morning, Lady Phel. How are you feeling?"

"Fine. Why isn't Gabriel awake?"

He kept his serene smile firmly in place, but his wizardblack eyes went opaque. "Sleep is the best thing for him. You know this from your schooling. Lord Phel expended an enormous amount of magic, and now he must replenish it naturally."

She did know that, but the frustration welled up in her. Why couldn't she inject her magic into him? Why did she have to wait for him to take it, when he was so incapacitated that he couldn't? "If we could wake him, he could drink of my magic and replenish that way."

"No sense wishing for things that cannot be," Asa said.

The frustration boiled over. "So you suggest I simply give up and do *nothing*?"

"I suggest that you go and eat, Lady Phel," Asa replied gently. "Clean up. Put on fresh clothes. Take care of the business of House Phel. Leave Lord Phel to me. This is my expertise."

She opened her mouth to retort but closed it again. She didn't necessarily believe Asa had any expertise in this situation—certainly he couldn't have previous experience with it—but then, neither did she. Sitting up, she stretched, her body much looser and energized this morning than when she'd woken in the night.

Asa came around, laying light fingers on her wrist as she stood, nodding to himself. "I treated you a bit ago, while you still slept. You're recovering nicely, and the babe is fine."

"Thank you." She glanced around, seeing that Jadren was gone and Selly appeared to be sleeping also. "Selly?"

Asa gestured in that direction, and they walked together to Selly's bedside. "Physically, she's greatly restored," he reported, sounding more clinical. "Lord Phel pulled the greatest charge off her stagnant magic, which is why he was worst hit, and Wizard Jadren was able to release a great deal more. After you, he drained Iliana, Han, and Narlis to do it. I've been able to tap a bit more this morning, but it's still stagnant stuff. Nothing yet that anyone can use. I can handle it on my own now, however, and I hope that eventually I can purge all of the repressed magic and allow the fresh to flow and finish the work of cleansing her magical being. Then we'll see."

Nic nodded to show she understood, though her thoughts had snagged on something Asa had said. "Narlis was of help?"

"I was surprised, too," Asa answered with a genuine grin that made his cheeks dimple. "The elderly lady has quite a nice punch to her now. The wonders a good home will do."

Apparently so—and Gabriel had been the one to give it to

her. "Asa... I apologize for being cranky earlier."

His smile softened, affection in it. "You're allowed, Lady Phel. Trust me to take care of him for you, just as we're trusting you to take care of House Phel and all of us."

SHE DID FEEL better for eating and getting cleaned up. Though she longed for a bath—especially as Alise had also installed water and fire elementals to provide instant hot water—she resolutely used the cleaning and grooming imps instead. The morning was advancing relentlessly, and there was a considerable backlog of problems to deal with, as they'd lost an entire day of work.

Sitting alone at her desk in the library, Nic organized the correspondence in order of priority, trying to summon some enthusiasm for tackling her many tasks. The weather had turned cold again, a greeting rain falling steadily and silently. Even the cheerful fire in the fireplace didn't seem to be dispersing the chill. Alise was busily installing fire elementals in the residential chambers, making sure everyone had at least one before distributing them through the rest of the manse. The library had only the fire for heating still.

The most pressing problem facing them was food, prosaically enough. With the rapidly increasing population of the manse, their food supply was diminishing at an even greater speed. Not to mention that they had a swamp monster to feed now. She spent a good couple of hours seeking out people to deliver food to the manse on a regular basis, and also sending out word that House Phel would pay for new suppliers.

That reminded her she hadn't balanced the house accounts for a couple of days. They were also diminishing at an alarming rate. They really needed to get some products to market. If Gabriel didn't wake, they'd be destitute in a couple of months—but she couldn't contemplate that. She'd really love to extract her dowry from House Elal, but the odds of that were dismally low.

To exacerbate it all, more wizards and familiars had continued to arrive, and they were out of copies of the NDA. So far the manse had plenty of space, but these people needed to create income for the house or they'd drain the coffers even faster. It was lowering to recall she had been the one to insist that Gabriel needed minions. They should've started slower: a few wizards, build up the product lines, then incorporate new people gradually. But then, she'd never imagined their call for applicants would be met with such enthusiasm.

Or that Gabriel would be out of commission.

Shaking off that gloomy thought, she mused over the fact that there was apparently a great deal more dissatisfaction in the Convocation than she'd realized. All this time, she'd thought it was only her who railed against convention—and she'd thought it was entirely because she was a familiar and not a wizard as she'd planned. From talking to Alise, however, and hearing the stories and conversations among the new arrivals, she was realizing that not many people in the Convocation were happy.

Food for thought, but she really needed food for people. And swamp monsters.

"Lady Phel?" Iliana eased in the library doors, which Nic had left ajar to facilitate the coming and going of her various messengers. "You wanted to see me?"

The pretty redhead came forward as Nic beckoned her, though trailing her feet reluctantly, as if being called before a thought-seeker for chastising. "Why did you stop calling me by my name?" Nic asked.

Iliana flushed lightly, the pink making her fawn freckles stand out. "I wasn't sure why I was summoned, I suppose."

"I wanted to ask about fish," Nic said gently, restraining her smile at Iliana's confused expression. "What kind the swamp monster likes. Some varieties are apparently easier to obtain than others. Cost is, unfortunately, a factor."

"Ah." Iliana studied the documents littering the desk. "I don't know if I ever told you, but my family's branch of House Ariel was impoverished. I'm quite good at budgeting, if you need help."

"I do need help," Nic confessed, feeling unreasonably emotional about it. She couldn't possibly start weeping over piles of paperwork. *Get a grip on yourself.* "What I need is a copying gremlin, but the things are ridiculously pricey." She waved the missive from House Xerograf.

"The copying gremlins are their only lucrative product." Iliana grimaced. "You're not the first to complain about the cost. But why buy a gremlin when you have people with idle hands?"

"You're supposed to be communicating with the sea monster," Nic reminded her. When she wasn't being called on to supplement emergency healing incantations, that was. Quinn had offered to help, too, she remembered—and Nic hadn't quite gotten around to setting her up to do the work.

Iliana shrugged. "It sleeps a lot, so I can only spend so much time on that. I'll test out different fish—feed it one kind and try to sense how it likes it. Maybe we can find a sweet spot of abundant, cheap, and tasty. In the meanwhile, what can I copy for you?"

"The NDAs, for starters," Nic said, unbearably grateful for the offer. "Though I'm out of blank ones."

"I can use my own as a template." Iliana accepted the paper and extra quill Nic offered her. "I'll just sit here and—"

"Not there," Nic corrected sharply when Iliana moved to Gabriel's empty desk. Then caught herself. "I mean… Never mind. That's fine."

Iliana gave her a look of sympathy. "I can sit in a chair. I see now that this is Lord Phel's desk. Of course you don't want me to sit here."

"No, don't be foolish. It's not as if he'll walk in and need to use it." Nic's voice broke a little, and she scrubbed a hand over her face.

"How about some tea?" Iliana went to a side table where someone had left a pot of tea warming over a tiny fire elemental. Nic had forgotten about it. "Tea always makes me feel better. Honey?"

"Yes, please. And help yourself to a cup."

Iliana brought the tea to Nic, keeping one for herself. "How is Lord Phel doing?"

"The same." At least, she figured he was the same. Asa had sent a strongly worded reply to her last inquiry telling her that she'd be the first to know about any change and to leave him alone. "Thank you for helping yesterday."

"We were happy we were able to. It was good to feel like we can do something to pay you back."

"You have no obligation to us."

"But we do," Iliana insisted. "Lord Phel asked Han to teach bladework to the familiars and non-magic workers, which is a great choice because Han spent a lot of time in weapons work electives while waiting to manifest. So, I'm happy to have this job helping you."

Nic hadn't known Gabriel had arranged for Han to teach. When had he done that? She found herself suddenly and furiously jealous of the time he'd spent away from her. She'd been so cavalier, not treasuring every moment together she could.

"Lord Phel will be all right, Nic," Iliana said with infinite gentleness, as if the words might break her if she said them too loudly. Nic wondered how long she'd been sitting there in silence to prompt that reassurance.

"How do you know?" she asked, meaning the question in all sincerity.

Iliana shrugged and smiled. "I know like I knew Han and I could escape. I just know."

Nic envied her that certainty. She was searching for something to say when Alise charged into the library, flinging the doors open so hard they banged against the walls, sending Nic's heart pounding. The expression on her sister's face frightened her even more. "Gabriel?" she asked, leaping to her feet.

"Worse," Alise replied grimly, gaze sliding to Iliana. "House Sammael."

~ 14 ~

NIC MOMENTARILY FLOUNDERED, enraged at the pair of them, Alise and Iliana, looking at her for instructions on what to do, both clearly terrified. And she was furious with Gabriel for being fucking *unconscious* and not here to help her. Especially when this was all his fault. He'd promised to protect them, and here was House Sammael on her doorstep—and she with nothing but a bunch of minor wizards, rogue familiars, and barely talented commoners.

They'd all be slaughtered.

If only she were a wizard, then... *Well,* she snapped at herself, *you are not a wizard. But you are Veronica Phel, an Elal by birth and breeding, and an Elal doesn't give up without a fight.*

"*Who* from House Sammael?" she asked coolly.

"We don't know yet," Alise replied, watching Nic with an odd expression. "One of my sentry spirits spotted the carriage with the House Sammael crest crossing from Sammael to Meresin and headed this way. They're a few hours away still, but I thought you'd want to know immediately."

All right, you have a few hours to make a plan. A single carriage might not mean anything. It depends on who it is. "You can't tell who's inside?" she asked Alise.

Alise flushed. "I'm still a student wizard, you know. Guiding a spirit to go inside a moving object and teaching it to recognize individuals is advanced work. There aren't many wizards, even with three or four times my age and experience, who can do that."

Nic held up a hand to stop the defensive rush of words. "I didn't mean to imply anything. I'm just trying to assemble my thoughts."

Alise blew out a breath. "No, I apologize. I'm just... really afraid." Her gaze slid to Iliana again, who stood like a rabbit frozen in the hawk's gaze, a pale statue of a young woman.

"We should run," Iliana whispered, as if the predator might overhear. "Han and I, we'll leave now. We'll run. Run far away and—"

"Iliana," Nic said sharply. "We don't know this has anything to do with you. We've been receiving visitors and delegations from all sorts of houses. There's no reason to panic."

Iliana stared at her, round-eyed and pupils dilated. "If it's Sabrina Sammael, there is *huge* reason to panic."

"Sabrina Sammael is at Convocation Academy," Nic reminded the younger woman crisply. "It is still in session with students expected to be in attendance, present company excepted."

Alise winced ruefully. "Still, Han and Iliana should hide. They're unbonded, so it's not wise to have them out where anyone can see and take a fancy to them."

Nic nodded, ringing for a page. "Fetch Rat for me, immediately," she directed, and the boy took off running. "Rat knows the wilds of the marshes better than anyone," she explained. "He can take the three of you to—"

"Not me," Alise interrupted. "I'm staying with you, Nic."

"You could be in danger, too," Nic reminded her.

"Yes, but I'm a wizard. They can't just abduct me. Papa might be pissed at me, but he's not going to let House Sammael perform an act of aggression on one of his own." She paused. "That goes for you, too, Nic."

Nic did not share her confidence, but she didn't say so. Papa might consider it a proper punishment, which was Sammael's purview, after all. "Iliana, in the meanwhile, go find Han and assemble some supplies. Then meet me back here."

Face pinched, Iliana scurried off. So much for getting those NDAs copied. Though Nic supposed those were the least of her problems. She picked up the tea Iliana had given her, finding it had already cooled, tasting more like honey-flavored water than tea. "What is your plan?" Alise asked tentatively.

Nic held back a bitter laugh. *Plan?* As if she knew.

Taking a breath, she struggled to get ahold of herself. *What would Papa do?* As angry and disappointed in him as she was, Papa had made House Elal unassailable. Of course, a great deal of that unassailability relied upon not letting the enemy onto Elal lands in the first place. The borders were famously impenetrable, passable only by permission or via the tattoo that residents bore on their forearms.

House Phel had no such border guardians. Nor did they have the status to prevent High Houses from visiting as they pleased. "I suppose I'll have to meet with whoever is in that carriage."

"But what if it's Sabrina Sammael?" Alise protested.

Now Nic did laugh. "I almost hope it is! I can handle Sabrina the teenage bitch." Or, rather, she hoped she could. "The real concern is what do I do if it's Lord Sammael? Worse, what if it's Lord Sammael, or his agent, come to take me into custody in the name of the Convocation?"

"Is that a possibility?" Alise asked faintly.

"My status as Lord Phel's familiar is still up for debate in some circles. My own fault, for running away."

"I'd heard you sent the Convocation proctor away just before I arrived, but I didn't realize." Alise chewed her lip. "I can help to defend you, should it come to that. My defensive magics aren't fantastic, but I have some tricks. I can ask the other wizards, too. I don't... I don't suppose there's much chance of Lord Phel being able to assist?"

Nic shook her head. "Who knows when he'll wake?" *If he ever will.* She shook away the rime of dread that she'd lost him forever. "Do that—ask the others, but we can't risk an outright confrontation that would end up with everyone dead and the manse razed."

"Sammael would not be in their rights to do that," Alise argued indignantly.

"Yes, well, they can include that in the epitaph of House Phel: once again removed from the Convocation roster, unjustly, and no doubt permanently this time."

NIC MADE WHAT plans she could for the confrontation and set as much to rights as possible, in case the worst happened. A still-exhausted but willing Rat arrived and spirited Han and Iliana into the depths of the marshes, promising he knew of a safe haven. Alise sent a spirit with them to keep an eye on the group and assure those back at the house of their continued safety.

With the Sammael carriage no more than half an hour out, Nic visited Gabriel.

Asa glanced up with considerable irritation when she entered his outer offices. "Lady Phel, I told you that I—"

"I'm just visiting," she snapped. "And House Sammael is due to arrive in half an hour. Forgive me for wanting to see my husband before that." She didn't want to think of it as saying goodbye, but a creeping foreboding made her certain it would be exactly that. The Hanneil blood from her mother's side wasn't an active psychic magic in her, naturally, but she sometimes wondered if it didn't passively warn her of danger, much as Iliana sensed the swamp monster's emotions.

"Sammael?" Asa replied, getting up from his desk where he'd apparently been recording notes. "Why would House Sammael come here?"

"I have a few guesses," Nic replied drily. Clearly Alise hadn't attempted to recruit Asa in her defense plan, which made sense, as his House Refoel vows prohibited him from using his healing magic to harm anyone, even if gentle Asa could bring himself to do it. "I'm going inside." She gestured to the infirmary unnecessarily.

"Fine." Asa sighed. "Just don't ... upset him."

How she could upset an unconscious man, Nic didn't know, but she agreed. Once inside the infirmary, she was surprised to see Narlis seated at Gabriel's bedside. She was stroking his hands, which were folded over his breast as he lay on his back, talking to him quietly. As Nic drew near, she heard Narlis telling Gabriel that he was a good boy, her usual mantra with him. The aged familiar beamed as Nic came into her line of sight. "He's a good boy," she confided to Nic.

"He is," she agreed, worried that Gabriel looked worse than he had that morning. More... sunken. She edged a hip onto the edge of the bed, the one she'd slept in beside him long since removed, and laid her hand over his heart. It beat steadily, but no sense of his silvery-bright magic greeted her touch.

"He's lost," Narlis said, bobbing her head when Nic's startled gaze flew to hers. "Can't find his way back."

"How do you know?" Nic stretched her senses, trying to feel what Narlis did. Unless, of course the older woman was suffering from some sort of delusion, which was far more likely. It was a mark of Nic's hope—and despair—that she was willing to grab onto any shred of possibility.

"I know." Narlis nodded wisely and tapped her temple. She returned her gaze to Gabriel and patted his hands. "He's a good boy."

Nic choked back the tears that had been wanting to spill all morning. She didn't feel like iron-willed Lady Veronica Phel. Losing Gabriel had hollowed her out in some essential way. *Lost.* Gabriel was lost. She was lost. They were all lost.

"Well, help him find his way home, would you?" she asked Narlis, managing a wobbly smile.

Narlis nodded gravely. "He's a good boy."

"Why don't you take a little break?" Nic suggested. "I'll sit with him."

"You're a good girl," Narlis replied, pushing slowly to her feet and going toward the relief room.

Nic scooted closer, then simply repositioned herself and lay down on the narrow edge beside Gabriel. Keeping her hand over his heart, she nuzzled into the side of his neck, kissing the soft spot under his ear that always made him light up with desire. Not this time. His skin remained cool to the touch, no answering flare of magic. Brushing her lips against his ear, she began whispering.

She didn't mention Sammael's approach. If Gabriel could hear her at all, she didn't want him worrying. "I love you," she told him, though he should know that by now. "If you really are lost, all you have to do is follow that thread. You and I are joined forever, and no matter what they do, they can't destroy our bond. I'm right here. All you have to do is open your eyes."

Nothing. She was absurdly disappointed, as if she'd truly expected him to simply follow instructions.

"Gabriel," she whispered more urgently. "You have to wake up. Even for a moment. Just for a little bit, so you can have some of my magic. You know I want you to have it. I'd push it into you if I could, but I … can't." Her voice broke, tears following. "Idiot wizard—just take it. Please."

She tried again to open that channel between them, to replicate how it felt when he drew magic from her. Water flowed downhill without help; why not magic? She'd replenished, and she wanted, more than anything, for him to have it. Over and over, she tried to push the magic into him, with no result. She simply couldn't do it. Never, not even in those early days of crashing denial when the oracle head spoke those dreaded words, had she hated being a familiar more.

It simply wasn't fair.

"Lady Phel." Asa spoke softly, putting a gentle hand on her shoulder. "Wizard Alise is here. She says it's time."

Nic nodded, surreptitiously wiping her tears on Gabriel's shirt. He wouldn't mind. If he were awake, he'd use the shirt to dry her tears himself. She sat, then stood. One step at a time. She eyed Asa, watching her with professional concern. "Why can't *you* take my magic and put it into Gabriel?"

Asa shook his head in slow-moving regret. "It doesn't work that way."

"Why not?" she demanded, as if he'd made the rule.

"Magic doesn't work that way. I could put it in him, but it would disperse again. He has to actively take it in for it to do any good."

Nic knew that. She didn't even know why she asked. "Take care of him, will you?"

Asa smiled ruefully. "As if his parents would let me do anything less." Then he frowned. "Watch yourself with Sammael."

"Excellent advice." She realized Jadren had also come to fetch her. "Ready to establish the wards?"

He dipped his bearded chin, wizard-black eyes serious. "No one will get through. In fact, unless Sammael brought a ward-breaker, the entire warded area should be invisible to any searchers."

That was as good as they could get. Alise was waiting for them in the outer offices, turning to walk by Nic's side without comment. Jadren and Alise flanked Nic as they walked together to the main hall, then out to the front porch. Sage and Quinn were waiting there, along with a cadre of other wizards and their familiars. Even Dahlia, the Ophiel wizard, was in attendance, and Nic wanted to ask if she planned to swath Sammael in fabric to slow any aggressive moves.

Alise met Nic's questioning gaze and shrugged. "They wanted to bear witness, at least."

Bear witness to what, exactly?

Dahlia moved forward as Nic did. "Lady Phel, may I?" She held up a hand sparkling with magic. "For the pride of the House," Dahlia added, by way of explanation, and Nic nodded permission. The gown shifted around her, changing to a heavier, more expensive fabric. A gleaming silver taffeta, it was embossed with slightly lighter and darker moons tumbling across the expanse in subtle shimmers. The taffeta itself had subtle waves that rippled like water in moonlight. The style changed somewhat, too—the neckline higher, the sleeves longer. More formal, she supposed. More impressive Lady Phel.

At least she looked it on the outside, even if she felt like a fraud inside.

The carriage came into view, the largest she'd ever seen, and ridiculously gilded. She knew that coach well: It had conveyed Lord Sergio Sammael to House Elal. Heir apparent to House Sammael—though not officially heir, as the current Lord Sammael was cagey about keeping his progeny on tenterhooks—Sergio had been Nic's first suitor, and first lover, if one could dignify their copulation with that word. For the first time since Gabriel had collapsed, Nic was fervently glad for his unconscious state. If Sergio Sammael was in that carriage, Gabriel might have carried out his threat to kill the wizard.

It might not be Sergio, she reassured herself.

Wishful—and foolish—thinking. The carriage drew to a halt in the circular drive, the elementals powering it gliding the enormous thing to a smooth and soundless stop. Magic crackled in the air, emanating mostly from her motley collection of partially trained wizards, but with a powerful charge throbbing off the Sammael conveyance. They'd come prepared to fight.

Alise's spirits hovered near Nic, unseen but prepared to protect her. Nic was desperately afraid they could do nothing to save her. Certainly not at a price Nic was willing to pay.

The doors slid open with a silken hiss that whispered of money and power. And out slunk a bevy of hunters. Beside Nic, Alise gasped, quickly swallowing the reaction. For her part, Nic flinched internally, though she refused to show any sign of weakness. Why did House Sammael have hunters at their command? Had the Convocation given them to Sammael in order to exact punishment? This did not bode well.

An unnatural creation, the hunters stood on two legs, had long, canine snouts, and moved like weasels. They sported fangs and claws, and couldn't be killed by normal methods, as Nic knew from personal experience. The only thing that had completely nullified them was an enchanted blade Gabriel had made, and the illegality of that artifact infringing on House El-Adrel's license had enabled Lady El-Adrel to strongarm them into taking on Jadren. Unfortunately for them at this moment, that lady had retained the knife as damning evidence against House Phel.

Really, that seemed like the least of their problems now.

The other method of disposing with hunters involved chopping them up into pieces so small that they couldn't do any harm, although nothing seemed to stop them from regenerating again. It suddenly occurred to Nic that she had no idea what Gabriel had done with the pieces of the lone hunter that had pursued them from Wartson. Hopefully that wasn't a bigger problem waiting to happen.

The hunters slunk out into a slavering circle, cutting off any avenue of escape for Nic, except for the house behind her. Well orchestrated, though they made no other move toward her. From the recesses of the carriage emerged a young woman with sleekly bobbed blond hair and wizard-black eyes. Correction: She was hardly a young woman, truly little more than a girl, though her arrogant mien well exceeded her youth. Nic didn't remember Sabrina Sammael from Convocation Academy, but her resemblance to her older brother was unmistakable.

Speaking of the odious fellow, Sergio Sammael emerged behind his younger sister, golden hair the same shade, though artfully tousled, his eyes equally as black. His self-satisfied smirk was the twin of hers, though he slid it greasily over Nic, lascivious gaze reminding her that he'd been inside her. Nic returned the look coolly, refusing to care, appearing not to remember how he'd treated her.

"Why, Alise," Sabrina cooed. "Imagine finding you here." She tapped a polished nail against her bow-shaped pink lips, then pointed it at Alise, the digit trembling with her anger. "I just *knew* you'd run to your outlaw sister with *my* familiars that you stole. Sergio, arrest them!"

Sergio threw his sister an irritated look. "Sabrina, darling, we can't gallivant around the countryside arresting people simply on your say-so. We must have a warrant from the Convocation." He smiled at Nic, not nicely at all. "The warrant we have isn't for *Alise* Elal."

Nic's blood ran cold. Sergio, noting the reaction she hadn't quite suppressed, grinned in self-satisfaction, savoring her fear.

Sabrina pouted prettily, though her wizard-black eyes were hard on Alise. "Return my familiars, you bitch, or I will make you suffer."

"I wasn't aware that you'd bonded a familiar," Alise replied with Elal poise, "much less several. Isn't that illegal?"

"You know perfectly well I'd arranged to bond Han and take Iliana into House Sammael," Sabrina hissed, her magic like a static charge in ozone-tainted air. House Sammael was unusual among the Convocation houses in that they accepted wizards with a variety of magic specializations. Anything suitable to punishment worked for them. The core family, however, tended toward high MP scores in psychic magic along with various elemental affinities. From the feel of her, Sabrina had the psychic magic in spades—no doubt part of why she wanted Han so badly with his strong Hanneil magic—along with something uncomfortably metallic.

Alise had widened her eyes, evincing innocent shock. "The Convocation already matched Han? He'd only just manifested as a familiar when I took a short holiday to visit my sister. By the way, have you met Lady Phel? Nic, this is Sabrina Sammael, a student wizard at the academy. I don't believe you knew her there."

"No," Nic replied politely. "But then, I paid little attention to the younger students."

"And where *is* Lord Phel?" Sergio asked lazily, eyes caressing Nic, as he didn't even bother to look around. With increasing chill, she realized Sergio wasn't expecting Gabriel to appear. He knew House Phel was largely undefended. "I find it quite rude," Sergio continued with a smirk, "that he hasn't bothered to greet us. I can't imagine he expects me to suffer conversation with a familiar, no matter how well titled she found herself."

"Lord Phel is otherwise occupied," Nic answered with regal boredom. That was her story, and she'd be cursed if she'd admit otherwise. "Did you have an appointment? I saw nothing in his calendar."

"I don't need an appointment," Sergio replied haughtily, waving his fingers dismissively. "Fetch your master, Familiar, if you can. You've already wasted enough of my time."

"He's occupied in his arcanium. I dare not interrupt him." Nic tried to sound meek, but Sergio eyed her with contempt.

"Without his familiar?" he sneered. "You'll have to lie better than that."

"Surely you're aware that Lord Phel is astonishingly powerful," Jadren said smoothly, stepping up on Nic's other side. "He can accomplish more without a familiar than most do *with* one." He made a show of peering around. "Oh, but you don't have a familiar yet, do you, Sergio?" He grimaced in false sympathy, tsking. "That Sammael infertility raising its ugly head in the next generation."

"Jadren El-Adrel," Sergio mused, as if trying to place the name. "I thought you were dead."

Jadren smiled thinly. "Rumors can be so misleading."

"I note you have no familiar, either," Sergio sneered. "Mommy still withholding that particular treat to extort you into good behavior?"

"At least I'm not having to service every high-MP-scoring familiar that pops up on the market," Jadren replied casually. "How many have you tried now—a dozen? More? Perhaps you should consult a Refoel healer specializing in whiskey dick."

"Watch yourself, El-Adrel," Sergio growled. "Someday, perhaps very soon, I will be Lord Sammael, head of a High, and you'll still be a junior minion, at best." Sergio made a show of looking around, unable to disguise his confidence, however. "And you won't have even that once House Phel crumbles back to the ashes it belongs to."

"Do you know something we don't?" Nic inquired in a polite tone, though she deliberately omitted any honorific. "As

Wizard Jadren notes, rumors can be so misleading."

Sergio settled his sneer on Nic. "How the mighty have fallen. Veronica Elal, disinherited, outlawed, knocked up by a house-poor wizard too afraid to show himself to his betters." He eyed her more closely, even scathingly. "Is he too impotent and incompetent to even bond you?"

"Lady Phel is duly bonded to Lord Phel," Alise retorted for her.

"I witnessed the Convocation proctor determine it herself," Jadren added. "As did we all, when Lord Phel commanded Lady Phel to take her alternate form."

Well, not everyone here, but Nic discreetly kept that tidbit to herself. She had enough to worry about with the direction this inquisition was going without fretting that someone would pipe up that *they* didn't see the proof. Gabriel and his reciprocal bonding nonsense continued to jeopardize them all. Unless his being so incapacitated had disrupted their bond. Supposedly only death could dissolve the wizard–familiar bond. But then, Gabriel was as close to death without being dead as anyone could get.

"She doesn't *look* bonded now," Sergio commented, speaking to Jadren and Alise. "Perhaps something else has occurred in the interim. You can confide in me," he added in a silky tone.

"Your wizard senses deceive you," Jadren replied on a yawn. "Not surprising, given your weak scores. Mostly sixes and sevens, aren't they?"

"Enough to punish you," Sergio spat, then recovered his composure. Eyeing Nic, he withdrew an envelope made of heavy, very expensive paper. Convocation stationery. "This discussion is moot regardless. I have here a directive to remand one Veronica Elal into custody, pending a decision by Convocation Center on her bonded status."

"This is House Tadkiel's purview," Jadren said. "You have no authority to—"

"This gives me the authority," Sergio replied, waving the document languidly. "Sammael borders Meresin, so I was in the neighborhood already. And darling Sabrina here wanted to visit her little school friends. I suggest you produce them, Nic, or things will go badly for you."

Nic held on to her composure with the shreds of mental fingernails. "Alise came to visit me alone. I have no idea where these misplaced familiars are." Mostly true, as she didn't know where Rat had taken Han and Iliana.

"Ah-ah-ah." Sergio waved a finger at her. "The only thing worse than a familiar who speaks without being asked a direct question is one who lies." He waggled the document. "I have here a letter from a member of House Phel certifying that you are harboring two escaped and unbonded familiars who match the description of House Sammael's property." He withdrew another document, one Nic recognized as a deed of agreement. "I also have proof of ownership of House Sammael of the two familiars. You may verify the authenticity of all."

Nic held out a hand to take them, but Sergio passed them to Jadren, blithely pretending she didn't exist. Jadren read the letter first and passed it to her, speaking in a low voice. "It's from Laryn, Wizard Asa's familiar."

So much for the NDA, Nic reflected with seething rage.

Did Asa know? She doubted it. Asa might argue with her, but he didn't have a duplicitous bone in his body. So infuriatingly ironic that a familiar's words and will were ignored until one decided to betray her entire house. Maybe Nic had been wrong to bring more people in. They'd have been safer being just the two of them. Her thoughts chased each other like songbirds scattered by a hawk, slamming into the glass windows thinking it was freedom. But the glass only reflected the sky, bringing mockery and death.

Nic finished examining the documents Jadren passed to her as he was done. She'd be irritated that he was so careful to read them first, but if this went the direction it looked to be going, then it would be good for him to have seen and witnessed everything. She handed the papers back to Sergio, who deigned to notice her this time. "I'm afraid I can't help you recover your lost property. There are no unbonded familiars in House Phel."

"Saving yourself," Sergio replied with an unfriendly smile. "Oh, and another, I understand. A Seliah Phel, Lord Phel's undocumented sister."

"Seliah Phel is not in residence at the moment," she smoothly lied. "I'm certain the Convocation proctor noted Seliah's escape into the wilds in her report." If she couldn't save herself, she could at least save Selly.

"This affidavit suggests she was recovered." Sergio waggled the letter.

Nic shrugged. "Such a pity you can't believe everything a liar and traitor tells you."

"We'll see what a search turns up."

"Lord Phel won't allow you to search his property."

"Too bad Lord Phel is *otherwise occupied*," Sergio retorted, "and unable to stop me." He watched her reaction with such obvious and cruel glee that Nic instantly realized what she should have the moment Laryn's role in House Sammael's appearance at this critical juncture truly meant. Laryn had also conveyed what few even in House Phel knew: that Gabriel was incapacitated, perhaps permanently.

Sergio smiled then, with true delight and no posturing. "I thought so. Come with me, Veronica Elal. Collar the familiar," he casually ordered one of the hunters.

"No!" Alise shouted, her spirits manifesting to protect Nic.

"Sabrina, sweetheart," Sergio drawled. "Why don't you show your little playmate that it's not nice to thwart us?"

Sabrina flipped her hair and smiled, her magic lancing through the air, hitting Alise like an invisible fireball. Everyone gasped, flinching back as Alise contorted in a rictus of agony, fingers curling into claws, a strangled scream wrenching out of her strained throat. She lost her grip on her own magic, the spirits vanishing again.

"Stop it." Nic ordered with cool authority, striving to appear unmoved. "I will obey the terms of the warrant and cooperate in being conducted to Convocation Center." Perhaps she could find a way to appeal her case there.

"But she stole my familiars," Sabrina whined, sending another jolt through Alise.

Nic fought for control, reminding herself that Sammael punishment rarely did physical damage—the Convocation valued its wizards and familiars intact, if only as magical commodities—and mostly worked via tricking the mind and nervous system. "Does House Sammael truly want to anger House Elal by harming Lord Elal's heir?" Nic asked Sergio, gambling that they couldn't know of Alise's reduced status. In truth, no one knew, as their father had yet to say anything about Alise's departure from Convocation Academy.

Sergio eyed her, then flicked a hand at Sabrina. "Playtime is over."

Sabrina stomped her foot in annoyance, but stopped. Alise collapsed to the ground, Jadren quickly moving to help her up. Sergio raised his voice, surveying the small gathering. "It would be unwise for anyone here to interfere with this lawful arrest." He gestured to the hunters. "I don't think you want to fight my deputies." Sergio laughed at his own joke, Sabrina joining in, while everyone else stood around stone-faced. "I said to collar the familiar," he ordered the hunter nearest him.

It advanced on Nic, another of the hated iron collars in its hands, the twin of the one she'd worn in Wartson. She squinted at the too-familiar thing. It could be the same one— and would be a fine joke from House Iblis to furnish the thing to the Convocation in a petty bit of retribution for Gabriel stealing their familiar. *You stole ours, so we'll be an agent of repossessing yours.*

Alise glared at her in fury and terror. "You can't mean to go with them, Nic."

"This is a battle we can't win. They have a warrant. I'll be remanded into Convocation custody, where I'll be examined, and Lord Phel's claim on me verified. I'm pregnant with a valuable child," she added in a lowered voice, touching Alise's arm to soothe her. "They won't dare hurt me."

"Not in a way that physically harms you, that is," Sergio inserted with unsettling enthusiasm. "Still, I look forward to renewing our acquaintance."

Nic forced herself to hold still as the hunter's foul breath washed over her. It smelled like the dead thing it was.

"Is that really necessary?" Jadren asked in a bored tone, though he kept an easy hold on Alise's arm, casually restraining her. "A collar is so gauche. Surely a pair of Sammael wizards aren't afraid of a mere familiar."

"Veronica Elal has always thought far too highly of herself," Sergio returned in a sorrowful tone, "or she wouldn't have dared attempt to escape the Convocation and her rightful role in life. She needs a bit of humbling. This is only the first step in breaking the false pride that has warped what could've been a brilliant familiar. But no worries: the Convocation trainers are eager to teach her the important lessons that will restore her early promise as a valuable cog in our well-oiled machine."

Though it took everything in her to submit to being collared again—and in front of all of House Phel—Nic quelled the urge to run. The hunters possessed supernatural speed, as she'd experienced, and they'd only pin her down and drag her away in chains. She should probably be past caring about her pride, but if she ever returned to House Phel, she'd rather not be shamed before her people more than she already was. Still, she turned her head away, unable to bear the hunter's dripping fangs so near her face... and she spotted Laryn, standing well off to the side, wearing an expression of unholy glee. The fool hadn't even had the sense to disappear. What did she imagine would result from this—that Asa would take her back to Convocation Center?

Perhaps so.

"I'm contacting our father," Alise gritted out, her hands clenched in fists. "You'll regret crossing House Elal."

Sergio snickered, swaggering forward to attach a lead to Nic's collar himself. "Lord Elal can take it up with the relevant authorities—though I doubt he'll have any luck, if he even cares—but the Convocation is extremely interested in making an example of this recalcitrant familiar." He yanked viciously on the chain, dropping Nic to her knees before she could resist. "House Sammael is ever loyal to the Convocation," he declared. "We are above such petty extortion and threats. Come along, pet. No time for napping." Winding the lead around his hand, he dragged Nic to her feet again and pulled her toward the carriage.

"Wait!" Sabrina shrieked, stomping her foot like a child. "What about *my* familiars?"

"Don't fret, silly Sabrina," Sergio chided, shoving Nic into the carriage. "The hunters have their scent now. They'll ferret out wherever the naughty things are hiding, and your pair of lovers will be at House Sammael in a heartbeat. You'll be able to play with them to your heart's content."

"Yay!" Sabrina clapped her hands together, following them into the carriage.

From the inside, the carriage was transparent, allowing Nic a good, last look at the graceful manse, her people, turning to each other in agitation, Alise in tears and Jadren looking stoic.

In the background, Laryn waved goodbye, and the hunters split into groups, dropping onto all fours to sniff the ground. Like a lethal river of blight, they streamed off to find Han and Iliana.

Nic closed her eyes and, for the first time, hoped that Gabriel wouldn't wake up, so he'd never know about this. In the meanwhile, she was on her own again, and it would be up to her to extract herself and the babe from the Convocation's trainers. If she was smart and kept her cool, she could do it. She would have to.

~ 15 ~

G ABRIEL WANDERED IN a mist. It was a peaceful place, reminiscent of his boyhood when he'd go out on cool mornings before the sun rose high enough to burn off the fog. He'd wander the orchards, hills, or marshes, alone but for his thoughts, the early birdsong weaving with the peeping of frogs. Unseen, he'd felt safe in being unobserved. No one could chide him about doing his chores or, much later, look at him askance as his eyes blackened and his hair turned silver.

His thoughts tripped over that. How old was he? Then he shook the uncertainty away. It was restful in this place, and he was happy to be back in that place of no responsibility.

Except that something niggled at him. He kept feeling like he'd forgotten something, as if he'd misplaced a valuable he'd intended to keep safe. The unease prompted him to search the mist, for what, he couldn't quite remember, the cloaking fog no longer restful. Thwarted by his inability to find his way, utterly depleted, he'd sleep for a while, enfolded by the once-again comforting fog, dreaming deeply of emerald eyes and fiery kisses.

Until the vague urgency spurred him to wakefulness. He was forgetting something, but what? Restless, he wandered through the mist again, searching with mounting frustration, until exhaustion claimed him, and he lay down on nothing to sleep.

At one point, he thought he heard someone calling him. He tried to follow the voice, feeling the warming of the cool mist, like the distant sun finally burning through. It must be summer, because he smelled roses. No—it was spring, because he was certain the blood poppies were in bloom. Perhaps he'd meant to find the meadow where the poppies bloomed. He'd certainly meant to show them to someone. Bloodred lips, magic as warm as a hearth in winter, eyes green as summer grass, an embrace lush as rose petals.

Love and loss intertwined, roses blooming crimson on black vines with piercing thorns.

You're a good boy. The voice was comforting, reminding him of his great-grandmother, who'd passed long ago. *You're lost is all.*

He was lost. Lost in the mist. And there was something wrong with that.

Forcing himself to move, he began searching again, blindly seeking that something. The ground squished beneath his feet, spongy with moisture. The peeping of frogs grew louder, the fog clearing to show a pond. Lily pads covered the surface, studded with blossoms of ethereal beauty, seeming to glow with their own light, ivory petals framing soft pink interiors that shaded into sunshine yellow at the tips.

A quiet splashing drew his attention to a tall, skinny-legged girl wading in the pond. Black hair tumbled long and tangled around her narrow frame, her brown eyes huge in her piquant face. She held a lily blossom in one hand and a bright-green frog in the other, and she regarded him solemnly. "I like the frogs just as much as the flowers," she told him. "Is that contradictory of me?"

"No." His voice was hoarse, almost soundless, as if he hadn't spoken in a long time. "They're both beautiful, just in different ways."

Her somber face broke into a wide grin. "That's what I think, too." She looked around. "I think we're not supposed to be here. This was a long time ago. Not today. Not real."

He nodded, though he didn't understand. "Where are we supposed to be?"

She frowned, then bent to ease the frog onto a lily pad. "That's a fine question, but I really thought you'd know the answer, Gabriel. That's a big brother's job, you know."

"Selly?" He should have recognized her right away, except... She was right that this was long ago.

She rolled her eyes, reminding him of someone else. "And here I thought *I* was the crazy one. You really didn't know who I was?"

"You're not crazy," he said, realizing she might not know. "You never were. You only lost your way for a while because you have magic like I do, only you're a familiar, so you couldn't release it on your own. It's been building up inside you, clouding your mind." He wasn't sure how he knew all of that. When he tried to put context to that information, his thoughts slid away again.

She regarded him gravely. "That explains things, and it doesn't. Still, I'd really like to not be crazy anymore." She glanced around at the thick fog ringing the small pond. "Are we dead?"

Are we? "I don't think so," he ventured. "I don't feel dead."

"What does dead feel like, though?" she replied philosophically. "Maybe it's like this."

"A daunting thought."

She shrugged. "Could be worse."

You're lost is all. "I don't think we're dead. I think we're lost."

"I've been here a long time, off and on. You only just arrived. Did you come to find me?" She looked suddenly sad and alone, heartbreakingly hopeful.

"I think so," he said, because he couldn't bear to tell her otherwise.

"I found this," Selly said. She now held a rose, bloodred against the silvery-pale shimmers of the lily pond, vivid and full of fire. "It must be yours."

Because she didn't come to him, he waded into the pond, the water pouring into his boots. Instead of it being annoying, he found the cool wet refreshing, and he drank it in. The fog seemed to brighten, and he looked up to find a full moon shining bright, shedding its light upon them. Selly looked up, too, holding open one palm. "It feels good." She extended the rose to him. "Is this what you were looking for?"

"Yes," he said, suddenly quite certain of it. He took it, feeling better, more grounded all the time, and held out a hand. "Shall we go home?"

"I'd really like that." Almost shyly, Selly laid her hand in his, also cool and wet, but he didn't mind. In fact, she shimmered with silvery calm magic.

"Would you share some of your magic with me?" he asked.

"Apparently I have more than enough," she answered. "And you always shared with me. You're a good brother."

See? You're a good boy.

"I don't know how to give it to you, though," Selly continued, brows drawing together in puzzlement.

"That's all right," he reassured her. "I know." And, though he didn't quite understand why, he found that he did. The scent of roses reminded him, and he drew on Selly's magic, the water relieving the parched soil of his being, the moonlight lightening his mind.

And he remembered everything.

HE OPENED HIS eyes to sunlight bright enough to make him squint. A beaming face hovered over his, lined with age, her silvery hair a halo around her head. Narlis patted his cheek. "You're a good boy. Have a bit more magic," she invited.

Because he felt starved for it, he drew on her magic, rich as aged wine, fertile as earth. "Thank you, Narlis," he croaked, his voice rough with disuse, as it had been in his dream. Not a dream? "Selly?"

"She just woke up, too." A dark-skinned man stepped into his field of vision, smile bright with lines of strain around the edges. Asa, the Refoel healer. "Welcome back to the land of the living, Lord Phel," he said. "We're mighty relieved to see you recovering."

Recovering from tapping Selly's magic. "How is Selly?"

"Healthy in body at least," Asa answered. "With your help and Wizard Jadren's, we've drained all the fetid magic from her, and she's now replenishing with fresh magic, as is normal. Time will tell on the rest."

I'd really like to not be crazy anymore.

He craned to see Selly, where he sensed her magic, watery soft and silvery bright now, and Asa obligingly moved to the side. Their parents flanked Selly, talking to her with watery laughter, her low voice replying too quietly for Gabriel to make out. But his mother saw him looking over. She nodded, eyes bright with tears, and blew him a kiss. The respect and love shining in her face meant everything. Nic would be so pleased.

Nic. Where was she? Not that he'd expected her to hold vigil at his bedside—she'd probably been pressed to hold things together with him unconscious—but he needed to see her to feel whole again. "Did you send for Nic?" he asked, trying not to feel sulky that she hadn't immediately raced to see him. Maybe he hadn't been out all that long, and she'd had no cause to be concerned.

Asa had rested gentle fingers on his forearm, face relaxed as he listened to what his magic told him. So Gabriel felt the tremor of apprehension in the wizard's magic. There and gone. Asa's black eyes focused, and he smiled that bland healer's smile. "Don't worry about anything but recovering right now, Lord Phel. You very nearly died. Respect that your body and your magic are still replenishing."

A non-answer was always ominous. He pushed himself up, his body creaking, horribly weak. "How long have I been out?"

"Seven days," Asa answered with gravity. "Which is why you need to rest and take this recovery slowly. See if you can drink this water. I've been using magic to keep your body going, but that doesn't replace real food and water."

Gabriel drank slowly, his throat feeling as stiff from disuse as the rest of him. Seven days. Nic should have been wild with worry. Something was very wrong that she wasn't here. "Where is Nic?"

"After this, we'll try some broth. Work you back into solid food slowly."

"Answer the question, Asa. It should be an easy one."

Asa winced. "There's nothing you can do and I'd really like you to be stronger before you have to confront unpleasant news."

Rage cleared away the cloying weakness like the sun burning through morning mist. Magic flowed into him, and he realized he was pulling still from Narlis, the woman gamely holding his hand. Abruptly he let go, guilt riding him as she swayed faintly. "I'm sorry, Narlis."

"You're a good boy," she replied with a sweet smile. "You needed my magic, and Nic needs you." She got up and tottered away at a slow pace, someone Gabriel didn't recognize coming to help her.

Gabriel pushed up to a sitting position, swinging his legs to the floor, ignoring his body's groaning protests and Asa's arguments. "Tell me, right now, what happened, or I swear, healer, I will break every bone in your body."

"She's gone," said a voice behind him, so like Nic's warm contralto that he twisted around, hope wild in his heart—and his head spun with it, pain stabbing sharp at his temples. Alise. With her dark curling hair bobbed short, her face familiar and not, eyes wizard-black instead of emerald green, the sight of her rent his heart. "House Sammael arrived with hunters and a Convocation warrant for her arrest," she told him flatly.

Gabriel struggled to assimilate all the horrible things Alise had packed into one sentence. "And you all just let them take her?" he inquired, keeping the roaring pain out of his voice by clamping it down to a steely whisper.

"They had no choice," Asa said, clamping a hand on his shoulder. "And you need to lie down."

Gabriel shrugged him off, the movement making his head spin. "I'm going after her."

"You are in no shape to do that," Asa retorted.

"I'm getting her back," Gabriel ground out. "I rescued her before, and I can do it again."

"Not if you're fainting on your feet," Asa insisted. "You can't fool me, Lord Phel. I can feel how weak you are."

Weak. And worthless. He'd promised to protect Nic, and he'd failed. "How long ago?" he asked Alise, who was apparently the only person willing to tell him the truth.

She grimaced. "Six days ago."

So long. She'd be at Convocation Center by now. Dark arts only knew what they were doing to her. "And you've heard nothing from her?"

"No more questions until you at least drink some broth,"

Asa declared. He pointed sternly at Alise. *"You* will cooperate, as I am lord of the infirmary. My word is law." Asa turned a fierce look on Gabriel. "I'll allow you to sit up, but you will drink this bone broth and, if I clear you, you can interrogate Wizard Alise further. Give me trouble, and I'll put you out. You've seen me do it."

Torn, Gabriel was tempted to test the healer. But his magic felt as tremulous as the rest of him. So he acceded, if ungracefully, scooting on the bed to lean against the wall, legs stretched out before him. He seemed to be wearing light, thin pants and a shirt, both in off white. They fit him perfectly, so he knew they must be Dahlia's work. Asa gestured to someone, another unfamiliar helper, who brought a bowl of steaming broth.

Gabriel took it and obediently sipped, the rich flavor seeming to go straight to his bones. He scanned the room. Noted Asa's tired mien. "Where is Laryn?"

Asa shook his head, expression deeply unhappy. "No more answers until the broth is gone."

Containing his impatience, Gabriel drank, slowing when Asa chided him that if he puked it up it would only take longer to get his answers. Alise pulled up a chair, waiting with considerably more patience, though her worry was clear in her face, deep shadows under her eyes. Finally, he finished, holding up the empty bowl for Asa, who'd gone to check on Selly. Grimly, Asa nodded permission to Alise.

She told him of House Sammael's arrival and how the confrontation had gone, culminating with Nic being collared and taken away. "She wouldn't let us fight for her," Alise explained, knotting her fingers in her lap. "She forbade us from it, saying that it was a battle we couldn't win and the end result would be the same."

But it wouldn't have been that way if Gabriel had been awake. He could've successfully fought for her. "The Sammael representatives," he said slowly, choosing his questions in case Asa cut him off again, "who were they?"

Alise hesitated before answering. "Sabrina and Sergio Sammael."

Sergio Sammael. Heir apparent to House Sammael. Just to be clear, he verified, "Sergio was one of Nic's suitors?"

"Yes. A real piece of work, that one. He was far too happy to see Nic collared. It was so unnecessary, as she went peacefully."

Gabriel wrestled back the blood rage at the thought of Nic in that sadistic bastard's hands. He wouldn't just kill Sergio; he'd slowly dismember him, piece by piece. "Are you sure they took her to Convocation Center?"

"Of course they did," Asa inserted, returning and putting a hand on Gabriel's forehead. It took considerable effort for Gabriel not to growl and fend him off. The more compliant he was, the sooner he'd escape Asa's tender care. "Why would they take her anywhere else?"

"I swear," Jadren exclaimed in exasperation as he strode into the room on the heels of Asa's words. "Is everyone in House Refoel an idealistic fool, or is it just you, Asa?" Jadren spared a glance for Gabriel. "You look like shit, Lord Phel, but at least you're alive."

"I am not a fool," Asa bit out, "nor am I an idealist. I believe in the rule of law."

Jadren snorted disdainfully. "Like that NDA your familiar violated?"

Asa stiffened. "That was Laryn's choice, and I remanded her into your custody pending Lord Phel's judgment. I don't know what else you expected me to do."

"I expected you to control your familiar," Jadren snarled. "But apparently that was too much to ask."

Before Asa could retort, Gabriel held up a hand to silence them, asking Alise. "What does Laryn have to do with this?"

Once again, Alise proved her worth by giving him a straight answer, no dancing around. "She sent a letter to the Convocation notifying them of Han and Iliana's presence in House Phel, and calling into question whether Nic had been properly bonded. We believe she also somehow conveyed that you'd been incapacitated. They knew about Selly, too."

Gabriel winced internally. All those times Nic had railed at him for wanting a reciprocal bonding, and she'd been right in the end. Hopefully she wasn't even now cursing him for all the ways he'd failed her. "So they took Han and Iliana?"

"No." Alise looked a bit surprised. "Sorry—I left out that bit. We did have some forewarning from the spirits I'd sent to watch the roads in, and Nic arranged with some fellow by the name of Rat to hide Han and Iliana in the marshes. Sammael left hunters to search for them, but I gave them a spirit to send to me if they were found. So far I haven't heard from them. I haven't summoned them back yet, because we weren't sure yet if it was safe, since..." She trailed off, flushing.

"Since you weren't sure if I'd wake up or if I'd be of any

use if I did," he finished for her. He pondered a moment. Nic had been clever to think of Rat, and Alise had been right to leave Han and Iliana where they were. "How many hunters?"

"A dozen," Jadren supplied.

"I counted ten," Alise corrected with a frown.

Jadren shrugged that off. "That enchanted dagger of yours—did it really work to kill them?"

"Sent them back to the piles of rotten goo they were born of," Gabriel replied, noting the gleam in Jadren's eye. Yes, they had hunters to fight. "Interested in making some enchanted artifacts, Wizard El-Adrel?"

"A wizard never gives up the hobbies of his youth," Jadren agreed with a slow smile. "A bit of amateur collaboration is to be expected."

"Excellent, because I'm going to need Han and Iliana." He looked to Alise. "We're going to summon them back—and we must anticipate that the hunters will be on their heels."

"I love me a good trap," Jadren declared happily. "Those things are an abomination, so it will be a pleasure to dissolve them."

Alise was less enthused. "Iliana and Han will no doubt be willing to donate their magic, but even you cannot take on Convocation Center, Lord Phel."

"Watch me," he replied grimly.

"Regardless, Lord Phel," Asa put in wearily, "you are doing nothing today. I can continue to treat you, but as you can imagine, my abilities are limited without Laryn's assistance. You must rest—and remain calm—or you'll undo all of my work. And be of no help to Lady Phel," he added, correctly reading the rebellious glint in Gabriel's eyes.

"Laryn is in custody, you say?" Gabriel asked carefully, trying to appear calm, though the murderous rage brewed in him. He couldn't kill Sergio Sammael—not yet—but he could take care of the trash in his own household.

"Locked in one of the guest rooms," Jadren answered. "Wizard Sage reinforced the windows so they cannot be broken, and I put a lock on the door myself."

What would they have done with her if he hadn't awakened? He looked to Asa, miserably averting his gaze. "What would you have me do with her?"

"Lord Phel..." Asa didn't meet his eyes. "There are essentially two options available. You'd be within your rights to kill her outright."

"Which is what I would do," Jadren put in, thoughtfully stroking his beard. Alise said nothing, staring stonily into the distance.

"I thought familiars are too valuable to the Convocation to kill," Gabriel said, taken aback by that news. Nursing thoughts of murderous revenge was different from entertaining the idea of killing Laryn in cold blood.

"The heads of the houses have considerable latitude," Jadren said, so drily that it was clear he covered some deeper emotion. His magic, usually so contained, left a bitter tinge in the air. "The Refoel familiar's actions could have resulted in your death, might still result in the loss of your lady and familiar. No one would blame you for killing a traitor of that magnitude."

Gabriel refused to consider the bleak future Jadren painted

for Nic. If he did, he'd lose his mind. *When Lyndella was abducted by Sylus's nemesis,* Nic's voice whispered in his memory, *she'd gone mad, locked in a cell while Sylus searched frantically for her. When he finally found her, she was too far gone. Lyndella died in his arms, insane and broken beyond repair. Then Sylus used all his magic wreaking revenge on his enemy, killing himself, but taking his nemesis with him.* Gabriel vividly and viscerally sympathized with Sylus in that moment. "Laryn is carrying your child, Asa," he pointed out, as no one else had mentioned it.

"Yes." Asa said nothing more than the simple, terse affirmative.

"What is the second option?" Gabriel asked, though he suspected he knew.

"Let the Convocation deal with her," Jadren supplied when Asa seemed too overcome to answer. "If your need for vengeance, which we all respect, would be satisfied, it's the course I'd recommend."

"I thought you said you'll kill her," Alise broke in.

Jadren slid her a cynical look. "What I do and what I advise are two different things." He returned his attention to Gabriel. "It's the civilized option. They'd keep the familiar healthy until the babe is born, which would be returned to Wizard Asa. Asa might have to stand trial to prove that his familiar acted without his knowledge and manipulation. It's an unlikely scenario, as familiars rarely act independently of their wizard, but it has been known to happen, and we can all bear witness that Asa was unaware of his familiar's betrayal. Else we'd have confined him as well, I hope you know, Lord Phel."

Alise nodded staunchly. "I broke the news to Wizard Asa and can confirm that he was astonished and devastated."

Gabriel could easily observe how Laryn's actions had affected Asa. Though he was soldiering on, something in the man had broken.

"I accept full responsibility for what Laryn did," he inserted, looking at a point on the wall over Gabriel's shoulder. "I didn't monitor Laryn's activities closely. I knew that she resented Lady Phel, but I thought she'd get over it in time. I never imagined she would..." He couldn't seem to finish.

"Asa," Gabriel said, holding out a hand. Asa met his gaze then and clasped Gabriel's hand, wary surprise in his wizard-black eyes. "That's the trouble with treating other people like human beings. Laryn isn't a dog to be kept on a leash. She's a woman with free will. It's not on you what she chose to do."

Asa smiled briefly, grief replacing it. "Thank you, Lord Phel."

Gabriel released the man's hand, thinking, which unfortunately made his head ache. What would Nic want him to do? "I assume turning Laryn over to the Convocation means they'll punish and retrain her using vile methods."

Jadren shrugged as if it were of little interest, though Alise shook her head. "They might not bother. Once separated from Asa, Laryn's mind would deteriorate from the attenuation of the bond." She tipped her head at Asa. "They would likely make her docile through psychic sedation and use her as a breeder. She doesn't need sanity to produce magical babies for the Convocation."

Gabriel couldn't even contemplate what that life would

look like. He felt certain that Nic, no matter her need for justice, wouldn't wish it on Laryn either. He'd just have to ask Nic, and they'd decide together. Any other scenario didn't bear contemplating.

"The downside for Asa, of course," Jadren continued, "is that he won't be able to bond a new familiar until the current one dies." Everyone, even Asa, stared at Jadren, aghast. He shrugged it off. "Even with that bond attenuated, that's how it works. It needs to be said." Jadren spoke to Gabriel directly now. "Wizard Asa will be hampered as a healer without a familiar. You'd have to replace or demote him as House Phel healer. Killing the traitor would be doing Asa a favor. The Convocation would likely offer him a new familiar. He wouldn't get another crack at the Betrothal Trials, naturally, and they'd almost certainly simply assign him a familiar, but it would still be a more favorable outcome."

"It's true," Asa said wearily. "Not that killing Laryn would be a favor to me. I don't wish for her death, despite everything, but I won't be an effective healer without her assistance. I'll resign, so you can replace me."

"Can't you use magic from unbonded familiars?" Gabriel asked. "We have Iliana, Han, and Narlis. Even Selly might be helpful, in time. I know you borrowed from them already."

"Short term, sure," Jadren answered for him, "but having unbonded familiars around is like leaving your coin sitting on the seat of a public carriage—you're just begging for them to be stolen."

"Clearly even bonded familiars can be taken from their wizards," Gabriel retorted, the worry for Nic climbing up his throat, bittersour. *When he finally found her, she was too far gone.*

"Yes, but—again—they don't survive the attenuation of the bond for long," Jadren replied, not without sympathy. "I don't like to say this, but it's already been six days. I wouldn't hold out much hope for Lady Phel's... mental health."

Lyndella died in his arms, insane and broken beyond repair. Alise made a small sound, like a swallowed sob. Gabriel didn't reply to Jadren's dour prediction. Hope was all he had. He tried reaching for Nic along their bond, uncertain if the echo of fire-warmed wine and the scent of bloodred roses came from her or from his memories.

"Laryn is fine where she is," Gabriel said, deciding to let this argument wait. "The priority is rescuing Nic. Laryn's crimes are primarily against her, so I'll wait until Nic can consult on the sentence." *And firmly believe that she'd be able to.*

The three wizards exchanged uncomfortable glances. "Lord Phel," Jadren ventured, "I feel I should reiterate Wizard Alise's point. You cannot expect to extract Lady Phel from Convocation Center. You are one wizard, and they are multitudes. Powerful, experienced multitudes. It would be suicide."

Sylus used all his magic wreaking revenge on his enemy, killing himself, but taking his nemesis with him. "It's not suicide if I survive," Gabriel returned grimly. "Besides, all that matters is that Nic is recovered. I promised to keep her safe, and I'll do that."

"No matter how it turns out," Jadren warned, "the Convocation will level judgment on House Phel. They *will* punish you for it. They'll at least revoke your house status, possibly worse."

Gabriel was heartily tired of the threat of the Convocation yanking away the treat they'd so grudgingly awarded him. Once upon a time, restoring House Phel had been all that mattered to him. Since then, his priorities had changed. Getting Nic back was what mattered.

She was the only thing that mattered.

~ 16 ~

I T TOOK ANOTHER full day for Gabriel to escape the infirmary. Despite being a broken and guilt-riddled man, Asa
continued to find his spine where his patient was concerned. In
all truth, he didn't have to fight Gabriel at all. When Gabriel
insisted he be released, Asa simply stood back and gestured for
Gabriel to leave. Gabriel made it two steps before the room
spun and his vision went black.

At least Asa had the grace to catch him before he hit the
floor.

After that, Gabriel ate and drank everything handed to him
with grim determination. He allowed Asa to work his healing
magic as often as he was able. He even suffered his parents'
fawning attention, figuring letting them pet him gave Selly a
break.

As for Selly, she wasn't exactly lucid—definitely not articulate—but she wasn't crazed either. No longer needing to be
strapped down, she was allowed to get up as she pleased—
which meant she often sat on the bench beneath the tall
windows, sniffing the spring breeze like a cat when the
windows were open. Wizards Wolfgang and Dahlia collabo-
rated to expand the bench into a deep window seat padded

with pillows. Selly beamed her happiness, even hugging the pair of wizards.

Gabriel watched Selly through the long hours of doing nothing but convalescing, recalling how she'd spoken in the mist they'd been lost in, her mind as sharp as ever. He hadn't told their parents about the conversation, as he wasn't sure if they'd understand that it hadn't been a dream. Sometimes Selly came to sit at his bedside, holding his hand and smiling sweetly at him. She seemed happy to simply be together like that, and he wasn't certain if she remembered the mist at all.

It also occurred to him that she'd been lost in that formless mist for a very long time, and he understood why everyone warned him that her mind might not recover from it. His own thoughts had a tendency to grow vague and formless. When exhaustion overwhelmed him, he wondered if *he* would ever be the same again.

When he managed to walk out of the infirmary under his own power, he climbed the stairs to the rooms he shared with Nic, ready to bathe and put on real clothes. He'd been braced for her lingering scent and vitality to hit him in the gut, but worse—there was no trace of her presence. Only her things, left behind, an open book discarded face down to mark her place. Her embroidery neatly folded on a side table. Her gowns, most of which he'd never gotten to see her wear, hanging like eviscerated ghosts in her wardrobe.

Afraid he might stand there fingering the fabric of her gowns, weeping like a child, he forced himself to walk away. Reasonably clean, shaved, and dressed, he went to the library and sent for Alise. She hadn't wanted to summon Iliana and

Han—along with the inevitable vicious pack of hunters on their trail—until Gabriel was able to fight. Jadren had been working on weapons to be enchanted, also refusing to show them to Gabriel until Asa gave approval.

Meanwhile, Nic was out there, somewhere, suffering and slowly losing her mind.

"Are you sure?" Alise asked dubiously. "Not to gainsay you, Lord Phel, but you've only just arisen from your sickbed. You're still replenishing your magic and—"

"That's why I need Han and Iliana," he interrupted. "I can't go after Nic without their help. Every day that passes is another day that—"

"I know that!" Alise nearly shouted. "You've been asleep for most of this, but I'm the one who's been counting the days, sick with worry. I even wrote to Papa, that's how desperate I was."

"You did what?" Gabriel asked, astonished.

"I wrote to Lord Elal," Alise answered, lifting her chin in stubborn pride, exactly as Nic would. "I offered to return as his heir if he would ransom Nic."

"What did he say?"

She laughed bitterly. "He didn't reply. I think I know why, too."

"And?"

Dropping into a chair, she put her face in her hands, then looked at him, black eyes haunted. "When Sammael took Nic, I sent a spirit with them, to keep an eye on her. Just in case."

Gabriel sat straighter, galvanized with excitement. "Then you know exactly where she is." If he could find a way to sneak into Convocation Center, he could break her out without confronting the multitudes Jadren warned of.

But Alise was shaking her head. "It vanished. Because it was taken away from me."

Gabriel urged his still sluggish brain to think. "What can do that?"

"*Who* can do that is the correct question. It would take an Elal wizard, and a decently powerful one, too. I'm not hugely powerful, but I'm no weakling either."

"Your father sent a wizard to assist Sammael in Nic's capture," Gabriel realized.

Alise nodded grimly. "Or someone is acting without Papa's knowledge. I know where I'd bet my coin."

Elal, up to their conniving noses in this, as usual. "Call Han and Iliana back, please. Don't make me make it an order."

She nodded in resignation, not entirely unhappy. There were no good answers to the situation they found themselves in. "Just be ready."

"I will be." He had to be.

THEREFORE, HE VISITED the arcanium. Alone. It felt hollow and wrong to walk the long tunnel under the lake without Nic. He sorely missed her running commentary of sardonic comments. Hesitating when he reached the final, round door, he recalled how Nic had said the arcanium required a mix of their magic.

Would he be able to open it? He was no longer drained to the point of death, but his magic hadn't yet fully rebounded.

Still, Nic had also theorized that the arcanium stored magic they'd combined. If any residual of Nic's powerful magic remained, it would be here. And he needed it if he was going to rescue her.

Laying his hand on the door, he summoned the water and moon magic that should open it. Trying to use his wizardry felt like trying to lift a sword after an injury. It hurt, and the pain made his stomach churn and head throb. Once, it had felt so easy. Of course, it had been easy with Nic's generously provided magic.

Take, she said in his mind, lush mouth curving with affectionate amusement. *Have.*

But she wasn't here. An echo of another conversation came back to him. Nic telling him that he'd taken her magic, transmuted it into water and moon magic, and stored it in the arcanium. When he'd said he didn't know that was possible, she'd replied she didn't think it was for any other wizard but him. Or that maybe all House Phel wizards could do it and that the arcanium functioning that way was a strong argument that they could. *I think you should experiment,* she whispered in his mind.

Beyond the door, surrounded by water, the dome of solidified moon magic hummed softly. Fire ran through the silver, summer heat gleaming in the glass. Nic *was* here, in a way. He reached for her with unbearable longing.

And the door spiraled open.

He stepped inside the silent space, well lit by the spring

sunshine filtering through the water above. The silver struts framing the windows sparkled with interior light, a hint of rose-gold in them. He could swear he smelled roses in the otherwise cool, still air.

Nic was everywhere and nowhere.

The silver bed with its chains caught his eye. It had once seemed so threatening, but his fears of becoming a monster seemed childish now. He didn't care what he did or became if it meant saving Nic. Nothing mattered but that.

With somber thoroughness, he searched the many cabinets and drawers studded around the dome in the interstices between windows and found plenty of useful tools and weapons. *See?* Nic chided in his mind. *I told you your ancestors created this stuff and left it to you for good reason. Foolish wizard that you were too afraid of what you'd find to look before this.*

"I'm looking now," he retorted to her ghost, his voice echoing oddly in the quiet space without ears to listen.

Having made a neat stack of blades, a couple of swords, and even a quiver of silver-tipped arrows, he left them by the door and seated himself beneath the circular moon window at the apex of the dome. It would be better to do this with direct moonlight, but the moon was always there, if unseen. And the water surrounded and soothed him.

Centering himself, he did his best to calm his mind with the disciplines Asa had begun to teach him. Memories of Nic in this place crowded into the empty spaces of his mind, her warm laughter, her sensual gasps and cries, the feel of her skin against his, hot and silken, redolent of wine and roses.

Though he wasn't doing it correctly, the arcanium answered. It responded as Nic responded to his kisses, to the caress of his hand, willingly and warmly. The magic spun into him, rich and ancient. Here was more than the sum of Nic and him; there were other magics sunk deep here, planted in love and eroticism, in the extremity of sensation, and powerful intensity.

For the first time, he considered that his ancestors might not have been universally terrible.

Finally replete, feeling something like his usual self, he rose and gathered the weapons and tools. He was ready to face the hunters.

"LOOKING TO TAKE my job?" Jadren asked with a raised brow, surveying the pile of weapons Gabriel had scattered on the workbench. He wasn't about to let the other wizard inside the arcanium, so they were using the workshop instead, with everyone but the swamp monster locked out.

"Planning to report me to your mother?" Gabriel returned, mirroring the raised brow.

Jadren raised his hands in mock surrender. "I'm sure all of this is grandparented in." Gingerly, he picked up a thick blade as long as his forearm. "Your ancestors didn't mess around."

Gabriel took it from him. "It's a machete, commonly used for clearing foliage, a perennial chore in Meresin."

"Looks good for clearing enemies, too," Jadren noted with

a jaunty grin.

"I'm fairly certain these are condensed from moonlight," Gabriel said, not responding to that comment, indicating the weapons he'd brought out of the arcanium. "And these are other weapons made with varying degrees of silver, plus alloys to strengthen them, but I don't know that we can make any of these work on the hunters. When I made the blade that did work, I used a silver alloy dagger I liked and infused it with moonlight over the course of months. We don't have time for that. Is there a shortcut?"

"Shortcuts and wizardry don't mix well," Jadren mused, sounding as if he quoted someone. He examined a small dagger. "Do you know why that enchanted blade worked against the hunters?"

"No, tell me."

Jadren gave him an exasperated look. "I'm asking *you*. You made the cursed, illegal thing. Why did it melt the hunters?"

"I don't know. I just happened to use it and it did."

Jadren tossed the blade down and leaned both hands on the workbench, frowning fiercely at Gabriel. "*Think*, man. Wizardry is about intention as much as anything. What was your intention when you bathed the blade under the light of the full moon as you danced naked around it, painting it with the blood of virgins?"

"Remind me that I never want a tour of House El-Adrel's manufacturing facilities," Gabriel noted dourly.

Jadren grinned. "Wise."

Gabriel thought back to that younger, far more naïve self. He'd been curious if the spell he'd found in the moldering

House Phel library would work, especially as he'd found little use for moon magic compared to water magic. He'd also been freshly returned from Convocation Center, more than a little concerned about the powerful wizards he'd encountered there, uncertain in his own skills. The elitists there had made their contempt for his ignorance and lack of education clear. He'd come back to Meresin relieved to be away from that suffocating atmosphere and determined to improve himself. Most of all, he'd wanted to be able to protect his people.

"I wanted... a weapon that could destroy any enemy," he said slowly.

"There you are, then." Jadren looked thoughtful, scratching his short auburn beard. "Should've been too nebulous to work well, but clearly it did. You're just not the typical wizard."

"Thank you, I think," Gabriel said drily. A spirit popped up beside him, taking the form of a ticking clock. "Apparently, our runaways will be here in about four hours. We need to be ready."

"All right, then." Jadren clapped his hands together, rubbing them briskly. With his feral grin showing white in the sleek frame of his dark red beard, he looked like the evil villain from one of Nic's novels. "Let's see if I can take your moon magic via my ability to embed enchantments into artifacts and recreate your kill-any-enemy blade, skipping the months of naked dancing and virginal bloodletting."

IT TOOK ALMOST all the time they had, but by the time Gabriel and Jadren emerged from the workshop, they had three swords, five daggers, and a full quiver of arrows that they hoped would work against the hunters. It had turned out to be easiest to work with the weapons Gabriel had brought out of the arcanium, as—according to Jadren—made of moonlight or not, they'd been primed to accept enchantments.

"I wish we had a way to test them before we actually confront the hunters," Jadren commented, uncharacteristically sober. "Unless you want to try one on Asa's traitorous familiar? She qualifies as an enemy, no doubt. Though she'd be easy to kill, regardless."

"Her name is Laryn," Gabriel said, irritated by Jadren's continued habit of speaking of her as something less than human.

Jadren shrugged that off. "I really don't care what that duplicitous bitch's name is."

Gabriel gave the man a sidelong speculative glance. "For a spy planted in my house by my enemy, you certainly have strong opinions about loyalty."

Jadren stared stonily ahead. "I may be a tool of my mother's, but I'm not one of her automatons. I'm capable of having my own moral code." He flicked a glance at Gabriel and away. "You've treated me fairly, Lord Phel. Far more so than I expected or likely deserve. So has Lady Phel, for that matter, though I gave her plenty of cause not to."

Aha. As he'd suspected—something unpleasant had passed between them, something Nic hadn't wanted him to know about. Always protecting him. He missed her presence with a sudden, fierce need. Worse, he mourned her with an agonizing grief, as if she were already lost to him.

"We'll get her back," Jadren said, divining the direction of Gabriel's thoughts. "We just need to melt some hunters first. I only wish we could test these things," he repeated, holding up the long sword he'd selected, scrutinizing it.

A thought occurred to Gabriel. "I actually *do* know of a hunter we can test it on."

JADREN MADE A face at the trunk Gabriel magically raised from the marsh. Dripping with mud and thick algae, the thing did look unprepossessing. "Explain this to me again," Jadren said. "You locked a hunter in the trunk and buried it in a swamp?"

"It showed up here and tried to attack Nic," Gabriel replied, setting the trunk down with an ungainly thump, as the water he'd used to mentally manipulate it had mostly dripped away. The silver chains he'd wrapped around the trunk as a safety measure unwound rapidly. "I didn't have my enchanted blade at that point, so I chopped the thing up into pieces, sealed it in this trunk, and sank it in the *marsh*."

"And that wasn't a tiny bit of overkill?" Jadren asked dubiously.

"I'd lay coin that, when we open this trunk, the hunter will be alive and whole—and ready to kill."

"Instead of coin, how about that machete? You're wrong and I get that, as well as the sword."

"You're on." Gabriel didn't bother to set stakes for the opposite outcome, as he knew he wasn't wrong. Drawing his own newly enchanted sword, he gave it a few test swings. It had a different balance than his favorite sword, but it was exquisitely made. Much as he'd like to have a bit of time to accustom himself to the new weapon, it wasn't meant to be. Hopefully the enchantment would make up for any clumsy wielding on his part. *If* the enchantment worked.

"Too bad there's only one hunter in there," Jadren noted. "That means we're testing just one these weapons. Not exactly comprehensive quality control."

"Be ready," Gabriel warned Jadren, who nodded and, despite his doubts, took up a defensive stance—an amateurish one. Gabriel frowned, opening his mouth to say something, then thought better of it. No time for that.

He had to use his free hand to undo the bronze latch on the trunk, then flung it open and danced back—barely dodging the slavering hunters that leapt out. Three of them. Smaller than the others but just as vicious, and unnaturally quick. Vicious claws swiping, two jumped at Jadren and one went for Gabriel. Though he'd warned Jadren to be ready, Gabriel was caught slightly flat-footed. He'd expected one hunter and had intended to stand aside for the other wizard to test his sword on it.

Thus the hunter caught Gabriel with a stinging swipe across his thigh before he managed to bring his sword around to decapitate the thing. He was already coming around with a follow-up swing, maximizing his momentum, when his brain caught up and realized the hunter had dissolved into goo.

"It worked!" he crowed, spinning to Jadren, then cursing under his breath.

The man was hard-pressed. The El-Adrel wizard held his sword with both hands, using it like a club trying to beat off the two hunters clinging to him like burrs, claws rending his sides, long jaws snapping at his throat. Gabriel waded in, grabbing one hunter by the back of the neck and pulling it away from Jadren just enough to run it through with his sword without stabbing Jadren in the process.

The thing collapsed into a foul stew of meat and bones—all over Jadren, who was contorting himself to strain away from the lethal fangs snapping at his throat. Gabriel spun to take the other hunter, and Jadren shouted, "No! I need to test my sword, too."

"Then do it," Gabriel snarled, greatly disliking standing back while Jadren wrestled the unnatural creature. "Slice or stab," he ordered. "Any cut will do."

Jadren contorted himself, trying to free his weapon from the hunter's barnacle-tight hold, bright blood running from the thing's claws where it dug into him. At this rate Jadren would be worthless to fight the fresh hunters that should arrive at any moment.

"That's enough," Gabriel declared, taking a step.

"Not yet!" Jadren yelped as a fang caught his collarbone,

but he managed to free his arm, slicing the hunter shallowly across the midsection. With a normal sword, the cut would barely have fazed a determined opponent. Fortunately, they'd created a sword far better than normal.

The hunter exploded, raining bits of rotten meat all around—mostly all over Jadren, who was at least evenly coated now. The El-Adrel wizard stood there, panting, bleeding, and looking like he might puke.

"Do you not know how to fight with a sword?" Gabriel inquired politely.

"I thought it was a magic sword," Jadren retorted, drawing himself up, bristling, and at least no longer looking likely to hurl up his breakfast.

"Magic, not autonomous," Gabriel explained, not above enjoying the arrogant wizard's embarrassment. "You still have to stick it in your opponent, which requires a modicum of skill."

"I'm a wizard, not a foot soldier," Jadren grumbled.

"You'll be training with Han."

"A familiar?" Jadren's scorn was clear.

"A familiar who can fight circles around you," Gabriel clarified. "That's an order, by the way. Meanwhile, we'd better get you cleaned up and healed before the next battle." He jerked his head at the pond. "Take a dip to get the worst off."

Jadren's already horrified scowl deepened as he looked at the green water. "In *that*? I'll get infected!"

"Your wounds are already infected with that rotten meat," Gabriel replied. "Asa can take care of both at once, but you're not tracking that shit into his infirmary."

Grumbling, Jadren tossed down his sword and waded into the water, algae swirling around him as he swiped at the goo, finally ducking his head and coming up sputtering. He clambered out again, still swiping at his hair and clothing. Gabriel gingerly picked up the man's sword and held it out. "Always clean your weapon first," he advised. He'd cleaned his own immediately.

Jadren gave him a sour look. "You're enjoying this, aren't you?"

As a matter of fact, he was—as much as he could enjoy anything while pretending that worry for Nic wasn't tearing him apart. Everyone in the Convocation had so scorned his tendency to use his body instead of his wizardry. Even Nic had teased him about the manual chop-chop method. "Growing up without being able to rely on magic teaches certain useful skills," he said by way of answering. "Let's get you to Asa."

Jadren shrugged off his offer of support. "I can walk on my own." He did, though slowly, trudging along in stoic silence. Gabriel took advantage of the conversational lull to sweep the surrounding landscape with his wizard senses. He'd detected the arrival of hunters before, but only when they'd gotten too close for comfort. Since then, he'd gotten more skilled at using his senses in this capacity, but he wasn't at all sure of his range. Still, Alise hadn't sent a recent update, so the trio must not be about to arrive at any moment.

"Why were there three?" Jadren sounded somewhat plaintive, no doubt from pain and blood loss. "You said you locked one in that trunk. I expected *one*."

Gabriel refrained from advising his impromptu student

never to make assumptions about the enemy. "I said I locked the pieces of one in the trunk. They must've regrown into three individuals. They were smaller than a standard hunter."

"You'd think it would've occurred to you to scatter the pieces," Jadren observed uncharitably.

"I didn't care for the idea of multiple points of attack, should they get free."

Jadren grunted but said nothing more.

ASA WASN'T PARTICULARLY pleased to have to heal Jadren, or the wound on Gabriel's thigh he'd already forgotten about. Narlis had remained in the infirmary, seeming to be happy to take care of small tasks, placidly donating magic to replenish Asa.

"You shouldn't be draining your magic already," Asa scolded Gabriel. "I might've let you out of bed, but you're far from fully recuperated."

"I have things to do," Gabriel replied, keeping his tone mild. It didn't fool Asa, who gave him a long, unhappy look.

"I know you want to recover Lady Phel," Asa began, "but—"

"But nothing," Gabriel said, cutting off the dire predictions he didn't want to hear. His wizard's instincts stirred with the distinctive stink of hunters. Still a ways off, but gaining. "Are we done here? The time for our next fight is upon us."

Jadren lifted his head like a bloodhound. "Is that what I sense? It feels like those things smell."

Asa stepped back, hands up in a gesture of resignation. "I suppose I should expect you brave idiots back here in even worse condition shortly."

Jadren grinned and clapped the Refoel healer on the shoulder. "Happy to help you feel indispensable."

Asa shrugged him off irritably and pointed at Gabriel. "*You* need to restore some of your magic."

"I won't need it," Gabriel replied, tapping his new, enchanted sword. "I have this."

Asa shook his head firmly. "Wrong. Magic is part of your health and vitality, even if you don't plan to use it."

"When we have Iliana and Han safe, I will," Gabriel promised, mostly to get Asa off his back. Or he'd visit the arcanium again. That had worked beautifully to top him off.

"You can have my magic," Selly said, shyly tugging on his elbow.

Gabriel gazed at her in some surprise. Did she even know what she was offering? Patting her hand, he smiled gently. "Maybe someday."

Her wide brown eyes narrowed. "It's mine to give, isn't it? You used the magic when we were in the mist. Let me help you this time, too."

She still sounded off, more like a child than a grown woman, but he recognized the determination in her posture. She seemed sane, seemed to know what she was offering—and had surprised him by remembering that moment in the mist. Still, he looked to Asa. The healer nodded. "It's good for her to release magic. I can't quite get a handle on it to transmute for healing. That water and moon magic is so odd. If you can use it, that will benefit you both."

"Are you sure?" he asked Selly tenderly.

She nodded vigorously. "I am part of House Phel, too," she said very seriously. Jadren, standing nearby, watched her with an inscrutable look on his face.

It was true that Selly was as much a member of House Phel as he was. Enfolding her hand in both of his, Gabriel reached for her magic, finding part of himself tense with apprehension. But this was nothing like the previous time, when her stagnant magic overwhelmed him, swept him up, and dragged him under to drown. Selly's magic was like his, and also not like. Pure water and pristine moonlight, deep as a mountain lake and brilliant as the full moon on a clear night. He drank her magic in, the transition to his own magic without flaw or hesitation. Where Nic was his mirror, compensating for what he lacked, Selly was like another face of himself. No wonder the Byssan sisters made such an effective team.

A spirit popped up just then, closely followed by the sound of running feet as Alise burst into the room. "They've been spotted! Hunters hard on their heels." She bared her teeth in a flesh-eating smile, disconcerting in her youthful face. She was all Elal in that moment, determined to win at all costs. Spirits swirled visibly around her, emitting a high-pitched keen of battle rage.

"We're ready," Gabriel replied. "Let's give them a solid House Phel welcome."

~ 17 ~

NIC PACED THE round, windowless chamber. It was comfortably appointed, all the furnishings the very finest, as they were at House Elal. The preponderance of black was a bit off-putting, but there were all the conveniences one could wish for, including fire elementals to heat the room, air elementals to provide oxygen—necessary without windows— water elementals for grooming and earth elementals to dispose of her waste. That also meant there was no bathtub, no cheerful fireplace, nothing that wasn't strictly serviceable. All very efficient and completely joyless.

It was a prison cell, after all.

Troubling most of all, it was also not Convocation Center.

She didn't remember falling asleep. Probably Sergio had used something to knock her unconscious, because she didn't remember much beyond getting in the carriage and watching House Phel recede in the distance. She'd awakened in this prison cell of a bedroom and known immediately that the Sammael siblings hadn't delivered her to the Convocation at all.

Given the over-the-top aesthetic of the décor, they'd brought her to House Sammael.

The room reminded her uncomfortably of the tower room she'd occupied at House Elal for those four months until Gabriel arrived as her unwitting rescuer. Indeed, she strongly suspected this room served as the House Sammael Betrothal Trials chamber, and she pitied the familiars of this house who spent their sequestration here. Unlike her old tower, this one had no books, no puzzles or crafts to occupy her hands. She supposed the claustrophobic boredom of the place gave them a powerful motivation to be compliant and conceive quickly. As if that was under their control.

The locked door clicked. Having quickly learned her lesson, she stood well back from it. The wizards that had brought her food and water the last several times had a tendency to jolt her with punishing pain—another indication she was in Sammael—if she stood too near the door.

There were no clocks in the room—apparently those weren't considered necessary to sustain life—but it seemed like the wrong time for the delivery of the adequately nourishing and totally boring meals. The lack of time also meant she wasn't entirely sure how many days she'd been kept captive. Maybe three, counting by fairly predictable routine. This visit was at the wrong time, she was sure of it, which did not bode well.

Sure enough, Sergio Sammael swanned into the room, smug smile distorting his handsome features as he looked her over. "Darling Veronica, you're looking lovely."

Nic plucked at the revealing black slip of lacy lingerie she'd been wearing when she awakened, her dress gone and no other clothing options available. At least they'd taken the collar off, too. "The latest fashion at Convocation Center? I must be behind the trends."

Sergio smiled thinly. "You belong to me now, so you will wear what I please." His gaze raked her with lewd interest, leaving her feeling soiled. "And your current apparel pleases me greatly. Mind your tongue, familiar, or I'll keep you entirely naked."

The threat worked all too well, and Nic bit her tongue, much as she wanted to point out that, in no permutation of Convocation law, did she belong to the odious wizard.

Appeased, Sergio glided toward her. "I've come to service you." His black eyes glittered with malicious glee, and she took an involuntary step back, hitting the curved wall of the small room immediately. "Not that," he snapped, though his gaze dipped to her scantily clad bosom. "Not until you're a bit more *tame*," he added silkily, absently fingering his bruised and bloodied lip.

He'd tried to embrace her in the carriage, and she'd fought him, managing to land several punches along with a bite on his lip. Sergio, a coward at heart, eyed her warily. He'd managed to immobilize her with pain so searing she'd dropped to the floor, unable to breathe—probably that's when she'd passed out—but he clearly hated experiencing any pain himself. There was a reason Maman had recommended him for a potential match. If Nic had been bonded to him, she could've found ways to use his fears and weak will against him.

She also would've suffered greatly in his hands, which she had no intention of doing now. She might be his prisoner, but she was far from helpless.

"I've come to tap your magic," Sergio informed her. "You must be needing the *relief* by now." He managed to make the word sound dirty. His wizard-black eyes glittered with lascivious greed.

"You can't," she replied firmly. "I'm a bonded familiar. My magic belongs to Lord Phel."

"Your former master is dead," Sergio spat. "We both know that. You weren't even clever about how you tried to conceal that from me, but I knew before we arrived. Such a pity House Phel commands so little loyalty from its minions. Sammael would never tolerate such latitude."

Nic swallowed back the bile and bitter hatred at Laryn's betrayal. And what had it gained the other woman beyond Nic's misery? Nothing, so clearly that single goal had been enough for Laryn. It was difficult to grapple, being hated that much, but it also wasn't her biggest problem at the moment. "If Lord Phel is dead—" She didn't, couldn't, believe it. "—then why am I still bonded to him?"

"Are you so sure you are?" He sounded pitying, insinuating that she didn't know her own mind.

"Yes. I know the bond survives, because my wizard is not dead." At least, he hadn't been when she was taken away. And now that they'd been separated by such a distance, she couldn't sense the bond between them at all. Something she tried not to dwell on. No sense losing her mind sooner than necessary.

Sergio waved that off as of negligible importance. "Comatose, then. An unoccupied corpse kept alive by Refoel magic, delaying the inevitable. Your wizard's spirit has already escaped his cage of flesh, and no amount of Refoel magic can put it back. Eventually that husk of an upstart wizard will cease to function." He leered at her, looming closer. "And guess who will be right here to bond you when that happy moment arrives? I will never be so weak and incompetent as to allow another wizard to steal you away, rest assured."

Nic was proud of herself for refusing to flinch—and declining to contemplate the scenario the vile Sammael wizard painted. Gabriel would live. He had to live. She would continue to believe. Otherwise, the despair would break her.

Sergio nodded, taking her silence for assent. "You may as well accept the inevitable, Familiar," Sergio crooned, his version of being charming, oily as it was. "You have always been destined to be mine. I was your first suitor, after all."

"That didn't work out so well for you," she pointed out coolly. "As Wizard Jadren noted, you had your shot and failed."

Petulant irritation contorted his face. "A chance of fate, of passing importance, and now remedied. That same fate has ensured I'll be your *last* suitor. You are pregnant, so when you are mine, the child will be, too. An heir to follow me in leading House Sammael to glory."

The prospect of her and Gabriel's child growing up in this travesty of a family made Nic feel sick—and frightened her more than any of his other threats. She wouldn't let it happen. Even if she had to crawl back to her father, beg him to forgive her, she'd protect this child. "I will never be yours."

Sergio tsked, making a show over looking around her prison. "Your intelligence sadly lags behind your MP scores. You already *are* mine."

"I am a prisoner, apparently, in House Sammael—but this is illegal. Clearly there was no warrant. The Convocation will never stand for—"

Sergio slammed a hand against the wall beside her head. So help her, she did flinch. Worse, he saw it and was pleased. "The warrant is valid, my disobedient familiar, and I have you here with full knowledge of the Convocation, as I volunteered to handle your punishment and retraining myself. Such is my duty to the Convocation."

It could be true. That was more believable than Sammael risking the Convocation's ire.

"You might be able to keep me prisoner," Nic retorted boldly, "but I am not bonded to you."

"You will be, in time. In the meanwhile, I intend to keep you healthy. We can't have you losing what little mind you have and wasting away while we wait for your travesty of a wizard to cease being an inconvenience and die already, which means tapping your magic."

"No." She firmed her jaw. "I refuse."

"You cannot refuse!"

"And yet, I am," she returned calmly.

With a growl, Sergio clamped a hand over her throat, forcing her chin higher, his fingers digging in like spidery claws. He leaned against the wall with his other hand, using the leverage to choke her lightly. She held his gaze, glaring her lack of fear. He wouldn't kill her. He wanted her too badly. "Yield, Familiar," he ordered. "Give me your magic."

"No." Oddly enough, sharing her magic with Jadren helped

in this moment, having given her insight into what made it more difficult for him. She'd also been practicing with Gabriel to govern the flow of her magic. Every little bit helped. Supposedly a wizard couldn't take magic from an unwilling, bonded familiar—but she also didn't want this to be how they discovered that her bond with Gabriel was gone.

Sergio's magic clamped onto hers, echoing the hand pinning her to the wall. He was a powerful wizard, despite Jadren's insults and his weak personality, and the pull was difficult to resist. Still, she was powerful, too, and being around Gabriel and his radical ideas had given her new confidence in her abilities.

Her magic was *hers*, to keep or give, and that certainty made all the difference. She would not give even a drop to Sammael.

Sergio's face reddened with effort. "Yield, curse you!" he shouted in her face. "It's your duty to submit to your betters."

"I see no one better than me," she choked out, and his hand spasmed on her throat, her vision darkening at the edges. Maybe he *would* kill her.

"I can give you pain," he said, leaning his face even closer to hers. "You know I can. There's a great deal of pain I can deliver without harming you. I can make you suffer so much that you'll be begging me to strip you of your magic, and the pain will only generate more." His magic blazed into her, setting her blood on fire with agony.

She gasped and writhed in his grip, fisting her hands and flailing at him. Sergio only laughed, savoring her suffering. "I can feel it even now, how your magic is growing like a bonfire.

You love this, as all familiars do. Abandon your pride and admit it to me."

Nic opened her mouth—and spat in his face.

With a screech, he leapt back, wiping away her spittle in disgust as she collapsed to the floor without his supporting throttle. Her body screamed in every pore, and she drew in great lungfuls of breath, trying to calm and restore her alarmed system. *The pain isn't real,* she told herself. *There's no injury. It's an illusion.*

Except the pain *was* real. Her nerves jangled at high alert from Sammael's magic, her body trying to make sense of how to react to an attack it couldn't otherwise perceive. Sergio's shiny black boots filled her vision before he crouched, vising a hand on her chin to force her gaze up to his—and to hold her jaw closed so she couldn't bite him again, she felt sure. "You can't win this fight," he said softly, false sympathy in his face as he shook his head. "You cannot hold out against me forever. As your sanity dissolves and your will softens, you won't be able to remember why you were so stubborn. Eventually you'll submit to me. And when I bond you to me, you'll adore doing it. I'll make you crawl as I lead you with a leash, and you'll delight in kissing my feet."

"Never," she ground through clamped teeth.

He laughed softly. "Time is on my side, naughty familiar. And I will enjoy breaking you."

Dropping her again, he stood and dusted off his hands. "I advise you to contemplate your situation. There is no rescue coming. The Convocation was happy to confer your punishment to House Sammael, which is legally binding. Even the house of your birth has turned its back on you, given your reckless and rebellious behavior. I am the only one who wants you, and I have complete power over you. You'd do well to appease me, as I am and ever will be your new master." He gave her a jolt of pain that made her nerves flare into panic again. She bit her lip to keep from screaming.

"I'll be back tomorrow," Sergio said cheerfully, as if saying farewell at a party. "Make sure you look pretty for me."

As the door closed and locked, Nic lay on the floor, too exhausted to move, dully contemplating her prospects. Had Lyndella endured this from her captors? Likely so, or similar, though Lyndella at least had the hope that Sylus would find and rescue her. Nic held out no such hope. Sergio was right: She would eventually break. She wouldn't be able to hold out against the combined force of his torment and her own unreleased magic. Something would give—either her will or her sanity.

Insanity was starting to sound pretty attractive.

"LET'S GO OVER the plan," Gabriel told the group. Iliana, Han, and Rat had arrived on nearly spent horses, all of them mud-spattered and smelling more like the bottom of a bog than any person should. But—largely due to Rat exploiting his intimate knowledge of the marshes—they'd arrived well ahead of their pursuers. The two familiars were in high spirits and ready to fight the hunters that had plagued them for days. Rat had already been sent off to the infirmary and had gone without protest, which was a greater mark of his exhaustion than his haggard face or the deep shadows under his eyes. He'd kept his charges alive, but he'd paid the price.

"Everyone select a weapon or two," Gabriel continued. He handed the machete to Jadren. "I believe you had your eye on this one."

Jadren took it warily. "But I lost the bet."

Gabriel shrugged and grinned. "I always planned to let you have it."

Scowling and muttering under his breath, Jadren unbuckled his belt to contrive a way to carry the big blade. Alise, playing with a pair of daggers she'd selected, rolled her eyes at him.

"I'm a decent archer," Iliana said, taking up the quiver of arrows, "if there's a bow to go with these."

Gabriel pointed his chin at the several recurve bows he'd asked his hunters to lend for the cause. "One of those should work for you."

Han had, meanwhile, selected a sword and short dagger and was testing them with a martial form that Jadren eyed with mixed envy and irritation. Gabriel distributed the remaining enchanted weapons to the assembly of volunteers—a mix of wizards, familiars, and nonmagical folk—explaining to all how the enchantment worked.

"Han and Iliana will be the bait," he told the group. "They'll appear to be trying to escape through the orchard, where we can hide ourselves in the trees. Once the hunters encircle these two, we'll surround them in turn and take them out."

"I don't think Iliana needs to be there," Han said with hard-jawed defiance. "Not on the ground. Let her hide in a tree with the bow and arrows, and I'll play bait alone. You don't need both of us."

"I am *not* leaving you alone to face the hunters," Iliana retorted with ferocity, her color high. "What if something goes wrong?"

"Exactly!" Han shot back. "If something goes wrong, I want you well away from the fighting."

"I'm not helpless, Han." Iliana waved the bow at him. "And I didn't defy the Convocation for you to sit idly by while you risk your life."

"Same." Han returned her glare, then opened his arms. Iliana flung herself against him with a sob, and he held her close, stroking her long red curls. He met Gabriel's gaze over her shoulder. "Lord Phel will protect us." He made it a question and a demand, and Gabriel nodded slowly. A promise.

"The hunters grow closer," he told the group. "It's time to set our ambush and banish these abominations."

Jadren whistled a jaunty tune. "This will be fun."

THE ORCHARD HE'D selected to set their trap was the most

mature in the vicinity of House Phel, with the tallest trees and densest foliage, but Gabriel still felt exposed. He didn't much care for sitting idly by while Iliana and Han pretended to be collapsed in exhaustion in plain sight below, even if it *was* his plan. Waiting, never his favorite activity, wore on him with slow drips of rising restless anxiety.

Worse, sitting in silence, with nothing to occupy his thoughts, meant that he couldn't suppress thoughts about Nic and what she might be enduring at Convocation Center. When she'd been taken, no one had been sure whether Gabriel would ever wake. Could she feel that he was alive, awake, and healthy? Did she have faith that he'd rescue her, or was she facing the despair of captivity and grief that she'd lost him?

He had to believe that she was holding strong. She was the most courageous, clever, and indomitable person he'd ever met. She'd find a way to survive this, he had to believe in that. But with every minute, every hour, every day that trickled by, he knew her chances of emerging unscathed dwindled. He chomped at the bit to race after her, to bring her home and begin the process of healing.

No other alternative bore contemplating.

Gabriel never thought he'd be happy to see hunters, but the strong, stinking sense of their imminent presence came as a relief. He whistled like one of the songbirds that frequented the orchard, three times in a row, their agreed signal. Alise's pet spirits scuttled through the branches, a second warning, in case anyone missed the first.

Iliana did an impressive job of appearing surprised and terrified to see the hunters loping toward her. She leapt to her feet, screaming shrilly, and began dashing away between the straight row of trees. Han jumped up, too, from his feigned sleep, squaring off with his sword in one hand and the dagger in the other. "Run, Iliana!" he shouted, their third and final signal, in case someone had managed to miss the rest.

Some of the hunters encircled Han, who turned warily, making a show of fighting panic, trying to keep an eye on them all at once. The rest sprinted after Iliana. With the herd of hunters duly separated, she stopped running, putting her back to a tree and nocking an arrow. Drawing her bow, she tremulously told them to stay away.

Holding himself in place, Gabriel counted, hunters and seconds. Reports from those who'd witnessed House Sammael's arrival and abduction of Nic had varied, some claiming there had been a dozen or more hunters, others insisting there'd been no more than nine. Or ten. People under strain tended not to remember details clearly, especially those unused to battle or facing any kind of intimidating enemy. Most everyone there had been too focused on trying to make sense of the existence of hunters in the first place, with little wit left over to count them.

Five hunters circled Han, and four formed a loose arc around Iliana. She trembled violently enough to be visibly shaking from this distance, her fear not faked now as she tried to choose a target. *Just a moment or two more,* Gabriel thought at her. *Hold steady.* He really didn't want to risk having extra hunters come up behind them. He also didn't want to betray their secret weapon too soon.

Hunters weren't terribly bright, but they weren't complete

fools either.

Gabriel had about decided that was all of them and was on the verge of giving the signal to attack when two more hunters strolled out of the trees from the sides, each carrying one of the loathsome iron collars that seemed part of their standard package for capturing and humiliating familiars. Eleven total. One loped in a tripod gallop, on two legs and one hand, toward Iliana, while the other walked upright toward Han, right below Gabriel's perch. Gabriel vibrated with the restrained impulse to kill it immediately.

"Familiar Haniel," the hissed, extending the collar. "You mussst be returned to the Convocation. Come quietly, and you will not be harmed."

"If I agree, will you let her go?" Han demanded. The hunter turned to look at Iliana—and Gabriel dropped on top of him.

It almost went too fast for his bloodthirst. Gabriel used the momentum of his controlled fall to hammer the enchanted broad-bladed hunting knife into the thing's back. The sudden collapse of his opponent turning to goo dropped him to the ground rather ignominiously—and fortuitously, as one of Iliana's arrows whizzed past where his head had been and *thunked* into a tree trunk. Iliana screamed, no pretense in it, and Han shouted her name, charging in her direction. *Not* in the plan, curse it.

One hunter down. Ten to go.

That left Gabriel, Jadren, and a couple of others facing off four hunters. Jadren looked determined, at least holding his sword at the correct angle this time, but he'd yet to dispose of any of the beasts.

One of the hunters skirted around Gabriel warily, staying out of reach of his sword, canine jaws lolling open, canting its head to study him with one yellow eye. "Lord Phel, I presssume," it said, sounding incongruously pleased. "Your reputation pressseedess you. You will turn over the familiarss to me."

"How about you die instead?" Gabriel invited, and lunged.

The hunter skipped back, fisted something, and hurled it like an invisible ball at Gabriel. The compulsion spell hit him, numbing his limbs, and the hunter laughed with feral glee. But Gabriel was no longer the ignorant country bumpkin he'd been when the hunters deployed that trick on him before. Though he'd promised Asa he'd conserve his magic and not use it in this fight, when he saw the spell coming, he had to react. He pulled reflective moon magic around himself at the last moment, bouncing it back at the hunter. The creature froze in place, almost comically, with its jaws parted and tongue hanging out.

One down, one immobilized. Nine to go.

Gabriel left the neutralized hunter for the moment, spinning to assist Alise, who was doing a creditable job of holding off another hunter with her paired daggers and a couple of air elementals buzzing around its eyes as it feinted, harrying her in an attempt to tire her enough for it to slip past her guard. Gabriel dispatched it from behind with one sweep of his sword.

Eight to go.

Jadren shouted in triumph, like a rowdy fan at a sporting

match, doing a dance of joy over a pile of goo. Good for him.

Seven to go.

The others in their group seemed to have the remaining two hunters cornered and under control, so Gabriel spun and ran toward Iliana.

Two more contained. Five to go.

He passed one pile of goo with an arrow sticking out of it, so not all of her shots had gone wild. Good for her.

Four to go.

Iliana, however, was splayed on the ground, a hunter pinning her there with slavering jaws clamped around her throat, impervious to her kicking and flailing. Gabriel recognized the tactic well, as they'd employed the same strategy against Nic, thinking to hold him off with the threat to her life. Han danced with agitation, furious and clearly frightened by the danger to Iliana. He held his sword at the ready, turning his dagger as if contemplating throwing it.

That could work if Han at least nicked the creature, but if his aim was off, they'd be down a blade.

The hunter that had brought the collar had set it aside on the ground and crouched beside Iliana, awkwardly holding a long knife in its taloned paws, with the point resting on Iliana's heart. "You cannot kill usss both at onsse," it was saying to Han. "Make one move, and we kill her."

"A bluff. You want us alive," Han ground out.

"We want *you* alive, Familiar Haniel," the hunter corrected with a grin. "Sshe iss sssuperflouss. A nissse bonuss, but nothing more. Cooperate, and ssshe will not be harmed. Resssisst, and ssshe diess before your eyess. Lay down your weaponss."

Iliana gave a strangled scream, blood blooming bright under the hunter's jaws where it had her by the throat, and Han nearly howled in fury.

"Let her go!"

"Lay down your weaponss," the hunter with the knife at Iliana's heart insisted. "Or watch her die."

"*You* will die," Gabriel declared, stepping up beside Han. He gestured at the diminished force of hunters. "You cannot stand against us. Surrender."

The hunter studied him, yellow eye bright, drool dripping from its fangs to splash on Iliana's skin above the neckline of her shirt. She flinched, then squeaked as the hunter at her throat tightened its jaws, squeezing out more blood. Han moaned low in his chest, and Gabriel feared the man wouldn't be able to stand the situation much longer.

"If it iss as you sssay, Lord Phel," the hunter finally replied, "then I have no insssentive to sssurrender. You will sssimply kill usss all."

It was unfortunately correct—and clearly more intelligent than the hunters previously sent against them. "If you agree to leave Meresin lands and never return, I'll promise you safe passage," he offered, perhaps recklessly. "But only if Iliana is not harmed any further."

The hunter considered, then sadly shook its head. "I cannot return without fulfilling my instructions. Both familiars come with me, and we will trouble you no further."

"No deal," Gabriel replied.

"A compromisse," the hunter suggested, jaw dropping

open in a parody of amusement. "I will release Familiar Iliana without further harm, and Familiar Haniel will come with me."

"Agreed," Han blurted, and Gabriel groaned internally. "Let her go and I'll comply," Han insisted to them both.

"No!" Iliana shrieked, immediately silenced into whimpers.

The hunter ignored both familiars and kept its wily gaze on Gabriel. "Lord Phel?"

Gabriel hesitated, assessing the situation. Han was the biggest problem here, unpredictable in his heightened emotional state. Two hunters in sight, possibly four still free to sneak up behind them, depending on what the others were doing. The back of his neck prickled at their vulnerability. He opened his mouth, hoping the right words would come, when something whizzed past him at impossibly high speed.

An arrow shot through the yellow eye of the hunter at Iliana's throat, the thing exploding into a rain of rotten meat. At the same moment, a strange-looking silver-winged thing slammed into the hunter holding the knife to Iliana's heart. The hunter reeled back for a long, frozen moment of astonishment, then melted more slowly, like butter in hot sun, words of denial burbling out of its softening jaws, until there was nothing left to make a sound.

Seven down. One hopefully still immobilized and no more than three to go.

Han launched himself at Iliana, helping her extract herself from the piles of goo, both of them trying to reassure the other. Gabriel spun, sword ready to take on the rest—and found himself facing a grinning Jadren and an equally pleased

Alise. "The other hunters?" he asked.

"All melted, Lord Phel." Jadren gave him a faux salute. "Except the one you froze. We saved it, since it seems harmless, in case you wanted it for something."

Did he? Perhaps so. "Thanks for the save," he told them both.

"I had air elementals carry one of Iliana's spent arrows," Alise informed him with a crow of delight. "Clever, huh?"

"Very clever," Gabriel acknowledged with a bow. "And timely. What was the metal flying thing?"

"I gave a dagger wings," Jadren said, going over to pluck it out of the hunter goo. Holding it gingerly, he shook clumps of dripping flesh and a chunk of bone off it, grimacing in disgust, before holding it up for Gabriel to see. "Clumsy and not as aerodynamic as I'd like, but it worked."

"Also clever," Gabriel said with a smile for Jadren's pride. The El-Adrel wizard looked happier than Gabriel had ever seen him.

"You inspired us," Alise confided, Jadren nodding in agreement. "Innovation on the fly!"

"Literally," Jadren added, and they both snickered.

Both of them giddy from their first real battle, Gabriel realized.

"I'm taking Iliana to Asa." Han stepped up beside Gabriel, Iliana in his arms. He'd improvised a bandage around her throat, but the blood bloomed on the cloth in bright red blossoms. She smiled bravely, but her complexion had the unhealthy green tinge of someone about to faint.

"Of course," Gabriel replied, chagrined that they'd been

making light of a bad situation that had nearly gone sideways in a terrible way. "Do you need help?"

"I can take care of her," Han snapped, then winced, as if regretting his tone. "Thank you, all, for risking your lives for us."

Gabriel bowed deeply to them. "House Phel stands together."

An odd look crossed Han's face, something deeply emotional, but he composed himself and nodded gravely to Gabriel. "Yes, we do, Lord Phel. Yes, we do."

Han carried Iliana down the lane between the spring blossoming trees, and Gabriel, Jadren, and Alise watched them go. "They're so sweet," Jadren commented.

"And hapless," Alise said in a rueful tone of agreement.

"Like the ill-fated lovers in a novel who are forever placing themselves in jeopardy for each other," Jadren added, nodding.

Alise gave him an askance look. "You read those novels?"

He glared. "There's not a lot to do at House El-Adrel, and the winters are long. We're not in the social whirl like the pretty princesses at House Elal."

"Why didn't you attend Convocation Academy, then?" she retorted, clearly stung.

Jadren stiffened. "I have work to do. Call me when it's time to go on our suicidal quest," he said to Gabriel, and stomped off, taking his winged dagger with him.

With a mental sigh, Gabriel noted that the wizard's sword and machete hung off his belt, still coated in gore.

"Sorry," Alise said. "I didn't realize it was such a sore point." Her black eyes sparkled with mischief, reminding

Gabriel of Nic at her most wicked. "Now I *really* want to know what his story is."

"Good luck getting it out of him," Gabriel said, walking toward the immobilized hunter.

"Sergio Sammael dropped an interesting tidbit when they were trading insults," Alise said, accompanying him. "Something about Lady El-Adrel dangling the promise of a familiar over Jadren's head to enforce his compliance."

"Hmm," Gabriel grunted in acknowledgment. Had it been the same with denying Jadren a Convocation education and somehow suppressing his MP scores? He hadn't expected to feel sorry for the El-Adrel wizard, but somewhere along the way, the prickly man had become something of a friend. Go figure. In that light, he added, "But maybe don't drive him out of his mind about it until after we've recovered Nic?"

"Oh, sure," Alise answered, nonchalantly enough to raise Gabriel's suspicions. But he didn't pursue it.

He faced the hunter, frozen in place but still snarling and gnashing its long jaws. Gabriel recalled that helpless feeling well—his limbs immobilized, though the rest of him worked well enough.

"Who sent you to recover these familiars?" he demanded of the creature.

It glared at him in impotent fury, clamping its jaws shut.

"Don't we know it was the Convocation?" Alise asked with some surprise.

"They arrived with House Sammael," Gabriel replied. "So I want to be sure. Answer my question, hunter."

"I do not ansssswer to you, Lord Phel."

Gabriel considered trying to bribe it, but that hadn't worked on the others. Maybe torture, though the things seemed impervious to pain, nor did they appear to fear for their lives. He should probably just melt it like its unfortunate cohort and have done.

"Shall I try compulsion on it?" Alise asked. "I have some ability, though I'm naturally not supposed to use that magic outside of school without House Hanneil's permission."

"Go ahead," Gabriel said with relief and more than a little curiosity. He'd tried some compulsion, without much success, and was interested to see how Alise performed it. "The Convocation can take it up with me."

Sadly, there wasn't much to see. He sensed her magic, and the hunter squirmed, but nothing he could readily emulate.

"Who sent you to recover these familiars?" Gabriel repeated as the thing fought the compulsion.

"We come on Convocation bussinesss," it snarled.

Which didn't answer the question. "At what person's behest, specifically?" he pressed.

The thing panted, fighting the spell that held it. "Sabrina Sammael," it finally confessed, eliciting a gasp from Alise.

Not a surprise to Gabriel, however. "Are you in the direct employ of House Sammael?"

"Yesss," it hissed unhappily.

"Does Convocation Center know?" Alise asked, voice faint with shock.

"We are on loan, until the problem of House Phel is settled," the hunter admitted wearily.

"Did Sergio Sammael intend to deliver Lady Phel to Convocation Center?" Gabriel asked on a hunch.

"No," the hunter replied. "They took her to House Sammael."

~ 18 ~

THE NEXT TIME Sergio Sammael came to visit, Nic was prepared to do battle: mentally and physically. To give herself more confidence, she'd used her time to improvise a more modest outfit from her bedsheets, thanking her past self for all those long hours spent doing needlework. Not that she had any sewing supplies, but she felt comfortable folding and manipulating the fabric.

She'd also selected a few implements that could be used as weapons and hidden them around the tower room. Sergio could paralyze her with pain, of course, but she could hurt him back. She didn't need magic to do that—something she'd learned from Gabriel—and Sergio was coward enough that a little damage would make him think twice the next time he tried to force her.

None of that took very long, so she spent her copious remaining time in meditation, exploring those nonphysical channels that opened when she voluntarily gave away magic and concentrating on strengthening her skills of keeping them barricaded shut. Her sanity was a small price to pay for depriving Sergio of the least drop of her magic. Petty of her, perhaps, but it also starved him of magic. She didn't have much power in this situation, but whatever leverage she could use, she intended to.

She'd come a long way since she'd believed her only power in life would come from manipulating her wizard master. If she'd learned anything from Gabriel, it was that controlling one's own life was a choice. She didn't have to accept that not being able to wield magic equated to having no power at all except through whatever wizard bonded her.

One thing she was sure of: She would never allow another wizard to bond her. Part of her hoped—perhaps irrationally, and perhaps as an early sign that her sanity was eroding—that Gabriel would wake up, somehow figure out where she was, and come to rescue her.

That was the Lyndella fantasy, however, captured by her wizard's enemies and wasting away while she awaited the rescue that came too late, for both of them. Tragic foolishness.

And Nic was no Lyndella.

If they couldn't triumph, she could at least take their enemies with her. She'd learned from poor Selly. If Nic could build up enough magic inside of her for long enough, the wizard who eventually forced their way in to tap into it would get an ugly surprise. She might never match the sheer compressed volume of years of magic going stagnant, but Nic was the most powerful familiar in the Convocation, with years of practice at cultivating magic. And Sergio was no Gabriel, nor did he have the help Gabriel had had.

With a bit of luck, if and when she broke, her magic would kill or maim Sergio at the same time. It wouldn't be an unequivocal victory, but it was better than submitting to defeat. So when Sergio unlocked her tower door, she was ready for him.

She was not, however, prepared for the sight of his companion.

"Papa?" she squeaked, her breath having gone entirely out of her. Her thoughts whirled through a gamut of relief, terror, joy, and cruel suspicion. How was Papa there, where House Sammael was holding her captive? She needed to think through the ramifications and possibilities. She couldn't think at all. Some pitiful childish part of her wanted him to be there to save her. The older, jaded adult knew that wasn't the case.

It hurt an astonishing amount.

"Kitten," Papa declared, calling her by her old pet name and opening his arms to her as if nothing between them had changed and she'd run to him for a hug. "It's so good to see you again," he said when she didn't move, prompting her. His magic sang sharp in the air, primed, invisible spirits milling palpably around him, and his black eyes glittered with expectant calculation.

No, he wasn't here as her beloved papa, no matter how he playacted at it. He was here on some mission of political conniving.

"I'm confused about why you're here, Lord Elal," she said formally.

Sergio folded his arms and raked her improvised outfit with an infuriated glare. Nic was doubly happy to have thwarted him. Having her father see her in that excuse for a negligee would've been especially humiliating. "What did I tell you, Lord Elal?" Sergio sneered. "Hopelessly recalcitrant."

"She wouldn't be if you'd bonded her already," Lord Elal snapped at the younger man. "I handed you a golden opportunity, a pearl beyond price, and what have you done with it? *Nothing.*"

"Her wizard is still alive," Sergio retorted, more than a hint of a whine in his voice. "I can't bond her while he lives."

"There's a simple solution to *that*, you idiot," Lord Elal sneered. "How difficult is it to dispatch a magicless living corpse? It's not as if he can defend himself. A toddler could take care of it."

Nic's blood ran cold, and she stared at her father, wondering how she'd ever loved him. And how she could still be taken by surprise at his duplicity. "You're talking about my husband, wizard, and the father of my child, as well as the lord of a rival house in the Convocation," she said softly, a clear warning in her tone. One which her father ignored completely.

"Phel has wizards around him," Sergio protested. "We can't simply waltz into House Phel and expect no one to fight us."

"Then take a force of your own," Lord Elal explained with exaggerated patience. "They are a motley crew of half-talents, with more commoners and familiars than wizards."

"Do you consider your daughter and heir, Alise, a half-talent?" Nic inquired, steeling herself not to flinch when her father rounded on her, wizard-black eyes blazing with fire.

"Have a care, kitten," he said with lethal quiet. "You serve a purpose, for the moment, but I won't hesitate to muzzle you as your wizard should've done. You have caused a number of problems for me, you and your delinquent sister. Do you know she wrote to me, begging me to help you?" He laughed, sounding genuinely amused. "She even offered to come home and accept whatever punishment I deemed necessary, like that was something I would ever want from that ungrateful brat."

Oh, Alise.

"Nander will be the next Lord Elal," her father continued, nodding to himself. "He shows great promise, and none of the unfortunate bad blood that seems to have infected you and your sister. Fortunately for you, kitten, you have an opportunity to redeem yourself. Once you bond with young Sergio here, you will cement our ties with House Sammael. And I'll consider forgiving you."

"I can never bond with Sammael." She held her head high. "I am Lady Phel. House Phel is mine, whether Lord Phel revives or not."

Her father laughed again, incredulity and contempt in it. "I thought I taught you better than that. It's just as well you turned out to be a familiar, as impotent in intelligence as you are in magic. House Phel will cease to exist," he explained. "Once Lord Phel is dispatched, his house status will be well and truly revoked."

"I carry the House Phel heir," Nic countered. "That parentage has been certified by the Convocation proctors."

Her father waved that consideration off with such ease that her worry increased. What would he do?

"Listen to me closely, pet," he instructed, his magic condensing around her. When she was a little girl and had committed some transgression, he'd used his tame spirits to frighten her, and now he tried the same tricks as if she weren't a grown woman. Besides that, she was an Elal herself, a trained familiar and well able to discern the spirits he tried to intimidate her with. He was miscalculating, underestimating her, and she kept the satisfaction of that to herself, waiting to use it to her advantage.

"If you want any sort of life," her father continued, speaking as if she were that child still, "then you will do as you're told. Look around you at all you can have. I'm sure you missed the wealth and comforts of a Convocation High House. You can be Lady Sammael in due course. No familiar can aspire to better than that." He held out his hands with open palms facing the sky. "Pain, misery, and insanity on one hand. Wealth, status, and the love of your family on the other. The choice is a simple one."

She pretended to consider, flicking her uncertain gaze between smug Sergio and her arrogantly preening father. "What would I have to do?"

"Submit to bonding with Sammael here, naturally," her father replied, confident in her capitulation already. "Once we've taken care of Phel, that is. And answer a few questions, make yourself useful that way."

"Questions?" made a show of looking puzzled, though she began to see where this was going. Why had House Elal—and likely others, such as Sammael?—sought the fall of House Phel generations ago? Though houses fought regularly, it was rare for one to be so decimated the family disappeared altogether. Or nearly so.

"Oh, details of House Phel. Reconnaissance. That sort of thing." Her father waved a hand, pretending to nonchalance, apparently oblivious to the fact that he'd always prided himself on gathering his own information. He thought Nic knew something he couldn't uncover on his own.

"House Phel?" she echoed, hoping she wasn't laying on the stupid-familiar routine too thick. "There's nothing much to know."

Her father shrugged a little, beaming, lapping it up. "I'm sure there isn't, but information is always useful. Maybe you know something worth all this trouble, something to redeem yourself in my eyes." He pretended to think. "I know—to begin with, you can tell me where the House Phel arcanium is."

Nic fought to keep her expression quizzical, not to allow the gleam of triumph to enter her gaze. This was it. Lord Elal was eager to know this specific thing. The pieces of the puzzle fell into place with startling clarity. Her father had engineered all of this, perhaps from the very beginning. She'd suspected before that he'd somehow induced the Fascination that made her want Gabriel, as she'd wanted no one else before him. And that he'd induced Maman to submit to his bonding her via the same method. The big question had been why. The alliance with Gabriel and House Phel had not been a jewel in House Elal's crown.

Now she knew the answer: her father wanted the House Phel arcanium.

However the plot had played out generations ago, the conspirators had succeeded in destroying the family and the house, but the arcanium had gone undetected, quietly submerged beneath the lake.

Her father must have seen the reappearance of magic in the form of Gabriel as an opportunity, a chance to obtain whatever he—or more likely, their Elal ancestors—believed the arcanium contained. Nic had certainly noted to Gabriel how the arcanium stored magic at an extraordinary level, far beyond what she knew of other arcaniums. Not all houses had them, of course, and many wizards created their own, making them look impressive from the outside. The joke in the Convocation went that the bigger the arcanium, the more substandard the wizard.

Apparently the House Phel arcanium, discreetly hidden away, was as special as she'd speculated.

Nic barely managed to conceal her excitement at this insight into her father's plans. Her best chance lay in making him believe her ignorance, in having him continue to underestimate her. Shaking her head, hoping to look a little daft, she tested the extent of his knowledge. "But there is no arcanium."

"Of course there is," her father returned impatiently, and her spirits sank. "I've read… information about it. And Jan indicated that Phel was waiting to bond you until he got you back to Meresin. We all know the only reason for him to delay was so he could access the power of his house arcanium. Clearly he needed the assist, as everyone has witnessed how he botched the eventual bonding anyway." Her father peered at her, wizard-black gaze penetrating, and she wondered what his wizard senses told him about their reciprocal bond. Whatever it was, it caused him to shake his head in apparent disgust. "One can't expect more from an uneducated rogue wizard."

Sergio snickered at that and Lord Elal cast him an irritated glance, then focused on Nic again. "Tell us where it is, and perhaps I can arrange for a treat. Something pretty to wear, perhaps."

Did her father even care that she was imprisoned here, dressed in an odd tunic of bedsheets? Clearly not, except to take advantage of the leverage that provided. She had to finally face the reality that her own father was her enemy, and act accordingly. Which meant using everything she knew about him against him. Putting on a disdainful tone, playing spoilt Elal princess, she waved off the possibility of an arcanium. "If there ever was an arcanium, Lord Phel doesn't know where it is. And I doubt he'd know how to use one—or have the wit to know what it was—if he managed to find it. I can't see that happening, as the manse is a disaster. Most of it sank long ago. The parts that are above water are dilapidated and moldering. If there was a tower, it rotted away with the last of the old family."

Her father frowned. "I have reports that the manse has been at least partially restored."

Aha! He *didn't* know everything. Careless of him to let slip his incomplete knowledge. Nic shook her head, feigning contempt and flopped herself down in a chair as if exhausted. "Phel drained me dry trying to restore that lost cause. It doesn't help that he has no idea how to use magic." She rolled her eyes, looking to both men for sympathy, grimly pleased when they nodded eagerly. So keen to believe in Gabriel's incompetence. "You're so right that it's probably that's why he botched the bonding, too. Maybe if he'd been able to use an arcanium, it would've helped."

Her father watched her closely, not entirely convinced. "Think! Are you sure you have no idea where it could be hidden? I have records that clearly indicate the presence of an arcanium. Indestructible, an arcanium constructed with the lost arts of the ancients, one like no other."

Nic looked as innocent and befuddled as she could, though that might be a hard sell. Still, her father seemed willing to believe his sharp-witted former heir had lost the mind he'd once praised when she failed to manifest with wizard abilities. "Records?" she repeated. "How would you have access to records about another house's arcanium?"

It was a really good question, given that wizards and their houses guarded the locations of and access to their arcaniums zealously. She supposed all information leaked. After all, she knew the location of the House Elal arcanium, though not how to enter it.

Her father looked smug rather than defensive. "Even after all that time under my tutelage, you still don't understand that I have ways of uncovering information. Knowledge is power, pet. And there's a reason I'm the most powerful wizard in the Convocation."

"My father would disagree," Sergio put in defensively.

Lord Elal eyed him with pity. "If Lord Sammael is so powerful, why am I in his house without his knowledge, conspiring with his son and heir to have him ousted and replaced?"

Sergio subsided, having no argument to that. But when Lord Elal turned his back, Sergio sent him a fuming glare. Nic filed that away as potentially useful. It was easy to dismiss Sergio as weak-willed and petulant. She certainly had, not without reason, but she was also surprised that Sergio had been bold enough to rebel against his father. He was sneaky, which bore remembering.

Nic's father studied her with that penetrating gaze. "I think you're lying to me, pet."

"What reason would I have to lie?" She managed to sound resigned and weary at once—not a stretch at all. Waving her hand at the round, windowless room, she continued. "I'm a prisoner here, dependent on you and Sammael for my very life. My husband and wizard will be dead soon, his house dissolved. I have nothing and am no one. I'm a realist, as you taught me to be, Papa." The taste of the affectionate moniker was like bile in her mouth. "I'm well aware of who holds my leash now."

Her father smiled, pleased with her capitulation, but not entirely convinced. "Forgive me if I don't entirely believe you, kitten." He glanced at Sergio. "Fetch Lady Elal."

ASA FOLDED HIS arms, looking more stubborn than usual. "There is no way that Iliana can accompany you on this quest. Not without a few days to recover."

Gabriel bit back his frustration. "Nic might not *have* a few days."

"We don't know that one way or the other," Asa countered. "What I *do* know is that, without my familiar, I am not able to heal injuries as severe as Iliana sustained. I was able to cleanse the wounds of infection and initiate healing, but her body will have to do the rest." He sagged a little, looking gray. "I only have so much innate magic, Lord Phel. Healing Wizard Jadren earlier set me back. That's on top of an intense sequence of days of healing emergencies, not to mention the chronic treatment of Selly. Without my familiar, I'm extremely limited. If you insist on leaving today, Lord Phel, you leave without Iliana."

"The entire point of recalling Iliana and Han was so that they could go with me," Gabriel argued.

"A questionable plan to begin with, and one that went awry." Asa sighed and unfolded his arms, holding up his hands in surrender. "Look, Lord Phel—you contracted me knowing that I wouldn't always cede to you and tell you what you wanted to hear. I'm not saying this to thwart you. Iliana is simply in no shape to do this."

Gabriel swallowed a growl that wanted to be a howl of rage. Beyond Asa, Iliana lay in one of the infirmary beds, looking small and fragile, her throat freshly bandaged. Han sat at her bedside, holding her hand and putting on a brave face, but obviously wrecked by Iliana's injuries. Her wounds had turned out to be far worse than anyone had realized in the moment, largely due to the fortitude belied by her sweet demeanor. The hunter at her throat had torn muscles, punctured a critical blood vessel, and even perforated her wind pipe. It was daunting, in retrospect, to realize just how willing the hunters had been to sacrifice Iliana in obtaining Han for Sabrina Sammael.

Even more difficult to face was the stark reality that tearing Han away from his beloved at this juncture would be beyond cruel. If it were Nic, Gabriel wouldn't want to leave her. How could he ask Han to do so? He couldn't. Scrubbing his hands over his face, he wearily considered his options.

"Lord Phel," Asa said gently, "you could also benefit from another day of rest or two. Let Iliana recover. Give yourself time to get back up to full health, and then go to Convocation Center to argue to have Lady Phel returned to you. She is in good hands there. They're not going to harm a familiar of her power, especially not when she's carrying a child that will possibly exceed you both in ability."

Gabriel dropped his hands and stared at Asa, realizing he'd forgotten to relate what they'd discovered. "Nic isn't at Convocation Center. She's been taken to House Sammael."

Asa looked confused. "House Sammael? But why would they take her there? Sammael has no claim on Lady Phel, unless…" He trailed off in dawning realization.

"Unless they believe I'm on the brink of death and Sergio Sammael wants to be poised to bond her as soon as my death dissolves our bond," Gabriel finished. "And in the meanwhile, who knows how he's tormenting her to break her spirit and enforce her eventual submission."

"I…" Asa rubbed a hand over his scalp. "It sounds so over the top, even for a Convocation power play. Sammael took Lady Phel into custody in the Convocation's name. Keeping her prisoner at House Sammael is a declaration of war against both the house of her birth and the house of her bonding."

"War against Elal and Phel?" Jadren asked derisively from

the nearby bed. He wasn't injured. He'd simply sprawled out lazily, hands propped behind his head, as he listened to the argument. "The first has made it clear that Nic has been disowned. The second…" He raised his brows at Gabriel.

"They believe me defanged and our house status soon to be revoked. Why would they be concerned?" Gabriel reflected bitterly.

"Something else to consider," Alise, who'd been standing by quietly, inserted, "is that my father could be working with Sammael in some way." She shrugged philosophically at Asa's and Jadren's startled expressions and repeated what she'd told Gabriel.

They were all silent, contemplating the ramifications of that.

"House Elal allying with House Sammael to plunder House Phel upon your demise is something my mother would be very interested to hear about," Jadren finally said. Everyone looked at him, waiting. "What? It's not as if you all don't know I'm a spy."

"Yes," Alise drawled, "but one would expect you to be more circumspect about it."

He shrugged that off. "That sounds like a great deal of trouble, especially for someone my mother is forever lamenting lacks proper initiative."

"Do you plan to tell Lady El-Adrel of this development?" Gabriel asked. He felt he *should* ask, that he needed to know, in case House El-Adrel joined the vultures planning to feast on his house's corpse, and his own. He doubted they much cared whether he or House Phel was actually dead yet. Scavengers were just as comfortable devouring the fatally disabled.

"Well, I do have to tell her *some* things." Jadren gazed at the ceiling, then his eyes cut to them. "Else she'd use her leverage on me, and I don't want that."

"What *does* she have on you?" Alise asked.

Jadren freed his hands to waggle a finger at her. "Ah-ah-ah, baby Elal. That would be telling. So, are we leaving today or what?"

"Yes," Gabriel replied decisively. "Within the hour."

"Wait," Asa protested. "You can't mean to go to House Sammael."

"That's where Nic is. That's where I'm going," Gabriel informed the healer.

"I mean," Asa said, clearly trying to sound patient and not succeeding, "you can't simply ride up to House Sammael, ask if they're keeping your lady familiar prisoner, and politely request her return."

"Why not?" Jadren stood up, rubbing his hands together with glee. "It's either that or storm the house with our army. Oh wait, we don't have an army. Knocking on the door and asking it is."

"Will that work?" Gabriel asked the El-Adrel wizard, sorely wishing for Nic's advice.

"The Convocation runs on manners," Jadren answered. "Exquisite politeness as a veneer over savagery. I'm betting that, if you show up on their doorstep, back from the dead, they'll have to offer some excuse, like that Lady Phel had only stopped to visit a few days, and turn her over to you. Nobody really wants outright war."

GREY MAGIC

"Asa? Alise?" Gabriel asked.

Asa sighed in resignation. "I don't have better advice."

"It's as good a plan as any," Alise agreed, "given the lack of an army. And if House Elal is involved, my presence will confuse the issue." Her gaze drifted to Han, his head bowed over Iliana's hand as she slept. "Will you ask Han to come along?"

He should. Nic would chide him for being soft-hearted and taunt him into being arrogant Lord of House Phel, conscripting everyone to do as he pleased. But he wasn't that. Couldn't be that and didn't want to be. He'd recovered Nic on his own before. He would do it again. "No," he informed them. "Nor am I asking either of you. In fact, I'm going alone."

That set them all off. Alise, Jadren, Asa all began exclaiming with versions of how he couldn't do that. Finally, he cut them off, apparently retaining enough intimidation factor that they immediately clamped their mouths shut. Nic would be proud, he reflected ruefully. "I've decided. I'm putting no one else at risk. One person can do what an army cannot. I can knock on a door by myself."

"Do you even know the etiquette involved, or what a High House is like?" Jadren demanded. "Let me answer for you: No. I'm betting the only Convocation house you've ever been to is House Elal for the Betrothal Trials, and they are famous for restricting visitors to particular areas and warding them from the rest."

"It's true," Alise allowed.

"Wrong," Gabriel shot back. "I've been to House Elal twice."

343

It had sounded better in his head. And, he had to admit, at least to himself, that he had been scrupulously shepherded in and out on both occasions, kept to blandly uninteresting spaces. Even Lord Elal's study where Gabriel had been received had held little evidence of the wizard's work. Gabriel had been in a fury over Nic's absence, but now that he looked back with clearer and calmer hindsight, it seemed clear that the space had been carefully staged, more like a set for a play than an actual working space.

Jadren watched him sardonically, waiting for the inevitable admission.

"Regardless," Gabriel told him, "I'm no fool. I can figure it out on my own. I'm certainly not taking a spy and enemy of House Phel along."

Far from offended, Jadren only grinned. "El-Adrel and Sammael have been at each other's metaphorical throats for nearly a century. Why do you think my esteemed lady mother was so eager to place me next door to Sammael lands? Alise can confirm."

"Confirmed," Alise said drily. "But the argument that the enemy of my enemy is my friend doesn't hold much water."

Jadren chucked her under the chin before she could bat his hand away. "Not long term, it's true," he conceded, "but situationally? My mother would be most displeased if I missed the opportunity to spit in Sammael's face. I'm going with you, even if I have to follow behind, all spy-like." He wiggled his fingers in what was probably supposed to be a spooky look, and failed.

Alise snorted, but Gabriel saw she suppressed a smile. "I'm

coming, too. Nic is my sister, and I won't be stopped from helping her this time."

"Great." Gabriel, aware of Asa's astute gaze on him, rubbed his throbbing temples. "So we have three wizards and zero familiars. This will go swimmingly." One part of him wryly observed how quickly he'd gone from refusing to use a familiar to being certain of failure without one.

"I'm going with you," Selly said, coming into the room. She'd changed into the tough, close-fitting clothing she preferred during her tenures in the wild. In addition, she sported several silver blades Gabriel recognized as the newly enchanted ones, plus a bow and the quiver of Iliana's arrows. She had her black hair braided back and, though her face looked far too thin and pale still, her brown eyes sparkled with determination, and her magic gleamed silvery sharp with a touch of steam.

To Gabriel's surprise, it was Jadren who protested first. "*You* are not going anywhere," he informed Selly. "I didn't risk my life and sanity to pull you out of that muck you made of your magic to have you run off and get yourself killed, injured, or captured by Sammael."

"Is that in order of importance?" she retorted coolly. Gabriel hadn't at all expected such ready wit from her, and stared at her in some shock.

Jadren, however, took it in stride. "Believe me," he said, thrusting a finger at her, "you'd rather be dead than Sammael's captive."

"That's why I'm going," she returned without hesitation. "Nic has been nothing but kind to me. I would be a poor sister to her if I were to sit here with my thumb up my ass when I could help her."

An awkward silence settled, Alise actually muffling a laugh and Jadren looking infuriated. Asa regarded Selly with academic interest. "Seliah's mind has been healing rapidly," he said to Gabriel. "She's making excellent progress."

Gabriel hastily revised his mental image of his little sister. She truly wasn't the skinny-legged gamine of his memories and the vision in the mist. Selly had seemed childlike for so long that he'd missed that she truly had grown up into a woman, older than Nic, even. "Excellent enough progress for her to come along?" he asked Asa without taking his eyes off Selly. She rewarded him with a brilliant smile.

"Yes," Asa agreed grudgingly. "There's nothing wrong with Selly's health at this point. At least, nothing that diligent attention on her part won't cure in time." He gave Selly a stern glare, and she simpered at him. "And it will be good for her to spend her magic."

"I think it's a bad idea," Jadren grumbled.

Alise, black eyes alight with speculation, looked back and forth between Jadren and Selly.

"Good for me that you're not in charge, then," Selly taunted, then looked to Gabriel. "I'm ready to go."

"So am I," Han said, joining them. He surveyed the small circle. "Why so shocked? This was the deal. Iliana can't go, but I'm fine." He patted his new enchanted sword. "I'm eager to see how this beauty works on something besides hunters." His striking blue eyes chilled. "And I have a score to settle with a certain spoilt teenage wizard."

"I'm not asking you to leave Iliana," Gabriel said, shaking his head.

Han shrugged. "Then I'm volunteering. Iliana would be disappointed in me if I let you down. Besides, she's in good hands here, yes?"

"Yes," Asa answered firmly, clapping the blond man on the shoulder. "By the time you come home, I'll have her back on her feet and running to greet you."

Han smiled wistfully. "Coming home. That sounds very good to me."

~ 19 ~

MAMAN WAS HERE? Nic's heart simultaneously leapt with joy and crashed with terror at her father's words. He'd kept Maman from Nic thus far, rather than bringing her with him, as Maman would've begged to do. Therefore, this was some new twist in the game her father played with them both. Indeed, Lord Elal watched her with a smug smile dancing on his lips.

She took refuge in revealing nothing, standing in polite expectation, keeping her expression calm and serenely pleased to be seeing her mother again. Pretending that her abused heart wasn't fluttering against her ribs, uncertain whether to break or fly.

Sergio, seeming oblivious to how easily he did Lord Elal's bidding—her father had a knack for turning everyone into a servant—returned quickly with a cloaked Lady Elal, locking the tower door behind them again.

Lord Elal held out a proprietary hand. "Come here, precious." And Maman went to him immediately, without even glancing in Nic's direction first. She laid her hand in his, then turned, using her free hand to sweep her voluminous hood back.

Nic gasped, unable to contain her shock, and her father's smile widened in satisfaction at her reaction. Maman gazed at her with vacant eyes, the pupils feline, as they would be in her alternate form of a cat. And they held no human intelligence to speak of, only bright curiosity.

"Maman..." Nic whispered, her uncertain heart settling on grief, charring to ash. "What has he done to you?"

"What she did to herself," her father snapped, finally revealing the vicious anger that had driven him to such an extreme, "was betray me, her house, and you."

"Maman never would!" Nic fired back, her magic, untapped for days and days, billowing up and burning the inside of her skin. "She loves me," she added, searching Maman's face for any evidence of the mother who'd cherished Nic and taught her everything she knew about being a familiar, worlds of wisdom the Convocation Academy could never teach.

"Did you think I wouldn't discover how she helped you?" her father ground out, his carefully banked fury finally burning through his façade. "Not only was that a profound betrayal of my trust, she nearly irreparably harmed our future. She could've ruined all of my plans, and for what? A moment of caprice. If you were smart, if you'd truly absorbed what I attempted to teach you when I thought you still might amount to something, then you would hate her."

"*You* are the one I hate," Nic whispered, fisting her hands at her sides, unable to continue her pretense at idiotic obedience.

Her father smiled thinly, then lifted a hand to caress Maman's cheek, turning her head so she gazed at him. She did so with perfect obedience, but without reaction, much like one of those El-Adrel automatons. "I have you to thank, in truth, kitten," her father murmured, still stroking Maman's cheek. "If you hadn't enraged me so, I'd never have kept my precious in alternate form for so long. When I finally brought her back to human form, she was... changed. And compliant as never before. I'm writing a paper on it for the Academic Society of Wizards. It's quite the breakthrough in control of familiars. And all because of you."

Nic had difficulty mastering the illness oozing through her. All of this because she hadn't had the courage to face what Gabriel represented. Unbelievable now that she'd thought she'd wanted a Sergio. Instead she'd been so afraid of how Gabriel opened her heart, how he so easily found and slipped through the cracks in the tough hide she'd developed under her father's tutelage. Terrified of the change he represented. Change she now embraced—and would continue to fight for, even if he was parted from her forever.

"I have complete access to her magic now," Lord Elal continued, still stroking Maman's cheek in a parody of affection. Or, perhaps, in the very real affection of a madman for a prized possession. For her father was crazed, that was clear to her now. Maybe he always had been, or he'd been growing more twisted over time, but he'd tipped over some threshold and become the monster Gabriel had so feared becoming, and never could be.

"Which is why she will be useful to me here," her father said, dropping his hand and leading Maman to her. "Though I have little psychic magic myself, at least of the sort suitable to thought-seeking, precious here has significant scores in it, from the Hanneil side, you know. I've discovered, with my in-creased access to her mind and will, that I can use that magic, amplifying my abilities considerably. I hope you understand how truly important this breakthrough is. We stand on the brink of a new society. We will usher in an exciting era of bolder magic use."

Nic tried to evade them, but she hit her back against the curved stone wall.

"And you'll teach me this?" Sergio asked eagerly. "You promised that I'll have access to Nic's abilities as well as mine."

"Yes, yes," Lord Elal answered with some irritation, not bothering to look back at Sergio. "As we agreed. Though you'll have to find a way to contain her in alternate form long enough. It requires tremendous self-discipline to forgo your familiar's magic long enough for their will to entirely dissolve." He eyed Nic curiously. "Is the proctor's report accurate, that your alternate form is a monstrous bird?"

"You are the monster," she whispered, trapped, unable to look away from her mother's blank and alien gaze.

"And you are my progeny," her father answered with a gentle smile. "As such, you will be a credit to House Elal, no matter how much of your mind and will we have to break in order for you to be properly reshaped. Leave us, Sergio."

"But I—"

"Go." Her father cracked out the command, power shiver-ing through the little room. "And lock the door. I'll summon you when I'm ready."

Sergio grumbled but obeyed. Her father focused on Nic, and his wizardry hit her like a vise clamped over her skull, clumsier than any thought-seeker she'd experienced. But then, he'd never trained in these skills. Only his megalomania made him believe he could do this without training. "Tell me where the House Phel arcanium is located."

Ham-fisted or not, he did have considerable power behind the command, and Nic fought the urge to tell him everything. The best she could do was a bit of side-stepping. "Sunk," she answered.

He frowned. "Sunk where?"

"Under the water." With her obedience and truthfulness, the pressure on her skull eased. "Lost," she added, which was also true. It had been lost for ages, until she and Gabriel found it.

"That can't be," her father growled, wizard-black eyes going depthless as he exerted the thought-seeking command upon her. "How was it lost?"

"The wizards died out, the family moved away. The house sank into the marshes." It was getting easier to offer a partial truth, though she was grimly amused that she was forced to use the correct term "marshes," instead of "swamps," as she'd intended. Gabriel would be proud, and the thought made her feel like she was bleeding inside. "Why do you want it?" she asked, more hoping to lessen the pressure on her mind for a moment by distracting her father than because she believed he'd tell her.

But he looked thoughtful. "Why does anyone want anything? Power. That's the only thing that matters in this world."

"That's the only thing that matters in *your* world." With the truth compulsion still on her, she spoke aloud what she'd intended to keep to the silence of her own thoughts.

Her father laughed, black eyes glittering like knives. "In all the world," he corrected gently. "Everything else is a lie, an illusion. I'm curious, though, what you think matters. Do tell."

"Love. Freedom. Working to better the lives of others," she answered with painful honesty, hating how her father curled his lip in contempt.

"Lies and illusions," he repeated. "Don't tell me you believe you love your wizard master?"

She said nothing, able to obey that command the way he phrased it, but he plowed on, face going hard with ruthless delight.

"I arranged that," he informed her. "What you experienced as the Fascination. It's an Aratron potion crafted in secrecy and shared with only a few. You will, by the way, never speak of that to anyone." He reinforced the command with an agonizing stab of Hanneil wizardry. "I'm only telling you this for your own good. I made you feel the Fascination for Gabriel Phel, just as I made my precious feel it for me. Did you know she thought to escape me?" He shook his head, hatred briefly flaring in his eyes as he gazed at Maman. "You familiars have a distressing tendency to think of yourselves as autonomous human beings, fatally unable to resign yourselves to the bare fact that your brains are inferior. We allow you to believe you love your wizards. We deliberately incorporated that into the bonding spell, because that makes everything easier for us, but it's not real." His face lit with manic glee. "And, with my discovery, it's not necessary. Precious does everything I say now, holding nothing back, even more purely than before.

Once you are properly bonded, you will do it for Sergio, too. After you reveal where the House Phel arcanium is. Enough of these games. Tell me everything you know about the arcanium."

She screamed at the increased pain—and began babbling. She'd been kidding herself that she was dodging her father's questions, thinking she fooled him with her evasions. Now she indeed told him everything she knew. Where the arcanium was. How to get there. She described its properties for him, and he voraciously drank in every detail of the stored power there, his magic glittering with excitement. He only sobered when she explained the access spell.

"It has to be water and moon magic?" he demanded, frowning.

"Yes."

"Applied in what way?"

"I don't know," she answered, the truth a relief. "I'm only a familiar."

No one would blame her for savoring how he ground his teeth in frustration. "Apparently we'd best not assassinate Lord Phel just yet," he bit out, and Nic's battered heart leapt with hope. Her father studied her thoughtfully. "Fortunately, I have the leverage I need to make him do my bidding. Does he believe he cares for you?"

"Yes," Nic answered reluctantly.

"Soft-headed, the pair of you," he grunted. "And you carry his heir, which is also useful. It seems I must see to it that he wakes up. Fortunately, I'm in possession of the perfect bait. You wait here," he told Nic, smiling at his joke. "I suggest you play nice with Sergio, as he will be your eventual master. If you want to have influence over your wizard master, then you will find sweetness gets you much farther than sarcastic words and dour moods."

He led Maman away—who never once gave any sign she knew her daughter—leaving Nic reeling with the realization that her mother's favorite advice had always come from her father's mouth.

VALE STRETCHED HIS legs in a ground-eating gallop, seeming to know that they raced on a mission to rescue Nic, one of the gelding's favorite people. It was good to be moving. Or at least to feel some sort of progress, rather than the endless waiting.

It hadn't helped that they'd taken a supply boat down the Dubglass River, which meant standing still, even though Gabriel knew in his head that they were making progress. It was the fastest and most anonymous way into Sammael lands. They'd disembarked well before Port Carica, taking the horses on back roads through the forested foothills of Sammael, the ground gradually rising as they made their way to the craggy peaks where House Sammael sat, perched like a vulture surveying the valley for the weak.

Of all of them, ironically enough, Selly was holding up the best. Her mental fragility didn't translate to a lack of physical endurance. In fact, her long tenures in the wilds had toughened her dramatically. That and extended time with intensive healing from Asa had her looking bright-eyed and brimming with vitality.

In contrast, Gabriel felt like shit, though he was careful not to let on to his companions. Jadren and Han were unlikely to interrogate him, as both of them were unused to traveling by horseback, and so were sore, exhausted, and cranky about it. Alise didn't complain, but she was also concentrating fiercely on using spirits to disguise evidence of their progress and intentions, as well as to guard against any spies that might be sent against them. They might be planning to knock on the front door, but they didn't want to give Sammael, or Elal, forewarning or time to set traps for them.

Because Alise's magic was critical to their approaching House Sammael undetected, only she was accessing Selly's and Han's magic. Gabriel's was slowly returning on its own, but— even though he'd topped off in the arcanium before they left— he was aware of his weakened state still. He wanted to spare the familiars as much as possible until the time came when they'd need everything they had.

They also had to stop more frequently than he would have on his own, for people to refresh themselves and for their horses to rest. Gabriel missed when it had been just him and Vale, when they'd chased after Nic with single-minded intensity.

"This is brutal," Jadren commented, stretching his body and grimacing, "how you backwoods types live. We invented carriages for a reason, you know."

"Poor little soft and spoilt wizard," Selly commented, digging some oranges out of her saddlebags and passing them around.

Jadren scowled at her but took one. "When you've bruised your balls against a saddle for a couple of days, you can talk to me about being soft and spoilt."

She smiled mirthlessly. "Like worm-ridden fruit, are they?"

Han snickered, and Jadren sputtered in outrage a moment before opening his mouth to retort.

"Enough," Gabriel inserted sharply. He already begrudged every rest they took, feeling Nic's time ticking away. "We're supposed to be a team."

Jadren muttered something darkly, but Gabriel let it go. "Alise, how are you holding up?"

The young wizard had collapsed against a tree trunk, legs splayed, holding an orange without seeming to register she did. Han went to her, setting the orange aside and taking her hands. "Alise, sweetheart," he said gently. "You need to take some magic."

"I don't want to drain you," she replied, tugging her hands away. "Lord Phel will need you soon."

"It won't do us any good to spare Han and Selly only to have your father catch us out here in the woods," Gabriel said, not for the first time. He'd tried using a shield of reflective moon magic, but it was difficult to cover the entire group, particularly when they were moving. They'd gone back to having Alise combat any questing spirits, of which there were plenty. She was sure either Lord Elal himself was in the vicinity—which seemed like an unlikely coincidence to them all—or one of his protégés.

Though, why would Lord Elal have sent one of his best wizard minions to Sammael? Gabriel couldn't shake the creeping certainty that Elal was behind all of this, just as his Elal ancestors had been behind the fall of House Phel.

"Take the magic, Alise," he ordered, just in case he hadn't been clear. She frowned but complied.

"At least we have plenty of water," Jadren noted, passing around the ever-replenishing flask.

"Too bad we only have my brother's prototype," Selly replied, taking another jab at the El-Adrel wizard. "It would be good to have more, in case we get separated."

"I've been busy," Jadren snarled, defending himself. "And I didn't have access to Lord Phel's half of the magic for the better part of a week, if you'll recall."

Gabriel walked down the road to get out of earshot, needing some peace and quiet to brood. The track they followed should lead to House Sammael via a back route, according to Alise's spies, but it was overgrown with disuse, meandering through the countryside and seeming to be going nowhere. Gabriel chafed at the slow progress, his thoughts turning down dark, twisted corridors of vengeance should they arrive too late to save Nic. Whatever plan they were trying to bend her to, she wouldn't cooperate. He knew her that well. She'd break first, and that was what worried him most.

Realizing that he was stalking furiously along, he made himself slow and take a few deep breaths, grounding himself again by studying the huge old trees of the forest. They'd thinned in this area, opening onto a barren meadow. Real spring had not yet made it this far north, though the land had freed itself from winter. Across the meadow, on a crag above, rose an unsettling edifice that could only be House Sammael.

Built of rock as black as the volcanic stuff of the surrounding peaks, the house seemed to be mostly a series of towers, sharp spikes spearing the overcast skies. Nic had commented sardonically about the Sammael aesthetic, and how their affinity for causing pain was mirrored by their ancestral home. Gabriel smiled to himself, appreciating her insight, missing her with a crazed intensity. His magic kept reaching for her of its own accord, snarled and miserable when it failed to connect.

Was she up in one of those towers? If so, why couldn't he feel her?

"Not very welcoming, is it?" Jadren asked, walking up behind him. Before Gabriel could growl that he'd walked this way to be alone, Jadren pressed the water flask into Gabriel's hand. "Selly says you need to hydrate." Then he gazed up at the forbidding citadel. "Downright menacing, that castle. Makes House El-Adrel look like a pretty beachside cottage by comparison."

"You've never been here?" Gabriel had assumed the other wizard had. It seemed like the head families of the High Houses had a custom of visiting each other, and he was sure Jadren had implied as much.

Jadren squinted at the towers. "Not me. I never got out much. Not until Mother darling brought me to Meresin."

"Explains your poor social skills."

"You have no idea," Jadren agreed.

"You ever going to tell us why you didn't attend Convocation Academy?"

"Why didn't you?"

"I didn't know any better," Gabriel replied equably.

"Ignorance is bliss, they say." Jadren took back the flask and took a healthy swallow, grunting in displeasure. "We need to make one of these with whiskey."

"I have water magic, not whiskey magic."

"We'd have to brew the whiskey, but if you could figure out the replenishing part, we'd be rich. Think of what we could charge for it!" Jadren smacked his lips in anticipation.

"Nic wants to grow grapes," Gabriel offered, not sure why he was mentioning it, except that it made him feel closer to her to talk about her. "To make wine."

"Wine flasks would be great, too." Jadren nodded sagely. "We'll keep the entire Convocation too drunk to realize how miserable they are."

Gabriel laughed, realizing as he did that it wasn't funny. Sobering, he turned back. The horses should be rested enough. Jadren walked alongside him.

"So what's your plan for approaching House Sammael if you've never been there?" he asked.

"*My* plan?" Jadren looked around as if one might appear.

Gabriel set his teeth, so as not to snap in sheer frustration. "Yes. Remember how you argued to come along because you know how to approach a High House and I don't?"

"Ohhh... *that* plan." Jadren nodded thoughtfully.

Gabriel waited pointedly. The rest of the group, spotting their approach, got up and prepared to ride on. "And?" he prompted Jadren.

"I'm sure something will come to me."

Wonderful. His mood blacker than ever, Gabriel checked Vale's tack. Vale twitched an ear, swinging his head to gaze at him in mild astonishment when Gabriel yanked too hard on the cinch. Apologizing to the steed, he went to check on Salve, too. He'd brought Nic's mare along in a burst of determined optimism, so she'd be able to ride home. That was the fantasy he clung to: that Nic would be fine, able to ride, and would return to House Phel beside him.

I have zero sympathy for fools. And idealists, Nic whispered in his mind.

Terribly afraid he was being both in this venture, and that these fatal flaws would spell Nic's doom, he leaned his forehead against Salve's pale hide, stroking her silky shoulder. The mare ruffled his hair with hay-scented breath, and for no good reason, that made him miss Nic more than ever.

"Hey," Jadren said quietly, for once entirely serious, no joking to him. "We'll get her back."

Gabriel closed his eyes, though the image of that forbidding, unassailable castle had seared itself into his brain. "How do you know?"

"We have to. Therefore we will."

Gabriel mulled that as they rode on, all of Nic's advice about intention filtering through his mind. *I have to,* he repeated to himself. *Therefore, I will.*

THERE WEREN'T MANY roads to House Sammael. So much so that it wasn't possible to approach the place undetected. At some point, someone would inevitably see them, if they hadn't been spotted already. That was something the High House shared with House Elal. Gabriel mused grimly over the contrast of those with House Phel. Even in its previous heyday, the grand manse in Meresin had never been designed as a fortress as these were. The entrée to both the Sammael and Elal family seats were explicitly made to be difficult for the uninvited—and no doubt treacherous for anyone with ill intentions.

"Is House El-Adrel like this?" he asked Jadren, who rode beside him. "Built like they expect an invading army to attack at any moment," he explained when Jadren raised an inquiring brow.

"Of course," Jadren answered, as if it were self-evident.

"So is House Hanneil," Han supplied from behind them. "And every other High House I've been to—along with a significant number of lower-tier houses hoping to elevate themselves."

"The history of the Convocation is a bloody and violent one, especially among the houses jockeying to become High Houses," Jadren added. "No one wins by underestimating their enemies. House Phel is unusual in that it's so easily approached."

Perhaps that explained why the Phel family was defeated back in the day. Gabriel rarely felt empathy for his unknown ancestors, but now it seemed perhaps they may have been what Nic accused him of being: too soft and concerned with all the wrong things. Gazing up at the malevolent architecture of House Sammael as it loomed over them, taking up most of the sky from this perspective, he recognized with visceral clarity how unlike the bulk of the Convocation he truly was.

But that didn't make him a victim. *They have no idea how dangerous you are,* Nic's voice echoed in his head. Well, soon they *would* know.

"Why are we simply riding up to the front doors again?" Gabriel asked, worry and suspicion tightening in his gut.

"The High Houses might be forever at each other's throats, but we do it politely," Jadren answered with an easy grin.

Abruptly, Gabriel turned Vale around, Salve whickering on her lead as she kicked into a trot to follow. The rest of his entourage scrambled out of his way to allow them through. Selly immediately turned her steed to follow along.

"Where are you going?" Alise demanded, dazed by the sudden shift. "We know Nic is up in one of those towers!" She'd been able to determine that much before the spirit spy she'd sent was ripped from her control by high Elal magic.

"We're walking into a trap," Gabriel threw over his shoulder, urging Vale and Salve into a faster pace. "No way am I just riding up to Sammael's front door and asking politely that they give my wife back."

"But they have to!" Jadren shouted after him. "She belongs to you by Convocation law. All you have to do is demonstrate that you're alive and that you've properly bonded her."

Gabriel brought Vale up short, wheeling him around again, poor, confused Salve following. The gelding, having caught his mood, pranced and pawed his displeasure. Selly drew her steed up, watching over her shoulder and waiting. "You just said that the history of the Convocation is a bloody and violent one," Gabriel nearly shouted at Jadren, "and that no one wins by underestimating their enemies. Do you really believe they're going to start playing by the rules with me now? Or is that your role in this little venture—to convince me to stumble blindly into this trap they've set for me?"

Jadren reddened, jaw tight. "I'm trying to give you the best advice I can."

"From a self-confessed spy," Gabriel snarled. He shouldn't have been lulled into thinking that Jadren was—what?—some sort of friend.

Face hardening, Jadren nudged his own steed forward. Like most everything the house-poor wizard possessed, the horse was borrowed from House Phel. The gelding danced sideways, unhappy, and Jadren had difficulty regaining control. "House El-Adrel has nothing to do with this... *collaboration* between Elal and Sammael. I'm a spy in your house entirely to discover these things."

"And report back," Gabriel retorted, his rage growing.

"Yes, obviously—which does not mean I'm working to harm House Phel." He laughed bitterly. "I'd be sabotaging my one opportunity to escape my mother's grip. Why would I do that?"

"To ingratiate yourself with your mother." Gabriel waited, but Jadren had no quick reply to that. He nodded, confirming his guess. "Tell me, Wizard Jadren, if there's no collaboration between Elal and El-Adrel, why did Nic see Elal-tamed spirits animating your automatons?"

Alise caught her breath, head whipping around to Jadren. "Is that true?"

"No!" Jadren denied the accusation immediately, but his brows drew together.

It was Alise's turn to nudge her horse forward, crowding Jadren. "Would you know?" she demanded coolly. "Your MP scorecard is a mystery, but I don't sense any magic in you suitable for communicating with or manipulating the spirit world."

Jadren glared at her—then relented as he thought through her words. "No," he admitted in a softer tone. "I wouldn't know. Are you sure of this?" he demanded of Gabriel.

"Nic was sure." And that was all Gabriel needed to know.

Alise craned her head up at the towering edifice. "If Elal is working with both Sammael and El-Adrel…" She leveled her wizard-black gaze on Jadren, fury in it as she spoke to Gabriel. "You're right. This is a trap."

"Not of my doing," Jadren ground out.

"We have no reason to trust you," Selly put in coolly. "In fact, we have every reason not to."

Jadren clenched his jaw, a muscle there bulging as he met Selly's accusing eyes. "I helped save your life, at great risk to my own health and sanity."

"The perfect subterfuge to gain trust," she countered.

Han, who'd been listening in stoic silence, spoke up then. "It does look damning, Wizard El-Adrel."

Concentrating on his restive mount—and likely attempting to compose himself—Jadren finally offered a response. "I don't see how I can prove a negative. I signed your bloody NDA, your bizarre contract, but I'll be seen as a person of suspicion until I commit a crime against the house."

"Yes, well, we've seen how well that NDA worked to control Laryn," Gabriel bit out.

"Only because you weren't awake to enforce it," Jadren countered. "You can take retribution against me at any time, should I fail to observe its strictures, and the contract's. You have the power."

"By the time I discover you've betrayed me, it might be too late," Gabriel noted.

Jadren opened his mouth. Closed it. Then shrugged. "Clearly only my death without incident will absolve me."

"I can live with that," Selly observed. When Gabriel glanced at her in question, startled by Selly's cold assessment, she shrugged. "I haven't been clear-headed for long, but it occurs to me that supposedly stepping in to heroically save your sister is the perfect way for Wizard Jadren to ingratiate himself in your confidence. It should be noted that he waited until you were incapacitated before he acted. If the plan had been to see you comatose or dead, as has turned out to be quite convenient for our enemies, it worked perfectly."

Gabriel couldn't help considering all the incidents where Jadren was nearby when trouble erupted. By the look on the El-Adrel wizard's face, the same had occurred to him. "I won't pass judgment on Wizard Jadren in the absence of firm evidence. I am, however, not taking suggestions from you," he added to Jadren. "Therefore, we're abandoning this approach." Wheeling Vale around, he urged him back the way they'd come.

"But we can't desert Nic!" Alise nearly wailed in despair.

Gabriel swallowed the urge to bite her head off for suggesting he might. "We're not abandoning her. We're simply not doing this the Convocation-approved way. I've succeeded in the past because I'm not of the Convocation. We're doing this my way." He flicked a glance at the still-fuming Jadren. "A way our enemies won't expect, in the eventuality that they have been forewarned."

"I tell you, I didn't—"

Gabriel cut Jadren off with a sharp chop of his hand, then raised it and pointed for the group to follow. As if obeying the command, his magic responded, rising up with the power he'd been familiar with before.

Good. For what he had in mind, he'd need it.

~ 20 ~

THEY RETURNED TO the overlook where Gabriel had first seen House Sammael. Everyone but Selly watched Gabriel askance as they unsaddled the horses and made themselves comfortable, staying within the cover of the ancient forest as he'd ordered. No one was outright questioning him, but they clearly found his behavior odd. For his part, it took no effort to sink into the role of brooding and arrogant Lord Phel. The need to get to Nic clawed like a wild beast inside him, his magic resisting that they'd gone away from her. He wouldn't be able to fake calm.

That resistance in his magic at least confirmed the hunter's information and his own instincts: Nic *was* in House Sammael. Now to extract her.

"I know you don't want to hear my advice, but—" Jadren began.

"But nothing," Gabriel interrupted, removing Vale's saddle. "I *don't* want to hear it."

Jadren palpably fumed, his indefinable magic curling in frustration. "You can't *do* anything from here, Gabriel," he nearly shouted, obviously determined to be heard. "Delaying like this only gives them more time to prepare and more time to hurt her."

"What do you care?" Gabriel snarled.

"I care, all right?" Jadren threw up his hands in the air. "I know you don't trust me, and I have no good argument for why you should, but you and Lady Phel are about the only decent people I've ever met—though you can be a real asshole—and I don't want to see you suffer."

Gabriel wanted to believe him—his too-soft heart at play, no doubt. "What about your mother?"

"What about her?" Jadren retorted. "I don't see Nic and Alise giving first loyalty to their father. My mother isn't like yours. You're fortunate to have the charming Daisy as your mother. Be happy, but maybe leave some room to believe that not everyone's family is like yours."

Gabriel finished brushing the sweaty hide under Vale's saddle pad, the gelding blowing out contented whuffles. "Make your point," he finally conceded.

Jadren paused, clearly taken aback by Gabriel's capitulation when he'd been ready to go another round. "I don't understand what you think you can do from this distance. You're powerful, no doubt of that, but even with Han and Selly feeding you magic, you're no Sylus destroying his enemies like a raging storm. You can't stand here and raze House Sammael."

"I don't plan to."

"Never mind that it's illegal, since Sammael had a legitimate warrant and likely dispensation to take Lady Phel there instead of Convocation Center," Jadren continued, undaunted, "there's no way to destroy the house and the people in it without harming her."

"I don't plan to," Gabriel repeated, more slowly, moving to groom Salve.

"And nobody, not even you, can perform a feat like that from this distance!" Jadren finished. "If anyone could, wizards would've been long-distance attacking each other's houses for centuries, and there would be no Convocation. Why do you think the houses are so far apart?"

"Good thing I don't plan to do that, then," Gabriel replied, amused, despite everything. Jadren was only confirming that his plan was a good one. No one would expect it.

This time Jadren seemed to hear him, muttering something unintelligible to himself. "Then what *do* you plan to do?"

Gabriel allowed himself a wicked smile. "Just watch."

NIC PACED THE round tower room, which was crazy-making, but better than sitting still and repeatedly poking at herself mentally in a futile effort to determine if her sanity was eroding yet. She'd gone longer than this before without having her magic tapped, so there really shouldn't be any corrosive effect yet. Maybe she was feeling the pressure of her magic so much because she'd been using it with Gabriel more than ever before in her life. More likely, she only thought it was building to boiling due to the galling combination of utter boredom and low-level terror.

She had way too much time to think about it. Days, though she wasn't sure how many. And way too little to do with her energy.

Except pace and fret.

On the upside, smarmy Sergio hadn't been back to pester her. Neither had her father. The downside of them leaving her alone was that she worried about what they were up to. Were they laying a trap for Gabriel, if he was even awake? Had they gone to House Phel in force and even now everyone there was dead? Had her father used the information she'd given him to take over the arcanium?

Pausing in her pacing, she slammed the meat of her fists against the stone wall, growling her frustration. Never had she felt so impotent to affect her fate, to save the people who meant everything to her. Though she knew she only harmed herself, she beat on the wall, venting her despair in incoherent half screams, stopping short of banging her head against it because that would really hurt.

Giving up on her tantrum, she slid down the wall, giving in to tears. She'd been good about not letting herself cry—mostly because if her father or Sergio did suddenly turn up, she didn't want them to see the evidence that they were making progress on breaking her. If the untapped magic didn't make her crazy, the boredom, isolation, and despair would.

But for the regularly delivered, bland-beyond-description meals, she'd worry that they'd left her there to die. "They won't do that, though, will they?" she muttered to the baby, the silent life inside her. At least then she could pretend she wasn't talking to herself. "Oh nooo. We're much too valuable.

We've always been kept in a cage by them. This one is just far more tangible." Giving in, she banged her head back against the wall. "Ow."

Bashing her head against stone walls was as futile, and painful, as she'd known without trying. Gabriel was the one who tried anyway.

Scrubbing the tears away, she tried to think—for the millionth time—of a way out of this predicament. Maybe it wasn't too late to save Gabriel and everyone in House Phel. If she could just warn them, then maybe… This was getting her nowhere. Instead, she let herself dwell in some memories of Gabriel. He'd been the first person in her life who hadn't wanted to cage her, intangibly or otherwise. He was the best thing that ever happened to her, and keeping their child alive was the only reason she wasn't considering suicide to escape the terrible fate that awaited her. Maybe after the baby was born… If she could keep a small corner of her will, she could find a way to finally escape her cage.

Firmly setting aside the invidious temptation of that last resort, sitting crumpled and listless against the unyielding wall, she let herself sink into happy memories. Gabriel's black eyes, filled with humor and warm affection. His hair, like moonlight, save for the single streak that matched his dark eyes. His magic curling around her, silvery cool, moon bright, a balm for all the aching empty pits inside her. She imagined she could sense him, his loving presence, the sensual caress of his hands, the firm embrace, his voice promising to protect her always. Her own magic leapt to him eagerly, flowing in a rush like an undammed river, churning when it met the wall of her channels.

I love you, Nic, he whispered in her mind.

She caught her breath on a sob. "I love you, Gabriel. Always."

Will you share your magic with me?

"Take. Have." She was weeping freely as she repeated the refrain, remembering how she'd first tantalized him with it, and how it had become a declaration of deepest love. She would give him everything of herself, if only he would live. She almost believed she could feel his magic strengthening around her, silver chains of moonlight under her skin, the refreshingly cool water that formed his silent core, and she reached for him in longing, pushing her magic toward him.

More, please. Just like that.

Letting out a watery laugh, because it felt so good to imagine that rapport with him again, she opened all those channels she'd been working so hard to keep closed. And it felt like unclenching a muscle grown tight with strain. The floodgates opened, and she poured her magic and love into Gabriel, giving him every last fiery bit of herself, imagining sending him a shower of bloodred rose petals.

He drank her in, his magic flowing into and around her, bracing and enveloping her in a bubble of fiercely protective love. She had the sudden urge to lie down and cover her head. Probably she had lost her mind, but this was so much better than sanity. So she allowed herself to sag into the hard cradle of wall and floor, curving her body into it, pressing her face into her hands so that all the world faded away and nothing remained but the sacred flow of her magic and his, freely exchanged in purest love.

So comforting was this imaginary embrace, that she didn't even startle when the roof came off.

MEDITATION WASN'T GABRIEL'S strong suit, so though he started out in a seated pose, trying to ignore the outside world, he ended up standing just inside the verge where the smaller saplings met the open meadow, House Sammael towering above in all its malevolent grandeur. With Selly's hand clasped in his, coolly fresh as water from hidden spring, huge and bright as a full moon just touching the horizon, he reached for one of those towers, seeking the bloom of rosy fire that was his beloved.

Alise stood nearby, Han behind her with his hands on her shoulders, ready to defend them against attack. And Jadren flanked their other side, sword in one hand and machete in the other, as he shifted from foot to foot restlessly. "Even if you can reach her, you can't access her magic without touching her," he argued, not for the first time, either. Another reason quiet meditation hadn't been an option.

Gabriel ignored the argument—not for the first time—and extended his senses toward Nic. She was there, hot and bright as midsummer sunshine, bursting with magic, frustration, and despair. *Oh, Nic...*

His heart bleeding for her, he sent all his love, wanting to wrap her up in it. She responded to him ardently, as she always did, her magic and love full of scarlet passion. He imagined asking her to share her magic, and she laughed that he asked. *Take. Have.*

It poured into him like a draught of the most potent wine conceivable. If wine could be made from roses, it would taste and feel like this. Gloriously inebriating, deeply nurturing. Beside him, Selly gasped.

"What?" Jadren demanded. "What's happening?"

"Shh!" Alise hushed him sharply.

Gabriel laughed, a breath of air, giddy with the flush of Nic's magic. She was there. Alive and well, sensually overpowering. He groaned his pleasure, the perfection of the exchange, feeling as if he'd sunk into the hot embrace of her body, shuddering with need only she could satiate. "Just like that," he murmured.

Hoping she understood, he urged her to take cover. Then, taking the bountiful magic she'd supplied, he pulled moonlight into hooks, digging them into the eaves of the slate roof capping the tower. Then pulled.

"Dark arts take me!" Jadren yelped as the roof spun up, then crashed into the crevasse below.

To be fair, all the others, even Selly, who'd felt him do it, exclaimed in astonishment. Gabriel smiled in grim satisfaction, tightening his hold on Nic, reassuring himself she was whole and well.

"That's all well and good," Jadren declared, sounding as if it were anything but—though a faintness to his voice showed he was impressed by the feat. "Now what? Are we going to fly over there and haul her out?"

"No," Gabriel answered, finding the silver threads that wove back and forth between them. "She's going to fly out."

NIC GAZED IN bewilderment at the open sky above, gray clouds scudding in a high wind. Apparently her insanity had progressed further than she'd guessed—though, did insane people know they were crazy?—leading her into illusions of freedom along with the wish-fulfillment of feeling Gabriel's magic intertwined with hers. Getting to her feet, she nevertheless gulped great lungfuls of fresh air, the chill bracing after the cloistered air of the tower.

For an illusion created by her own longings, it was surprisingly realistic. It even felt like her blood brightened, her system energized by the sight of a world beyond her dismal prison. Silvery moon magic sang along her nerves, and cool water coursed through her bloodstream, Gabriel's essence running along her skin with sensual caresses. As in the arcanium, the silver threads he'd embedded in her with erotic precision glowed just beneath her skin, tightening in a web that—

She barely managed a gasp of astonishment before she morphed into alternate form. The room suddenly looked much smaller, the bland curving walls taking on strange new dimensions. And the sky… Oh, the sky called to her.

Fly. Fly to me, my heart.

Gabriel was here. No one else could have pushed her into alternate form. Unless this was all a dream.

Well, if so, then she was going to fly in her dreams. They would give her the escape she craved. Though she'd never actually flown, a dream would be a wonderful place to try it out. She spread her wings, the sensitive feather tips brushing the walls on either side, and pumped down.

And crow-hopped a minute bit into the air before landing with a thud.

Dreams were *not* supposed to be this realistic. Maybe it was simply another depressing nightmare.

Fly. I know you can.

You are not real, she crossly informed the sense of Gabriel. Hmm. Maybe they were both dead, and they were struggling through some sort of purgatory of the afterlife. Like an old tale, where the lovers struggled to find each other. As with all those tales, it seemed, living it wasn't nearly so swooningly romantic. It was just a miserable slog.

Her keen hearing picked up the sound of boots on the tower stairs, soldiers calling to each other in excited tones. Huh. Maybe some of this *was* real and the roof *had* blown off, attracting attention from her captors. In which case...

The Iblis lock on the door clicked open.

In which case, this was her one chance at escape. Summoning all the spine and determination she possessed, she launched herself to the top of the wall, talons digging in as she bobbled there. The drop below was precipitous and terrifyingly deep, made all the more alarming by her acute long vision. She could actually see the sharp rocks far below at the bottom of the crag, and her avian brain assessed the distance with brutal clarity. If she didn't manage to take wing, the fall would kill her.

"Stop!" A Sammael wizard shrieked, while another hit her with a dose of nerve-frying pain.

Of course, if she stayed, she'd just wish she were dead. Better to reach than fail for not trying.

She took the leap and fell through the air.

~ 21 ~

THE GROUP AT the forest's verge exclaimed as one. Even Gabriel, who'd felt Nic become the silver phoenix, who'd been viscerally connected to her as she wondered at the change and decided to try. He'd seen the dizzying drop through her eyes and feared along with her, felt her pain as the Sammael wizards tried to immobilize her.

He both watched and felt her fall from the tower, his stomach dropping as they shared the exhilarating terror and wild hope, the wizards' magic quickly shredding as she escaped their field of power. "*Fly,*" he urged her, sending magic into her through the silver web they shared. "Fly!"

Alise wailed, clapping her hands over her mouth as the distant silver bird plummeted into the abyss. Then choked on a gasp when Nic popped into sight again.

They all broke into cheers, even Jadren, and Gabriel's spirits soared, exultant, along with her, the beat of her wings his own, the thundering of her great heart pounding through him. Unerringly, she arrowed toward him, crossing the distance at amazing speed.

"Incoming!" Alise shouted as a group of aerial spirits condensed to hound Nic, and she jogged in the air, distressed, her flight faltering.

"Help Alise?" Gabriel asked Selly, who was already moving to join Han in feeding magic to Alise. The spirits harrying Nic peeled away, attacked in turn, and she shot toward him again.

Now that Gabriel was connected to Nic once more, her fiery magic billowing into him with all her generosity of spirit, wine-red, rose-warm, he no longer needed anyone else. Nic filled him as no one else could, shoring up those lingering weaknesses left by the struggle to save Selly, bringing him singingly alive. Nic drew closer, skimming low over the meadow, Alise's wizardry battling the pursuing spirits. Jadren had joined the knot around Alise, offering terse advice. Gabriel couldn't tell if it was helpful or not, but he was focused on Nic anyway.

He ran out of the sheltering saplings as she landed, her wings flapping furiously, dirt and winter-cured plants kicking up in a rooster-tail wake. The moment she halted, he yanked on the threads, still running toward her, bringing her back to human form moments before she flung herself into his embrace.

They stood there, sealed together, shuddering, laughing and weeping as one, and he buried his face in her silky black curls, savoring being able to touch her again. "My heart," he chanted over and over, feeling indeed as if his heart had been restored, filling the gaping, agonizing hole left by her absence.

She pulled back enough to crane her head back, extracting her hands to frame his face in her palms. "You're alive," she breathed. "Aren't you? This is real, I hope."

"More real than anything else in the world," he promised,

dropping his mouth to hers. Lush, heated, richer than the finest wine, her mouth opened to him, her magic flowing into him and his back into her in a cycle old as time.

Jadren dragged them back, literally, grabbing them both by the shoulders and yanking them toward the dubious cover of the forest. "Dark arts save me from the stupidity of true love," he snarled. "We're not out of trouble yet."

Gabriel's gaze followed Jadren's pointing finger, spotting the undulating river of hunters coursing down the lower crags, straight toward them. "To the horses!" he shouted, taking Nic by the hand and running with her, glad they'd thought to— after the horses had rested—have them all saddled and ready to go, just in case of this very thing.

"Can we outrun them?" Jadren demanded.

"Maybe. With a head start," Gabriel answered, lifting Nic onto Salve's back. Her bare thighs flashed as the sheet thing she wore parted, and she made a noise of disgust as she wrestled herself into a more modest covering.

"That's a no," Jadren said.

"That's a maybe," Gabriel retorted. Assured that Nic had her situation in hand, he swung up on Vale. "Getting on your horse now ups our chances," he told Jadren.

Jadren squinted at the onrushing river of hunters. "I'll play rearguard," he decided.

"Don't be ridiculous," Nic fired at him. "You can't fight them."

He brandished his machete with a broad grin. "We made more enchanted weapons, Lady Phel. I'm a wicked-good hunter slayer now."

Gabriel nearly rolled his eyes, gratified when Nic actually did.

"You can't stay," Alise said, sidling her horse close. "You'll be slaughtered."

"I didn't know you cared, baby Elal." He snickered.

Alise's eyes flashed. "I'll stay with you, then."

"No." Jadren was firm. "*You* have to stay with them, guard them from those spirits of your father's. This is something I can do."

"I'll stay," Han offered, still on the ground, holding his sword. "I can offer magic and a second enchanted blade."

"I'm staying, too," Selly declared, dismounting again. "I still have a lot of magic left, if Jadren can figure out something useful to do with it."

"Charming," he retorted, and she grinned, brandishing her bow and quiver.

"Plus I have a lot of arrows," she added. Gabriel was opening his mouth to argue when she pinned him with a severe look. "Don't try to tell me not to do this," she warned. "You have Nic back. Get her home and safe. We'll be right behind you."

He had to swallow his fear for her, but he nodded. "See you at home."

Selly faltered, as if she'd been prepared to argue more, then nodded. "Tell Mom not to worry so much."

A laugh burst out of Gabriel. "I'll let you tell her that."

"Coward."

"You know it." They shared a smile, and it was if the years had faded away, memories rushing back of how close he and

Selly had once been. "It's good to have you back," he told her. "Don't screw that up."

"I hate to say it," Nic put in, "but Han should come with us. If House Sammael gets their hands on him, Sabrina will bond him, or they'll use him as leverage."

"We know how determined those hunters will be to take him," Gabriel agreed.

Han hesitated, clearly torn. Jadren clapped him on the shoulder. "Give me a last shot of magic and go. Lady Phel is right on this one."

In another moment, they were off, leaving Jadren and Selly with all the enchanted weapons they could spare. Gabriel had to force himself not to look over his shoulder, hoping it wouldn't be his last glimpse of the sister he'd only just regained.

RIDING HARD WITH nothing between her and the saddle was an excruciating experience, but Nic gritted down and revealed no sign of discomfort. Gabriel, Alise, and the others, who owed her nothing, had suffered more to rescue her. Besides, any pain was worth being free again. In truth, she could hardly believe that she *was* free. Part of her suspected she remained in the tower room, imprisoned and tormented, hallucinating about being with her husband, family, and friends again. It would be exactly the sort of mental torment a Hanneil thought-seeker would use to break her spirit and will. Offer her everything, only to yank it away.

Gabriel glanced over at her, his silver hair whipping in the wind of their passage, wizard-black eyes intent as he offered her an encouraging smile. She attempted to return it, but she could never fool him.

"Hold up!" he shouted to Alise, slowing Vale, Salve gratefully dropping her own pace to a walk. Nic patted the mare's shoulder, murmuring a reassurance. Even the horses were suffering to help her. It shouldn't make her want to cry. She'd shed enough tears.

"What's wrong?" Alise asked, circling back from the lead position where she'd been scanning for ambush and hiding them from spies with her wizardry. "Nic?"

"She's fine. The horses need a break," Gabriel temporized. Nic wasn't fine, but he doubted she'd want her sister to know that. "Any pursuers?"

"We've lost them for now. That could change."

"I've replenished some magic," Han said, catching up from where he'd been playing rearguard. "Let me top you off, Alise. You're looking drawn."

"We won't stop long," Gabriel promised. Already dismounted, he came around to help Nic down. "Come here, my heart," he murmured, and she let him lift her down. He led her a few steps away, then enfolded her in a strong embrace. "It's real," he whispered. "You're safe with me. Never fear. I'm right here."

She nodded against his chest as he held her, momentarily overcome with emotion. "Can you read my every thought now?" she asked, trying to sound wry, though the words wobbled badly.

"I don't know," he answered softly. "We're more... entwined than before, it feels like."

"Yes, it does." She looked up at him as much as she could while maintaining as much physical contact as possible, feeling as if she needed to soak him in, to saturate herself with his nearness so she'd never doubt again. "I don't mind."

"Neither do I." He caressed her back, his touch steadying and soothing at once. "I'm sorry I bungled bringing you back to human form."

"What do you mean?"

"This sheet thing." He tugged at it. "I don't know where it came from, and now you're naked beneath."

"Oh, that." She was indeed naked beneath, as she'd torn Sergio's negligee into tiny strips, shredding it to vent her fury. But how to explain to Gabriel without risking him losing his temper?

Too late. The anger built in his eyes, magic going silver-sharp in the air, his face hard. "He kept you naked," Gabriel stated.

"Not exactly," she temporized. "But I didn't care for what he did give me to wear."

"I already vowed to kill that bottom dweller," Gabriel replied conversationally. "All that's changed is now I'll enjoy it that much more." He frowned then, searching her face. "Are you injured at all?"

"I'm perfectly healthy, and the babe is fine. Time enough to trade tales later."

He wasn't satisfied, an awful fear creeping into his face. "Did he…" He fought to find the words.

"No!" She pushed the truth of it through their connection, so he'd feel it. "I hurt him when he tried. Mostly he wanted my magic, anyway—and I didn't let him have that either."

Gabriel visibly calmed himself. "I'm still going to kill him."

"I think you'd be doing the world a service," she replied with a smile that felt genuine this time. "Although, he means to supplant his father, so you could let Lord Sammael do it for you."

"And deprive myself of the pleasure?" Gabriel's lips crooked in a half smile, but his eyes held lethal intent, deadly danger in his magic. She shivered despite herself. Silvery calm and black as the dark side of the moon, that was her wizard.

"We should probably move on," Alise said from where she and Han had been walking the horses to cool them gradually, apology in her tone.

Nic went to her sister, hugging her hard. "Thank you for coming to rescue me," she said. "I didn't get to say so before."

Alise held on to her a long moment, her grip nearly desperate. "Was our father there?"

Surprised, Nic let her go. "How did you know?"

"I sensed him. This changes a great deal."

"You have no idea." Nic hesitated. "Maman was with him."

Alise's face lit up. "Oh, such good news! How is she?"

Much as she hated to break the bad news—and Alise's heart along with it—she shook her head. "Not good at all. I'll tell you everything. But we have to save her."

Alise searched her face, then nodded crisply. "We'll find a way. There must be one."

When Nic went back to Salve, she found Gabriel had attached the mare to a lead behind Vale. "Ride with me," he suggested. Mounting up, he held a hand down to her.

Nic hesitated. "Won't that be hard on Vale?"

"Just for a short time," Gabriel coaxed. "I need to hold you for a little while longer." As if agreeing, Vale swung his great head around and snorted at her, clearly disdainful of her concerns.

With a laugh that was only a little watery, she patted his muzzle, pressing a kiss to the velvety skin. "You're my hero, too," she told him. "Every time." Taking Gabriel's extended hand, she let him lift her with his easy strength to sit crosswise in his lap, wrapping her arms around his waist and leaning in. He put one strong arm around her and urged Vale into a fast clip.

It was better this way. Wrapped in Gabriel's arms, she began to believe in the reality of her escape. Parts of her she hadn't realized were tense, braced in anticipation of crushing disappointment, finally relaxed and calmed. For his part, Gabriel held her tightly, pressing his cheek into her hair, seeming to need the contact just as much. His magic smoothed out, no longer churning with spikes, the moon turning to its brighter face, the rippling sense of him under her skin like an intimate caress. In turn, she embraced him with her magic, letting it flow without reservation, so grateful he could receive it from her again.

THEY RODE WITH only short breaks, otherwise not stopping until they reached the Dubglass River, where they'd left a barge secured. Though Gabriel had hidden it with a spell of reflective moon magic, everyone was relieved to find it still there.

Unfortunately, Selly and Jadren had yet to catch up with them. Gabriel stared off the way they'd come, trying to conceal his worry, looking as if he were trying to sense where they might be. Alise had sent a spirit to look for them, but she was exhausted, and even with Han's help, her range was too diminished for her to send it far enough. The fact that the pair were beyond her reach was a distressing sign in and of itself, though no one wanted to articulate that.

Nic slipped her hand into his. They'd loaded the horses onto the barge, Alise already lying down to rest, her head propped on Han's knee, eyes closed. "They're strong and smart," she told Gabriel. "Selly knows how to survive, and Jadren is a powerful wizard, whatever his magic is."

"He's a shitty fighter, though, did I tell you?" Gabriel essayed a smile.

"Maybe you can tell me about it on the barge," she suggested gently. "I don't want to strand them either, but they have horses, supplies, and weapons. Selly knows the land and can find her way back. They wouldn't thank us for rendering their sacrifice moot or jeopardizing the safety of everyone back at House Phel because we waited too long for them."

Sighing, he nodded. "Ever my practical Nic." He studied her face. "There's something you're not telling me."

"There are a lot of things we haven't had opportunity to tell each other," she replied, her heart quaking. She dreaded confessing how she'd betrayed the secrets of the House Phel arcanium, but there was no way around it. Even now, her father might be there, greedily gorging on the stored magic, Maman an unwitting accomplice. The thought of him taking what she and Gabriel had spun out of their purest connection and taking it for his twisted ends made her feel ill at the violation.

Gabriel watched her, no doubt sensing her tumult of emotion. "Whatever it is, we'll handle it together," he told her, silvery cool magic soothing and caressing.

"And if we can't?"

"Then we're still together. That's what matters most."

She nodded, stepping with him onto the barge, their hands still joined, feeling the truth of it. "I can't believe you've managed to get me to voluntarily step foot on another barge," she said archly.

He grinned, real humor in it. "Romantic, yes?"

"No," she answered firmly, but when he gathered her close for a long, lingering kiss, she melted into him. The barge moved under her feet, lurching a little as it caught the current, his water magic moving them upstream. It was difficult to remember the time when she was consumed with keeping her distance from him, especially now when not touching him affected her with a physical pain. Fortunately, he seemed to need it, too, both of them clinging to each other to keep from drowning. It would take time, she suspected, for them to recover enough to feel safe separating.

Until then, she was more than happy to curl up in his lap, even if it meant telling him the terrible news.

~ 22 ~

HE'D LIVED HIS entire life up until just recently without the arcanium, Gabriel told himself as they finally reached the land he'd grown up on, so it didn't matter what Elal had done to it. What *did* matter was the people at House Phel. Much as it twisted his gut to think of Elal violating the place that had become sacred to him, because of and for Nic, he'd give up the arcanium to have everyone safe from harm.

Including Selly... But Nic was correct. He had to trust in her, and Jadren, that they'd survive. Grimly, he reflected on the irony of trusting the El-Adrel spy to keep his sister safe, but everything had turned upside down, it seemed. Telling his parents that he'd lost Selly yet again would be unpleasant. Even worse would be if his parents weren't alive to be told.

Nic rode beside him, low over Salve's neck as they raced the final distance to the manse, wearing the riding clothes Alise had wisely brought with her and stowed on the barge. She caught his eye, her smile grave, her eyes full of understanding and regret. She blamed herself for giving up their secrets, even though she also admitted that no one could stand up to Hanneil thought-seeking. It tormented her, too, knowing how her mother had been reduced, and she also blamed herself for that. Guilt wasn't a rational thing, and Gabriel knew he couldn't talk her out of it.

What he could do was hand her the tools and opportunity to make it right. Or take revenge.

The answering glitter in her dark emerald gaze told him she understood, and agreed.

This new mental and emotional intimacy between them wasn't something Nic had precedent for. They'd spent the trip upriver talking, comparing notes, and sharing stories. According to Convocation teaching, what they'd done hadn't been possible. He should not have been able to access her magic from that distance, nor should he have been able to push her into alternate form without touching her. Even more dramatically, she insisted that there was no way she'd sent her magic into him, as he was sure he'd experienced—and as he felt still. He no longer needed to touch her to consciously sip from her magic. It flowed into him with a steady warmth, curling around him with love he couldn't doubt. Her father may have induced the Fascination with an Aratron potion, but Nic loved him, just as he loved her.

They might not need to touch to transfer magic, but they couldn't seem to bear to have much distance between them. Nic thought it was the bond at work, reestablishing and strengthening their connection, rebuilding what had been strained to breaking. He was sure he'd been able to do the supposedly impossible because of their reciprocal bond. Nic, true to her nature, doubted that—but she also had no better explanation.

The fields and orchards were empty as they passed

through, which was all wrong for the middle of a balmy spring day. He feared the worst.

House Phel still stood, seeming intact, white and graceful against the lush green lawn and blossoming orchards. Like the arcanium, the manse—at least in its current glory—hadn't been part of his life for long, but it was more than simply a very large house. It was the historical home of his family, of the wizards who'd come before him. As the metaphorical house had fallen, eradicated from the Convocation, so had the literal manifestation of House Phel, sinking into the surrounding marshes, rotting away uncared for, largely forgotten except by children like himself who'd played in its bones. Now the manse was something he and Nic had created together, as much a triumph of their combined energies as the child she'd bear.

He wouldn't cede any of it to the rapacious greed of their enemies.

Alise pulled her horse to a halt on the far side of the lake, just inside the bordering trees, holding up a hand. She was pale and drawn, her dusky skin, usually the same shade as Nic's, had lost all its glow, more ashen than anything. Han galloped up from his rearguard position, holding out a hand to her. She waved him off, not because she didn't need the magic, Gabriel knew, but because Han was nearly tapped out, too. Once they were closely grouped, Gabriel pulled reflective moon magic around them, hiding their presence. "Our father is here," she told Nic, who nodded without surprise.

"Where is he?" she asked.

"I can't tell, but he's sent sentry spirits."

"Can you get around them?" Gabriel asked. "It would be good to find out where everyone is."

"Maybe," she said, her voice weary. "I don't have much magic left in me."

"You can have mine," Han insisted.

"If I take more from you, it could cause you harm," she replied with regret.

"I don't care," he retorted with heat. "Iliana is in there somewhere. I'll give anything to see that she survives."

"Have some of my magic," Nic said, nudging Salve forward and holding a hand out to Alise.

But Alise refused it. "You two have a battle ahead and will need everything you have if you're going to win. Let me try this on my own."

They waited while she concentrated, the silence only broken by the sound of the horses grabbing mouthfuls of the lush grass, taking advantage of the short opportunity to eat. Gabriel, needing the contact, held out a hand to Nic, and she sidled Salve closer, giving him a smile that had a tinge of sadness to it. "Can you feel the arcanium?" she asked quietly.

He could. And there was something wrong with it. The taint of other magic like a bitter taste in the back of his throat. "I hadn't realized I was that connected to it."

"We both are," she returned softly, the green of her eyes sharpening with determination. "It's a part of us now, and we're getting it back."

Finally, Alise blew out a frustrated breath. "My control is no good. I can't get anything past them."

"Gabriel and I will need to get past the sentry spirits in

person, regardless," Nic said with asperity, tugging her hand from Gabriel's and nudging Salve back toward Alise. "I have a lot of magic. Take what you need. We'll be counting on you to handle those sentries or there won't be any fight at all."

Alise frowned, clearly warring with herself. "But what point of that if—"

An eruption of lake water interrupted her, the horses rearing and whinnying their distress, except for Vale, who'd seen far worse than... whatever was rising from the water. Gabriel gathered his magic, preparing to defend them, but held off for a long, astonished moment, staring in disbelief at the candy-pink head, delicate spines traveling the arch of its horselike head then down its curving neck. A lavender eye with absurdly long lashes gazed at them with apparent curiosity, set in a narrow head with a tapering snout. It looked like—

"Is that a seahorse?" Han demanded, expertly wrangling his horse back under control.

"If seahorses are pink and grow big as a house," Nic answered, bringing Salve around.

The giant pink seahorse was still rising from the water, something wet and bedraggled clinging to its neck. Gabriel marshalled his magic, reaching for the lake water, ready to drown both creatures in a deadly wave.

"Iliana!" Han shouted, flinging himself from his mount and racing to the water's edge. Gabriel cursed, urging Vale after him, Nic and Alise following suit.

Iliana leapt from the creature's neck and into the water, wading to Han until her lissome form disappeared in his embrace. The seahorse bobbed placidly, looking brightly interested.

"Where in the dark arts did that thing come from?" Gabriel demanded, as if anyone could answer.

"I think that's our swamp monster," Nic replied slowly. She pointed to the surface of the water, where an array of tentacles gently waved, treading water to keep the creature afloat.

"Her name is Nathi," Iliana declared happily, wiping her hair, dark red with water, from her face. "She appreciates the fish you sent her," she added to Nic, who looked as bemused as he felt. "We're both very happy to see you well and back home where you belong."

"And *how* did you get her out of the pit in the workshop?" Gabriel asked, feeling very slow but nearly unable to assimilate any of this.

"It turns out the pit is connected to the lake," Iliana answered in a matter-of-fact tone. "The Sammael siblings and Lord Elal locked us all in the workshop—everyone is fine, by the way—and sealed the door with a new Iblis lock that only they can open, but then Nathi here showed me there was a way out. We just waited until she felt you arrive—she's very fond of you, Lord Phel—to come out to you."

Indeed, the seahorse batted the absurdly long lashes fringing her lavender eyes, looking quite flirtatious. "Fond... of me?" he echoed.

"Well, as the prime wizard of House Phel," Iliana explained. "The communication isn't perfect. I mainly get her emotions. She feels very loving toward you, Lord Phel."

"I'm soul sisters with a giant candy-pink seahorse," Nic

murmured.

"Anyway," Iliana said, giving Han a last kiss, then going to Alise, who dismounted. "I assume you need my magic to get around Lord Elal's guardians. The invaders are all in the manse somewhere," she added, "doing villainous things, no doubt."

"Did Sabrina hurt you?" Han demanded.

Iliana shook her head. "Asa hid me from her in the workshop. Then they decided to lock everyone in there, and it was so crowded, it was easy for me to hide. The Sammaels are waiting for you all to arrive, thinking that you'll stumble into some sort of surprise trap. But Nathi and I outwitted them!" she crowed in delighted triumph. Several of Nathi's deep-purple tentacles lifted from the water, waving in celebration. Iliana sobered, scanning the group. "Shouldn't Wizard Jadren and Selly be with you, too?"

"Long story," Gabriel answered. "What about Lord Elal?"

"He was going on about locating the arcanium, apparently." She blanched, giving Nic and Alise an apologetic glance. "You knew he was involved, yes? I'm so sorry."

"We knew," Nic confirmed, then looked to him. "So, we ride up to the house, dispatch the Sammael siblings, then kick my father out of the arcanium?"

"And be done in time for formal dinner," he replied, bowing in the saddle. If only it would be so easy, and yet he felt a kind of giddiness rather than apprehension. It could be the utter absurdity of their current circumstances, but he found he wasn't worried about the outcome. He and Nic could do this. In truth, the prospect of finally being able to unleash their magic on deserving targets came as a relief. "Alise, let us know when the way is clear, and Nic and I will handle the rest."

"You sure you want to approach the manse directly?" Nic asked, but her eyes were shining with similar fervor.

"It's our house," he confirmed, drawing the moon and water magic close, the massive charge feeling like pressurized lightning, ready to wreak havoc. "They should be afraid of us."

NIC HAD NEVER been prouder of, or more entranced by, her wizard. She could swear he glowed with silvery light, even in the bright sunshine, as they circumnavigated the lake. Vale and Salve paced each other at a gentle gallop. She felt like the avenging hero come to save the day, something akin to her early fantasies of the sort of wizard she'd be—and something she'd never expected to be as a mere familiar.

But she *was* something more than that, wasn't she? The magic cycling back and forth between her and Gabriel, growing, amplifying, felt as much hers as his. As if hearing the thought, Gabriel grinned over at her. Together, they were greater than either of them alone.

They rode right up to the steps that rose to the wide front porch, the manse eerily still. So far as traps went, it wasn't a subtle one. But then, the Sammaels had never been known for their guile. They tended to blast and bluster, getting their way through cruelty. Gabriel leapt down and, even at this extremity, took the time to help her down. Together, her hand tucked through his arm, they ascended the steps, Gabriel's moon magic shimmering in a protective shell around them that she sensed more than saw, her own magic woven into it, also.

Silence reined, as if the manse itself held its breath, the ancient architecture humming in the back of her mind. Like their connection to the arcanium, but larger, more diffuse. Whatever had changed and grown between Gabriel and her, it seemed they'd be a long time exploring the parameters. For the moment, she imagined the Phel ancestors had gathered, ghostlike and shimmering, with long-ago magic, invested in the proceedings.

Gabriel nodded toward the library, and she acknowledged, fighting down the irritation and sense of violation at the thought that slimy Sergio had ensconced himself there. Gabriel flung open the doors so they banged hard against the flanking walls.

Sergio, lounging in one of their armchairs, facing the doors and clearly expecting Gabriel's arrival, still jumped slightly, a hint of nerves crossing his face before he managed to assume his indolent pose again. "Why, if it isn't the absent landlord," he crooned, "come to deliver my property to me."

Nic rolled her eyes at the obviously rehearsed line. "I belong to no one," she replied, "least of all you."

Sergio laughed. "We'll see about that. Elal's spies said you somehow ripped off the roof, but I didn't believe it. How did you get inside House Sammael?" he demanded of Gabriel.

Gabriel smiled thinly. "I'm more powerful than you can imagine."

"Or stupider, as you've walked right into my trap. Sabrina!"

Behind them, Sabrina slammed and locked the doors, putting her back to them with a sly grin. "You should've run while you had the chance," she cooed. "Instead, you slunk back here thinking you'd be safe. How sweet of you to bring my toys right to me."

Nic eyed her with disgusted pity. "You've read all the wrong novels if that's the best dialogue you can come up with." When Sabrina opened her mouth, a hiss forming, Nic cut her off with a wave of her hand. "Save it. I advise you to leave. The grownups have business, and this is no place for a child. Go back to school and see if you can learn something." She actually said it kindly. Sabrina might be horrible, but she was also young, even younger than Alise, and—despite her scheming and tantrums—didn't truly understand what she dabbled with.

Quite dumbstruck, Sabrina stared back at her. Probably few people had ever been unafraid of the little hellion. Deliberately, Nic turned her back on the teen.

"So, how does this trap work?" Gabriel asked Sergio conversationally. "I'm not familiar with Convocation conniving. What happens next?"

He sounded so cool, even as his magic flickered like sharp silver knives in the air, that Sergio shifted uncomfortably, closing the book he'd been reading and setting it aside. "Now you die," he declared, sounding even more like a parody of a villain than Sabrina had. "Never fear, however," he added with a leer at Nic, "your familiar won't be widowed for long."

Sergio's magic lashed out, a whip of intended agony Nic

remembered well. She flinched despite her resolve—and it bounced off Gabriel's shield. Gabriel smiled mirthlessly. "Was that supposed to hurt?" he inquired, drawing his sword. It was the enchanted blade he and Jadren had crafted to defeat the hunters. Gabriel advanced on Sergio, who took a step back, sly gaze flicking behind them. He nodded.

Sabrina launched herself at them, bursting between their linked arms, separating them with a hoot of laughter. Faster than Nic had expected from Sergio, he blasted Gabriel with power, the screech of it almost audible as it hit the shield of moonlight. Sabrina grasped Nic's arm, sending a jolt of agony into her. Though Nic fought not to show a reaction, the pain screaming along her nerves was too intense, and Sabrina cackled with glee.

"Now what will you do!" Sergio shouted. "Separated from your familiar, you cannot stand against me for long."

Nic mustered her strength, supplemented by Gabriel's cooling silver, drawing herself up to glare at Sabrina. "Bad girl," she gritted out, and slapped her across the face, hard enough to draw blood. Sabrina staggered, putting a hand to her bleeding lip, stared at the blood in confusion, and began to cry.

Whipping around, Nic moved to help Gabriel, but found she wasn't needed. Gabriel had slowly, mercilessly, backed Sergio against the wall, the point of his sword at the hollow of the Sammael wizard's throat. Their clashing magic fulminated visibly in the air, Sergio desperately trying to reach Gabriel, who remained impervious.

"You can't kill me," Sergio gasped, seeming to finally understand his peril. "The Convocation won't stand for it."

"You abducted my wife and familiar," Gabriel said in a lethally quiet tone.

"It was legal!" Sergio nearly shrieked, trying to worm away, immediately pinned as the point of the sword pressed into his skin, eliciting a trickle of blood.

"I don't care much for Convocation laws," Gabriel mused.

"Sergio!" Sabrina cried, starting to climb to her feet.

Nic pinned the girl down with the simple expedient of stepping on her silken skirts. "Sit," Nic commanded. "Stay." And earned a simmering glare full of impotent fury.

"Regardless, what the Convocation considers legal is not something that concerns me," Gabriel continued softly. "I only care about what is right. You'll die for what you've done."

Sergio's eyes bugged out. "My father will kill you."

"He's welcome to try," Gabriel replied, and sliced Sergio's throat.

The motion was so fast, the blade so sharp, that Nic didn't fully process what had happened until the blood poured out, Sergio's lifeless body sagging after it like detritus swept over a crimson waterfall. Nic held her breath in shock, Sabrina's wails a distant sound. Gabriel stood over Sergio's corpse, bloodied sword in one hand, the tip pointing at an angle to the floor, the dark side of his moon magic dense in the air, the water magic deep as a bottomless ocean. Dangerous, as she'd known long ago. Also hers.

Then, as if sensing her gaze on him, he turned to her. "Are you all right?" he asked, gaze flicking to the now-sobbing heap of young blond wizard at her feet.

"I'm fine." She managed a smile. Her reaction was her own, and she wouldn't put it on Gabriel. Besides, for all the apparent barbarity of Gabriel's actions, it had been a clean death, and far more merciful than Sammael—or truly, most Convocation wizards—would visit on their enemies.

"Let's take back our arcanium then," Gabriel said, holding out a hand to her.

She took it, grateful for the steadying contact. "You haven't cleaned your sword," she noted. He always immediately cleaned his weapons.

He didn't bother to glance at it. "I want to meet your father with Sammael's blood fresh for him to see."

She nodded, understanding and also terrified of his intentions. "Do you plan to kill him, too?"

Gabriel stilled, searching her face. "What would you have me do?"

Nic pressed her lips together, the emotion rising up, turbulent and unnamable. If her father died, Maman would be free. But... he was still her father. "I don't want him to die," she whispered, aware of the plea in her voice.

Nodding, unsurprised, Gabriel released her hand and caressed her cheek. "We'll find a way, then."

Finding her eyes had filled with tears, she laid her hand over his, mutual understanding humming between them. Love, respect, and magic.

~ 23 ~

"WHAT DO WE do with her, though?" Nic asked him, and Gabriel reluctantly took his eyes off his beautiful wife—too pale, her eyes bright with shock—to glance at the pitifully sobbing Sabrina.

It was tempting to simply run her through also, if only to shut her up, but that, Nic wouldn't forgive. If he were honest with himself, once the murderous fury left him, he'd regret it also.

"She's still a child," Nic explained, though she hardly needed to. "Yes, she's a monster, but she's been raised by monsters."

"If we send her home," he reasoned, meeting Nic's emerald-green, somber gaze, "she'll only continue down this path."

"She should be back in school," Nic replied, her face filled with compassion as she looked at the girl. He was tempted to tease her about where her practical nature had fled to now, but he restrained it. Nic had never had the hardness and cruelty of these people. She'd simply learned to hide her soft heart away, carefully protecting it behind the façade she'd used to masquerade as one of them. Nic looked at him again. "Though, if we send her back to Convocation Academy, there won't be anyone to teach her she doesn't have to be what they've shaped her into."

"Will you take on that project?" he asked, intending to point out the absurdity of it, but Nic considered it thoughtfully.

"I don't know. Can I decide later?"

"We're already harboring at least one traitor," he reminded her, making the warning clear. "We can lock her up like Laryn and figure out next steps once this is done."

She looked startled. "Laryn is still alive?"

Realizing they hadn't discussed it, he nodded. "In custody, but alive, awaiting your judgment. At least, that was the case when I left."

"I figured you'd killed her."

"I wanted to, but I wanted to decide with you more."

Her smile lit up her face. "This is why I love you."

He rather wished it were for other reasons, but he'd take it. With a thought—and very little effort, he was so replete with magic—he extruded chains to bind Sabrina, leaving her to weep there on the rug.

"Should we move her to another room?" Nic ventured, averting her gaze from Sergio's bloody corpse.

"Let her remain here," Gabriel answered, "and sit with the results of Sergio's actions."

Nic didn't protest, accepting his hand and going with him to the back kitchen, where the door to the cellar stood open. If he'd hoped that Lord Elal hadn't been able to follow the information he'd extorted from Nic, that faint hope was dashed. They moved quietly down the rickety old stairs, finding the door to the tunnel had been hacked apart.

Gabriel paused to examine the destruction. "What magic did this?"

"A spirit manifestation. It takes a lot out of him to produce this much physical damage, but he has Maman's magic and the promise of a glut of more from our arcanium," she answered quietly.

"Do you sense any sentry spirits guarding the way?"

She shook her head. "No, but I might not. Or," she considered, "Alise might've dealt with them."

"Wouldn't your father sense that?"

Nic cocked her head doubtfully. "It very much depends on how focused he is on what he's doing."

"He's doing *something*." Gabriel had sensed it from the other side of the lake. It was even stronger her, the arcanium keening inaudibly, the embedded magic vibrating on some other plane he couldn't quite define clearly.

"Yes," Nic agreed, confirming that she sensed it, too, "though I can't tell what."

"Me neither. We approach carefully."

"And here I was all for charging down the tunnel, waving a bloody sword like an avenging angel."

"You can't have my bloody sword," he replied, not understanding the black humor they shared in this moment but beyond grateful for it. He squeezed her hand, then let it go. "Stay behind me."

"No, this time you stay behind me." She stepped in front of him on the narrow strip of flat walkway in the round passage. "My father won't attack me, because he still thinks to use me. You, he'd go after without hesitation."

"I'd welcome that, in truth," he growled but held himself back.

She gave him a brilliant smile over her shoulder. "Thank you for agreeing not to kill him."

"Not on purpose, anyway," he qualified under his breath, and she shot him a stern look, then proceeded onward. He truly would make an effort not to kill Elal, for Nic's sake, but if it came down to it... Well, he wouldn't grieve for the man who'd done so much wrong.

Nic might be preceding him, but he was significantly taller than her, so he could see that the spiraling silver door at the entrance to the arcanium also stood open. He set his teeth against the rising fury. Nic had told him long ago that no wizard allowed any other wizard inside their arcanium— something Elal would also know. He knew full well the kind of theft he attempted. It was, perhaps, not the greatest of his transgressions, but it communicated Elal's lack of regard for House Phel. Even when Lord Elal had encouraged, even worked his guile to promote, the match between Nic and him, the man had never meant his words. When he'd told his daughter that Gabriel deserved the chance to rebuild his house, he'd only wanted to seize this very opportunity.

Gabriel would see to it that he choked on it.

They reached the round entrance, the arcanium luminescent beyond from sunshine filtering through the lake water. The light glanced through the domed room, gleaming off the silver struts, turning the glittering mosaic-tiled floor into a whirl of color. The built-in cabinets and drawers all stood open, clearly ransacked, and a bag by the door bulged with

Elal's scavenged treasures.

Nic gave a soft cry, and Gabriel saw what alarmed her—her mother slumped unconscious on the floor, crumpled in the shadows of the curving wall, along with other things that had been dug out and discarded. As for Lord Elal himself, he stood at the center of the tiled spiral, arms upraised to the moon window above, his body a rictus of effort.

He turned slowly at Nic's exclamation, like a man in a daze. Focusing, he dropped his arms, his face a picture of offended incredulity that Gabriel found immensely satisfying. Stepping to the side, he nodded at Nic to tend to her mother and confronted the invader. "Elal," he ground out. "You trespass unforgivably."

Lord Elal goggled a moment longer, his black eyes going to the bloodied sword. "I don't know how you penetrated House Sammael to reclaim my daughter," he said, his gaze flicking to Nic. "Either way, you're meant to be dead, Phel."

Gabriel allowed a slight smile. "I elected to live—and to kill your lackey."

Elal gathered his self-possession, very much as his daughters did, firming his chin. "Sammael was a poor tool, easily bent and broken. If you expect me to mourn his loss, you'll be disappointed. You've actually done me a favor, ridding me of excess baggage."

The wizard was stalling, gathering his magic for an attack. Gabriel had encountered Elal's power once before, when he challenged the wizard over Nic's absence, and he was quite certain it had been stronger then. The Elal wizard had clearly drained Nic's mother to the point of unconsciousness and, though he'd managed to penetrate and loot the Phel arcanium, Gabriel very much doubted whether the man had gleaned much magic.

"Have you found yourself able to use water and moon magic?" Gabriel inquired silkily, following Elal as he pivoted, keeping the sword pointed squarely at him.

Lord Elal smirked. "Have *you?*" he retorted. "They're not terribly useful magics, after all."

"Useful enough for my purposes," Gabriel replied, mentally assembling his own arsenal. "Not that I'd expect an outsider like you to understand."

Lord Elal laughed heartily at that. Gesturing widely to the dome, he took on a condescending tone. "Young wizard, *you* are the outsider. And you have no idea what you have—or should I say, *had*—here. A tool like this is wasted on an uneducated buffoon. In a way, I'm doing you a favor by taking it over and tuning it to my own magic. If you'd attempted anything more than your trifling games, you could have released uncontrolled magics that would leave a bottomless pit where this lake and manse once sat. You, my dear boy, are like a monkey that discovered a magic sword: you're more likely to kill yourself with it than make any use of it."

"Is that so?" Gabriel followed Elal's slight turning, keeping him squarely before him, edging slightly closer. "I think I'll take my chances. You will leave, immediately."

"Or what?" Lord Elal looked terribly amused. "I don't take orders from low-level rogue wizards who wouldn't qualify to be an apprentice anywhere in the Convocation." He pretended to glance at the nearest window, turning ever so slightly with the movement, and Gabriel followed.

"I promised your daughter I wouldn't kill you," Gabriel replied easily, "but not that I wouldn't make you suffer. Leave now, and you'll escape with your limbs intact."

Lord Elal produced a serene smile. "Oh, you really are a naïve fool. Pitiful, really. If you'd been identified as a lad, brought to the Convocation for training, we might've made a wizard of you. As it is, you're the magical equivalent of a babbling idiot, blundering about and making fatal errors."

"Final warning," Gabriel said. "Leave, or I start carving pieces off you."

Elal chuckled, folding his hands together. "Such a commoner that you think we'll fight with blades." He sobered abruptly, which was all the warning Gabriel got. A spirit manifested inside Gabriel's reach, a suddenly physical blade slicing down his chest. With a snarl, Gabriel flung a hail of silver at Elal, breaking his concentration so the spirit vanished. Blood ran hot down his skin.

"An entertaining start," Lord Elal declared, unbothered, the air around him whirling with tiny spirits deflecting the silver. "Too bad the ending will come so soon."

A whirlwind of spirits surrounded him, slashing with blades that appeared and vanished with the speed of thought. Others sought to blind him, to thrust into his mouth and nose and smother him. But he'd faced fighters wilier than these, puppeted as they were, and didn't fall for the trick of trying to fight them one by one. Instead he focused on the source, pulling water from outside the dome and surrounding Elal in a bubble of it.

The spirits disappeared as suddenly as they'd attacked, leaving Lord Elal flailing in the bubble of water. A swarm of water elementals arrived, piercing the surface tension of Gabriel's watery creation, popping it so water abruptly gushed over the floor. Elal slipped a little as his feet hit the floor, but his wizard-black eyes held fury. His magic snapped out, and fire elementals leapt at Gabriel, air elementals spinning like tiny dervishes, fanning the flames that set fire to his hair and clothing.

Gabriel vaporized the water on the floor, drenching himself so the flames died away. At the same time, he flung a series of silver spikes at Lord Elal. Several spirit sentries intervened, batting them away with apparent ease.

"You're tiring," Lord Elal taunted, "and I have barely begun."

"This is my arcanium," Gabriel ground out, edging just a bit closer while Elal gloated.

"It *was*." The wizard pulled a sad face. "It answers to me now. The benefit of training and experience you lack. It didn't take long to attune it to me. Magic is magic, after all, and there is a nigh infinite amount stored here. I can go on forever while *you* have made a critical erro. A beginner's mistake." He grinned in triumph. "I am between you and your familiar. You cannot reach her. Meanwhile, I'll bleed you dry and finally rid us of your pestilent presence."

"You're celebrating too soon," Gabriel informed him. Beyond the wizard, on the other side of the room, Nic stood, meeting his gaze with firm devotion. She nodded her readiness. "And your thinking is limited by your archaic

Convocation traditions. I never went to House Sammael, because Nic and I don't need to touch to combine magic."

Lord Elal's instant sneer of disdain shattered into astonishment, then fear as Gabriel received Nic's magic, spinning it with his into an amalgam of moon, water, and spirit fire. He wrested the spirits and elementals from Elal's dwindling grasp, then slammed the wizard with steam boiling up from the floor. Elal shrieked, high and frantic, twisting and contorting as silver spikes pierced him from all directions, his blood falling to the floor like the richest of his wines.

With a final wail, he collapsed, holding both hands to his head, sobbing piteously as he tried to pluck the spike embedded in his right eye. Gabriel stood over him, then looked to Nic. "An eye for an eye."

"Is it enough for you?" she asked softly, no judgment in her gaze.

He considered, the monster within craving more, the man who Nic called foolishly noble uncertain for once of the balance that needed to be struck. "It can be enough," he told her, "if you tell me it is."

"It's enough." She offered a rueful smile. "There's been sufficient bloodshed today, and I'd like to be done with it."

"What shall we do with him, then?"

Nic let out a long sigh, drifting closer, though she spared no glance for her defeated father. "Put him in his carriage and send him back to Elal. Alise can direct the elemental to take him. I want him gone from here."

"And your mother?"

"Maman stays with us," Nic answered firmly.

"Won't she pine after him, try to return?"

"I have an idea." Finally, she glanced down. "Lord Elal. I am confiscating your familiar as payment for crimes against our family."

He stared up at her, face contorted as his mouth worked, and she looked away from the spike embedded in his ruined eye. "You can't," he croaked.

"I can." She turned away from him, then spoke over her shoulder. "You should've paid my dowry."

~ 24 ~

I T TOOK THE rest of the day to simply reestablish a semblance of normality.

They released the prisoners in the workshop, and Nic made Gabriel sit down right there for Asa to heal his wounds. He was covered, head to toe, in shallow slices and angry burns. How he'd stayed on his feet, much less unleashed that storm of magic on her father, Nic would never know. Though he fretted at having to sit, he yielded to her insistence.

While Gabriel was being taken care of, she set teams to work, cleaning up the blood from the library, confining Sabrina to her assigned room, and disposing of Sergio's corpse by sending him back to House Sammael in the carriage he and Sabrina had taken to House Phel, much as her father was sent, bleeding and broken, back to House Elal. Alise happily instructed the air elementals to travel without pause to deliver their passengers, along with the implicit message that House Phel was not to be trifled with.

As soon as Alise finished with that task, she joined Nic in helping settle Maman. Alise gave over her spacious rooms to Maman, saying she could set herself up elsewhere. Maman was nonresponsive. Not asleep, but also not seeming present at all.

Her cat's eyes stared vacantly at the ceiling and, when Asa arrived—greeting Nic's raised brow with the assurance that Gabriel was fine and had gone to deal with the mess in the arcanium—he examined Maman. After bolstering her vitality, he pronounced nothing else physically wrong with her.

"Her magic is already regenerating," Asa explained, "which is, of course, an excellent sign. The impact of alternate form on her psyche, however—well, there's no precedent that I know of. Perhaps with time and rest, she'll recover on her own." He met Nic's eyes, his own full of reticent sorrow. "She'll suffer, though, being parted from her wizard. I know you know that, but we can't pretend that's not the case."

Nic nodded thoughtfully. "If I told you that I have an idea, something that might sever the wizard–familiar bond, would you be willing to let us experiment on the bond you have with Laryn?"

Asa sucked in a breath, eyes going wide. "How would you do this?"

"Not me," Nic answered, then turned to her sister. "Alise would do it."

Alise, who'd been sitting on the bed, holding Maman's hand, jerked her head up. "Me?" she squeaked. "I don't know how to do that."

"I think you can do it," Nic said. "I had a lot of time to think in that tower, and I mulled over some of the things we'd been talking about, pieces coming together. I can sense Elal magic, and it seems to me the method you use to bond spirits and elementals is very much the same as the wizard–familiar bond."

Alise slowly stood. "They do *look* the same, but that doesn't mean…"

"We don't know, do we?" This was her opportunity to convince her small audience to give this serious thought. "Have you been taught yet how to bind a familiar?"

Alise exchanged a look with Asa, then nodded. "We're sworn to secrecy—and placed under a geas that won't allow us to speak of it, so I can't tell you details—but it's one of the first things we're taught when we advance to the wizard-only training."

Just as Nic had suspected. "I knew enough of the basics to tell Gabriel what to do for our bonding, but it occurred to me since that our father was counting on the bonding being inadequate or nonstandard. Because only wizards are taught the key. It has to be an embedded spell, if any wizard, regardless of magical type, can trigger it, and I'm betting it's embedded in the familiars."

The way both Asa and Alise had their lips clamped firmly shut, black eyes wide in astonishment, told Nic she was right on target. "I remember when I was categorized," she told them. "It's a vivid memory, as you can imagine, made sharper by the emotional intensity. I recall everything—the proctor, the oracle head, the words that changed my life… and then there's a small gap. That's when they do it, I'm guessing. They embed the spell in us that a wizard later triggers."

Neither of the wizards moved, almost holding their breath so as not to activate the geas. "Gabriel and I created a bond between us," Nic continued, "but it looks strange, and acts differently from other wizard–familiar bonds, because he never triggered that spell. He simply didn't know how."

Alise relaxed slightly, experimentally opening her mouth. "That explains a great deal."

Asa nodded judiciously. "I would not argue with that conclusion."

With a surge of excitement, Nic smiled at the healer. "I think we should try. The spell should only affect Laryn, if my conclusions are correct. If it works, then we can sever Maman from her wizard, too."

She held Alise's dubious gaze. "It would be worth it, if this can be done."

"It would change everything," Alise breathed, pale with the enormity of what Nic proposed.

"I know it. Familiars will be able to elect to leave the partnerships they were forced, arguably tricked, into."

"We're talking about a world filled with unbonded familiars," Asa warned, brow furrowed.

"A world where familiars can *choose* who to share their magic with," Nic returned crisply. "You don't have to agree to this, Asa, but I'm offering you an opportunity to be free of Laryn. It's an alternative to seeing her executed," she added more gently. "If it goes wrong, then we'll know—and the fallout will likely be less than whatever punishment we or the Convocation would sentence her to."

Asa scrubbed his hands over his scalp, then nodded. "Only if she agrees. She is a traitor, but she should have the choice: execution, delivery to Convocation Center for them to do as they see fit, or this."

"If it works," Alise put in, "then what do we do with her?"

Nic looked to Asa for the answer. He looked pained. "House Refoel will take her in, at least until the child is born, and they'll see to it that she doesn't cause trouble. No one will question that, and my house will expect it. After that, well, then we'll have to see."

Alise and Nic nodded sympathetically, and Nic found herself laying a protective hand over the flicker of life she carried. She wouldn't want to be the one to separate a mother from her child, but given what she'd observed of Laryn, the other woman hadn't seemed excited about the pregnancy. Perhaps she'd be willing to give the child up to Asa, so they could be raised by a parent who wanted them, in a loving home.

Every child—no, every person—deserved that much.

"I'M STILL THINKING through the ramifications that the bonding can be broken," Gabriel said much later that night, when they had finally handled everything and the manse had settled into the peace of people returning to their routines. "You're truly amazing to have figured that out."

Nic preened a little, feeling quite deserving of the praise. She hadn't gone with Asa, Gabriel, and Alise to put the question to Laryn. She didn't feel any need to confront the bitter woman ever again. Unsurprisingly, Laryn had elected to be experimented upon, in return for the amnesty that at least the remainder of her pregnancy would grant. Alise had reported that severing the bond was remarkably simple, when she thought of it in terms of the Elal spirit-bonding skills she already possessed.

Nic had attended when Alise severed the bond between Maman and their father. She seemed unchanged thus far, and Nic very much hoped her father felt it and knew who was responsible.

Nic and Alise had decided to postpone further discussion of the implications—that House Elal had to be behind the creation of the spell in the first place. Also, the invisible, giant pink seahorse in the room was the power they now possessed to free all familiars of their enchantment. That Gabriel would insist they had a moral obligation to do so wasn't in doubt. Nic, true to her nature, harbored reservations. The Convocation wizards wouldn't sit idly by for an enterprise that would deprive them of their familiars. If House Phel wasn't already at war, that would do it.

But for at least this, her first night home, with both of them safe and sound, Nic wanted to savor being with Gabriel. There'd been no sign yet of Jadren and Selly. Hopefully they'd turn up the following day. If not, then they'd organize a search. In the meanwhile, Nic didn't want Gabriel dwelling on his worries. Thus, she planned to distract her wizard quite thoroughly. "You know, my father told me we stood on the brink of a new society. We do, but not at all in the way he thought. I always knew you'd turn the Convocation upside down."

"That *we* would," he corrected with a half smile. "I still have no idea how you put that together, about the bonding."

She moved to him, adding an extra swish to her hips, just to enjoy the silvery-bright surge of desire from him, and trailed her finger down his muscled chest. "I happen to be exceedingly clever," she informed him.

"That you are," he agreed warmly, snagging her provocative fingers and lifting them to his mouth, brushing a kiss over her sensitive fingertips, nipping just enough to make her shudder. "As well as innovative, powerful, loving, sensual, and staggeringly beautiful."

"Are those qualities listed in order of preference?" she teased.

"I like the entire package," he answered, wizard-black eyes like a starless night.

"I like your package, too," she murmured, swaying close enough to rub against him.

"Excellent news, as I have need of your assistance, familiar."

She caught her breath, knees going weak with her dizzying reaction. No longer able to play coy, she nodded. "Whatever my wizard desires of me."

He swept her up into the balcony of his arms, carrying her out of their bedchamber. "We have an arcanium to cleanse and retune to the proper magics."

"Oh," she breathed, not daring to hope. "That will take considerable work, but we must do our duty to House Phel."

The look he gave her scorched from the inside out. "Just so. I plan to spend all night on the project."

She shivered, unbearable need taking her, a sweet counterpoint to the lulling comfort of being held close to his heart, enfolded in his strong embrace. "I confess, I love it when you carry me," she murmured.

He brushed a kiss against her hair. "I know. I can feel it."

He carried her all the way to the arcanium, through the temporary doors that they planned to reinforce. Everyone now had a very good idea of where the arcanium was located, so relying on secrecy to protect it was no longer an option. Gabriel, the master of innovation, had already been thinking up various magical tricks to provide additional defenses.

"Close your eyes," he murmured as they reached the final door. His magic took hers in a sweet embrace, laying their joined mental hands on the silver circle, and she felt it open. The arcanium didn't smell of blood as she'd feared. Instead, the heated scent of candles and roses filled her senses.

Gabriel set her on her feet. "You can look now."

Opening her eyes, she gasped in wonder. The center circle of the tiled floor was ringed with lit candles and red roses. Inside, directly under the moon window, sat the silver bed—complete with a mattress and black bedding, neatly turned down to show the scattering of rose petals. Gabriel encircled her wrist with a firm grip, gaze firing as he sensed her heated curl of desire. "I thought you'd look good, spreadeagled naked on black, but I might have to try other colors."

"It's important for a wizard to experiment," she acknowledged, mouth dry with anticipation. "Incantations of this complexity require meticulous fine-tuning."

"Exactly what I thought. Stand still."

She obeyed, heart thundering, as he undressed her. Taking his time, he slowly peeled the gown off of her, kissing, nipping, and licking her bare skin as he uncovered it, until she was melting, trembling so much that she thought she might not be able to stand any longer.

Sensing he had her exactly as he wanted her, Gabriel swept her up into his arms again, carrying her to the bed. Laying her down, he arranged her as he'd promised, arms and legs spread widely. Holding her gaze, he smiled slightly as the silver chains responded to their magic, snaking around her wrists and ankles. Experiencing both moving the chains and the sensation of being bound, she writhed, body singing with erotic passion and magical need.

Gabriel kissed her, long and lingering, soothing and silvery, then brushing kisses over her cheeks, forehead, and eyelids, a rain of love. His excitement flared through her, magnifying her own. "Do you feel this, too?" she asked, opening her eyes.

He ran a hand down her body, tracing the curves, eyes glittering as she moved into the caress, pleading without words. "Yes," he answered. "I understand now why you wanted this." Then he gave her a stern look. "And I should inform you that I have plans for your helpless body. You can beg and plead all you like, but I won't be moved. Look up."

He moved out of her line of sight, and she gasped in wonder at the sight of the full moon, exactly framed in the moon window, huge and luminescent, light rippling through the clear water. "Perfect timing," she breathed. The chains tightened on her, stretching her body taut, and she moaned at the thrill of anticipation.

"Moon and water magic," Gabriel murmured huskily. "I'll be using both to drive you wild, and you won't have surcease until the dawn." The moonlight shivered over her skin, titillating pinpricks just short of pain. Gasping, she tugged against the restraints, helpless indeed. Water slid over her, cooling the prickles of silver, then heating to a near burn before steaming away. Before she could take a breath, Gabriel's mouth followed the same path, soothing and sensitizing her skin.

Her magic billowed like fire, reaching for him, embraced in return. He began again, tormenting her with moonlight. Overhead, the moon shone like a beacon, flickers of silver traveling through the glass and struts of the dome.

It would be a very long night, indeed.

And there would be many more to come over a long life together, she'd make sure of it—and House Phel would flourish as a result.

"Are you paying attention, familiar?" Gabriel asked, nipping her sharply.

"Yes, wizard," she answered on a delicious sigh.

Oh, yes.

Worried about Jadren and Selly?
Their story continues in the next trilogy
Renegades of Magic
Beginning with SHADOW WIZARD

TITLES BY JEFFE KENNEDY

FANTASY ROMANCES

BONDS OF MAGIC
Dark Wizard
Bright Familiar
Grey Magic
Familiar Winter Magic (In Fire of the Frost)

RENEGADES OF MAGIC
Shadow Wizard

HEIRS OF MAGIC
The Long Night of the Crystalline Moon
(also available in *Under a Winter Sky*)
The Golden Gryphon and the Bear Prince
The Sorceress Queen and the Pirate Rogue
The Dragon's Daughter and the Winter Mage
The Storm Princess and the Raven King

THE FORGOTTEN EMPIRES
The Orchid Throne

The Fiery Crown
The Promised Queen

THE TWELVE KINGDOMS
Negotiation
The Mark of the Tala
The Tears of the Rose
The Talon of the Hawk
Heart's Blood
The Crown of the Queen

THE UNCHARTED REALMS
The Pages of the Mind
The Edge of the Blade
The Snows of Windroven
The Shift of the Tide
The Arrows of the Heart
The Dragons of Summer
The Fate of the Tala
The Lost Princess Returns

THE CHRONICLES OF DASNARIA
Prisoner of the Crown
Exile of the Seas
Warrior of the World

SORCEROUS MOONS
Lonen's War
Oria's Gambit
The Tides of Bára
The Forests of Dru

Oria's Enchantment

Lonen's Reign

A COVENANT OF THORNS

Rogue's Pawn

Rogue's Possession

Rogue's Paradise

CONTEMPORARY ROMANCES

Shooting Star

MISSED CONNECTIONS

Last Dance

With a Prince

Since Last Christmas

CONTEMPORARY EROTIC ROMANCES

Exact Warm Unholy

The Devil's Doorbell

FACETS OF PASSION

Sapphire

Platinum

Ruby

Five Golden Rings

FALLING UNDER

Going Under

Under His Touch

Under Contract

EROTIC PARANORMAL

MASTER OF THE OPERA E-SERIAL
Master of the Opera, Act 1: Passionate Overture
Master of the Opera, Act 2: Ghost Aria
Master of the Opera, Act 3: Phantom Serenade
Master of the Opera, Act 4: Dark Interlude
Master of the Opera, Act 5: A Haunting Duet
Master of the Opera, Act 6: Crescendo
Master of the Opera

BLOOD CURRENCY
Blood Currency

BDSM FAIRYTALE ROMANCE
Petals and Thorns

Thank you for reading!

ABOUT JEFFE KENNEDY

Jeffe Kennedy is a multi-award-winning and best-selling author of epic fantasy romance. She is the current president of the Science Fiction and Fantasy Writers Association (SFWA) and is a member of Romance Writers of America (RWA), and Novelists, Inc. (NINC). She is best known for her RITA® Award-winning novel, *The Pages of the Mind*, the recent trilogy, *The Forgotten Empires*, and the wildly popular, *Dark Wizard*. Jeffe lives in Santa Fe, New Mexico.

Jeffe can be found online at her website: JeffeKennedy.com, on her podcast First Cup of Coffee, every Sunday at the popular SFF Seven blog, on Facebook, on Goodreads, on BookBub, and pretty much constantly on Twitter @jeffekennedy. She is represented by Sarah Younger of Nancy Yost Literary Agency.

jeffekennedy.com

facebook.com/Author.Jeffe.Kennedy

twitter.com/jeffekennedy

goodreads.com/author/show/1014374.Jeffe_Kennedy

bookbub.com/profile/jeffe-kennedy

Sign up for her newsletter here.

jeffekennedy.com/sign-up-for-my-newsletter

www.ingramcontent.com/pod-product-compliance
Lightning Source LLC
Chambersburg PA
CBHW031029030726
47497CB00004B/1061